Dan Simmons, a former teacher and director of programmes for gifted children, now writes full time. He lives with his wife and daughter in Colorado, USA. He has always been interested in writing, composing his first short stories at the age of nine. Since then he has been co-winner of the first *Twilight Zone Magazine* short story contest, winner of the Rod Serling Memorial Award, and winner of the World Fantasy Award for Best Novel with *Song of Kali*. He is also the author of the much-acclaimed horror novel *Carrion Comfort*, winner of the 1990 Bram Stoker Award, the Locus Award for Best Horror Novel and the British Fantasy Award.

Hyperion is the winner of the 1990 Hugo Award and Locus Award for Best Science Fiction Novel.

Hyperion

Dan Simmons

First published in Great Britain 1990
by HEADLINE BOOK PUBLISHING

First published in paperback in 1990
by HEADLINE BOOK PUBLISHING

First HEADLINE FEATURE paperback in 1991

20 19 18 17 16 15 14 13

ISBN 0 7472 3482 5

Typeset in 10/10½ pt English Times
by Colset Private Limited, Singapore

Printed and bound in Great Britain by
Clays Ltd, St Ives plc

HEADLINE BOOK PUBLISHING
A division of Hodder Headline
338 Euston Road
London NW1 3BH

This is for Ted

PROLOGUE

The Hegemony Consul sat on the balcony of his ebony spaceship and played Rachmaninoff's Prelude in C-sharp Minor on an ancient but well-maintained Steinway while great, green, saurian things surged and bellowed in the swamps below. A thunderstorm was brewing to the north. Bruise-black clouds silhouetted a forest of giant gymnosperms while stratocumulus towered nine kilometers high in a violent sky. Lightning rippled along the horizon. Closer to the ship, occasional vague, reptilian shapes would blunder into the interdiction field, cry out, and then crash away through indigo mists. The Consul concentrated on a difficult section of the Prelude and ignored the approach of storm and nightfall.

The fatline receiver chimed.

The Consul stopped, fingers hovering above the keyboard, and listened. Thunder rumbled through the heavy air. From the direction of the gymnosperm forest there came the mournful ululation of a carrion-breed pack. Somewhere in the darkness below, a small-brained beast trumpeted its answering challenge and fell quiet. The interdiction field added its sonic undertones to the sudden silence. The fatline chimed again.

'Damn,' said the Consul and went in to answer it.

While the computer took a few seconds to convert and decode the burst of decaying tachyons, the Consul poured himself a glass of Scotch. He settled into the cushions of the projection pit just as the diskey blinked green. 'Play,' he said.

'You have been chosen to return to Hyperion,' came a woman's husky voice. Full visuals had not yet formed; the air remained empty except for the pulse of transmission

1

codes which told the Consul that this fatline squirt had originated on the Hegemony administrative world of Tau Ceti Center. The Consul did not need the transmission coordinates to know this. The aged but still beautiful voice of Meina Gladstone was unmistakable. 'You have been chosen to return to Hyperion as a member of the Shrike Pilgrimage,' continued the voice.

The hell you say, thought the Consul and rose to leave the pit.

'You and six others have been selected by the Church of the Shrike and confirmed by the All Thing,' said Meina Gladstone. 'It is in the interest of the Hegemony that you accept.'

The Consul stood motionless in the pit, his back to the flickering transmission codes. Without turning, he raised his glass and drained the last of the Scotch.

'The situation is very confused,' said Meina Gladstone. Her voice was weary. 'The consulate and Home Rule Council fatlined us three standard weeks ago with the news that the Time Tombs showed signs of opening. The anti-entropic fields around them were expanding rapidly and the Shrike has begun ranging as far south as the Bridle Range.'

The Consul turned and dropped into the cushions. A holo had formed of Meina Gladstone's ancient face. Her eyes looked as tired as her voice sounded.

'A FORCE:space task force was immediately dispatched from Parvati to evacuate the Hegemony citizens on Hyperion before the Time Tombs open. Their time-debt will be a little more than three Hyperion years.' Meina Gladstone paused. The Consul thought he had never seen the Senate CEO look so grim. 'We do not know if the evacuation fleet will arrive in time,' she said, 'but the situation is even more complicated. An Ouster migration cluster of at least four thousand . . . units . . . has been detected approaching the Hyperion system. Our evacuation task force should arrive only a short while before the Ousters.'

The Consul understood Gladstone's hesitation. An Ouster migration cluster might consist of ships ranging in size from single-person ramscouts to can cities and

2

comet forts holding tens of thousands of the interstellar barbarians.

'The FORCE joint chiefs believe that this is the Ousters' big push,' said Meina Gladstone. The ship's computer had positioned the holo so that the woman's sad brown eyes seemed to be staring directly at the Consul. 'Whether they seek to control just Hyperion for the Time Tombs or whether this is an all-out attack on the Worldweb remains to be seen. In the meantime, a full FORCE:space battle fleet complete with a farcaster construction battalion has spun up from the Camn System to join the evacuation task force, but this fleet may be recalled depending upon circumstances.'

The Consul nodded and absently raised the Scotch to his lips. He frowned at the empty glass and dropped it onto the thick carpeting of the holopit. Even with no military training he understood the difficult tactical decision Gladstone and the joint chiefs were faced with. Unless a military farcaster were hurriedly constructed in the Hyperion system – at staggering expense – there would be no way to resist the Ouster invasion. Whatever secrets the Time Tombs might hold would go to the Hegemony's enemy. If the fleet *did* construct a farcaster in time and the Hegemony committed the total resources of FORCE to defending the single, distant, colonial world of Hyperion, the Worldweb ran the terrible risk of suffering an Ouster attack elsewhere on the perimeter, or – in a worst-case scenario – having the barbarians actually seizing the farcaster and penetrating the Web itself. The Consul tried to imagine the reality of armored Ouster troops stepping through farcaster portals into the undefended home cities on a hundred worlds.

The Consul walked through the holo of Meina Gladstone, retrieved his glass, and went to pour another Scotch.

'You have been chosen to join the pilgrimage to the Shrike,' said the image of the old CEO whom the press loved to compare to Lincoln or Churchill or Alvarez-Temp or whatever other pre-Hegira legend was in historical vogue at the time. 'The Templars are sending their treeship *Yggdrasill*,' said Gladstone, 'and the

3

evacuation task force commander has instructions to let it pass. With a three-week time-debt, you can rendezvous with the *Yggdrasill* before it goes quantum from the Parvati system. The six other pilgrims chosen by the Shrike Church will be aboard the treeship. Our intelligence reports suggest that at least one of the seven pilgrims is an agent of the Ousters. We do not . . . at this time . . . have any way of knowing which one it is.'

The Consul had to smile. Among all the other risks Gladstone was taking, the old woman had to consider the possibility that *he* was the spy and that she was fatlining crucial information to an Ouster agent. Or *had* she given him any crucial information? The fleet movements were detectable as soon as the ships used their Hawking drives, and if the Consul *were* the spy, the CEO's revelation might be a way to scare him off. The Consul's smile faded and he drank his Scotch.

'Sol Weintraub and Fedmahn Kassad are among the seven pilgrims chosen,' said Gladstone.

The Consul's frown deepened. He stared at the cloud of digits flickering like dust motes around the old woman's image. Fifteen seconds of fatline transmission time remained.

'We need your help,' said Meina Gladstone. 'It is essential that the secrets of the Time Tombs and Shrike be uncovered. This pilgrimage may be our last chance. If the Ousters conquer Hyperion, their agent must be eliminated and the Time Tombs sealed at all cost. The fate of the Hegemony may depend upon it.'

The transmission ended except for the pulse of rendezvous coordinates. 'Response?' asked the ship's computer. Despite the tremendous energies involved, the spacecraft was capable of placing a brief, coded squirt into the incessant babble of FTL bursts which tied the human portions of the galaxy together.

'No,' said the Consul and went outside to lean on the balcony railing. Night had fallen and the clouds were low. No stars were visible. The darkness would have been absolute except for the intermittent flash of lightning to the north and a soft phosphorescence rising from the marshes. The Consul was suddenly very aware that

4

he was, at that second, the only sentient being on an unnamed world. He listened to the antediluvian night sounds rising from the swamps and he thought about morning, about setting out in the Vikken EMV at first light, about spending the day in sunshine, about hunting big game in the fern forests to the south and then returning to the ship in the evening for a good steak and a cold beer. The Consul thought about the sharp pleasure of the hunt and the equally sharp solace of solitude: solitude he had earned through the pain and nightmare he had already suffered on Hyperion.

Hyperion.

The Consul went inside, brought the balcony in, and sealed the ship just as the first heavy raindrops began to fall. He climbed the spiral staircase to his sleeping cabin at the apex of the ship. The circular room was dark except for silent explosions of lightning which outlined rivulets of rain coursing the skylight. The Consul stripped, lay back on the firm mattress, and switched on the sound system and external audio pickups. He listened as the fury of the storm blended with the violence of Wagner's 'Flight of the Valkyries.' Hurricane winds buffeted the ship. The sound of thunderclaps filled the room as the skylight flashed white, leaving afterimages burning in the Consul's retinas.

Wagner is good only for thunderstorms, he thought. He closed his eyes but the lightning was visible through closed eyelids. He remembered the glint of ice crystals blowing through the tumbled ruins on the low hills near the Time Tombs and the colder gleam of steel on the Shrike's impossible tree of metal thorns. He remembered screams in the night and the hundred-facet, ruby-and-blood gaze of the Shrike itself.

Hyperion.

The Consul silently commanded the computer to shut off all speakers and raised his wrist to cover his eyes. In the sudden silence he lay thinking about how insane it would be to return to Hyperion. During his eleven years as Consul on that distant and enigmatic world, the mysterious Church of the Shrike had allowed a dozen barges of offworld pilgrims to depart for the windswept barrens around the Time Tombs, north of the mountains. No one had returned. And that had been in normal times, when the Shrike had been prisoner to the tides of time and forces no one understood, and the anti-entropic fields had been contained to a few dozen meters around the Time Tombs. And there had been no threat of an Ouster invasion.

The Consul thought of the Shrike, free to wander everywhere on Hyperion, of the millions of indigenies and thousands of Hegemony citizens helpless before a creature which defied physical laws and which communicated only through death, and he shivered despite the warmth of the cabin.

Hyperion.

The night and storm passed. Another stormfront raced ahead of the approaching dawn. Gymnosperms two hundred meters tall bent and whipped before the coming torrent. Just before first light, the Consul's ebony spaceship rose on a tail of blue plasma and punched through thickening clouds as it climbed toward space and rendezvous.

ONE

The Consul awoke with the peculiar headache, dry throat, and sense of having forgotten a thousand dreams which only periods in cryogenic fugue could bring. He blinked, sat upright on a low couch, and groggily pushed away the last sensor tapes clinging to his skin. There were two very short crew clones and one very tall, hooded Templar with him in the windowless ovoid of a room. One of the clones offered the Consul the traditional post-thaw glass of orange juice. He accepted it and drank greedily.

'The Tree is two light-minutes and five hours of travel from Hyperion,' said the Templar, and the Consul realized that he was being addressed by Het Masteen, captain of the Templar treeship and True Voice of the Tree. The Consul vaguely realized that it was a great honor to be awakened by the Captain, but he was too groggy and disoriented from fugue to appreciate it.

'The others have been awake for some hours,' said Het Masteen and gestured for the clones to leave them. 'They have assembled on the foremost dining platform.'

'Hhrghn,' said the Consul and took a drink. He cleared his throat and tried again. 'Thank you, Het Masteen,' he managed. Looking around at the egg-shaped room with its carpet of dark grass, translucent walls, and support ribs of continuous, curved weirwood, the Consul realized that he must be in one of the smaller environment pods. Closing his eyes, he tried to recall his memories of rendezvous just before the Templar ship went quantum.

The Consul remembered his first glimpse of the kilometer-long treeship as he closed for rendezvous, the treeship's details blurred by the redundant machine and

7

erg-generated containment fields which surrounded it like a spherical mist, but its leafy bulk clearly ablaze with thousands of lights which shone softly through leaves and thin-walled environment pods, or along countless platforms, bridges, command decks, stairways, and bowers. Around the base of the treeship, engineering and cargo spheres clustered like oversized galls while blue and violet drive streamers trailed behind like ten-kilometer-long roots.

'The others await,' Het Masteen said softly and nodded toward low cushions where the Consul's luggage lay ready to open upon his command. The Templar gazed thoughtfully at the weirwood rafters while the Consul dressed in semiformal evening wear of loose black trousers, polished ship boots, a white silk blouse which ballooned at waist and elbows, topaz collar cinch, black demi-coat complete with slashes of Hegemony crimson on the epaulets, and a soft gold tricorne. A section of curved wall became a mirror and the Consul stared at the image there: a more than middle-aged man in semiformal evening wear, sunburned skin but oddly pale under the sad eyes. The Consul frowned, nodded, and turned away.

Het Masteen gestured and the Consul followed the tall, robed figure through a dilation in the pod onto an ascending walkway which curved up and out of sight around the massive bark wall of the treeship's trunk. The Consul paused, moved to the edge of the walkway, and took a quick step back. It was at least six hundred meters down – down being created by the one-sixth standard gravity being generated by the singularities imprisoned at the base of the tree – and there were no railings.

They resumed their silent ascent, turning off from the main trunk walkway thirty meters and half a trunk-spiral later to cross a flimsy suspension bridge to a five-meter-wide branch. They followed this outward to where the riot of leaves caught the glare of Hyperion's sun.

'Has my ship been brought out of storage?' asked the Consul.

8

'It is fueled and ready in sphere eleven,' said Het Masteen. They passed into the shadow of the trunk and stars became visible in the black patches between the dark latticework of leaves. 'The other pilgrims have agreed to ferry down in your ship if the FORCE authorities give permission,' added the Templar.

The Consul rubbed his eyes and wished that he had been allowed more time to retrieve his wits from the cold grip of cryonic fugue. 'You've been in touch with the task force?'

'Oh, yes, we were challenged the moment we tunneled down from quantum leap. A Hegemony warship is . . . escorting us . . . this very moment.' Het Masteen gestured toward a patch of sky above them.

The Consul squinted upward but at that second segments of the upper tiers of branches revolved out of the treeship's shadow and acres of leaves ignited in sunset hues. Even in the still shadowed places, glowbirds nestled like Japanese lanterns above lighted walkways, glowing swingvines, and illuminated hanging bridges, while fireflies from Old Earth and radiant gossamers from Maui-Covenant blinked and coded their way through labyrinths of leaves, mixing with constellations sufficiently to fool even the most starwise traveler.

Het Masteen stepped into a basket lift hanging from a whiskered-carbon cable which disappeared into the three hundred meters of tree above them. The Consul followed and they were borne silently upward. He noted that the walkways, pods, and platforms were conspicuously empty except for a few Templars and their diminutive crew clone counterparts. The Consul could recall seeing no other passengers during his rushed hour between rendezvous and fugue, but he had put that down to the imminence of the treeship going quantum, assuming then that the passengers were safe in their fugue couches. Now, however, the treeship was traveling far below relativistic velocities and its branches should be crowded with gawking passengers. He mentioned his observation to the Templar.

'The six of you are our only passengers,' said Het Masteen. The basket stopped in a maze of foliage and the treeship captain led the way up a wooden escalator worn with age.

The Consul blinked in surprise. A Templar treeship normally carried between two and five thousand passengers; it was easily the most desirable way to travel between the stars. Treeships rarely accrued more than a four- or five-month time-debt, making short, scenic crossings where star systems were a very few light-years apart, thus allowing their affluent passengers to spend as little time as necessary in fugue. For the treeship to make the trip to Hyperion and back, accumulating six years of Web time *with no paying passengers* would mean a staggering financial loss to the Templars.

Then the Consul realized, belatedly, that the treeship would be ideal for the upcoming evacuation, its expenses ultimately to be reimbursed by the Hegemony. Still, the Consul knew, to bring a ship as beautiful and vulnerable as the *Yggdrasill* – one of only five of its kind – into a war zone was a terrible risk for the Templar Brotherhood.

'Your fellow pilgrims,' announced Het Masteen as he and the Consul emerged onto a broad platform where a small group waited at one end of a long wooden table. Above them the stars burned, rotating occasionally as the treeship changed its pitch or yaw, while to either side a solid sphere of foliage curved away like the green skin of some great fruit. The Consul immediately recognized the setting as the Captain's dining platform, even before the five other passengers rose to let Het Masteen take his place at the head of the table. The Consul found an empty chair waiting for him to the left of the Captain.

When everyone was seated and quiet, Het Masteen made formal introductions. Although the Consul knew none of the others from personal experience, several of the names were familiar and he used his diplomat's long training to file away identities and impressions.

To the Consul's left sat Father Lenar Hoyt, a priest of the old-style Christian sect known as Catholic. For a second the Consul had forgotten the significance of the black clothing and Roman collar, but then he remembered St Francis Hospital on Hebron where he had received alcohol trauma therapy after his disastrous first diplomatic assignment there almost four standard decades earlier. And at the mention of Hoyt's name he remembered another priest, one who had disappeared on Hyperion halfway through his own tenure there.

Lenar Hoyt was a young man by the Consul's reckoning – no more than his early thirties – but it appeared that something had aged the man terribly in the not too distant past. The Consul looked at the thin face, cheekbones pressing against sallow flesh, eyes large but hooded in deep hollows, thin lips set in a permanent twitch of muscle too downturned to be called even a cynical smile, the hairline not so much receding as ravaged by radiation, and he felt he was looking at a man who had been ill for years. Still, the Consul was surprised that behind that mask of concealed pain there remained the physical echo of the boy in the man – the faintest remnants of the round face, fair skin, and soft mouth which had belonged to a younger, healthier, less cynical Lenar Hoyt.

Next to the priest sat a man whose image had been familiar to most citizens of the Hegemony some years before. The Consul wondered if the collective attention span in the Worldweb was as short now as it had been when he had lived there. Shorter, probably. If so, then Colonel Fedmahn Kassad, the so-called Butcher of South Bressia, was probably no longer either infamous or famous. To the Consul's generation and to all those who lived in the slow, expatriate fringe of things, Kassad was not someone one was likely to forget.

Colonel Fedmahn Kassad was tall – almost tall enough to look the two-meter Het Masteen in the eye – and dressed in FORCE black with no rank insignia or citations showing. The black uniform was oddly similar to Father Hoyt's garb, but there was no real resemblance between the two men. In lieu of Hoyt's wasted appearance, Kassad was brown, obviously fit, and whip-handle lean, with strands of muscle showing in shoulder, wrist, and throat. The Colonel's eyes were small, dark, and as all-encompassing as the lenses of some primitive video camera. His face was all angles:

shadows, planes, and facets. Not gaunt like Father Hoyt's, merely carved from cold stone. A thin line of beard along his jawline served to accent the sharpness of his countenance as surely as blood on a knife blade.

The Colonel's intense, slow movements reminded the Consul of an Earth-bred jaguar he had seen in a private seedship zoo on Lusus many years before. Kassad's voice was soft but the Consul did not fail to notice that even the Colonel's silences commanded attention.

Most of the long table was empty, the group clustered at one end. Across from Fedmahn Kassad sat a man introduced as the poet Martin Silenus.

Silenus appeared to be quite the opposite of the military man across from him. Where Kassad was lean and tall, Martin Silenus was short and visibly out of shape. Countering Kassad's stone-cut features, the poet's face was as mobile and expressive as an Earth primate's. His voice was a loud, profane rasp. There was something, thought the Consul, almost pleasantly demonic about Martin Silenus, with his ruddy cheeks, broad mouth, pitched eyebrows, sharp ears, and constantly moving hands sporting fingers long enough to serve a concert pianist. Or a strangler. The poet's silver hair had been cropped into rough-hewn bangs.

Martin Silenus seemed to be in his late fifties, but the Consul noticed the telltale blue tinge to throat and palms and suspected that the man had been through more than a few Poulsen treatments. Silenus's true age might be anywhere from ninety to a hundred and fifty standard years. If he were close to the latter age, the Consul knew, the odds were that the poet was quite mad.

As boisterous and animated as Martin Silenus seemed upon first encounter, so the next guest at the table exuded an immediate and equally impressive sense of intelligent reticence. Sol Weintraub looked up upon introduction and the Consul noted the short gray beard, lined forehead, and sad, luminous eyes of the well-known scholar. The Consul had heard tales of the Wandering Jew and his hopeless quest, but he was shocked to realize that the old man now held the infant in his arms – his daughter Rachel, no more than a few weeks old. The Consul looked away.

The sixth pilgrim and only woman at the table was Brawne Lamia. When introduced, the detective stared at the Consul with such intensity that he could feel the pressure of her gaze even after she looked away.

A former citizen of the 1.3-g world of Lusus, Brawne Lamia was no taller than the poet two chairs to her right, but even her loose corduroy shipsuit did not conceal the heavy layers of muscle on her compact form. Black curls reached to her shoulders, her eyebrows were two dark lines dabbed horizontally across a wide brow, and her nose was solid and sharp, intensifying the aquiline quality of her stare. Lamia's mouth was wide and expressive to the point of being sensuous, curled slightly at the corners in a slight smile which might be cruel or merely playful. The woman's dark eyes seemed to dare the observer to discover which was the case.

It occurred to the Consul that Brawne Lamia might well be considered beautiful.

Introductions completed, the Consul cleared his throat and turned toward the Templar. 'Het Masteen, you said that there were seven pilgrims. Is M. Weintraub's child the seventh?'

Het Masteen's hood moved slowly from side to side. 'No. Only those who make a conscious decision to seek the Shrike may be counted among the pilgrims.'

The group at the table stirred slightly. Each must know what the Consul knew; only a group comprising a prime number of pilgrims might make the Shrike Church-sponsored trip north.

'I am the seventh,' said Het Masteen, captain of the Templar treeship *Yggdrasill* and the True Voice of the Tree. In the silence which followed the announcement, Het Masteen gestured and a group of crew clones began serving the pilgrims their last meal before planetfall.

'So the Ousters are not in-system yet?' asked Brawne Lamia. Her voice had a husky, throaty quality which strangely stirred the Consul.

'No,' said Het Masteen. 'But we cannot be more than a few standard days ahead of them. Our instruments have detected fusion skirmishes within the system's Oört cloud.'

'Will there be war?' asked Father Hoyt. His voice seemed as fatigued as his expression. When no one volunteered a response, the priest turned to his right as if retroactively directing the question to the Consul.

The Consul sighed. The crew clones had served wine; he wished it had been whiskey. 'Who knows what the Ousters will do?' he said. 'They no longer appear to be motivated by human logic.'

Martin Silenus laughed loudly, spilling his wine as he gestured. 'As if we fucking *humans* were ever motivated by human logic!' He took a deep drink, wiped his mouth, and laughed again.

Brawne Lamia frowned. 'If the serious fighting starts too soon,' she said, 'perhaps the authorities will not allow us to land.'

'We will be allowed to pass,' said Het Masteen. Sunlight found its way past folds in his cowl to fall on yellowish skin.

'Saved from certain death in war to be delivered to certain death at the hands of the Shrike,' murmured Father Hoyt.

'There is no death in all the Universe!' intoned Martin Silenus in a voice which the Consul felt sure could have awakened someone deep in cryogenic fugue. The poet drained the last of his wine and raised the empty goblet in an apparent toast to the stars:

'No smell of death – there shall be no death, moan, moan;
Moan, Cybele, moan; for thy pernicious Babes
Have changed a god into a shaking palsy.
Moan, brethren, moan, for I have no strength left;
Weak as the reed – weak – feeble as my voice—
Oh, oh, the pain, the pain of feebleness.
Moan, moan, for still I thaw . . .'

Silenus abruptly broke off and poured more wine, belching once into the silence which had followed his recitation. The other six looked at one another. The Consul noticed that Sol Weintraub was smiling slightly until the baby in his arms stirred and distracted him.

14

'Well,' said Father Hoyt hesitantly, as if trying to retrieve an earlier strand of thought, 'if the Hegemony convoy leaves and the Ousters take Hyperion, perhaps the occupation will be bloodless and they'll let us go about our business.'

Colonel Fedmahn Kassad laughed softly. 'The Ousters don't want to *occupy* Hyperion,' he said. 'If they take the planet they'll loot what they want and then do what they do best. They'll burn the cities into charred rubble, break the rubble into smaller pieces, and then bake the pieces until they glow. They'll melt the poles, boil the oceans, and then use the residue to salt what's left of the continents so nothing will ever grow there again.'

'Well . . .' began Father Hoyt and then trailed off.

There was no conversation as the clones cleared the soup and salad dishes and brought on the main course.

'You said that there was a Hegemony warship escorting us,' the Consul said to Het Masteen as they finished their roast beef and boiled sky squid.

The Templar nodded and pointed. The Consul squinted but could make out nothing moving against the rotating starfield.

'Here,' said Fedmahn Kassad and leaned across Father Hoyt to hand the Consul a collapsible pair of military binoculars.

The Consul nodded his thanks, thumbed on the power, and scanned the patch of sky Het Masteen had indicated. Gyroscopic crystals in the binoculars hummed slightly as they stabilized the optics and swept the area in a programmed search pattern. Suddenly the image froze, blurred, expanded, and steadied.

The Consul could not avoid an involuntary intake of breath as the Hegemony ship filled the viewer. Neither the expected field-blurred seed of a solo ramscout nor the bulb of a torchship, the electronically outlined image was of a matte-black attack carrier. The thing was impressive in the way only warships through the centuries had succeeded in being. The Hegemony spinship was incongruously streamlined with its four sets of boom arms retracted in battle readiness, its sixty-meter command probe sharp as a Clovis point, and its Hawking drive and fusion blisters set far back along the launch shaft like feathers on an arrow.

The Consul handed the binoculars back to Kassad without comment. If the task force was using a full attack carrier to escort the *Yggdrasill*, what kind of firepower were they setting in place to meet the Ouster invasion?

'How long until we land?' asked Brawne Lamia. She had been using her comlog to access the treeship's datasphere and obviously was frustrated with what she had found. Or had not found.

'Four hours until orbit,' murmured Het Masteen. 'A few minutes more by dropship. Our consular friend has offered his private craft to ferry you down.'

'To Keats?' said Sol Weintraub. It was the first time the scholar had spoken since dinner had been served.

The Consul nodded. 'It's still the only spaceport on Hyperion set to handle passenger vehicles,' he said.

'Spaceport?' Father Hoyt sounded angry. 'I thought that we were going straight to the north. To the Shrike's realm.'

Het Masteen patiently shook his head. 'The pilgrimage always begins from the capital,' he said. 'It will take several days to reach the Time Tombs.'

'Several *days*,' snapped Brawne Lamia. 'That's absurd.'

'Perhaps,' agreed Het Masteen, 'but it is the case, nonetheless.'

Father Hoyt looked as if something in the meal had caused him indigestion even though he had eaten almost nothing. 'Look,' he said, 'couldn't we change the rules this once – I mean, given the war scare and all? And just land near the Time Tombs or wherever and get it over with?'

The Consul shook his head. 'Spacecraft and aircraft have been trying to take the short route to the northern moors for almost four hundred years,' he said. 'I know of none who made it.'

'May one inquire,' said Martin Silenus, happily raising

his hand like a schoolboy, 'just what the gibbering fuck *happens* to these legions of ships?'

Father Hoyt frowned at the poet. Fedmahn Kassad smiled slightly. Sol Weintraub said, 'The Consul did not mean to suggest that the area is inaccessible. One may travel by ship or various land routes. Nor do spacecraft and aircraft disappear. They easily land near the ruins or the Time Tombs and just as easily return to whatever point their computers command. It is merely the pilots and passengers who are never seen again.' Weintraub lifted the sleeping baby from his lap and set her in an infant carrier slung around his neck.

'So the tired old legend goes,' said Brawne Lamia. 'What do the ship logs show?'

'Nothing,' said the Consul. 'No violence. No forced entry. No deviation from course. No unexplained time lapses. No unusual energy emissions or depletions. No physical phenomena of any sort.'

'No passengers,' said Het Masteen.

The Consul did a slow double take. If Het Masteen had, indeed, just attempted a joke, it was the first sign in all of the Consul's decades of dealing with the Templars that one of them had shown even a nascent sense of humour. What the Consul could see of the Captain's vaguely oriental features beneath the cowl gave no hint that a joke had been attempted.

'Marvelous melodrama,' laughed Silenus. 'A real-life, Christ-weeping Sargasso of Souls and we're for it. Who orchestrates this shitpot of a plot, anyway?'

'Shut up,' said Brawne Lamia. 'You're drunk, old man.'

The Consul sighed. The group had been together for less than a standard hour.

Crew clones swept away the dishes and brought dessert trays showcasing sherbets, coffees, treeship fruit, draums, tortes, and concoctions made of Renaissance chocolate. Martin Silenus waved away the desserts and told the clones to bring him another bottle of wine. The Consul reflected a few seconds and then asked for a whiskey.

*　　*　　*

17

'It occurs to me,' Sol Weintraub said as the group was finishing dessert, 'that our survival may depend upon our talking to one another.'

'What do you mean?' asked Brawne Lamia.

Weintraub unconsciously rocked the child sleeping against his chest. 'For instance, does anyone here know why he or she was chosen by the Shrike Church and the All Thing to go on this voyage?'

No one spoke.

'I thought not,' said Weintraub. 'Even more fascinating, is anyone here a member or follower of the Church of the Shrike? I, for one, am a Jew, and however confused my religious notions have become these days, they do not include the worship of an organic killing machine.' Weintraub raised eyebrows and looked around the table.

'I am the True Voice of the Tree,' said Het Masteen. 'While many Templars believe that the Shrike is the Avatar of punishment for those who do not feed from the root, I must consider this a heresy not founded in the Covenant or the writings of the Muir.'

To the Captain's left, the Consul shrugged. 'I am an atheist,' he said, holding the glass of whiskey to the light. 'I have never been in contact with the Shrike cult.'

Father Hoyt smiled without humor. 'The Catholic Church ordained me,' he said. 'Shrike-worship contradicts everything the Church defends.'

Colonel Kassad shook his head, whether in refusal to respond or to indicate that he was not a member of the Shrike Church, it was not clear.

Martin Silenus made an expansive gesture. 'I was baptized a Lutheran,' he said. 'A subset which no longer exists. I helped create Zen Gnosticism before any of your parents were born. I have been a Catholic, a revelationist, a neo-Marxist, an interface zealot, a Bound Shaker, a satanist, a bishop in the Church of Jake's Nada, and a dues-paying subscriber to the Assured Reincarnation Institute. Now, I am happy to say, I am a simple pagan.' He smiled at everyone. 'To a pagan,' he concluded, 'the Shrike is a most acceptable deity.'

'I ignore religions,' said Brawne Lamia. 'I do not succumb to them.'

'My point has been made, I believe,' said Sol Weintraub. 'None of us admits to subscribing to the Shrike cult dogma, yet the elders of that perceptive group have chosen us over many millions of the petitioning faithful to visit the Time Tombs . . . and their fierce god . . . in what may be the last such pilgrimage.'

The Consul shook his head. 'Your point may be made, M. Weintraub,' he said, 'but I fail to see it.'

The scholar absently stroked his beard. 'It would seem that our reasons for returning to Hyperion are so compelling that even the Shrike Church and the Hegemony probability intelligences agree that we deserve to return,' he said. 'Some of these reasons – mine, for instance – may appear to be public knowledge, but I am certain that none are known in their entirety except to the individuals at this table. I suggest that we share our stories in the few days remaining to us.'

'Why?' said Colonel Kassad. 'It would seem to serve no purpose.'

Weintraub smiled. 'On the contrary, it would – at the very least – amuse us and give at least a glimpse of our fellow travelers' souls before the Shrike or some other calamity distracts us. Beyond that, it might just give us enough insight to save all of our lives if we are intelligent enough to find the common thread of experience which binds all our fates to the whim of the Shrike.'

Martin Silenus laughed and closed his eyes. He said:

> *'Straddling each a dolphin's back*
> *And steadied by a fin,*
> *Those Innocents re-live their death,*
> *Their wounds open again.'*

'That's Lenista, isn't it?' said Father Hoyt. 'I studied her in seminary.'

'Close,' said Silenus, opening his eyes and pouring more wine. 'It's Yeats. Bugger lived five hundred years before Lenista tugged at her mother's metal teat.'

'Look,' said Lamia, 'what good would telling each other stories do? When we meet the Shrike, we tell *it* what we want, one of us is granted the wish, and the others die. Correct?'

'So goes the myth,' said Weintraub.

'The Shrike is no myth,' said Kassad. 'Nor its steel tree.'

'So why bore each other with stories?' asked Brawne Lamia, spearing the last of her chocolate cheesecake.

Weintraub gently touched the back of his sleeping infant's head. 'We live in strange times,' he said. 'Because we are part of that one tenth of one tenth of one percent of the Hegemony's citizens who travel *between* the stars rather than along the Web, we represent odd epochs of our own recent past. I, for example, am sixty-eight standard years old, but because of the time-debts my travels could have incurred, I might have spread these threescore and eight years across well more than a century of Hegemony history.'

'So?' said the woman next to him.

Weintraub opened his hand in a gesture which included everyone at the table. 'Among us we represent islands of time as well as separate oceans of perspective. Or perhaps more aptly put, each of us may hold a piece to a puzzle no one else has been able to solve since humankind first landed on Hyperion.' Weintraub scratched his nose. 'It is a mystery,' he said, 'and to tell the truth, I am intrigued by mysteries even if this is to be my last week of enjoying them. I would welcome some glimmer of understanding but, failing that, working on the puzzle will suffice.'

'I agree,' said Het Masteen with no emotion. 'It had not occurred to me, but I see the wisdom of telling our tales before we confront the Shrike.'

'But what's to keep us from lying?' asked Brawne Lamia.

'Nothing.' Martin Silenus grinned. 'That's the beauty of it.'

'We should put it to a vote,' said the Consul. He was thinking about Meina Gladstone's contention that one of the group was an Ouster agent. Would hearing the stories be a way of revealing the spy? The Consul smiled at the thought of an agent so stupid.

'Who decided that we are a happy little democracy?' Colonel Kassad asked dryly.

'We had better be,' said the Consul. 'To reach our individual goals, this group needs to reach the Shrike regions together. We require some means of making decisions.'

'We could appoint a leader,' said Kassad.

'Piss on that,' the poet said in a pleasant tone. Others at the table also shook their heads.

'All right,' said the Consul, 'we vote. Our first decision relates to M. Weintraub's suggestion that we tell the stories of our past involvement with Hyperion.'

'All or nothing,' said Het Masteen. 'We each share our story or none does. We will abide by the will of the majority.'

'Agreed,' said the Consul, suddenly curious to hear the others tell their stories and equally sure that he would never tell his own. 'Those in favor of telling our tales?'

'Yes,' said Sol Weintraub.

'Yes,' said Het Masteen.

'Absolutely,' said Martin Silenus. 'I wouldn't miss this little comic farce for a month in the orgasm baths on Shote.'

'I vote yes also,' said the Consul, surprising himself. 'Those opposed?'

'Nay,' said Father Hoyt but there was no energy in his voice.

'I think it's stupid,' said Brawne Lamia.

The Consul turned to Kassad. 'Colonel?'

Fedmahn Kassad shrugged.

'I register four yes votes, two negatives, and one abstention,' said the Consul. 'The ayes have it. Who wants to start?'

The table was silent. Finally Martin Silenus looked up from where he had been writing on a small pad of paper. He tore a sheet into several smaller strips. 'I've recorded numbers from one to seven,' he said. 'Why don't we draw lots and go in the order we draw?'

'That seems rather childish, doesn't it?' said M. Lamia.

'I'm a childish fellow,' responded Silenus with his

satyr's smile. 'Ambassador' – he nodded toward the Consul – 'could I borrow that gilded pillow you're wearing for a hat?'

The Consul handed over his tricorne, the folded slips were dropped in, and the hat passed around. Sol Weintraub was the first to draw, Martin Silenus the last.

The Consul unfolded his slip, making sure that no one else could see it. He was number seven. Tension ebbed out of him like air out of an overinflated balloon. It was quite possible, he reasoned, that events would intercede before he had to tell his story. Or the war would make everything academic. Or the group could lose interest in stories. Or the king could die. Or the horse could die. Or he could teach the horse how to talk.

No more whiskey, thought the Consul.

'Who's first?' asked Martin Silenus.

In the brief silence, the Consul could hear leaves stirring to unfelt breezes.

'I am,' said Father Hoyt. The priest's expression showed the same barely submerged acceptance of pain which the Consul had seen on the faces of terminally ill friends. Hoyt held up his slip of paper with a large 1 clearly scrawled on it.

'All right,' said Silenus. 'Start.'

'Now?' asked the priest.

'Why not?' said the poet. The only sign that Silenus had finished at least two bottles of wine was a slight darkening of the already ruddy cheeks and a somewhat more demonic tilt to the pitched eyebrows. 'We have a few hours before planetfall,' he said, 'and I for one plan to sleep off the freezer fugue when we're safely down and settled among the simple natives.'

'Our friend has a point,' Sol Weintraub said softly. 'If the tales are to be told, the hour after dinner each day is a civilized time to tell them.'

Father Hoyt sighed and stood. 'Just a minute,' he said and left the dining platform.

After some minutes had passed, Brawne Lamia said, 'Do you think he's lost his nerve?'

'No,' said Lenar Hoyt, emerging from the darkness at the head of the wooden escalator which served as the main staircase. 'I needed these.' He dropped two small, stained notebooks on the table as he took his seat.

'No fair reading stories from a primer,' said Silenus. 'These are to be our own tall tales, Magus!'

'Shut up, damn it!' cried Hoyt. He ran a hand across his face, touched his chest. For the second time that night, the Consul knew that he was looking at a seriously ill man.

'I'm sorry,' said Father Hoyt. 'But if I'm to tell my . . . my tale, I have to tell someone else's story as well. These journals belong to the man who was the reason for my coming to Hyperion . . . and why I am returning today.' Hoyt took a deep breath.

The Consul touched the journals. They were begrimed and charred, as if they had survived a fire. 'Your friend has old-fashioned tastes,' he said, 'if he still keeps a written journal.'

'Yes,' said Hoyt. 'If you're all ready, I will begin.'

The group at the table nodded. Beneath the dining platform, a kilometer of treeship drove through the cold night with the strong pulse of a living thing. Sol Weintraub lifted his sleeping child from the infant carrier and carefully set her on a cushioned mat on the floor near his chair. He removed his comlog, set it near the mat, and programmed the diskey for white noise. The week-old infant lay on her stomach and slept.

The Consul leaned far back and found the blue and green star which was Hyperion. It seemed to grow larger even as he watched. Het Masteen drew his cowl forward until only shadows showed for his face. Sol Weintraub lighted a pipe. Others accepted refills of coffee and settled back in their chairs.

Martin Silenus seemed the most avid and expectant of the listeners as he leaned forward and whispered:

> *'He seyde, "Syn I shal bigynne the game,*
> *What, welcome be the cut, a Goddes name!*
> *Now lat us ryde, and herkneth what I seye."*
> *And with that word we ryden forth oure weye;*
> *And he bigan with right a myrie cheere*
> *His tale anon, and seyde as ye may heere.'*

23

THE PRIEST'S TALE:
'The Man Who Cried God'

'Sometimes there is a thin line separating orthodox zeal from apostasy,' said Father Lenar Hoyt.

So began the priest's story. Later, dictating the tale into his comlog, the Consul remembered it as a seamless whole, minus the pauses, hoarse voice, false starts, and small redundancies which were the timeless failings of human speech.

Lenar Hoyt had been a young priest, born, raised, and only recently ordained on the Catholic world of Pacem, when he was given his first offworld assignment: he was ordered to escort the respected Jesuit Father Paul Duré into quiet exile on the colony world of Hyperion.

In another time, Father Paul Duré certainly would have become a bishop and perhaps a pope. Tall, thin, ascetic, with white hair receding from a noble brow and eyes too filled with the sharp edge of experience to hide their pain, Paul Duré was a follower of St Teilhard as well as an archaeologist, ethnologist, and eminent Jesuit theologian. Despite the decline of the Catholic Church into what amounted to a half-forgotten cult tolerated because of its quaintness and isolation from the main-stream of Hegemony life, Jesuit logic had not lost its bite. Nor had Father Duré lost his conviction that the Holy Catholic Apostolic Church continued to be humankind's last, best hope for immortality.

To Lenar Hoyt as a boy, Father Duré had been a somewhat godlike figure when glimpsed during his rare visits to the preseminary schools, or on the would-be seminarian's even rarer visits to the New Vatican. Then, during the years of Hoyt's study in seminary, Duré had been on an important Church-sponsored archaeological dig on the nearby world of Armaghast. When the Jesuit returned, a few weeks after Hoyt's ordination, it had been under a cloud. No one outside the highest circles of the New Vatican knew precisely what had happened, but there were whispers of excommunication and even of a hearing before the Holy Office of the Inquisition, dormant the four centuries since the confusion following the death of Earth.

Instead, Father Duré had asked for a posting to Hyperion, a world most people knew of only because of the bizarre Shrike cult which had originated there, and Father Hoyt had been chosen to accompany him. It would be a thankless job, traveling in a role which combined the worst aspects of apprentice, escort, and spy without even the satisfaction of seeing a new world; Hoyt was under orders to see Father Duré down to the Hyperion spaceport and then reboard the same spinship for its return voyage to the Worldweb. What the bishopric was offering Lenar Hoyt was twenty months in cryogenic fugue, a few weeks of in-system travel at either end of the voyage, and a time-debt which would return him to Pacem eight years behind his former classmates in the quest for Vatican careers and missionary postings.

Bound by obedience and schooled in discipline, Lenar Hoyt accepted without question.

Their transport, the aging spinship *HS Nadia Oleg*, was a pockmarked metal tub with no artificial gravity of any sort when it was not under drive, no viewports for the passengers, and no on-board recreation except for the stimsims piped into the datalink to keep passengers in their hammocks and fugue couches. After awakening from fugue, the passengers – mostly offworld workers and economy-rate tourists with a few cult mystics and would-be Shrike suicides thrown in for good measure – slept in those same hammocks and fugue couches, ate recycled food in featureless mess decks, and generally tried to cope with spacesickness and boredom during their twelve-day, zero-g glide from their spinout point to Hyperion.

Father Hoyt learned little from Father Duré during those days of forced intimacy, nothing at all about the events on Armaghast which had sent the senior priest into exile. The younger man had keyed his comlog implant to seek out as much data as it could on Hyperion and, by the time they were three days out from planetfall,

Father Hoyt considered himself somewhat of an expert on the world.

'There are records of Catholics coming to Hyperion but no mention of a diocese there,' said Hoyt one evening as they hung talking in their zero-g hammocks while most of their fellow passengers lay tuned into erotic stimsims. 'I presume you're going down to do some mission work?'

'Not at all,' replied Father Duré. 'The good people of Hyperion have done nothing to foist their religious opinions on me, so I see no reason to offend them with my proselytizing. Actually, I hope to travel to the southern continent – Aquila – and then find a way inland from the city of Port Romance. But not in the guise of a missionary. I plan to set up an ethnological research station along the Cleft.'

'Research?' Father Hoyt had echoed in surprise. He closed his eyes to key his implant. Looking again at Father Duré, he said, 'That section of the Pinion Plateau isn't inhabited, Father. The flame forests make it totally inaccessible most of the year.'

Father Duré smiled and nodded. He carried no implant and his ancient comlog had been in his luggage for the duration of the trip. 'Not quite inaccessible,' he said softly. 'And not quite uninhabited. The Bikura live there.'

'Bikura,' Father Hoyt said and closed his eyes. 'But they're just a legend,' he said at last.

'Hmmm,' said Father Duré. 'Try cross-indexing through Mamet Spedling.'

Father Hoyt closed his eyes again. General Index told him that Mamet Spedling had been a minor explorer affiliated with the Shackleton Institute on Renaissance Minor who, almost a standard century and a half earlier, had filed a short report with the Institute in which he told of hacking his way inland from the then newly settled Port Romance, through swamplands which had since been reclaimed for fiberplastic plantations, passing through the flame forests during a period of rare quietude, and climbing high enough on the Pinion Plateau to encounter the Cleft and a small tribe of humans

26

who fit the profile of the legendary Bikura.

Spedling's brief notes hypothesized that the humans were survivors of a missing seedship colony from three centuries earlier and clearly described a group suffering all of the classic retrograde cultural effects of extreme isolation, inbreeding, and overadaptation. In Spedling's blunt words, '. . . even after less than two days here it is obvious that the Bikura are too stupid, lethargic, and dull to waste time describing.' As it turned out, the flame forests then began to show some signs of becoming active and Spedling had *not* wasted any more time observing his discovery but had rushed to reach the coast, losing four indigenie bearers, all of his equipment and records, and his left arm to the 'quiet' forest in the three months it took him to escape.

'My God,' Father Hoyt had said as he lay in his hammock on the *Nadia Oleg*, 'why the Bikura?'

'Why not?' had been Father Duré's mild reply. 'Very little is known about them.'

'Very little is known about *most* of Hyperion,' said the younger priest, becoming somewhat agitated. 'What about the Time Tombs and the legendary Shrike north of the Bridle Range on Equus?' he said. 'They're *famous*!'

'Precisely,' said Father Duré. 'Lenar, how many learned papers have been written on the Tombs and the Shrike creature? Hundreds? Thousands?' The aging priest had tamped in tobacco and now lighted his pipe: no small feat in zero-g, Hoyt observed. 'Besides,' said Paul Duré, 'even if the Shrike-thing is real, it is not human. I am partial to human beings.'

'Yes,' said Hoyt, ransacking his mental arsenal for potent arguments, 'but the Bikura are such a *small* mystery. At the most you're going to find a few dozen indigenies living in a region so cloudy and smoky and . . . *unimportant* that even the colony's own mapsats haven't noticed them. Why choose them when there are *big* mysteries to study on Hyperion . . . like the labyrinths!' Hoyt had brightened. 'Did you know that Hyperion is one of the nine labyrinthine worlds, Father?'

'Of course,' said Duré. A rough hemisphere of smoke expanded from him until air currents broke it into tendrils and tributaries. 'But the labyrinths have their researchers and admirers throughout the Web, Lenar, and the tunnels have been there – on all nine worlds – for how long? Half a million standard years? Closer to three quarters of a million, I believe. Their secret will last. But how long will the Bikura culture last before they're absorbed into modern colonial society or, more likely, are simply wiped out by circumstances?'

Hoyt shrugged. 'Perhaps they're already gone. It's been a long time since Spedling's encounter with them and there haven't been any other confirmed reports. If they *are* extinct as a group, then all of your time-debt and labor and pain of getting there will be for nothing.'

'Precisely,' was all that Father Paul Duré had said and puffed calmly on his pipe.

It was in their last hour together, during the dropship ride down, that Father Hoyt had gained the slightest glimpse into his companion's thoughts. The limb of Hyperion had been glowing white and green and lapis above them for hours when suddenly the old dropship had cut into the upper layers of atmosphere, flame had briefly filled the window, and then they were flying silently some sixty kilometers above dark cloud masses and starlit seas with the hurtling terminator of Hyperion's sunrise rushing toward them like a spectral tidal wave of light.

'Marvelous,' Paul Duré had whispered, more to himself than to his young companion. 'Marvelous. It is at times like this that I have the sense . . . the slightest sense . . . of what a sacrifice it must have been for the Son of God to condescend to become the Son of Man.'

Hoyt had wanted to talk then, but Father Duré had continued to stare out the window, lost in thought. Ten minutes later they had landed at Keats Interstellar, Father Duré was soon swept into the whirlpool of customs and luggage rituals, and twenty minutes after that a thoroughly disappointed Lenar Hoyt was rising toward space and the *Nadia Oleg* once again.

* * *

'Five weeks later of my time, I returned to Pacem,' said Father Hoyt. 'I had mislaid eight years but for some reason my sense of loss ran deeper than that simple fact. Immediately upon my return, the bishop informed me that there had been no word from Paul Duré during the four years of his stay on Hyperion. The New Vatican had spent a fortune on fatline inquiries, but neither the colonial authorities nor the consulate in Keats had been able to locate the missing priest.'

Hoyt paused to sip from his water glass and the Consul said, 'I remember the search. I never met Duré, of course, but we did our best to trace him. Theo, my aide, spent a lot of energy over the years trying to solve the case of the missing cleric. Other than a few contra-dictory reports of sightings in Port Romance, there was no trace of him. And those sightings went back to the weeks right after his arrival, years before. There were hundreds of plantations out there with no radios or comlines, primarily because they were harvesting boot-leg drugs as well as fiberplastic. I guess we never talked to the people at the right plantation. At least I know Father Duré's file was still open when I left.'

Father Hoyt nodded. 'I landed in Keats a month after your replacement had taken over at the consulate. The bishop had been astonished when I volunteered to return. His Holiness himself granted me an audience. I was on Hyperion less than seven of its local months. By the time I left to return to the Web, I had discovered the fate of Father Duré.' Hoyt tapped the two stained leather books on the table. 'If I am to complete this,' he said, his voice thick, 'I must read excerpts from these.'

The treeship *Yggdrasill* had turned so the bulk of the tree had blocked the sun. The effect was to plunge the dining platform and the curved canopy of leaves beneath it into night, but instead of a few thousand stars dotting the sky, as would have been the case from a planet's surface, literally a million suns blazed above, beside, and beneath the group at the table. Hyperion was a distinct sphere now, hurtling directly at them like some deadly missile.

'Read,' said Martin Silenus.

FROM THE JOURNAL OF
FATHER PAUL DURÉ:

Day 1:

So begins my exile.

I am somewhat at a loss as to how to date my new journal. By the monastic calendar on Pacem, it is the seventeenth day of Thomasmonth in the Year of Our Lord 2732. By Hegemony Standard, it is October 12, 589 P.C. By Hyperion reckoning, or so I am told by the wizened little clerk in the old hotel where I am staying, it is the twenty-third day of Lycius (the last of their seven forty-day months), either 426 A.D.C. (after dropship crash!) or the hundred and twenty-eighth year of the reign of Sad King Billy, who has not reigned for at least a hundred of those years.

To hell with it. I'll call it Day 1 of my exile.

Exhausting day. (Strange to be tired after months of sleep, but that is said to be a common reaction after awakening from fugue. My cells feel the fatigue of these past months of travel even if I do not remember them. I don't remember feeling this tired from travel when I was younger.)

I felt bad about not getting to know young Hoyt better. He seems a decent sort, all proper catechism and bright eyes. It's no fault of youngsters like him that the Church is in its final days. It's just that his brand of happy naiveté can do nothing to arrest that slide into oblivion which the Church seems destined for.

Well, my contributions have not helped either.

Brilliant view of my new world as the dropship brought us down. I was able to make out two of the three continents – Equus and Aquila. The third one, Ursa, was not visible.

Planetfall at Keats and hours of effort getting through customs and taking ground transit into the city. Confused images: the mountain range to the north with its shifting, blue haze, foothills forested with orange and yellow trees, pale sky with its green-blue undercoating,

30

the sun too small but more brilliant than Pacem's. Colors seem more vivid from a distance, dissolving and scattering as one approaches, like a pointillist's palette. The great sculpture of Sad King Billy which I had heard so much about was oddly disappointing. Seen from the highway, it looked raw and rough, a hasty sketch chiseled from the dark mountain, rather than the regal figure I had expected. It does brood over this ramshackle city of half a million people in a way that the neurotic poet-king probably would have appreciated.

The town itself seems to be separated into the sprawling maze of slums and saloons which the locals call Jacktown and Keats itself, the so-called Old City although it dates back only four centuries, all polished stone and studied sterility. I will take the tour soon.

I had scheduled a month in Keats but already I am eager to press on. Oh, Monsignor Edouard, if you could see me now. Punished but still unrepentant. More alone than ever but strangely satisfied with my new exile. If my punishment for past excesses brought about by my zeal is to be banishment to the seventh circle of desolation, then Hyperion was well chosen. I could forget my self-appointed mission to the distant Bikura (are they real? I think not this night) and content myself with living out the remainder of my years in this provincial capital on this godforsaken backwater world. My exile would be no less complete.

Ah, Edouard, boys together, classmates together (although I was not so brilliant nor so orthodox as you), now old men together. But now you are four years wiser and I am still the mischievous, unrepentant boy you remember. I pray that you are alive and well and praying for me.

Tired. Will sleep. Tomorrow, take the tour of Keats, eat well, and arrange transport to Aquila and points south.

Day 5:

There is a cathedral in Keats. Or, rather, there was one. It has been abandoned for at least two standard centuries. It lies in ruins with its transept open to the green-blue skies, one of its western towers unfinished, and the other tower a skeletal framework of tumbled stone and rusted reinforcement rods.

I stumbled upon it while wandering, lost, along the banks of the Hoolie River in the sparsely populated section of town where the Old City decays into Jacktown amid a jumble of tall warehouses which prevent even a glimpse of the ruined towers of the cathedral until one turns a corner onto a narrow cul-de-sac and there is the shell of the cathedral; its chapter house has half fallen away into the river, its facade is pocked with remnants of the mournful, apocalyptic statuary of the post-Hegira expansionist period.

I wandered through the latticework of shadows and fallen blocks into the nave. The bishopric on Pacem had not mentioned any history of Catholicism on Hyperion, much less the presence of a cathedral. It is almost inconceivable that the scattered seedship colony of four centuries ago could have supported a large enough congregation to warrant the presence of a bishop, much less a cathedral. Yet there it was.

I poked through the shadows of the sacristy. Dust and powdered plaster hung in the air like incense, outlining two shafts of sunlight streaming down from narrow windows high above. I stepped out into a broader patch of sunlight and approached an altar stripped of all decoration except for chips and cracks caused by falling masonry. The great cross which had hung on the east wall behind the altar had also fallen and now lay in ceramic splinters among the heap of stones there. Without conscious thought I stepped behind the altar, raised my arms, and began the celebration of the Eucharist. There was no sense of parody or melodrama in this act, no symbolism or hidden intention; it was merely the automatic reaction of a priest who had said Mass almost daily for more than forty-six years of his life and who now faced the prospect of never again participating in the reassuring ritual of that celebration.

It was with some shock that I realized I had a congregation. The old woman was kneeling in the fourth row of pews. The black of her dress and scarf blended so perfectly with the shadows there that only the pale oval of her face was visible, lined and ancient, floating disembodied in the darkness. Startled, I stopped speaking the litany of consecration. She was looking at me but something about her eyes, even at a distance, instantly convinced me that she was blind. For a moment I could not speak and stood there mute, squinting in the dusty light bathing the altar, trying to explain this spectral image to myself while at the same time attempting to frame an explanation of my own presence and actions.

When I did find my voice and called to her – the words echoing in the great hall – I realized that she had moved. I could hear her feet scraping on the stone floor. There was a rasping sound and then a brief flare of light illuminated her profile far to the right of the altar. I shielded my eyes from the shafts of sunlight and began picking my way over the detritus where the altar railing had once stood. I called to her again, offered reassurances, and told her not to be afraid, even though it was I who had chills coursing up my back. I moved quickly but when I reached the sheltered corner of the nave she was gone. A small door led to the crumbling chapter house and the riverbank. There was no sign of her. I returned to the dark interior and would have gladly attributed her appearance to my imagination, a waking dream after so many months of enforced cryogenic dreamlessness, but for a single, tangible proof of her presence. There in the cool darkness burned a lone red votive candle, its tiny flame flickering to unseen drafts and currents.

I am tired of this city. I am tired of its pagan pretensions and false histories. Hyperion is a poet's world devoid of poetry. Keats itself is a mixture of tawdry, false classicism and mindless, boomtown energy. There are three Zen Gnostic assemblies and four High Muslim mosques in the town, but the real houses of worship are the countless saloons and brothels, the huge marketplaces handling the fiberplastic shipments from the south, and the Shrike Cult temples where lost souls hide their suicidal hopelessness behind a shield of shallow mysticism. The whole planet reeks of mysticism without revelation.

To hell with it.

Tomorrow I head south. There are skimmers and other aircraft on this absurd world but, for the Common Folk, travel between these accursed island continents seems restricted to boat – which takes forever, I am told – or one of the huge passenger dirigibles which departs from Keats only once a week.

I leave early tomorrow by dirigible.

Day 10:

Animals.

The firstdown team for this planet must have had a fixation on animals. Horse, Bear, Eagle. For three days we were creeping down the east coast of Equus over an irregular coastline called the Mane. We've spent the last day making the crossing of a short span of the Middle Sea to a large island called Cat Key. Today we are offloading passengers and freight at Felix, the 'major city' of the island. From what I can see from the observation promenade and the mooring tower, there can't be more than five thousand people living in that random collection of hovels and barracks.

Next the ship will make its eight-hundred-kilometer crawl down a series of smaller islands called the Nine Tails and then take a bold leap across seven hundred kilometers of open sea and the equator. The next land we see then is the northwest coast of Aquila, the so-called Beak.

Animals.

To call this conveyance a 'passenger dirigible' is an exercise in creative semantics. It is a huge lifting device with cargo holds large enough to carry the town of Felix out to sea and still have room for thousands of bales of fiberplastic. Meanwhile, the less important cargo – we passengers – make do where we can. I have set up a cot near the aft loading portal and made a rather comfortable niche for myself with my personal luggage and three large trunks of expedition gear. Near me is a family of eight – indigenie plantation workers returning from a biannual shopping expedition of their own to Keats – and although I do not mind the sound or scent of their caged pigs or the squeal of their food hamsters, the incessant, confused crowing of their poor befuddled rooster is more than I can stand some nights.

Animals!

Day 11:

Dinner tonight in the salon above the promenade deck with Citizen Heremis Denzel, a retired professor from a small planters' college near Endymion. He informed me that the Hyperion firstdown team had no animal fetish after all; the official names of the three continents are not Equus, Ursa, and Aquila, but Creighton, Allensen, and Lopez. He went on to say that this was in honor of three middle-level bureaucrats in the old Survey Service. Better the animal fetish!

It is after dinner. I am alone on the outside promenade to watch the sunset. The walkway here is sheltered by the forward cargo modules so the wind is little more than a salt-tinged breeze. Above me curves the orange and green skin of the dirigible. We are between islands; the sea is a rich lapis shot through with verdant undertones, a reversal of sky tones. A scattering of high cirrus catches the last light of Hyperion's too-small sun and ignites like burning coral. There is no sound except for the faintest hum of the electric turbines. Three hundred meters below, the shadow of a huge, mantalike undersea creature keeps pace with the dirigible. A second ago an insect or bird the size and color of a hummingbird but with gossamer wings a meter across paused five meters out to inspect me before diving toward the sea with folded wings.

Edouard, I feel very alone tonight. It would help if I knew you were alive, still working in the garden, writing evenings in your study. I thought my travels would stir my old beliefs in St Teilhard's concept of the God in Whom the Christ of Evolution, the Personal, and the Universal, the *En Haut* and the *En Avant* are joined, but no such renewal is forthcoming.

It is growing dark. I am growing old. I feel something . . . not yet remorse . . . at my sin of falsifying the evidence on the Armaghast dig. But, Edouard, Your Excellency, if the artifacts *had* indicated the presence of a Christ-oriented culture there, six hundred light-years from Old Earth, almost three thousand years *before* man left the surface of the homeworld . . .

Was it so dark a sin to interpret such ambiguous data in a way which would have meant the resurgence of Christianity in our life-time?

Yes, it was. But not, I think, because of the sin of tampering with the data, but the deeper sin of thinking that Christianity could be saved. The Church is dying, Edouard. And not merely our beloved branch of the Holy Tree, but all of its offshoots, vestiges and cankers. The entire Body of Christ is dying as surely as this poorly used body of mine, Edouard. You and I knew this in Armaghast, where the blood-sun illuminated only dust and death. We knew it that cool, green summer at the College when we took our first vows. We knew it as boys in the quiet playfields of Villefranche-sur-Saône. We know it now.

The light is gone now; I must write by the slight glow from the salon windows a deck above. The stars lie in strange constellations. The Middle Sea glows at night with a greenish, unhealthy phosphorescence. There is a dark mass on the horizon to the southeast. It may be a storm or it may be the next island in the chain, the third of the nine 'tails.' (What mythology deals with a cat with nine tails? I know of none.)

For the sake of the bird I saw earlier – if it was a bird – I pray that it is an island ahead and not a storm.

Day 28:

I have been in Port Romance eight days and I have seen three dead men.

The first was a beached corpse, a bloated, white parody of a man, that had washed up on the mud flats beyond the mooring tower my first evening in town. Children threw stones at it.

The second man I watched being pulled from the burned wreckage of a methane-unit shop in the poor section of town near my hotel. His body was charred beyond recognition and shrunken by the heat, his arms and legs pulled tight in the prizefighter posture burning victims have been reduced to since time immemorial. I had been fasting all day and I confess with shame that I began to salivate when the air filled with the rich, frying-fat odor of burned flesh.

The third man was murdered not three meters from me. I had just emerged from the hotel onto the maze of mud-splattered planks that serve as sidewalks in this miserable town when shots rang out and a man several paces ahead of me lurched as if his foot had slipped, spun toward me with a quizzical look on his face, and fell sideways into the mud and sewage.

He had been shot three times with some sort of projectile weapon. Two of the bullets had struck his chest, the third entered just below the left eye. Incredibly, he was still breathing when I reached him. Without thinking about it, I removed my stole from my carrying bag, fumbled for the vial of holy water I had carried for so long, and proceeded to perform the sacrament of Extreme Unction. No one in the gathering crowd objected. The fallen man stirred once, cleared his throat as if he were about to speak, and died. The crowd dispersed even before the body was removed.

The man was middle-aged, sandy-haired, and slightly overweight. He carried no identification, not even a universal card or comlog. There were six silver coins in his pocket.

For some reason, I elected to stay with the body the rest of that day. The doctor was a short and cynical man who allowed me to stay during the required autopsy. I suspect that he was starved for conversation.

'This is what the whole thing's worth,' he said as he opened the poor man's belly like a pink satchel, pulling the folds of skin and muscle back and pinning them down like tent flaps.

'What thing?' I asked.

'His life,' said the doctor and pulled the skin of the corpse's face up and back like a greasy mask. 'Your life. My life.' The red and white stripes of overlapping muscle turned to blue bruise around the ragged hole just above the cheekbone.

'There has to be more than this,' I said.

The doctor looked up from his grim work with a bemused smile. 'Is there?' he said. 'Please show me.' He lifted the man's heart and seemed to weigh it in one hand. 'In the Web worlds, this'd be worth some money on the open market. There're those too poor to keep vat-grown, cloned parts in store, but too well off to die just for want of a heart. But out here it's just offal.'

'There has to be more,' I said, although I felt little conviction. I remembered the funeral of His Holiness Pope Urban XV shortly before I left Pacem. As has been the custom since pre-Hegira days, the corpse was not embalmed. It waited in the anteroom off the main basilica to be fitted for the plain wooden coffin. As I helped Edouard and Monsignor Frey place the vestments on the stiffened corpse I noticed the browning skin and slackening mouth.

The doctor shrugged and finished the perfunctory autopsy. There was the briefest of formal inquiries. No suspect was found, no motive put forward. A description of the murdered man was sent to Keats but the man himself was buried the next day in a pauper's field between the mud flats and the yellow jungle.

Port Romance is a jumble of yellow, weirwood structures set on a maze of scaffolds and planks stretching far out onto the tidal mud flats at the mouth of the Kans. The river is almost two kilometers wide here where it spills out into Toschahai Bay, but only a few channels are navigable and the dredging goes on day and night. I

38

lie awake each night in my cheap room with the window open to the pounding of the dredge-hammer sounding like the booming of this vile city's heart, the distant susurration of the surf its wet breathing. Tonight I listen to the city breathe and cannot help but give it the flayed face of the murdered man.

The companies keep a skimmerport on the edge of town to ferry men and matériel inland to the larger plantations, but I do not have enough money to bribe my way aboard. Rather, I could get *myself* aboard but cannot afford to transport my three trunks of medical and scientific gear. I am still tempted. My service among the Bikura seems more absurd and irrational now than ever before. Only my strange need for a destination and a certain masochistic determination to complete the terms of my self-imposed exile keep me moving upriver.

There is a riverboat departing up the Kans in two days. I have booked passage and will move my trunks onto it tomorrow. It will not be hard to leave Port Romance behind.

Day 41:

The *Emporotic Girandole* continues its slow progress upriver. No sight of human habitation since we left Melton's Landing two days ago. The jungle presses down to the riverbank like a solid wall now; more, it almost completely overhangs us in places where the river narrows to thirty or forty meters. The light itself is yellow, rich as liquid butter, filtered as it is through foliage and fronds eighty meters above the brown surface of the Kans. I sit on the rusted tin roof of the center passenger barge and strain to make out my first glimpse of a tesla tree. Old Kady sitting nearby pauses in his whittling, spits over the side through a gap in his teeth, and laughs at me. 'Ain't going to be no flame trees this far down,' he says. 'If they was the forest sure all hell wouldn't look like this. You got to get up in the Pinions before you see a tesla. We ain't out of the rain forest yet, Padre.'

It rains every afternoon. Actually, rain is too gentle a term for the deluge that strikes us each day, obscuring the shore, pounding the tin roofs of the barges with a deafening roar, and slowing our upstream crawl until it seems we are standing still. It is as if the river becomes a vertical torrent each afternoon, a waterfall which the ship must climb if we are to go on.

The *Girandole* is an ancient, flat-bottomed tow with five barges lashed around it like ragged children clinging to their tired mother's skirts. Three of the two-level barges carry bales of goods to be traded or sold at the few plantations and settlements along the river. The other two offer a simulacrum of lodging for the indigenies traveling upriver, although I suspect that some of the barge's residents are permanent. My own berth boasts a stained mattress on the floor and lizard-like insects on the walls.

After the rains everyone gathers on the decks to watch the evening mists rise from the cooling river. The air is very hot and supersaturated with moisture most of the day now. Old Kady tells me that I have come too late to make the climb through the rain and flame forests before the tesla trees become active. We shall see.

Tonight the mists rise like the spirits of all the dead who sleep beneath the river's dark surface. The last tattered remnants of the afternoon's cloud cover dissipate through the treetops and color returns to the world. I watch as the dense forest shifts from chrome yellow to a translucent saffron and then slowly fades through ocher to umber to gloom. Aboard the *Girandole*, Old Kady lights the lanterns and candle-globes hanging from the sagging second tier and, as if not to be outdone, the darkened jungle begins to glow with the faint phosphorescence of decay while glowbirds and multihued gossamers can be seen floating from branch to branch in the darker upper regions.

Hyperion's small moon is not visible tonight but this world moves through more debris than is common for a planet so close to its sun and the night skies are illuminated by frequent meteor showers. Tonight the heavens are especially fertile and when we move onto wide

40

sections of the river we can see a tracery of brilliant meteor trails weaving the stars together. Their images burn the retina after a while and I look down at the river only to see the same optic echo there in the dark waters.

There is a bright glow on the eastern horizon and Old Kady tells me that this is from the orbital mirrors which give light to a few of the larger plantations.

It is too warm to return to my cabin. I spread my thin mat on the rooftop of my barge and watch the celestial light show while clusters of indigenie families sing haunting songs in an argot I have not even tried to learn. I wonder about the Bikura, still far away from here, and a strange anxiety rises in me.

Somewhere in the forest an animal screams with the voice of a frightened woman.

Day 60:

Arrived Perecebo Plantation. Sick.

Day 62:

Very ill. Fever, fits of shaking. All yesterday I was vomiting black bile. The rain is deafening. At night the clouds are lit from above by orbital mirrors. The sky seems to be on fire. My fever is very high.

A woman takes care of me. Bathes me. Too sick to be ashamed. Her hair is darker than most indigenies'. She says little. Dark, gentle eyes.

Oh, God, to be sick so far from home.

Day

sheis waiting spying comesin from the rain the thin shirt

on purpose to tempt me, knows what iam my skin burning on fire thin cotton nipples dark against it i knowwho they are they are watching, here hear their voices at night they bathe me in poison burns me they think I dont know but i hear their voices above the rain when the screaming stops stop stop

My skin is almost gone. red underneath can feel the hole in my cheek. when I find the bullet iwill spit it out it out. agnusdeiquitolispecattamundi miserer nobis misere nobis miserere

Day 65:

Thank you, dear Lord, for deliverance from illness.

Day 66:

Shaved today. Was able to make it to the shower.

Semfa helped me prepare for the administrator's visit. I expected him to be one of the large, gruff types I've seen out the window working in the sorting compound, but he was a quiet black man with a slight lisp. He was most helpful. I had been concerned about paying for my medical care but he reassured me that there would be no charge. Even better – he will assign a man to lead me into the high country! He says it is late in the season but if I can travel in ten days we should be able to make it through the flame forest to the Cleft before the tesla trees are fully active.

After he left I sat and talked to Semfa a bit. Her husband died here three local months ago in a harvesting accident. Semfa herself had come from Port Romance; her marriage to Mikel had been a salvation for her and she has chosen to stay on here doing odd jobs rather than go back downriver. I do not blame her.

After a massage, I will sleep. Many dreams about my mother recently.

Ten days. I will be ready in ten days.

Day 75:

Before leaving with Tuk, I went down to the matrix paddies to say goodbye to Semfa. She said little but I could see in her eyes that she was sad to see me go. Without premeditation, I blessed her and then kissed her on the forehead. Tuk stood nearby, smiling and bobbing. Then we were off, leading the two packbrids. Supervisor Orlandi came to the end of the road and waved as we entered the narrow lane hacked into the aureate foliage.

Domine, dirige nos.

Day 82:

After a week on the trail – what trail? – after a week in the trackless, yellow rain forest, after a week of exhausting climb up the ever steeper shoulder of the Pinion Plateau, we emerged this morning onto a rocky outcropping that allowed us a view back across an expanse of jungle toward the Beak and the Middle Sea. The plateau here is almost three thousand meters above sea level and the view was impressive. Heavy rain clouds spread out below us to the foot of the Pinion Hills, but through gaps in the white and gray carpet of cloud we caught glimpses of the Kans in its leisurely uncoiling toward Port R. and the sea, chrome-yellow swatches of the forest we had struggled through, and a hint of magenta far to the east that Tuk swore was the lower matrix of fiberplastic fields near Perecebo.

We continued onward and upward late into the evening. Tuk is obviously worried that we will be caught in the flame forests when the tesla trees become active. I struggle to keep up, tugging at the heavily laden 'brid and saying silent prayers to keep my mind off my aches, pains, and general misgivings.

Day 83:

Loaded and moving before dawn today. The air smells of smoke and ashes.

The change in vegetation here on the Plateau is startling. No longer evident are the ubiquitous weirwood and leafy chalma. After passing through an intermediate zone of short evergreens and everblues, then after climbing again through dense strands of mutated lodgepole pines and triaspen, we came into the flame forest proper with its groves of tall prometheus, trailers of ever present phoenix, and round stands of amber lambents. Occasionally we encountered impenetrable breaks of the white-fibrous, bifurcated bestos plants that Tuk picturesquely referred to as '. . . looking like de rotting cocks o' some dead giants what be buried shallow here, dat be sure.' My guide has a way with words.

It was late afternoon before we saw our first tesla tree. For half an hour we had been trudging over an ash-covered forest floor, trying not to tread on the tender shoots of phoenix and firewhip gamely pushing up through the sooty soil, when suddenly Tuk stopped and pointed.

The tesla tree, still half a kilometer away, stood at least a hundred meters tall, half again as high as the tallest prometheus. Near its crown it bulged with the distinctive onion-shaped dome of its accumulator gall. The radial branches above the gall trailed dozens of nimbus vines, each looking silver and metallic against the clear green and lapis sky. The whole thing made me think of some elegant High Muslim mosque on New Mecca irreverently garlanded with tinsel.

'We got to get de 'brids and our asses de hell out o' here,' grunted Tuk. He insisted that we change into flame forest gear right then and there. We spent the rest of the afternoon and evening trudging on in our osmosis masks and thick, rubber-soled boots, sweating under layers of leathery gamma-cloth. Both of the 'brids acted nervous, their long ears pricking at the slightest sound. Even through my mask I could smell

44

the ozone; it reminded me of electric trains I had played with as a child on lazy Christmas Day afternoons in Villefranche-sur-Saône.

We are camping as close as we can to a bestos break this night. Tuk showed me how to set out the ring of arrestor rods, all the time clucking dire warnings to himself and searching the evening sky for clouds.

I plan to sleep well in spite of everything.

Day 84:

0400 hours—
Sweet Mother of Christ.

For three hours we have been caught up in the middle of the end of the world.

The explosions started shortly after midnight, mere lightning crashes at first, and against our better judgment Tuk and I slid our heads through the tent flap to watch the pyrotechnics. I am used to the Matthew-month monsoon storms on Pacem, so the first hour of lightning displays did not seem too unusual. Only the sight of distant tesla trees as the unerring focus of the aerial discharge was a bit unnerving. But soon the forest behemoths were glowing and spitting with their own accumulated energy and then – just as I was drifting off to sleep despite the continued noise – true Armageddon was unleashed.

At least a hundred arcs of electricity must have been released in the first ten seconds of the tesla trees' opening spasms of violent energy. A prometheus less than thirty meters from us exploded, dropping flaming brands fifty meters to the forest floor. The arrestor rods glowed, hissed, and deflected arc after arc of blue-white death over and around our small campsite. Tuk screamed something but no mere human sound was audible over the onslaught of light and noise. A patch of trailing phoenix burst into flame near the tethered 'brids and one of the terrified animals – hobbled and blindfolded as it was – broke free and lunged through the circle of glowing arrestor rods. Instantly half a dozen bolts of lightning from the nearest tesla arced to the hapless animal. For a mad second I could have sworn I saw the beast's skeleton glowing through boiling flesh and then it spasmed high into the air and simply ceased to be.

For three hours we have watched the end of the world. Two of the arrestor rods have fallen but the other eight continue to function. Tuk and I huddle in the hot cave of our tent, osmosis masks filtering enough cool oxygen out of the superheated, smoky air to allow us to breathe. Only the lack of undergrowth and Tuk's skill in placing our tent away from other targets and near the sheltering bestos plants have allowed us to survive. That and the eight whiskered-alloy rods that stand between us and eternity.

'They seem to be holding up well!' I shout to Tuk over the hiss and crackle, crash and split of the storm.

'Dey be made to stand de hour, mebbe two,' grunts my guide. 'Any time, mebbe sooner, dey fuse, we die.'

I nod and sip at lukewarm water through the slipstrip of my osmosis mask. If I survive this night, I shall always thank God for His generosity in allowing me to see this sight.

Day 87:

Tuk and I emerged from the smoldering northeastern edge of the flame forest at noon yesterday, promptly set up camp by the edge of a small stream, and slept for eighteen hours straight; making up for three nights of no sleep and two grueling days moving without rest through a nightmare of flame and ash. Everywhere we looked as we approached the hogback ridge that marked the terminus of the forest, we could see seedpods and cones burst open with new life for the various fire species that had died in the conflagration of the previous two nights. Five of our arrestor rods still functioned, although neither Tuk nor I was eager to test them another night. Our surviving packbrid collapsed and died the instant the heavy load was lifted off its back.

I awoke this morning at dawn to the sound of running water. I followed the small stream a kilometer to the northeast, following a deepening in its sound, until suddenly it dropped from sight.

The Cleft! I had almost forgotten our destination. This morning, stumbling through the fog, leaping from one wet rock to another alongside the widening stream, I took a leap to a final boulder, teetered there, regained my balance, and looked straight down above a waterfall that dropped almost three thousand meters to mist, rock, and river far below.

The Cleft was not carved out of the rising plateau as was the legendary Grand Canyon on Old Earth or World Crack on Hebron. In spite of its active oceans and seemingly earthlike continents, Hyperion is tectonically quite dead; more like Mars, Lusus, or Armaghast in its total lack of continental drift. And like Mars and Lusus, Hyperion is afflicted with its Deep Ice Ages, although here the periodicity is spread to thirty-seven million years by the long ellipse of the currently absent binary dwarf. The comlog compares the Cleft to the pre-terraformed Mariner Valley on Mars, both being caused by the weakening of crust through periodic freeze and thaw over the aeons, followed by the flow of subterranean rivers such as the Kans. Then the massive collapse, running like a long scar through the mountainous wing of the continent Aquila.

Tuk joined me as I stood on the edge of the Cleft. I was naked, rinsing the ash smell from my traveling clothes and cassock. I splashed cold water over my pale flesh and laughed out loud as the echoes of Tuk's shouts came back from the North Wall two thirds of a kilometer away. Because of the nature of the crust collapse, Tuk and I stood far out on an overhang that hid the South Wall below us. Although perilously exposed, we assumed that the rocky cornice which had defied gravity for millions of years would last a few more hours as we bathed, relaxed, shouted echoing hallos until we were hoarse, and generally acted like children liberated from school. Tuk confessed that he had never penetrated the full width of the flame forest – nor known anyone who had in this season – and announced that, now that the tesla trees were becoming fully active, he would have at least a three-month wait until he could return. He did not seem too sorry and I was glad to have him with me.

In the afternoon we transported my gear in relays, setting up camp near the stream a hundred meters back from the cornice and stacking my flowfoam boxes of scientific gear for further sorting in the morning.

It was cold this evening. After dinner, just before sunset, I pulled on my thermal jacket and walked alone to a rocky ledge southwest of where I had first encountered the Cleft. From my vantage point far out over the river, the view was memorable. Mists rose from unseen waterfalls tumbling to the river far below, spray rising in shifting curtains of mist to multiply the setting sun into a dozen violet spheres and twice that many rainbows. I watched as each spectrum was born, rose toward the darkening dome of sky, and died. As the cooling air settled into the cracks and caverns of the plateau and the warm air rushed skyward, pulling leaves, twigs, and mist upward in a vertical gale, a sound ebbed up out of the Cleft as if the continent itself was calling with the voices of stone giants, gigantic bamboo flutes, church organs the size of palaces, the clear, perfect notes ranging from the shrillest soprano to the deepest bass. I speculated on wind vectors against the fluted rock walls, on caverns far below venting deep cracks in the motionless crust, and on the illusion of human voices that random harmonics can generate. But in the end I set aside speculation and simply listened as the Cleft sang its farewell hymn to the sun.

I walked back to our tent and its circle of bioluminescent lantern light as the first fusillade of meteor showers burned the skies overhead and distant explosions from the flame forests rippled along the southern and western horizons like cannon fire from some ancient war on pre-Hegira Old Earth.

Once in the tent I try the long-range comlog bands but there is nothing but static. I suspect that even if the primitive comsats that serve the fiberplastic plantations were ever to broadcast this far east, anything but the tightest laser or fatline beams would be masked by the mountains and tesla activity. On Pacem, few of us at the monastery wore or carried personal comlogs, but the datasphere was always there if we needed to tap into it. Here there is no choice.

I sit and listen to the last notes from the canyon wind die, watch the skies simultaneously darken and blaze, smile at the sound of Tuk's snoring from his bedroll outside the tent, and I think to myself, *If this is exile, so be it.*

Day 88:

Tuk is dead. Murdered.

I found his body when I left the tent at sunrise. He had been sleeping outside, not more than four meters from me. He had said that he wished to sleep under the stars.

The murderers cut his throat while he slept. I heard no cry. I did dream, however: dreams of Semfa ministering to me during my fever. Dreams of cool hands touching my neck and chest, touching the crucifix I have worn since childhood. I stood over Tuk's body, staring at the wide, dark circle where his blood had soaked into Hyperion's uncaring soil, and I shivered at the thought that the dream had been more than a dream – that hands *had* touched me in the night.

I confess that I reacted more like a frightened old fool than as a priest. I did administer Extreme Unction, but then the panic struck me and I left my poor guide's body, desperately searched through the supplies for a weapon, and took away the machete I had used in the rain forest and the low-voltage maser with which I had planned to hunt small game. Whether I would have used a weapon on a human being, even to save my own life, I do not know. But, in my panic, I carried the machete, the maser, and the powered binoculars to a high boulder near the Cleft and searched the region for any signs of the murderers. Nothing stirred except the tiny arboreals and gossamers we had seen flitting through the trees yesterday. The forest itself seemed

49

abnormally thick and dark. The Cleft offered a hundred terraces, ledges, and rock balconies to the northeast for entire bands of savages. An army could have hidden there in the crags and ever present mists.

After thirty minutes of fruitless vigilance and foolish cowardice, I returned to the campsite and prepared Tuk's body for burial. It took me well over two hours to dig a proper grave in the rocky soil of the plateau. When it was filled and the formal service was finished, I could think of nothing personal to say about the rough, funny little man who had been my guide. 'Watch over him, Lord,' I said at last, disgusted at my own hypocrisy, sure in my heart that I was mouthing words only to myself. 'Give him safe passage. Amen.'

This evening I have moved my camp half a kilometer north. My tent is pitched in an open area ten meters away but I am wedged with my back against the boulder, sleeping robes pulled around, the machete and maser nearby. After Tuk's funeral I went through the supplies and boxes of equipment. Nothing had been taken except for the few remaining arrestor rods. Immediately I wondered if someone had followed us through the flame forest in order to kill Tuk and strand me here, but I could think of no motive for such an elaborate action. Anyone from the plantations could have killed us as we slept in the rain forest or – better yet from a murderer's point of view – deep in the flame forest where no one would wonder at two charred corpses. That left the Bikura. My primitive charges.

I considered returning through the flame forest without the rods but soon abandoned the idea. It is probable death to stay and certain death to go.

Three months before the teslas become dormant. One hundred twenty of the twenty-six-hour local days. An eternity.

Dear Christ, why has this come to me? And why was I spared last night if I am merely to be offered up this night . . . or next?

I sit here under the darkening crag and I listen to the suddenly ominous moaning rising with the night wind from the Cleft and I pray as the sky lights with the blood-red streaks of meteor trails.

Mouthing words to myself.

Day 95:

The terrors of the past week have largely abated. I find that even fear fades and becomes commonplace after days of anticlimax.

I used the machete to cut small trees for a lean-to, covering the roof and side with gamma-cloth and caulking between the logs with mud. The back wall is the solid stone of the boulder. I have sorted through my research gear and set some of it out, although I suspect that I will never use it now.

I have begun foraging to supplement my quickly diminishing cache of freeze-dried food. By now, according to the absurd schedule drawn up so long ago on Pacem, I was to have been living with the Bikura for some weeks and trading small goods for local food. No matter. Besides my diet of bland but easily boiled chalma roots, I have found half a dozen varieties of berries and larger fruits that the comlog assures me are edible; so far only one has disagreed with me enough to keep me squatting all night near the edge of the nearest ravine.

I pace the confines of the region as restlessly as one of those caged pelops that were so prized by the minor padishahs on Armaghast. A kilometer to the south and four to the west, the flame forests are in full form. In the morning, smoke vies with the shifting curtains of mist to hide the sky. Only the near-solid breaks of bestos, the rocky soil here on the summit plateau, and the hogback ridges running like armor-plated vertebrae northeast from here keep the teslas at bay.

To the north, the plateau widens out and the undergrowth becomes denser near the Cleft for some fifteen kilometers until the way is blocked by a ravine a third as deep and half as wide as the Cleft itself. Yesterday I reached this northernmost point and stared across the gaping barrier with some frustration. I will try again someday, detouring to the east to find a crossing point, but from the telltale signs of phoenix across the chasm and the pall of smoke along the northeastern horizon, I suspect I will find only the chalma-filled canyons and steppes of flame forest that are roughed in on the orbital survey map I carry.

Tonight I visited Tuk's rocky grave as the evening wind began to wail its aeolian dirge. I knelt there and tried to pray but nothing came.

Edouard, nothing came. I am as empty as those fake sarcophagi that you and I unearthed by the score from the sterile desert sands near Tarum bel Wadi.

The Zen Gnostics would say that this emptiness is a good sign; that it presages openness to a new level of awareness, new insights, new experience.

Merde.

My emptiness is only . . . emptiness.

Day 96:

I have found the Bikura. Or, rather, they have found me. I will write what I can before they come to rouse me from my 'sleep.'

Today I was doing some detail mapping a mere four kilometers north of camp when the mists lifted in the midday warmth and I noticed a series of terraces on my side of the Cleft that had been hidden until then. I was using my powered glasses to inspect the terraces – actually a series of laddered ledges, spires, shelves, and tussocks extending far out onto the overhang – when I realized that I was staring at man-made habitations. The dozen or so huts were crude – rough hovels of heaped chalma fronds, stones, and spongeturf – but they were unmistakably of human origin.

I was standing there irresolute, binoculars still lifted, trying to decide whether to climb down to the exposed ledges and confront the inhabitants or to retreat to my camp, when I felt that lifting chill along the back and neck that tells one with absolute certainty that he is no longer alone. I lowered the binoculars and turned slowly. The Bikura were there, at least thirty of them, standing in a semi-circle that left me no retreat to the forest.

I do not know what I expected; naked savages, perhaps, with fierce expressions and necklaces of teeth. Perhaps I had half expected to find the kind of bearded, wild-haired hermits that travelers sometimes encountered in the Moshé Mountains on Hebron. Whatever I had held in mind, the reality of the Bikura did not fit the template.

The people who had approached me so silently were short – none came higher than my shoulder – and swathed in roughly woven dark robes that covered them from neck to toe. When they moved, as some did now, they seemed to glide over the rough ground like wraiths. From a distance, their appearance reminded me of nothing so much as a gaggle of diminutive Jesuits at a New Vatican enclave.

I almost giggled then, but realized that such a response might well be a sign of rising panic. The Bikura showed no outward signs of aggression to cause such a panic; they carried no weapons, their small hands were empty. As empty as their expressions.

Their physiognomy is hard to describe succinctly. They are bald. All of them. That baldness, the absence of any facial hair, and the loose robes that fell in a straight line to the ground, all conspired to make it very difficult to tell the men from the women. The group now confronting me – more than fifty by this time – looked to be all of roughly the same age: somewhere between forty and fifty standard years. Their faces were smooth, the skin tinged with a yellowish cast that I guessed might be associated with generations of ingesting trace minerals in the chalma and other local plant life.

One might be tempted to describe the round faces of the Bikura as cherubic until, upon closer inspection, that impression of sweetness fades and is replaced by another interpretation – placid idiocy. As a priest, I have spent enough time on backward worlds to see the effects of an ancient genetic disorder variously called Down's syndrome, mongolism, or generation-ship legacy. This, then, was the overall impression created by the sixty or so dark-robed little people who had approached me – I was being greeted by a silent, smiling band of bald, retarded children.

I reminded myself that these were almost certainly the same group of 'smiling children' who had slit Tuk's throat while he slept and left him to die like a butchered pig.

The closest Bikura stepped forward, stopped five paces from me, and said something in a soft monotone.

'Just a minute,' I said and fumbled out my comlog. I tapped in the translator function.

'Beyetet ota menna lot cresfem ket?' asked the short man in front of me.

I slipped on the hearplug just in time to hear the comlog's translation. There was no lag time. The apparently foreign language was a simple corruption of archaic seedship English not so far removed from the indigene argot of the plantations. 'You are the man who belongs to the cross shape/cruciform,' interpreted the comlog, giving me two choices for the final noun.

'Yes,' I said, knowing now that these were the ones who had touched me the night I slept through Tuk's murder. Which meant that these were the ones who had murdered Tuk.

I waited. The hunting maser was in my pack. The pack was set against a small chalma not ten paces from me. Half a dozen Bikura stood between me and it. It did not matter. I knew at that instant that I would not use a weapon against another human being, even a human being who had murdered my guide and might well be planning to murder me at any second. I closed my eyes and said a silent Act of Contrition. When I opened my eyes, more of the Bikura had arrived. There was a cessation of movement, as if a quorum had been filled, a decision reached.

'Yes,' I said again into the silence, 'I am the one who wears the cross.' I heard the comlog speaker pronounce the last word 'cresfem.'

54

The Bikura nodded in unison and – as if from long practice as altar boys – all went to one knee, robes rustling softly, in a perfect genuflection.

I opened my mouth to speak and found that I had nothing to say. I closed my mouth.

The Bikura stood. A breeze moved the brittle chalma fronds and leaves together to make a dry, end-of-summer sound above us. The Bikura nearest to me on the left stepped closer, grasped my forearm with a touch of cool, strong fingers, and spoke a soft sentence that my comlog translated as, 'Come. It is time to go to the houses and sleep.'

It was midafternoon. Wondering if the comlog had translated the word 'sleep' properly or if it might be an idiom or metaphor for 'die,' I nodded and followed them toward the village at the edge of the Cleft.

Now I sit in the hut and wait. There are rustling sounds. Someone else is awake now. I sit and wait.

Day 97:

The Bikura call themselves the 'Three Score and Ten.'

I have spent the past twenty-six hours talking to them, observing, making notes when they take their two-hour, midafternoon 'sleep,' and generally trying to record as much data as I can before they decide to slit my throat.

Except now I am beginning to believe that they will not hurt me.

I spoke to them yesterday after our 'sleep.' Sometimes they do not respond to questions and when they do the responses are little better than the grunts or divergent answers one receives from slow children. After their initial question and invitation at our first encounter, none of them originated a single query or comment my way.

I questioned them subtly, carefully, cautiously, and with the professional calm of a trained ethnologist. I asked the simplest, most factual questions possible to

55

make sure that the comlog was functioning properly. It was. But the sum total of the answers left me almost as ignorant as I had been twenty-some hours before.

Finally, tired in body and spirit, I abandoned professional subtlety and asked the group I was sitting with, 'Did you kill my companion?'

My three interlocutors did not look up from the weaving they were doing on a crude loom. 'Yes,' said the one I have come to think of as Alpha because he had been the first to approach me in the forest, 'we cut your companion's throat with sharpened stones and held him down and silent while he struggled. He died the true death.'

'Why?' I asked after a moment. My voice sounded as dry as a corn husk crumbling.

'Why did he die the true death?' said Alpha, still not looking up. 'Because all of his blood ran out and he stopped breathing.'

'No,' I said. 'Why did you kill him?'

Alpha did not respond, but Betty – who may or may not be female and Alpha's mate – looked up from her loom and said simply, 'To make him die.'

'Why?'

The responses invariably came back and just as invariably failed to enlightened me one iota. After much questioning, I had ascertained that they had killed Tuk to make him die and that he had died because he had been killed.

'What is the difference between death and true death?' I asked, not trusting the comlog or my temper at this point.

The third Bikura, Del, grunted a response that the comlog interpreted as, 'Your companion died the true death. You did not.'

Finally, in frustration far too close to rage, I snapped, 'Why not? Why didn't you kill me?'

All three stopped in the middle of their mindless weaving and looked at me. 'You cannot be killed because you cannot die,' said Alpha. 'You cannot die because you belong to the cruciform and follow the way of the cross.'

I had no idea why the damn machine would translate cross as 'cross' one second and as 'cruciform' the next. *Because you belong to the cruciform.*

A chill went through me, followed by the urge to laugh. Had I stumbled into that old adventure holo cliché – the lost tribe that worshiped the 'god' that had tumbled into their jungle until the poor bastard cuts himself shaving or something, and the tribespeople, assured and a bit relieved at the obvious mortality of their visitor, offer up their erstwhile deity as a sacrifice?

It would have been funny if the image of Tuk's bloodless face and raw-rimmed, gaping wound was not so fresh.

Their reaction to the cross certainly suggested that I had encountered a group of survivors of a once Christian colony – Catholics? – even though the data in the comlog insisted that the dropship of seventy colonists who had crashed on this plateau four hundred years ago had held only Neo-Kerwin Marxists, all of whom should have been indifferent if not openly hostile to the old religions.

I considered dropping the matter as being far too dangerous to pursue, but my stupid need to know drove me on. 'Do you worship Jesus?' I asked.

Their blank expressions left no need for a verbal negative.

'Christ?' I tired again. 'Jesus Christ? Christian? The Catholic Church?'

No interest.

'Catholic? Jesus? Mary? St Peter? Paul? St Teilhard?'

The comlog made noises but the words seemed to have no meaning for them.

'You follow the cross?' I said, flailing for some last contact.

All three looked at me. 'We belong to the cruciform,' said Alpha.

I nodded, understanding nothing.

This evening I fell asleep briefly just before sunset and when I awoke it was to the organ-pipe music of the Cleft's nightfall winds. It was much louder here on the village ledges. Even the hovels seemed to join the chorus as the rising gusts whistled and whined through stone gaps, flapping fronds, and crude smokeholes.

Something was wrong. It took me a groggy minute to realize that the village was abandoned. Every hut was empty. I sat on a cold boulder and wondered if my presence had sparked some mass exodus. The wind music had ended and meteors were beginning their nightly show through cracks in low clouds when I heard a sound behind me and turned to find all seventy of the Three Score and Ten behind me.

They walked past without a word and went to their huts. There were no lights. I imagined them sitting in their hovels, staring.

I stayed outside for some time before returning to my own hut. After a while I walked to the edge of the grassy shelf and stood where rock dropped away into the abyss. A cluster of vines and roots clung to the cliff face but appeared to end a few meters into space and hang there above emptiness. No vine could have been long enough to offer a way to the river two kilometers below.

But the Bikura had come from this direction.

Nothing made sense. I shook my head and went back to my hut.

Sitting here, writing by the light of the comlog diskey, I try to think of precautions I can take to insure that I will see the sunrise.

I can think of none.

Day 103:

The more I learn, the less I understand.

I have moved most of my gear to the hut they leave empty for me here in the village.

I have taken photographs, recorded video and audio chips, and imaged a full holoscan of the village and its inhabitants. They do not seem to care. I project their images and they walk right through them, showing no interest. I play back their words to them and they smile and go back into their hovels to sit for hours, doing nothing, saying nothing. I offer them trade trinkets and they take them without comment, check to see if they are edible, and then leave them lying. The grass is littered with plastic beads, mirrors, bits of colored cloth, and cheap pens.

I have set up the full medical lab but to no avail; the Three Score and Ten will not let me examine them, will not let me take blood samples, even though I have repeatedly shown them that it is painless, will not let me scan them with the diagnostic equipment – will not, in short, cooperate in any way. They do not argue. They do not explain. They simply turn away and go about their nonbusiness.

After a week I still cannot tell the males from the females. Their faces remind me of those visual puzzles that shift forms as you stare; sometimes Betty's face looks undeniably female and ten seconds later the sense of gender is gone and I think of her (him?) as Beta again. Their voices undergo the same shift. Soft, well modulated, sexless . . . they remind me of the poorly programmed homecomps one encounters on backward worlds.

I find myself hoping to catch a glimpse of a naked Bikura. This is not easy for a Jesuit of forty-eight standard years to admit. Still, it would not be an easy task even for a veteran voyeur. The nudity taboo seems absolute. They wear the long robes while awake and during their two-hour midday nap. They leave the village area to urinate and defecate, and I suspect that they do not remove the loose robes even then. They do not seem to bathe. One would suspect that this would cause olfactory problems, but there is no odor about these primitives except for the slight, sweet smell of chalma. 'You must undress sometimes,' I said to Alpha one day, abandoning delicacy in favor of information. 'No,' said Al and went elsewhere to sit and do nothing while fully dressed.

They have no names. I found this incredible at first, but now I am sure.

'We are all that was and will be,' said the shortest

Bikura, one I think of as female and call Eppie. 'We are the Three Score and Ten.'

I searched the comlog records and confirmed what I suspected: in more than sixteen thousand known human societies, none are listed where there are no individual names at all. Even in the Lusus hive societies, individuals respond to their class category followed by a simple code.

I tell them my name and they stare. 'Father Paul Duré, Father Paul Duré,' repeats the comlog translator but there is no attempt at even simple repetition.

Except for their mass disappearances each day before sunset and their common two-hour sleep time, they do very little as a group. Even their lodging arrangements appear random. Al will spend one naptime with Betty, the next with Gam, and the third with Zelda or Pete. No system or schedule is apparent. Every third day the entire group of seventy goes into the forest to forage and returns with berries, chalma roots and bark, fruit, and whatever else might be edible. I was sure they were vegetarians until I saw Del munching on the cold corpse of an infant arboreal. The little primate must have fallen from the high branches. It seems then that the Three Score and Ten do not disdain meat; they simply are too stupid to hunt and kill it.

When the Bikura are thirsty they walk almost three hundred meters to a stream that cascades into the Cleft. In spite of this inconvenience, there are no signs of water skins, jugs, or any type of pottery. I keep my reserve of water in ten-gallon plastic containers but the villagers take no notice. In my plummeting respect for these people, I do not find it unlikely that they have spent generations in a village with no handy water source.

'Who built the houses?' I ask. They have no word for village.

'The Three Score and Ten,' responds Will. I can tell him from the others only by a broken finger that did not mend well. Each of them has at least one such distinguishing feature, although sometimes I think it would be easier to tell crows apart.

'When did they build them?' I ask, although I should know by now that any question that starts with 'when' will not receive an answer.

I receive no answer.

They do go into the Cleft each evening. Down the vines. On the third evening, I tried to observe this exodus but six of them turned me back from the edge and gently but persistently brought me back to my hut. It was the first observable action of the Bikura that had hinted at aggression and I sat in some apprehension after they had gone.

The next evening as they departed I went quietly to my hut, not even peering out, but after they returned I retrieved the imager and its tripod from where I had left them near the edge. The timer had worked perfectly. The holos showed the Bikura grabbing the vines and scrambling down the cliff face as nimbly as the little arboreals that fill the chalma and weirwood forest. Then they disappeared under the overhang.

'What do you do when you go down the cliff each evening?' I asked Al the next day.

The native looked at me with the seraphic, Buddha smile I have learned to hate. 'You belong to the cruciform,' he said as if that answered everything.

'Do you worship when you go down the cliff?' I asked.

No answer.

I thought a minute. 'I also follow the cross,' I said, knowing that it would be translated as 'belong to the cruciform.' Any day now I will not need the translator program. But this conversation was too important to leave to chance. 'Does this mean that I should join you when you go down the cliff face?'

For a second I thought that Al was thinking. His brow furrowed and I realized that it was the first time that I had seen one of the Three Score and Ten come close to frowning. Then he said, 'You cannot. You belong to the cruciform but you are not of the Three Score and Ten.'

I realized that it had taken every neuron and synapse in his brain to frame that distinction.

'What would you do if I did go down the cliff face?' I asked, expecting no response. Hypothetical questions almost always had as much luck as my time-based queries.

This time he did respond. The seraphic smile and untroubled countenance returned and Alpha said softly, 'If you try to go down the cliff we will hold you down on the grass, take sharpened stones, cut your throat, and wait until your blood stops flowing and your heart stops beating.'

I said nothing. I wondered if he could hear the pounding of my heart at that moment. *Well*, I thought, *at least you don't have to worry any longer that they think you are a god.*

The silence stretched. Finally Al added one more sentence that I have been thinking about ever since. 'And if you did it again,' he said, 'we would have to kill you again.'

We stared at each other for some time after that; each convinced, I am sure, that the other was a total idiot.

Day 104:

Each new revelation adds to my confusion.

The absence of children here has bothered me since my first day in the village. Looking back through my notes, I find frequent mention of it in the daily observations I have dictated to my comlog, but no record of it in the personal mishmash here that I call a journal. Perhaps the implications were too frightening.

To my frequent and clumsy attempts at piercing this mystery, the Three Score and Ten have offered their usual enlightenment. The person questioned smiles beatifically and responds in some non sequitur that would make the babble of the Web's worst village idiot seem like sage aphorisms in comparison. More often than not, they do not answer at all.

One day I stood in front of the one I have tagged as Del, stayed there until he had to acknowledge my presence, and asked, 'Why are there no children?'

'We are the Three Score and Ten,' he said softly.

'Where are the babies?'

No response. No sense of evading the question, merely a blank stare.

I took a breath. 'Who is the youngest among you?'

Del appeared to be thinking, wrestling with the concept. He was overmatched. I wondered if the Bikura had lost their time sense so completely that any such question was doomed. After a minute of silence, however, Del pointed to where Al was crouched in the sunlight, working with his crude hand loom, and said, 'There is the last one to return.'

'To return?' I said. 'From where?'

Del stared at me with no emotion, not even impatience. 'You belong to the cruciform,' he said. 'You must know the way of the cross.'

I nodded. I knew enough to recognize that in this direction lay one of the many conversational illogic-loops that usually derailed our dialogues. I hunted for some way to keep a grasp of the thin thread of information. 'Then Al,' I said and pointed, 'is the last to be born. To return. But others will . . . return?'

I was not sure that I understood my own question. How does one inquire about birth when the interviewee has no word for child and no concept of time? But Del seemed to understand. He nodded.

Encouraged, I asked, 'Then when will the next of the Three Score and Ten be born? Return?'

'No one can return until one dies,' he said.

Suddenly I thought I understood. 'So no new children . . . no one will be returned until someone dies,' I said. 'You replace the missing one with another to keep the group at Three Score and Ten?'

Del responded with the type of silence I had come to interpret as assent.

The pattern seemed clear enough. The Bikura were quite serious about their Three Score and Ten. They kept the tribal population at seventy – the same number recorded on the passenger list of the dropship that crashed here four hundred years ago. Little chance of coincidence there. When someone died, they allowed a

63

child to be born to replace the adult. Simple.

Simple but impossible. Nature and biology do not work that neatly. Besides the problem of minimum-herd population, there were other absurdities. Even though it is difficult to tell the ages of these smooth-skinned people, it is obvious that no more than ten years separates the oldest from the youngest. Although they act like children, I would guess their average age to be in the late thirties or mid-forties in standard years. So where are the very old? Where are the parents, aging uncles, and unmarried aunts? At this rate, the entire tribe will enter old age at approximately the same time. What happens when they all pass beyond childbearing age and it comes time to replace members of the tribe?

The Bikura lead dull, sedentary lives. The accident rate – even while living on the very edge of the Cleft – must be low. There are no predators. the seasonal variations are minimal and the food supply almost certainly remains stable. But, granted all this, there must have been times in the four-hundred-year history of this baffling group when disease swept the village, when more than the usual number of vines gave way and dropped citizens into the Cleft, or when *something* caused that abnormal cluster of sudden deaths that insurance companies have dreaded since time immemorial.

And then what? Do they breed to make up the difference and then revert to their current sexless behavior? Are the Bikura so different from every other recorded human society that they have a rutting period once every few years – once a decade? – once in a lifetime? It is doubtful.

I sit here in my hut and review the possibilities. One is that these people live *very* long lifetimes and can reproduce during most of that time, allowing for simple replacement of tribal casualties. Only this does not explain their common ages. And there is no mechanism to explain any such longevity. The best anti-aging drugs the Hegemony has to offer only manage to extend an active lifetime a bit over the hundred standard-year mark. Preventive health measures have spread the vitality of early middle age well into the late sixties – my age – but except for clonal transplants, bioengineering, and other perqs for the very rich, no one in the Worldweb can expect to begin planning a family when they are seventy or expect to dance at their hundred-and-tenth birthday party. If eating chalma roots or breathing the pure air of the Pinion Plateau had a dramatic effect on retarding aging, it would be a sure bet that everyone on Hyperion would be living here munching chalma, that this planet would have had a farcaster centuries ago, and that every citizen of the Hegemony who has a universal card would be planning to spend vacations and retirement here.

No, a more logical conclusion is that the Bikura live normal-length lives, have children at a normal rate, but kill them unless a replacement is required. They may practice abstinence or birth control – other than slaughtering the newborn – until the entire band reaches an age where new blood will soon be needed. A mass-birthing time explains the apparent common age of the members of the tribe.

But who teaches the young? What happens to the parents and other older people? Do the Bikura pass along the rudiments of their crude excuse for a culture and then allow their own deaths? Would this be a 'true death' – the rubbing out of an entire generation? Do the Three Score and Ten murder individuals at both ends of the bell-shaped age curve?

This type of speculation is useless. I am beginning to get furious at my own lack of problem-solving skills. Let's form a strategy here and act on it, Paul. Get off your lazy, Jesuit ass.

PROBLEM: How to tell the sexes apart?

SOLUTION: Cajole or coerce a few of these poor devils into a medical exam. Find out what all the sex-role mystery and nudity taboo is about. A society that depends upon years of rigid sexual abstinence for population control is consistent with my new theory.

PROBLEM: Why are they so fanatical about maintaining the same Three Score and Ten population that the lost dropship colony started with?

SOLUTION: Keep pestering them until you find out.

PROBLEM: Where are the children?

SOLUTION: Keep pressing and poking until you find out. Perhaps the evening excursion down the cliff is related to all of this. There may be a nursery there. Or a pile of small bones.

PROBLEM: What *is* this 'belong to the cruciform' and 'way of the cross' business if not a contorted vestige of the original colonists' religious belief?

SOLUTION: Find out by going to the source. Could their daily descent down the cliff be religious in nature?

PROBLEM: What *is* down the cliff face?

SOLUTION: Go down and see.

Tomorrow, if their pattern holds true, all threescore and ten of the Three Score and Ten will wander into the woods for several hours of foraging. This time I will go with them.

This time I am going over the edge and down the cliff.

Day 105:

0930 hours – Thank you, O Lord, for allowing me to see what I have seen today.

Thank you, O Lord, for bringing me to this place at this time to see the proof of Your Presence.

1125 hours – Edouard . . . Edouard!

I have to return. To show you all! To show everyone.

I've packed everything I need, putting the imager disks and film in a pouch I wove from bestos leaves. I have food, water, the maser with its weakening charge. Tent. Sleep robes.

If only the arrestor rods had not been stolen!

The Bikura might have kept them. No, I've searched the hovels and the nearby forest. They would have no use for them.

It doesn't matter!

I'll leave today if I can. Otherwise, as soon as I can.

Edouard! I have it all here on the film and disks.

1400—

There is no way through the flame forests today. The smoke drove me back even before I penetrated the edge of the active zone.

I returned to the village and went over the holos. There is no mistake. The miracle is real.

1530 hours—

The Three Score and Ten will return any moment. What if they know . . . what if they can tell by looking at me that I have been *there*?

I could hide.

No, there is no need to hide. God did not bring me this far and let me see what I have seen only to let me die at the hands of these poor children.

1615 hours—

The Three Score and Ten returned and went to their huts without giving me a glance.

I sit here in the doorway of my own hut and cannot keep from smiling, from laughing, and from praying. Earlier I walked to the edge of the Cleft, said Mass, and took Communion. The villagers did not bother to watch.

How soon can I leave? Supervisor Orlandi and Tuk had said that the flame forest was fully active for three local months – a hundred and twenty days – then relatively quiet for two. Tuk and I arrived here on Day 87 . . .

I cannot wait another hundred days to bring the news to the world . . . to all of the worlds.

If only a skimmer would brave the weather and flame forests and pluck me out of here. If only I could access one of the datafix sats that serve the plantations.

Anything is possible. More miracles will occur.

2350 hours—

The Three Score and Ten have gone down into the Cleft. The voices of the evening wind choir are rising all around.

How I wish I could be with them now! There, below.

I will do the next best thing. I will drop to my knees here near the cliff edge and pray while the organ notes of the planet and sky sing what I now know is a hymn to a real and present God.

Day 106:

I awoke today to a perfect morning. The sky was a deep turquoise; the sun was a sharp, blood-red stone set within. I stood outside my hut as the mists cleared, the arboreals ended their morning screech concert, and the air began to warm. Then I went in and viewed my tapes and disks.

I realize that in yesterday's excited scribblings I mentioned nothing of what I found down the cliff. I will do so now. I have the disks, filmtapes, and comlog notes, but there is always the chance that only these personal journals will be found.

I lowered myself over the cliff edge at approximately 0730 hours yesterday morning. The Bikura were all foraging in the forest. The descent on vines had looked simple enough – they were bound around one another sufficiently to create a sort of ladder in most places – but as I swung out and began to let myself down, I could feel my heart pounding hard enough to be painful. There was a sheer three-thousand-meter drop to the rocks and river below. I kept a tight grip on at least two vines at all times and centimetered my way down, trying not to look at the abyss beneath my feet.

It took me the better part of an hour to descend the hundred and fifty meters that I am sure the Bikura can cover in ten minutes. Eventually I reached the curve of an overhang. Some vines trailed away into space but most of them curled under the sheer slab of rock toward the cliff wall thirty meters in. Here and there the vines appeared to have been braided to form crude bridges upon which the Bikura probably walked with little or no help from their hands. I crawled along these braided strands, clutching other vines for support and uttering prayers I had not said since my boyhood. I stared straight ahead as if I could forget that there was only a seemingly infinite expanse of air under those swaying, creaking strands of vegetable matter.

There was a broad ledge along the cliff wall. I allowed three meters of it to separate me from the gulf before I squeezed through the vines and dropped two and a half meters to the stone.

The ledge was about five meters wide and it terminated a short distance to the northeast where the great mass of the overhang began. I followed a path along the ledge to the southwest and had gone twenty or thirty paces before I stopped in shock. It was a *path*. A path worn out of solid stone. Its shiny surface had been pushed centimeters below the level of the surrounding rock. Farther on, where the path descended a curving lip of ledge to a lower, wider level, steps had been cut into the stone but even these had been worn to the point that they seemed to sag in the middle.

I sat down for a second as the impact of this simple fact struck me. Even four centuries of daily travel by the Three Score and Ten could not account for such erosion of solid rock. Someone or something had used this path long before the Bikura colonists crashed here. *Someone or something had used this path for millennia.*

I stood and walked on. There was little noise except for the wind blowing gently along the half-kilometer-wide Cleft. I realized that I could hear the soft sound of the river far below.

The path curved left around a section of cliff and ended. I stepped out onto a broad apron of gently descending stone and stared. I believe I made the sign of the cross without thinking.

Because this ledge ran due north and south for a hundred-meter cut of cliff, I could look due west along a thirty-kilometer slash of Cleft to open sky where the plateau ended. I realized at once that the setting sun would illuminate this slab of cliff wall under the overhang each evening. It would not have surprised me if – on the spring or autumn solstice – Hyperion's sun would, from this vantage point, appear to set directly into the Cleft, its red sides just touching the pink-toned rock walls.

I turned left and stared at the cliff face. The worn path led across the wide ledge to doors carved into the vertical slab of stone. No, these were not merely doors, they were portals, intricately carved portals with elaborate stone casements and lintels. To either side of these twin doors spread broad windows of stained glass, rising

69

at least twenty meters toward the overhang. I went closer and inspected the facade. Whoever had built this had done so by widening the area under the overhang, slicing a sheer, smooth wall into the granite of the plateau, and then tunneling directly into the cliff face. I ran my hand over the deeply cut folds of ornamental carving around the door. Smooth. Everything had been smoothed and worn and softened by time, even here, hidden away from most of the elements by the protective lip of overhang. How many thousands of years had this . . . temple . . . been carved into the south wall of the Cleft?

The stained glass was neither glass nor plastic but some thick, translucent substance that seemed as hard as the surrounding stone to the touch. Nor was the window a composite of panels; the colors swirled, shaded, melded, and blended into one another like oil on water.

I removed my flashlight from the pack, touched one of the doors, and hesitated as the tall portal swung inward with frictionless ease.

I entered the vestibule – there is no other word for it – crossed the silent ten-meter space, and paused in front of another wall made from the same stained-glass material that even now glowed behind me, filling the vestibule with thick light of a hundred subtle hues. I realized instantly that at the sunset hour the direct rays of the sun would fill this room with incredibly deep shafts of color, would strike the stained-glass wall in front of me, and would illuminate whatever lay beyond.

I found the single door, outlined by thin, dark metal set into the stained-glass stone, and I passed through it.

On Pacem we have – as best we could from ancient photos and holos – rebuilt the basilica of St Peter's exactly as it stood in the ancient Vatican. Almost seven hundred feet long and four hundred and fifty feet wide, the church can hold fifty thousand worshipers when His Holiness says Mass. We have never had more than five thousand faithful there even when the Council of Bishops of All the Worlds is in assembly every forty-three years. In the central apse near our copy of Bernini's Throne of St Peter, the great dome rises more than a hundred and thirty meters above the floor of the altar. It is an impressive space.

This space was larger.

In the dim light I used the beam of my flashlight to ascertain that I was in a single great room – a giant hall hollowed out of solid stone. I estimated that the smooth walls rose to a ceiling that must be only a few meters beneath the surface of the crag where the Bikura had set their huts. There was no ornamentation here, no furniture, no sign of any concession to form or function except for the object that sat squarely in the center of this huge, echoing cave of a room.

Centered in the great hall was an altar – a five-meter-square slab of stone left when the rest was hollowed out – and from this altar rose a cross.

Four meters high, three meters wide, carved in the old style of the elaborate crucifixes of Old Earth, the cross faced the stained-glass wall as if awaiting the sun and the explosion of light that would ignite the inlaid diamonds, sapphires, blood crystals, lapis beads, queen's tears, onyxes, and other precious stones that I could make out in the light of the flashlight as I approached.

I knelt and prayed. Shutting off the flashlight, I waited several minutes before my eyes could discern the cross in the dim, smoky light. This was, without a doubt, the cruciform of which the Bikura spoke. And it had been set here a minimum of many thousands of years ago – perhaps tens of thousands – long before mankind first left Old Earth. Almost certainly before Christ taught in Galilee.

I prayed.

Today I sit out in the sunlight after reviewing the holodisks. I have confirmed what I barely noticed during my return up the cliff after discovering what I now think of as 'the basilica.' On the ledge outside the basilica there are steps descending farther into the Cleft. Although not as worn as the path leading to the basilica, they are equally intriguing. God alone knows what other wonders wait below.

I *must* let the worlds know of this find!

The irony of my being the one to discover this is not lost on me. If it had not been for Armaghast and my exile, this discovery might have waited more centuries. The Church might have died before this revelation could have brought new life to it.

But I *have* found it.

One way or the other, I will leave or get my message out.

Day 107:

I am a prisoner.

This morning I was bathing in my usual place near where the stream drops over the cliff edge when I heard a sound and looked up to see the Bikura I call Del staring at me with wide eyes. I called a greeting but the little Bikura turned and ran. It was perplexing. They rarely hurry. Then I realized that even though I had been wearing trousers at the time, I had undoubtedly violated their nudity taboo by allowing Del to see me naked from the waist up.

I smiled, shook my head, finished dressing, and returned to the village. If I had known what awaited me there, I would not have been amused.

The entire Three Score and Ten stood watching as I approached. I stopped a dozen paces from Al. 'Good morning,' I said.

Alpha pointed and half a dozen of the Bikura lunged toward me, seized my arms and legs, and pinned me to the ground. Beta stepped forward and removed a sharp-edged stone from his or her robes. As I struggled in vain to pull free, Beta cut my clothes down the front and pulled apart the shreds until I was all but naked.

I ceased struggling as the mob pressed forward. They stared at my pale, white body and murmured to themselves. I could feel my heart pounding. 'I am sorry if I have offended your laws,' I began, 'but there is no reason . . .'

'Silence,' said Alpha and spoke to the tall Bikura with the scar on his palm – the one I call Zed. 'He is not of the cruciform.'

Zed nodded.

'Let me explain,' I began again, but Alpha silenced me

with a backhanded slap that left my lip bleeding and my ears ringing. There had been no more sense of hostility in his action than I would have shown in silencing a comlog by throwing a switch.

'What are we to do with him?' asked Alpha.

'Those who do not follow the cross must die the true death,' said Beta and the crowd shifted forward. Many had sharpened stones in their hands. 'Those not of the cruciform must die the true death,' said Beta and her voice held the tone of complacent finality common to oft-repeated formulae and religious litanies.

'I *follow* the cross!' I cried out as the crowd tugged me to my feet. I grabbed at the crucifix that hung around my neck and struggled against the pressure of many arms. Finally I managed to lift the little cross over my head.

Alpha held up his hand and the crowd paused. In the sudden silence I could hear the river three kilometers below in the Cleft. 'He does carry a cross,' said Alpha.

Del pressed forward. 'But he is not of the cruciform! I saw. It was not as we thought. He is not of the cruciform!' There was murder in his voice.

I cursed myself for being careless and stupid. The future of the Church depended upon my survival and I had thrown both away by beguiling myself into believing that the Bikura were dull, harmless children.

'Those who do not follow the cross must die the true death,' repeated Beta. It was a final sentencing.

Stones were being raised by seventy hands when I shouted, knowing that it was either my last chance or my final condemnation. 'I have been down the cliff and worshiped at your altar! I follow the cross!'

Alpha and the mob hesitated. I could see that they were wrestling with this new thought. It was not easy for them.

'I follow the cross and wish to be of the cruciform,' I said as calmly as I could. 'I have been to your altar.'

'Those who do not follow the cross must die the true death,' called Gamma.

'But he follows the cross,' said Alpha. 'He has prayed in the room.'

'This cannot be,' said Zed. 'The Three Score and Ten pray there and he is not of the Three Score and Ten.'

'We knew before this that he is not of the Three Score and Ten,' said Alpha, frowning slightly as he dealt with the concept of past tense.

'He is not of the cruciform,' said Delta-two.

'Those who are not of the cruciform must die the true death,' said Beta.

'He follows the cross,' said Alpha. 'Can he not then become of the cruciform?'

An outcry arose. In the general babble and shuffle of forms I pulled against restraining hands but their grips remained firm.

'He is not of the Three Score and Ten and is not of the cruciform,' said Beta, sounding more puzzled than hostile now. 'How is it that he should not die the true death? We must take the stones and open his throat so that the blood flows until his heart stops. He is not of the cruciform.'

'He follows the cross,' said Alpha. 'Can he not become of the cruciform?'

This time silence followed the question.

'He follows the cross and has prayed at the room of the cruciform,' said Alpha. 'He must not die the true death.'

'All die the true death,' said a Bikura whom I did not recognize. My arms were aching from the strain of holding the crucifix above my head. 'Except the Three Score and Ten,' finished the anonymous Bikura.

'Because they followed the cross, prayed at the room, and became of the cruciform,' said Alpha. 'Must he not then become of the cruciform?'

I stood there gripping the cold metal of the small cross and awaited their verdict. I was afraid to die – I *felt* afraid – but the larger part of my mind seemed almost detached. My greatest regret was that I would not be able to send out the news of the basilica to an unbelieving universe.

'Come, we will talk of this,' Beta said to the group and they pulled me with them as they trod silently back to the village.

They have imprisoned me here in my hut. There was no chance to try for the hunting maser; several of them held me down while they emptied the hut of most of my possessions. They took my clothing, leaving me only one of their rough-woven robes to cover myself with.

The longer I sit here the more angry and anxious I become. They have taken my comlog, imager, disks, chips . . . everything. I have a single, unopened crate of medical diagnostic equipment left up at the old site, but that cannot help me document the miracle in the Cleft. If they destroy the things they have taken – and then destroy me – there will be no record of the basilica.

If I had a weapon I could kill the guards and

Oh dear God what am I thinking? Edouard, what am I to do?

And even if I survive this – make my way back to Keats – arrange travel back to the Web – who would believe me? – after nine years' absence from Pacem because of the quantum-leap time-debt – just an old man returning with the same lies he was exiled for—

Oh, dear God, if they destroy the data let them destroy me as well.

Day 110:

After three days they have decided my fate.

Zed and the one I think of as Theta-Prime came to get me shortly after midday. I blinked as they led me out into the light. The Three Score and Ten stood in a wide semicircle near the cliff edge. I fully expected to be thrown over that edge. Then I noticed the bonfire.

I had assumed that the Bikura were so primitive that they had lost the art of making and using fire. They did not warm themselves with fire and their huts were always dark. I had never seen them cook a meal, not even the rare corpse of an arboreal they devoured. But now the fire was burning strongly and they were the only ones who could have started it. I looked to see what fueled the flames.

They were burning my clothes, my comlog, my field

notes, the tape cassettes, video chips, data disks, the imager . . . everything that had held information. I screamed at them, tried to throw myself at the fire, and called them names I had not used since the street days of my childhood. They ignored me.

Finally Alpha came close. 'You will become of the cruciform,' he said softly.

I did not care. They led me back to my hut where I wept for an hour. There is no guard at the door. A minute ago I stood at the doorway and considered running for the flame forests. Then I thought of a much shorter but no less fatal run to the Cleft.

I did nothing.

The sun will be setting in a short time. Already the winds are rising. Soon. Soon.

Day 112:

Has it been only two days? It has been forever.

It did not come off this morning. *It did not come off.*

The medscanner's image wafer is right here in front of me but I still cannot believe it. And yet I do. I am of the cruciform now.

They came for me just before sunset. All of them. I did not struggle as they led me to the edge of the Cleft. They were more agile on the vines than I could have imagined. I slowed them down but they were patient, showing me the easiest footholds, the fastest route.

Hyperion's sun had dropped below low clouds and was visible above the rim wall to the west as we walked the final few meters to the basilica. The evening windsong was louder than I had anticipated; it was as if we were caught amid the pipes of a gigantic church organ. The notes rose from bass growls so deep that my bones and teeth resonated in sympathy to high, piercing screams that slid easily into the ultrasonic.

Alpha opened the outer doors and we passed through the antechamber into the central basilica. The Three Score and Ten made a wide circle around the altar and its tall cross. There was no litany. There was no singing.

There was no ceremony. We simply stood there in silence as the wind roared through the fluted columns outside and echoed in the great empty room carved into the stone – echoed and resonated and grew in volume until I clapped my hands over my ears. And all the while the streaming, horizontal rays of sunlight filled the hall with deepening hues of amber, gold, lapis, and then amber again – colors so deep that they made the air thick with light and lay like paint against the skin. I watched as the cross caught this light and held it in each of its thousand precious stones, held it – it seemed – even after the sun had set and the windows had faded to a twilight gray. It was as if the great crucifix had absorbed the light and was radiating it toward us, into us. Then even the cross was dark and the winds died and in the sudden dimness Alpha said softly, 'Bring him along.'

We emerged onto the wide ledge of stone and Beta was there with torches. As Beta passed them out to a selected few, I wondered if the Bikura reserved fire for ritual purposes only. Then Beta was leading the way and we descended the narrow staircase carved into the stone.

At first I crept along, terrified, clutching at the smooth rock and searching for any reassuring projection of root or stone. The drop to our right was so sheer and endless that it bordered on being absurd. Descending the ancient staircase was far worse than clutching at vines on the cliff face above. Here I had to look down each time I placed a foot on the narrow, age-slickened slabs. A slip and fall at first seemed probable, then inevitable.

I had the urge to stop then, to return at least to the safety of the basilica, but most of the Three Score and Ten were behind me on the narrow staircase and there seemed little chance that they would stand aside to let me pass. Besides this, and even greater than my fear, was the nagging curiosity about what was at the bottom of the staircase. I did pause long enough to glance up at the lip of the Cleft three hundred meters above and to see that the clouds were gone, the stars were out, and the nightly ballet of meteor trails was bright against a sable sky. Then I lowered my head, began a whispered recitation of the rosary, and followed the torchlight and the Bikura into the treacherous depths.

I could not believe that the staircase would take us all the way to the bottom of the Cleft, but it did. When, sometime after midnight, I realized that we would be descending all the way down to the level of the river, I estimated that it would take us until noon of the next day, but it did not.

We reached the base of the Cleft shortly before sunrise. The stars still shone in the aperture of sky between cliff walls that rose an impossible distance on either side. Exhausted, staggering downward step by step, recognizing slowly that there were no more steps, I stared upward and wondered stupidly if the stars remained visible there in the daylight as they did in a well I had lowered myself into once as a child in Villefranche-sur-Saône.

'Here,' said Beta. It was the first word uttered in many hours and was barely audible over the roar of the river. The Three Score and Ten stopped where they were and stood motionless. I collapsed to my knees and fell on my side. There was no possibility that I could climb that stairway we had just descended. Not in a day. Not in a week. Perhaps never. I closed my eyes to sleep but the dull fuel of nervous tension continued to burn inside me. I looked out across the floor of the ravine. The river here was wider than I had anticipated, at least seventy meters across, and the noise of it was beyond mere noise; I felt that I was being consumed by a great beast's roar.

I sat up and stared at a patch of darkness in the opposing cliff wall. It was a shadow darker than the shadows, more regular than the serrated patchwork of buttresses and crevices and columns that mottled the face of the cliff. It was a perfect square of darkness, at least thirty meters to a side. A door or hole in the cliff wall. I struggled to my feet and looked downriver along the wall we had just descended; yes, it was there. The other entrance, the one toward which Beta and the others even now were walking, was faintly visible in the starlight.

I had found an entrance to Hyperion's labyrinth.

'Did you know that Hyperion was one of the nine labyrinthine worlds?' someone had asked me on the dropship. Yes, it was the young priest named Hoyt. I had said yes and dismissed the fact. I was interested in the Bikura – actually more in the self-inflicted pain of my own exile – not the labyrinths or their builders.

Nine worlds have labyrinths. Nine out of a hundred seventy-six Webworlds and another two hundred-some colonial and protectorate planets. Nine worlds out of eight thousand or more worlds explored – however cursorily – since the Hegira.

There are planetary archaeohistorians who devote their lives to the study of the labyrinths. Not I. I had always found them a sterile topic, vaguely unreal. Now I walked toward one with the Three Score and Ten as the Kans River roared and vibrated and threatened to douse our torches with its spray.

The labyrinths were dug . . . tunneled . . . *created* more than three quarters of a million standard years ago. The details were inevitably the same, their origins inevitably unsolved.

Labyrinthine worlds are always Earthlike, at least to 7.9 on the Solmev Scale, always circling a G-type star, and yet always restricted to worlds that are tectonically dead, more like Mars than Old Earth. The tunnels themselves are set deep – usually a minimum of ten kilometers but often as deep as thirty – and they catacomb the crust of the planet. On Svoboda, not far from Pacem's system, over eight hundred thousand kilometers of labyrinth have been explored by remotes. The tunnels on each world are thirty meters square and carved by some technology still not available to the Hegemony. I read once in an archaeological journal that Kemp-Höltzer and Weinstein had postulated a 'fusion tunneler' that would explain the perfectly smooth walls and lack of tailings, but their theory did not explain where the Builders or their machines had come from or why they had devoted centuries to such an apparently aimless engineering task. Each of the labyrinthine worlds – including Hyperion – has been probed and researched. Nothing has ever been found. No signs of excavation machinery, no rusting miners' helmets, not a single piece of shattered plastic or decomposing stimstick wrapper. Researchers have not even identified entrance and exit shafts. No suggestion of heavy metals or precious ores has been sufficient to explain such a monumental effort. No legend or artifact of the Labyrinth Builders has survived. The mystery had mildly intrigued me over the years but never concerned me. Until now.

We entered the tunnel mouth. It was not a perfect square. Erosion and gravity had turned the perfect tunnel into a rough cave for a hundred meters into the cliff wall. Beta stopped just where the tunnel floor grew smooth and extinguished his torch. The other Bikura did likewise.

It was very dark. The tunnel had turned enough to block out any starlight that might have entered. I had been in caves before. With the torches extinguished, I did not expect my eyes to adapt to the near-total darkness. But they did.

Within thirty seconds I began to sense a roseate glow, dim at first, then ever richer until the cave was brighter than the canyon had been, brighter than Pacem under the glow of its triune moons. The light came from a hundred sources – a thousand sources. I was able to make out the nature of these sources just as the Bikura dropped reverently to their knees.

The cave walls and ceiling were encrusted with crosses ranging in size from a few millimeters to almost a meter long. Each glowed with a deep, pink light of its own. Invisible in the torchlight, these glowing crosses now suffused the tunnel with light. I approached one embedded in the wall nearest me. Thirty or so centimeters across, it pulsed with a soft, organic flow. This was not something that had been carved out of stone or attached to the wall; it was definitely organic, definitely alive, resembling soft coral. It was slightly warm to the touch.

There came the slightest whisper of sound – no, not sound, a disturbance in the cool air, perhaps – and I turned in time to see something enter the chamber.

The Bikura were still kneeling, their heads down, eyes lowered. I remained standing. My gaze never left the thing which moved among the kneeling Bikura.

It was vaguely man-shaped but in no way human. It stood at least three meters tall. Even when it was at rest, the silvered surface of the thing seemed to shift and flow like mercury suspended in midair. The reddish glow from the crosses set into the tunnel walls reflected from sharp surfaces and glinted on the curved metal blades protruding from the thing's forehead, four wrists, oddly jointed elbows, knees, armored back, and thorax. It flowed between the kneeling Bikura, and when it extended four long arms, hands extended but fingers clicking into place like chrome scalpels, I was absurdly reminded of His Holiness on Pacem offering a benediction to the faithful.

I had no doubt that I was looking at the legendary Shrike.

At that moment I must have moved or made a sound, for large red eyes turned my way and I found myself hypnotized by the dance of light within the multifaceted prisms there: not merely reflected light but a fierce, blood-bright glow which seemed to burn within the creature's barbed skull and pulse in the terrible gems set where God meant eyes to be.

Then it moved . . . or, rather, it did not move but ceased being *there* and was *here*, leaning less than a meter from me, its oddly jointed arms encircling me in a fence of body-blades and liquid silver steel. Panting hard but unable to take a breath, I saw my own reflection, face white and distorted, dancing across the surface of the thing's metallic shell and burning eyes.

I confess that I felt something closer to exaltation than fear. Something *inexplicable* was happening. Forged in Jesuit logic and tempered in the cold bath of science, I nevertheless understood at that second the ancient obsession of the God-fearing for another kind of fear: the thrill of exorcism, the mindless whirl of Dervish possession, the puppet-dance ritual of Tarot, and the almost erotic surrender of séance, speaking in tongues, and Zen Gnostic trance. I realized at that instant just

81

how surely the affirmation of demons or the summoning of Satan somehow can affirm the reality of their mystic antithesis – the God of Abraham.

Thinking none of this but feeling all of it, I awaited the embrace of the Shrike with the imperceptible tremble of a virgin bride.

It disappeared.

There was no thunderclap, no sudden smell of brimstone, not even a scientifically sound inrush of air. One second the thing was there, surrounding me with its beautiful certainty of sharp-edged death, and the next instant it was gone.

Numbed, I stood there and blinked as Alpha rose and approached me in the Bosch-tinted gloom. He stood where the Shrike had stood, his own arms extended in a pathetic imitation of the deadly perfection I had just witnessed, but there was no sign on Alpha's bland, Bikura face that he had seen the creature. He made an awkward, open-handed gesture which seemed to include the labyrinth, cave wall, and scores of glowing crosses embedded there.

'Cruciform,' said Alpha. The Three Score and Ten rose, came closer, and knelt again. I looked at their placid faces in the soft light and I also knelt.

'You will follow the cross all of your days,' said Alpha, and his voice carried the cadence of litany. The rest of the Bikura repeated the statement in a tone just short of a chant.

'You will be of the cruciform all of your days,' said Alpha, and as the others repeated this he reached out and pulled a small cruciform away from the cave wall. It was not more than a dozen centimeters long and it came away from the wall with the faintest of snaps. Its glow faded even as I watched. Alpha removed a small thong from his robe, tied it around small knobs at the top of the cruciform, and held the cross above my head. 'You will be of the cruciform now and forever,' he said.

'Now and forever,' echoed the Bikura.

'Amen,' I whispered.

Beta signaled that I should open the front of my robe. Alpha lowered the small cross until it hung around my neck. It felt cool against my chest; the back of it was perfectly flat, perfectly smooth.

The Bikura stood and wandered toward the cave entrance, apparently apathetic and indifferent once again. I watched them leave and then I gingerly touched the cross, lifted and inspected it. The cruciform was cool, inert. If it had truly been living a few seconds earlier, it showed no sign of it now. It continued to feel more like coral than crystal or rock; there was no sign of any adhesive material on the smooth back of it. I speculated on photochemical effects that would have created the luminescent quality. I speculated on natural phosphors, bioluminescence, and on the chances that evolution would shape such things. I speculated on what, if anything, their presence here had to do with the labyrinth and on the aeons necessary to raise this plateau so the river and canyon could slice through one of the tunnels. I speculated on the basilica and its makers, on the Bikura, on the Shrike, and on myself. Eventually I ceased speculating and closed my eyes to pray.

When I emerged from the cave, the cruciform cool against my chest under the robe, the Three Score and Ten were obviously ready to begin the three-kilometer climb up the staircase. I looked up to see a pale slash of morning sky between the walls of the Cleft.

'No!' I shouted, my voice almost lost against the roar of the river. 'I need rest. *Rest!*' I sank to my knees on the sand but half a dozen of the Bikura approached, pulled me gently to my feet, and moved me toward the staircase.

I tried, the Lord knows that I tried, but two or three hours into the climb I felt my legs give way and I collapsed, sliding across the rock, unable to stop my six-hundred-meter fall to the rocks and river. I remember grasping at the cruciform under the thick robe and then half a dozen hands stopped my slide, lifted me, carried me. Then I remember no more.

Until this morning. I woke to a sunrise pouring light through the opening of my hut. I wore only the robe and a touch assured me that the cruciform was still hanging from its fibrous thong. As I watched the sun lift over the forest, I realized that I had lost a day, that somehow I had slept through not only my ascent up that endless staircase (how could these little people carry me two and a half vertical kilometers?) but through the next day and night as well.

I looked around my hut. My comlog and other recording devices were gone. Only my medscanner and a few packets of anthropological software made useless by the destruction of my other equipment remained. I shook my head and went up to the stream to wash.

The Bikura appeared to be sleeping. Now that I had participated in their ritual and 'become of the cruciform,' they seemed to have lost interest in me. As I stripped to bathe, I decided to take no interest in them. I decided that I would leave as soon as I was strong enough. I would find a way around the flame forests if necessary. I could descend the staircase and follow the Kans if I had to. I knew more than ever that word of these miraculous artifacts had to be brought to the outside world.

I pulled off the heavy robe, stood pale and shivering in the morning light, and went to lift the small cruciform from my chest.

It did not come off.

It lay there as if it were part of my flesh. I pulled, scraped, and tore at the thong until it snapped and fell away. I clawed at the cross-shaped lump on my chest. *It did not come off.* It was as if my flesh had sealed itself around the edges of the cruciform. Except for the scratches from my fingernails, there was no pain or physical sensation in the cruciform or surrounding flesh, only sheer terror in my soul at the thought of this thing attached to me. After the first rush of panic subsided, I sat a minute and then hastily pulled on my robe and ran back to the village.

My knife was gone, my maser, scissors, razor – everything that might have helped me peel back the growth on my chest. My nails left bloody tracks across the red welt and my chest. Then I remembered the medscanner. I passed the transceiver over my chest, read the diskey display, shook my head in disbelief, and then ran an entire body scan. After a while I keyed in a request for hard copies of the scan results and sat motionless for a very long time.

I sit here now holding the image wafers. The cruciform is quite visible on both the sonic and k-cross images . . . as are the internal fibers that spread like thin tentacles, like *roots*, throughout my body.

Excess ganglia radiate from a thick nucleus above my sternum to filaments everywhere – a nightmare of nematodes. As well as I can tell with my simple field scanner, the nematodes terminate in the amygdala and other basal ganglia in each cerebral hemisphere. My temperature, metabolism, and lymphocyte level are normal. There has been no invasion of foreign tissue. According to the scanner, the nematodic filaments are the result of extensive but simple metastasis. According to the scanner, the cruciform itself is composed of familiar tissue . . . *the DNA is mine*.

I am of the cruciform.

Day 116:

Each day I pace the confines of my cage – the flame forests to the south and east, the forested ravines to the northeast, and the Cleft to the north and west. The Three Score and Ten will not let me descend into the Cleft beyond the basilica. The *cruciform* will not let me get more than ten kilometers from the Cleft.

At first I could not believe this. I had resolved to enter the flame forests, trusting to luck and to God's help to see me through. But I had gone no more than two kilometers into the fringes of the forest when pain struck me in the chest and arms and head. I was sure that I was having a massive heart attack. But as soon as I turned back toward the Cleft the symptoms ceased. I experimented for some time and the results were invariably the same. Whenever I ventured deeper into the flame forest, away from the Cleft, the pain would return and increase in severity until I turned back.

I begin to understand other things. Yesterday I

happened across the wreckage of the original seedship shuttle as I explored to the north. Only a rusted, vine-enmeshed wreck of metal remains among the rocks at the edge of the flame forest near the ravine. But crouching among the exposed alloy ribs of the ancient craft, I could imagine the rejoicing of the seventy survivors, their short voyage to the Cleft, their eventual discovery of the basilica, and . . . and what? Conjectures beyond that point are useless, but suspicions remain. Tomorrow I will attempt another physical exam of one of the Bikura. Perhaps now that I am 'of the cruciform' they will allow it.

Each day I do a medscan of myself. The nematodes remain – perhaps thicker, perhaps not. I am convinced that they are purely parasitic although my body has shown no signs of this. I peer at my face in the pool near the waterfall and see only the same long, aging countenance that I have learned to dislike in recent years. This morning, while gazing at my image in the water, I opened my mouth wide, half thinking that I would see gray filaments and nematode clusters growing from the roof of my mouth and the back of my throat. There was nothing.

Day 117:

The Bikura are sexless. Not celibate or hermaphroditic or undeveloped – sexless. They are as devoid of external or internal genitalia as a child's flowfoam doll. There is no evidence that the penis or testes or comparable female organs have atrophied or been surgically altered. *There is no sign that they ever existed.* Urine is conducted through a primitive urethra terminating in a small chamber contiguous with the anus – a sort of crude cloaca.

Beta allowed the examination. The medscanner confirmed what my eyes would not believe. Del and Theta also agreed to be scanned. I have absolutely no doubt that the rest of the Three Score and Ten are equally sexless. There is no sign that they have been . . . altered.

I would suggest that they had all been *born* that way but from what kind of parents? And how do these sexless lumps of human clay plan to reproduce? It must be tied in with the cruciform in some way.

When I was finished with their medscans I stripped and studied myself. The cruciform rises from my chest like pink scar tissue, but I am still a man.

For how long?

Day 133:

Alpha is dead.

I was with him three mornings ago when he fell. We were about three kilometers east, hunting for chalma tubers in the large boulders near the edge of the Cleft. It had been raining most of the past two days and the rocks were quite slippery. I looked up from my own scrambling just in time to see Alpha lose his footing and go sliding down a broad slab of stone, over the edge. He did not shout. The only sound was the rasp of his robe against the rock, followed several seconds later by the sickening dropped-melon sound of his body striking a ledge eighty meters below.

It took me an hour to find a route down to him. Even before I began the treacherous descent I knew it was too late to help. But it was my duty.

Alpha's body was half wedged between two large rocks. He must have died instantly; his arms and legs were splintered and the right side of his skull had been crushed. Blood and brain tissue clung to the wet rock like the refuse of a sad picnic. I wept as I stood over the little body. I do not know why I wept, but I did. And as I wept I administered Extreme Unction and prayed that God would accept the soul of this poor, sexless little person. Later I wrapped the body in vines, laboriously climbed the eighty meters of cliff, and – pausing frequently to pant with exhaustion – pulled the broken corpse up to me.

There was little interest as I carried the body of Alpha into the Bikura village. Eventually Beta and half a dozen

87

others wandered over to stare down indifferently at the corpse. No one asked me how he had died. After a few minutes the small crowd dispersed.

Later I carried Alpha's body to the promontory where I had buried Tuk so many weeks earlier. I was digging the shallow grave with a flat stone when Gamma appeared. The Bikura's eyes widened and for a brief second I thought I saw emotion cross those bland features.

'What are you doing?' asked Gamma.

'Burying him.' I was too tired to say more. I leaned against a thick chalma root and rested.

'No.' It was a command. 'He is of the cruciform.'

I stared as Gamma turned and walked quickly back to the village. When the Bikura was gone, I pulled off the crude fiber tarp I had draped over the corpse.

Alpha was, without any doubt, truly dead. It no longer mattered to him or the universe whether he was of the cruciform or not. The fall had stripped him of most of his clothes and all of his dignity. The right side of his skull had been cracked and emptied like a breakfast egg. One eye stared sightlessly toward Hyperion's sky through a thickening film while the other looked out lazily from under a drooping lid. His rib cage had been splintered so thoroughly that shards of bone protruded from his flesh. Both arms were broken and his left leg had been twisted almost off. I had used the medscanner to perform a perfunctory autopsy and it had revealed massive internal injuries; even the poor devil's heart had been pulped by the force of the fall.

I reached out and touched the cold flesh. Rigor mortis was setting in. My fingers brushed across the cross-shaped welt on his chest and I quickly pulled my hand away. The cruciform was warm.

'Stand away.'

I looked up to see Beta and the rest of the Bikura standing there. I had no doubt that they would murder me in a second if I did not move away from the corpse. As I did so, an idiotically frightened part of my mind noted that the Three Score and Ten were now the Three Score and Nine. It seemed funny at the time.

The Bikura lifted the body and moved back toward the village. Beta looked at the sky, looked at me, and said:

'It is almost time. You will come.'

We went down into the Cleft. The body was carefully tied into a basket of vines and lowered with us.

The sun was not yet illuminating the interior of the basilica when they set Alpha's corpse on the broad altar and removed his remaining rags.

I do not know what I expected next – some ritual act of cannibalism perhaps. Nothing would have surprised me. Instead, one of the Bikura raised his arms, just as the first shafts of colored light entered the basilica, and intoned, 'You will follow the cross all of your days.'

The Three Score and Nine knelt and repeated the sentence. I remained standing. I did not speak.

'You will be of the cruciform all of your days,' said the little Bikura and the basilica echoed to the chorus of voices repeating the phrase. Light the color and texture of clotting blood threw a huge shadow of the cross on the far wall.

'You will be of the cruciform now and forever and ever,' came the chant as the winds rose outside and the organ pipes of the canyon wailed with the voice of a tortured child.

When the Bikura stopped chanting I did not whisper 'Amen.' I stood there while the others turned and left with the sudden, total indifference of spoiled children who have lost interest in their game.

'There is no reason to stay,' said Beta when the others had gone.

'I want to,' I said, expecting a command to leave. Beta turned without so much as a shrug and left me there. The light dimmed. I went outside to watch the sun set and when I returned it had begun.

Once, years ago in school, I saw a time-lapse holo showing the decomposition of a kangaroo mouse. A week's slow work of nature's recycling had been accelerated to thirty seconds of horror. There was the sudden, almost comic bloating of the little corpse, then the stretching of flesh into lesions, followed by the sudden appearance of maggots in the mouth, eyes, and open sores, and finally the sudden and incredible corkscrew cleaning of meat from the bones – there is no other phrase that fits the image – as the pack of maggots spiraled right to left, head to tail, in a time-lapsed helix of carrion consumption that left behind nothing but bones and gristle and hide.

Now it was a man's body I watched.

I stopped and stared, the last of the light fading quickly. There was no sound in the echoing silence of the basilica except for the pounding of my pulse in my own ears. I stared as Alpha's corpse first twitched and then visibly vibrated, almost levitating off the altar in the spastic violence of sudden decomposition. For a few seconds the cruciform seemed to increase in size and deepen in color, glowing as red as raw meat, and I imagined then that I caught a glimpse of the network of filaments and nematodes holding the disintegrating body together like metal fibers in a sculptor's melting model. *The flesh flowed.*

I stayed in the basilica that night. The area around the altar remained lit by the glow of the cruciform on Alpha's chest. When the corpse moved the light would cast strange shadows on the walls.

I did not leave the basilica until Alpha left on the third day, but most of the visible changes had taken place by the end of that first night. The body of the Bikura I had named Alpha was broken down and rebuilt as I watched. The corpse that was left was not quite Alpha and not quite *not* Alpha, but it was intact. The face was a flowfoam doll's face, smooth and unlined, features stamped in a slight smile. At sunrise of the third day, I saw the corpse's chest begin to rise and fall and I heard the first intake of breath – a rasp like water being poured into a leather pouch. Shortly before noon I left the basilica to climb the vines.

I followed Alpha.

He has not spoken, will not reply. His eyes have a fixed, unfocused look and occasionally he pauses as if he hears distant voices calling.

No one paid attention to us when we returned to the

village. Alpha went to a hut and sits there now. I sit in mine. A minute ago I opened my robe and ran my fingers across the welt of the cruciform. It lies benignly under the flesh of my chest. Waiting.

Day 140:

I am recovering from my wounds and the loss of blood. It cannot be cut out with a sharpened stone.

It does not like pain. I lost consciousness long before the pain or loss of blood demanded it. Each time I awoke and resumed cutting, I would be made to pass out. It does not like pain.

Day 158:

Alpha speaks some now. He seems duller, slower, and only vaguely aware of me (or anyone else) but he eats and moves. He appears to recognize me to some extent. The medscanner shows the heart and internal organs of a young man – perhaps of a boy of sixteen.

I must wait about another Hyperion month and ten days – about fifty days in all – until the flame forests become quiet enough for me to try to walk out, pain or no pain. We will see who can stand the most pain.

Day 173:

Another death.

The one called Will – the one with the broken finger – had been missing for a week. Yesterday the Bikura went several kilometers northeast as if following a beacon, and found the remains near the great ravine.

Evidently a branch had snapped while he was climbing to grasp some chalma fronds. Death must have been instantaneous when he broke his neck, but it is where he fell that is important. The body – if one could call it that – was lying between two great mud cones marking the burrows of the large red insects that Tuk called fire mantises. Carpet beetles might have been a more apt phrase. In the past few days the insects had stripped the corpse clean to the bone. Little was left to be found except the skeleton, some random shreds of tissue and tendon, and the cruciform – still attached to the rib cage like some splendid cross packed in the sarcophagus of a long-dead pope.

It is terrible, but I cannot help but feel some small sense of triumph beneath the sadness. There is no way that the cruciform can regenerate something out of these bare bones; even the terrible illogic of this accursed parasite must respect the imperative of the law of conservation of mass. The Bikura I called Will has died the true death. The Three Score and Ten truly are the Three Score and Nine from this time on.

Day 174:

I am a fool.

Today I inquired about Will, about his dying the true death. I was curious at the lack of reaction from the Bikura. They had retrieved the cruciform but left the skeleton lying where they had found it; there was no attempt to carry the remains to the basilica. During the night I had become concerned that I would be made to fill the roll of the missing member of the Three Score and Ten. 'It is very sad,' I said, 'that one of you has died the true death. What is to become to the Three Score and Ten?'

Beta stared at me. 'He cannot die the true death,' said the bald little androgyny. 'He is of the cruciform.'

Somewhat later, while continuing my medscans of the tribe, I discovered the truth. The one I have tagged as Theta looks the same and acts the same, but now carries two cruciforms embedded in his flesh. I have no doubt that this is one Bikura who will tend toward corpulence in coming years, swelling and ripening like some obscene *E coli* cell in a petri dish. When he/she/it dies, two will leave the tomb and the Three Score and Ten will be complete once more.

I believe I am going mad.

Day 195:

Weeks of studying the damn parasite and still no clue as to how it functions. Worse, I no longer care. What I care about now is more important.

Why has God allowed this obscenity?

Why have the Bikura been punished this way?

Why was I chosen to suffer their fate?

I ask these questions in nightly prayers but I hear no answers, only the blood song of the wind from the Cleft.

Day 214:

The last ten pages should have covered all of my field notes and technical conjectures. This will be my last entry before attempting the quiescent flame forest in the morning.

There is no doubt that I have discovered the ultimate in stagnant human societies. The Bikura have realized the human dream of immortality and have paid for it with their humanity and their immortal souls.

Edouard, I have spent so many hours wrestling with my faith – my lack of faith – but now, in this fearful corner of an all but forgotten world, riddled as I am with this loathsome parasite, I have somehow rediscovered a strength of belief the likes of which I have not known since you and I were boys. I now understand the *need* for faith – pure, blind, fly-in-the-face-of-reason faith – as a small life preserver in the wild and endless sea of a universe ruled by unfeeling laws and totally indifferent to the small, reasoning beings that inhabit it.

Day after day I have tried to leave the Cleft area and day after day I have suffered pain so terrible that it has become a tangible part of my world, like the too small sun or the green and lapis sky. Pain has become my ally, my guardian angel, my remaining link with humanity. The cruciform does not like pain. Nor do I but, like the cruciform, I am willing to use it to serve my purposes. And I will do so consciously, not instinctively like the mindless mass of alien tissue embedded in me. This thing only seeks a mindless avoidance of death by any means. I do not wish to die, but I welcome pain and death rather than an eternity of mindless life. Life is sacred – I still hold to that as a core element of the Church's thought and teachings these past twenty-eight hundred years when life has been so cheap – but even more sacred is the soul.

I realize now that what I was trying to do with the Armaghast data was offer the Church not a rebirth but only a transition to a false life such as these poor walking corpses inhabit. If the Church is meant to die, it must do so – but do so gloriously, in the full knowledge of its rebirth in Christ. It must go into the darkness not willingly but well – bravely and firm of faith – like the millions who have gone before us, keeping faith with all those generations facing death in the isolated silence of death camps and nuclear fireballs and cancer wards and pogroms, going into the darkness, if not hopefully, then prayerfully that there is some reason for it all, something worth the price of all that pain, all those sacrifices. All those before us have gone into the darkness without assurance of logic or fact or persuasive theory, with only a slender thread of hope or the all too shakable conviction of faith. And if they have been able to sustain that slim hope in the face of darkness, then so must I . . . and so must the Church.

I no longer believe that any surgery or treatment can cure me of this thing that infests me, but if someone can separate it and study it and destroy it, even at the cost of my death, I will be well satisfied.

The flame forests are as quiet as they will ever be. To bed now. I leave before dawn.

Day 215:

There is no way out.

Fourteen kilometers into the forest. Stray fires and bursts of current, but penetrable. Three weeks of walking would have got me through.

The cruciform will not let me go.

The pain was like a heart attack that would not stop. Still I staggered forward, stumbling and crawling through the ash. Eventually I lost consciousness. When I came to I was crawling *toward* the Cleft. I would turn away, walk a kilometer, crawl fifty meters, then lose consciousness again and awake back where I had started. All day this insane battle for my body went on.

Before sunset the Bikura entered the forest, found me five kilometers from the Cleft, and carried me back.

Dear Jesus, why have you let this be?

There is no hope now unless someone comes looking for me.

Day 223:

Again the attempt. Again the pain. Again the failure.

Day 257:

I am sixty-eight standard years old today. Work goes on with the chapel I am building near the Cleft. Attempted to descend to the river yesterday but was turned back by Beta and four others.

Day 280:

One local year on Hyperion. One year in purgatory. Or is it hell?

Day 311:

Working on quarrying stones on the ledges below the shelf where the chapel is going up and I made the discovery today: the arrestor rods. The Bikura must have thrown them over the edge when they murdered Tuk that night two hundred and twenty-three days ago.

These rods would allow me to penetrate the flame forest at any time if the cruciform would allow it. But it will not. If only they had not destroyed my medkits with the painkillers! But still, sitting here holding the rods today, I have an idea.

My crude experiments with the medscanner have continued. Two weeks ago when Theta broke his leg in three places, I observed the reaction of the cruciform. The parasite did its best to block the pain; Theta was unconscious much of the time and his body was producing incredible quantities of endorphins. But the break was a very painful one and after four days the Bikura slashed Theta's throat and took his body to the basilica. It was easier for the cruciform to resurrect his corpse than to tolerate such pain over a long period. But before his murder my scanner showed an appreciable retreat of the cruciform nematodes from some parts of the central nervous system.

I do not know if it would be possible to inflict on oneself – or to tolerate – levels of nonlethal pain sufficient to drive the cruciform out completely, but I am sure of one thing: the Bikura would not allow it.

Today I sit on the ledge below the half-finished chapel and I consider possibilities.

Day 438:

The chapel is finished. It is my life's work.

Tonight, when the Bikura went down into the Cleft for their daily parody of worship, I said Mass at the altar of the newly erected chapel. I had baked the bread from chalma flour and I am sure that it must have tasted of that bland, yellow leaf, but to me the taste was exactly like that of the first Host I had partaken of during my first Holy Communion in Villefranche-sur-Saône some sixty standard years earlier.

In the morning I will do what I have planned. Everything is in readiness: my journals and the medscan wafers will be in the pouch of woven bestos fibers. That is the best I can do.

The consecrated wine was only water, but in the dim light of sunset it looked blood red and tasted of communion wine.

The trick will be to penetrate deep enough into the flame forest. I will have to trust that there is enough incipient activity in and from the tesla trees even during the quiet periods.

Goodbye, Edouard. I doubt if you are still alive, and should you be, I see no way that we could be reunited, separated as we are not only by years of distance but by a much wider gulf in the form of a cross. My hope of seeing you again shall not be placed on this life but on the one to come. Strange to hear me speak like this again, is it not? I must tell you, Edouard, that after all these decades of uncertainty, and with great fear of what lies ahead, my heart and soul are nonetheless at peace.

Oh, my God,
I am heartily sorry for having offended Thee,
And I detest all my sins,
Because of the loss of heaven
And the pains of hell,
But most of all because I have offended Thee,
My God,
Who art all good
And deserving of all my love.
I firmly resolve with the help of Thy grace to
   confess my sins, to do penance,
And to amend my life,
Amen.

2400 hours:
The sunset comes through the open chapel window and bathes the altar, the crudely carved chalice, and me

97

in light. The wind from the Cleft rises in the last such chorus that – with luck and God's mercy – I will ever hear.

'That is the final entry,' said Lenar Hoyt.

When the priest quit reading, the six pilgrims at the table raised their faces toward him as if they were awakening from a common dream. The Consul glanced upward and saw that Hyperion was much closer now, filling a third of the sky, banishing the stars with its cold radiance.

'I arrived some ten weeks after I had last seen Father Duré,' continued Father Hoyt. His voice was a hoarse rasp. 'More than eight years had passed on Hyperion . . . seven years since the last entry in Father Duré's journal.' The priest was visibly in pain now, his face paled to a sick luminescence and filmed with perspiration.

'Within a month I found my way to Perecebo Plantation upriver from Port Romance,' he continued, forcing some strength into his voice. 'My assumption was that the fiberplastic growers might tell me the truth even if they would have nothing to do with the consulate or Home Rule Authorities. I was right. The administrator at Perecebo, a man named Orlandi, remembered Father Duré, as did Orlandi's new wife, the woman named Semfa whom Father Duré mentioned in his journals. The plantation manager had tried to mount several rescue operations onto the Plateau, but an unprecedented series of active seasons in the flame forests had made them abandon their attempts. After several years they had given up hope that Duré or their man Tuk could still be alive.

'Nonetheless, Orlandi recruited two expert bush pilots to fly a rescue expedition up the Cleft in two plantation skimmers. We stayed in the Cleft itself for as long as we could, trusting to terrain-avoidance instruments and luck to get us to Bikura country. Even with bypassing most of the flame forest that way, we lost one of the skimmers and four people to tesla activity.'

Father Hoyt paused and swayed slightly. Gripping the

edge of the table to steady himself, he cleared his throat and said, 'There's little else to tell. We located the Bikura village. There were seventy of them, each as stupid and uncommunicative as Duré's notes had suggested. I managed to ascertain from them that Father Duré had died while trying to penetrate the flame forest. The bestos pouch had survived and in it we found his journals and medical data.' Hoyt looked at the others a second and then glanced down. 'We persuaded them to show us where Father Duré had died,' he said. 'They . . . ah . . . they had not buried him. His remains were badly burned and decomposed but complete enough to show us that the intensity of the tesla charges had destroyed the . . . the cruciform . . . as well as his body.

'Father Duré had died the true death. We returned the remains to the Perecebo Plantation where he was buried following a full funeral Mass.' Hoyt took a deep breath. 'Over my strong objections, M. Orlandi destroyed the Bikura village and a section of the Cleft wall with shaped nuclear charges he had brought from the plantation. I do not believe that any of the Bikura could have survived. As far as we could tell, the entrance to the labyrinth and the so-called basilica also must have been destroyed in the landslide.

'I had sustained several injuries during the expedition and thus had to remain at the plantation for several months before returning to the northern continent and booking passage to Pacem. No one knows of these journals or their contents except M. Orlandi, Monsignor Edouard, and whichever of his superiors Monsignor Edouard chose to tell. As far as I know, the Church has issued no declaration relating to the journals of Father Paul Duré.'

Father Hoyt had been standing and now he sat. Sweat dripped from his chin and his face was blue-white in the reflected light of Hyperion.

'Is that . . . all?' asked Martin Silenus.

'Yes,' managed Father Hoyt.

'Gentlemen and lady,' said Het Masteen, 'it is late. I suggest that you gather your luggage and rendezvous at our friend the Consul's ship on sphere eleven in thirty minutes or sooner. I will be using one of the tree's drop-ships to join you later.'

Most of the group was assembled in less than fifteen minutes. The Templars had rigged a gangway from a work pier on the interior of the sphere to the ship's top-tier balcony, and the Consul led the way into the lounge as crew clones stowed luggage and departed.

'A fascinating old instrument,' said Colonel Kassad as he ran one hand across the top of the Steinway. 'Harpsichord?'

'Piano,' said the Consul. 'Pre-Hegira. Are we all here?'

'Everyone except Hoyt,' said Brawne Lamia as she took a seat in the projection pit.

Het Masteen entered. 'The Hegemony warship has granted permission for you to descend to Keats's space-port,' said the Captain. He glanced around. 'I will send a crew member to see if M. Hoyt needs assistance.'

'No,' said the Consul. He modulated his voice. 'I'd like to get him. Can you tell me the way to his quarters?'

The treeship Captain looked at the Consul for a long second and then reached into the folds of his robe. '*Bon voyage*,' he said, handing over a wafer. 'I will see you on the planet, sometime before our midnight departure time from the Shrike's Temple in Keats.'

The Consul bowed. 'It was a pleasure traveling within the protective branches of the Tree, Het Masteen,' he said formally. Turning to the others, he gestured. 'Please make yourselves comfortable in the lounge or the library on the desk below this. The ship will see to your needs and answer any questions you might have. We will depart as soon as Father Hoyt and I return.'

The priest's environment pod was halfway up the treeship, far out on a secondary branch. As the Consul expected, the comlog direction wafer Het Masteen had given him also served as a palmlock override. After useless minutes tapping the announcer chime and pounding on the access portal, the Consul triggered the override and stepped into the pod.

Father Hoyt was on his knees, writhing in the center of the grass carpet. Bedclothes, gear, garments, and the contents of a standard medkit were strewn on the floor around him. He had torn off his tunic and collar and sweated through his shirt so that it now hung in damp folds, ripped and tattered where he had clawed through the fabric. Hyperion light seeped through the pod wall, making the bizarre tableau appear to be staged under-water – or, thought the Consul, in a cathedral.

Lenar Hoyt's face contorted in agony as his hands raked at his chest. Muscles on his exposed forearms writhed like living creatures moving beneath his pale tarp of a skin. 'The injector . . . *malfunctioned*,' gasped Hoyt. '*Please*.'

The Consul nodded, commanded the door to close, and knelt next to the priest. He removed the useless injector from Hoyt's clenched fist and ejected the syrette ampule. Ultramorphine. The Consul nodded again and took out an injector from the medkit he had brought from his ship. It took less than five seconds to load the ultramorph.

'*Please*,' begged Hoyt. His whole body spasmed. The Consul could almost see the waves of pain passing through the man.

'Yes,' said the Consul. He took a ragged breath. 'But first the rest of the story.'

Hoyt stared, reached weakly for the injector.

Sweating himself now, the Consul held the instrument just out of reach. 'Yes, in a second,' he said. 'After the rest of the story. It's important that I *know*.'

'Oh, God, sweet Christ,' sobbed Hoyt. '*Please!*'

'Yes,' gasped the Consul. 'Yes. As soon as you tell me the truth.'

Father Hoyt collapsed onto his forearms, breathing in quick pants. 'You fucking bastard,' he gasped. The priest took several deep breaths, held one until his body quit shaking, and tried to sit up. When he looked at the Consul, there was something like relief in the maddened eyes. 'Then . . . you'll give me . . . the shot?'

'Yes,' said the Consul.

'All right,' Hoyt managed in a sour whisper. 'The

truth. Perecebo Plantation . . . like I said. We flew in
. . . early October . . . Lycius . . . eight years after
Duré . . . disappeared. Oh, *Christ*, it hurts! Alcohol
and endos don't work at all anymore. Only . . . pure
ultramorph . . .'

'Yes,' whispered the Consul. 'It's ready. As soon as
the story is done.'

The priest lowered his head. Sweat dripped from his
cheeks and nose onto the short grass. The Consul saw
the man's muscles tense as if he were going to attack,
then another spasm of pain wracked the thin body and
Hoyt sagged forward. 'Skimmer wasn't destroyed . . .
by tesla. Semfa, two men, and I . . . forced down near
the Cleft while . . . while Orlandi searched upriver. His
skimmer . . . had to wait while the lightning storm died
down.

'Bikura came in the night. Killed . . . killed Semfa,
the pilot, the other man . . . forget his name. Left me
. . . alive.' Hoyt reached for his crucifix, realized that he
had torn it off. He laughed briefly, stopping before the
laughter turned to sobs. 'They . . . told me about the
way of the cross. About the cruciform. Told me about
. . . the Son of the Flames.

'Next morning, they took me to see the Son. Took me
. . . to see him.' Hoyt struggled upright and clawed at
his own cheeks. His eyes were wide, the ultramorph
obviously forgotten despite the pain. 'About three
kilometers into the flame forest . . . big tesla . . . eighty,
a hundred meters tall, at least. Quiet then, but still a lot
. . . a lot of charge in the air. Ash everywhere.

'The Bikura wouldn't . . . wouldn't go too close. Just
knelt there with their goddamned bald heads bowed. But
I . . . went close . . . had to. Dear God . . . Oh, Christ,
it was him. Duré. What was *left* of him.

'He'd used a ladder to get three . . . maybe four
meters . . . up on the bole of the tree. Built a sort of
platform. For his feet. Broken the arrestor rods off . . .
little more than spikes . . . then sharpened them.
Must've used a rock to drive the long one through his
feet into the bestos platform and tree.

'His left arm . . . he'd pounded the stake between the

radius and ulna . . . missed veins . . . just like the goddamned Romans. Very secure as long as his skeleton was intact. Other hand . . . right hand . . . palm down. He'd driven the spike first. Sharpened both ends. Then . . . impaled his right hand. Somehow bent the spike over. Hook.

'Ladder'd fallen . . . long ago . . . but it was bestos. Hadn't burned. Used it to climb up to him. Everything'd burned away years ago . . . clothes, skin, top layers of flesh . . . but the bestos pouch was still around his neck.

'The alloy spikes still conducted current even when . . . I could see it . . . *feel* it . . . surging through what was left of the body.

'*It still looked like Paul Duré.* Important. I told Monsignor. No skin. Flesh raw or boiled away. Nerves and things visible . . . like gray and yellow roots. Christ, the smell. *But it still looked like Paul Duré*!

'I understood then. Understood it all. Somehow . . . even before reading the journals. Understood he'd been hanging there . . . oh, dear God . . . seven years. Living. Dying. The cruciform . . . forcing him to live again. Electricity . . . surging through him every second of those . . . those seven years. Flames. Hunger. Pain. Death. But somehow the goddamned . . . cruciform . . . leeching substance from the tree maybe, the air, what was left . . . rebuilding what it could . . . forcing him to *live*, to feel the pain, over and over and over . . .

'But he *won*. Pain was his ally. Oh, Jesus, not a few hours on the tree and then the spear and rest, but *seven years*!

'But . . . he won. When I removed the pouch, the cruciform on his chest fell away also. Just . . . fell right off . . . long, bloody roots. Then the thing . . . the thing I'd been sure was a corpse . . . the man raised its head. No eyelids. Eyes baked white. Lips gone. But it looked at me and smiled. *He* smiled. And he died . . . really died . . . there in my arms. The ten thousandth time, but *real* this time. He smiled at me and died.'

Hoyt stopped, communed in silence with his own pain, and then continued between bouts of clenching his teeth. 'Bikura took me . . . back to . . . Cleft. Orlandi came the next day. Rescued me. He . . . Semfa . . . I couldn't . . . he lasered the village, burned the Bikura where they stood like stupid sheep. I didn't . . . didn't argue with him. I *laughed*. Dear God, forgive me. Orlandi nuked the site with shaped charges they used to . . . to clear the jungle . . . fiberplastic matrix.'

Hoyt looked directly at the Consul and made a contorted gesture with his right hand. 'The painkillers worked all right at first. But every year . . . every day . . . got worse. Even in fugue . . . the pain. I would have had to come back anyway. How could he . . . *seven years*! Oh, Jesus,' said Father Hoyt and clawed at the carpet.

The Consul moved quickly, injecting the full ampule of ultramorph just under the armpit, catching the priest as he collapsed, and gently lowering the unconscious form to the floor. His vision unclear, the Consul ripped open Hoyt's sweat-sodden shirt, casting the rags aside. It was there, of course, lying under the pale skin of Hoyt's chest like some great, raw, cross-shaped worm. The Consul took a breath and gently turned the priest over. The second cruciform was where he had expected to find it, a slightly smaller, cross-shaped welt between the thin man's shoulder blades. It stirred slightly as the Consul's fingers brushed the fevered flesh.

The Consul moved slowly but efficiently – packing the priest's belongings, straightening the room, dressing the unconscious man with the gentle care one would use in clothing the body of a dead family member.

The Consul's comlog buzzed. 'We need to go,' came Colonel Kassad's voice.

'We're coming,' replied the Consul. He coded the comlog to summon crew clones to fetch the luggage, but lifted Father Hoyt himself. The body seemed to weigh nothing.

The pod door dilated open and the Consul stepped out, moving from the deep shadow of the branch into the blue-green glow of the world which filled the sky. Deciding what cover story he would tell the others, the Consul paused a second to look at the sleeping man's face. He glanced up at Hyperion and then moved on.

Even if the gravity field had been full Earth standard, the Consul knew, the body in his arms would have been no burden.

Once a parent to a child now dead, the Consul walked on, knowing once again the sensation of bearing a sleeping son to bed.

TWO

It had been a warm, rainy day in Keats, Hyperion's capital, and even after the rains stopped a layer of clouds moved slow and heavy over the city, filling the air with the salt scent of the ocean twenty kilometers to the west. Toward evening, as the gray daylight was beginning to fade into gray twilight, a double sonic boom shook the town and then echoed from the single, sculpted peak to the south. The clouds glowed blue-white. Half a minute later an ebony spacecraft broke through the overcast and descended carefully on a tail of fusion flame, its navigation lights blinking red and green against the gray.

At one thousand meters the craft's landing beacons flared and three beams of coherent light from the spaceport north of town locked the ship in a welcoming ruby tripod. The spacecraft hovered at three hundred meters, slipped sideways as smoothly as a mug sliding on a wet table top, and then settled weightlessly into a waiting blast pit.

High-pressure jets of water bathed the pit and the base of the ship, sending up billows of steam to blend with the curtain of drizzle blowing across the paved plain of the spaceport. When the water jets ceased there was no noise except the whisper of rain and the random ticks and creaks of the cooling spaceship.

A balcony extruded itself from the ship's bulkhead twenty meters above the pit wall. Five figures emerged. 'Thank you for the ride, sir,' Colonel Kassad said to the Consul.

The Consul nodded and leaned on the railing, taking in deep breaths of fresh air. Droplets of rain beaded on his shoulders and eyebrows.

Sol Weintraub lifted his baby from her infant carrier.

Some change in pressure, temperature, scent, motion, noise, or a combination of all of these had awakened her and now she began to cry lustily. Weintraub bounced her and cooed to her but the wailing continued.

'An appropriate comment upon our arrival,' said Martin Silenus. The poet wore a long purple cape and a red beret which slouched to his right shoulder. He took a drink from a wineglass he had carried out from the lounge. 'Christ on a stick, this place looks different.'

The Consul, who had been away only eight local years, had to agree. The spaceport had been a full nine klicks from the city when he lived in Keats; now shacks, tents, and mud streets surrounded the landing field's perimeter. In the Consul's day, no more than a ship a week had put in at the tiny spaceport; now he counted more than twenty spacecraft on the field. The small administration and customs building had been superseded by a huge, prefabricated structure, a dozen new blast pits and dropship grids had been added where the field had been hastily extended to the west, and the perimeter now was littered with scores of camouflage-sheathed modules which the Consul knew must serve as everything from ground control stations to barracks. A forest of exotic antennae grew skyward from a cluster of such boxes at the far end of the landing apron. 'Progress,' murmured the Consul.

'War,' said Colonel Kassad.

'Those are *people*,' said Brawne Lamia, pointing toward the main terminal gates on the south side of the field. A wave of drab colors crashed like a silent surf against the outer fence and the violet containment field.

'My God,' said the Consul, 'you're right.'

Kassad produced his binoculars and they took turns staring at the thousands of forms tugging at the wire, pressing against the repelling field.

'Why are they here?' asked Lamia. 'What do they want?' Even from half a kilometer away, the mindless will of the mob was daunting. Dark forms of FORCE: Marines could be seen patrolling just within the perimeter. The Consul realized that between the wire, the containment field, and the Marines a strip of raw earth almost surely signified mines or a deathbeam zone, or both.

'What do they want?' repeated Lamia.

'They want out,' said Kassad.

Even before the Colonel spoke, the Consul realized that the shack city around the spaceport and the mob at the gates were inevitable; the people of Hyperion were ready to *leave*. He guessed that there must be such a silent surge toward the gates each time a ship landed.

'Well, there's one who'll be staying,' said Martin Silenus and pointed toward the low mountain across the river to the south. 'Old Weeping William Rex, God rest his sinful soul.' The sculpted face of Sad King Billy was just visible through the light rain and growing darkness. 'I knew him. Horatio,' said the drunken poet. 'A man of infinite jest. Not one of them funny. A real horse's ass, Horatio.'

Sol Weintraub stood just inside the ship, shielding his baby from the drizzle and removing her cries from the vicinity of the conversation. He pointed. 'Someone is coming.'

A groundcar with its camouflage polymer inert and a military EMV modified with hoverfans for Hyperion's weak magnetic field were crossing the damp hardpan.

Martin Silenus's gaze never left Sad King Billy's dour visage. Silenus said in a voice almost too soft to be heard:

> *'Deep in the shady sadness of a vale*
> *Far sunken from the healthy breath of morn,*
> *Far from the fiery noon, and eve's one star,*
> *Sat gray-hair'd Saturn, quiet as a stone,*
> *Still as the silence round about his lair;*
> *Forest on forest hung above his head*
> *Like cloud on cloud . . .'*

Father Hoyt came onto the balcony, rubbing his face with both hands. His eyes were wide and unfocused, a child rising from his nap. 'Are we there?' he asked.

'Fucking aye,' cried Martin Silenus, returning the binoculars to the Colonel. 'Let's go down and greet the gendarmes.'

*   *   *

The young Marine lieutenant seemed unimpressed with the group even after he had scanned the authorization wafer Het Masteen had passed along from the task force commander. The lieutenant took his time scanning their visa chips, letting them wait in the drizzle, occasionally making a comment with the idle arrogance common to such nobodies who have just come into a small bit of power. Then he came to Fedmahn Kassad's chip and looked up with the expression of a startled stoat. 'Colonel Kassad!'

'Retired,' said Kassad.

'I'm sorry, sir,' said the lieutenant, stumbling over his words as he fumbled the visas back to everyone. 'I had no idea you were with this party, sir. That is . . . the Captain just said . . . I mean . . . my uncle was with you on Bressia, sir. I mean, I'm sorry . . . anything I or my men can do to . . .'

'At ease, Lieutenant,' said Kassad. 'Is there any chance of getting some transport into the city?'

'Ah . . . well, sir . . .' The young Marine started to rub his chin and then remembered that he was wearing his helmet. 'Yes, sir. But the problem is, sir, the mobs can get pretty nasty and . . . well, the damn EMVs don't work for shit on this . . . uh, pardon me, sir. You see, the ground transports're limited to cargo and we don't have any skimmers free to leave the base until 2200 hours but I'll be happy to get your party on the roster for . . .'

'Just a minute,' said the Consul. A battered passenger skimmer with the gold geodesic of the Hegemony painted on one flare skirt had landed ten meters away. A tall, thin man stepped out. 'Theo!' cried the Consul.

The two men stepped forward, started to shake hands, and then hugged each other instead. 'Damn,' said the Consul, 'you look good, Theo.' It was true. His former aide had gained half a dozen years on the Consul, but the younger man still had the boyish smile, thin face, and thick red hair that had attracted every unmarried woman – and not a few married ones – on the consulate staff. The shyness which had been part of Theo Lane's vulnerability was still there, as evidenced by the way he now needlessly adjusted his archaic horn-rimmed glasses – the young diplomat's one affectation.

'It's good to have you back,' said Theo.

The Consul turned, started to introduce his friend to the group, and then stopped. 'My God,' he said, 'you're Consul now. I'm sorry, Theo, I wasn't thinking.'

Theo Lane smiled and adjusted his glasses. 'No problem, sir,' he said. 'Actually, I'm no longer Consul. For the last few months I've been acting Governor-General. The Home Rule council finally requested – and received – formal colonial status. Welcome to the newest world in the Hegemony.'

The Consul stared a second and then hugged his former protégé again. 'Congratulations, Your Excellency.'

Theo grinned and glanced at the sky. 'It's going to rain in earnest before long. Why don't we get your group aboard the skimmer and I'll drive you into town.' The new Governor-General smiled at the young Marine. 'Lieutenant?'

'Uh . . . yes, *sir*?' The officer had snapped to attention.

'Could you get your men to load these good people's luggage, please? We'd all like to get in out of the rain.'

The skimmer flew south above the highway at a steady sixty meters. The Consul rode in the front passenger seat; the rest of the group relaxed in flowfoam recliners behind. Martin Silenus and Father Hoyt appeared to be asleep. Weintraub's baby had ceased crying in favor of nursing on a soft bottle of synthesized mother's milk.

'Things have changed,' said the Consul. He rested his cheek against the rain-spattered canopy and looked down at the chaos.

Thousand of shacks and lean-tos covered the hillsides and gullies along the three-klick ride to the suburbs. Fires were being lighted under wet tarps and the Consul watched mud-colored figures moving between mud-colored shacks. High fences had been rigged along the old Spaceport Highway and the road itself had been widened and regraded. Two lanes of truck and hover traffic, most of it military green or shrouded with inactive camouflage polymer, moved sluggishly in both directions. Ahead, the lights of Keats seemed to have multiplied and spread across new sections of the river valley and hills.

'Three million,' said Theo, as if reading his former boss's mind. 'At least three million people and growing every day.'

The Consul stared. 'There were only four and a half million people on the *planet* when I left.'

'Still are,' said the new Governor-General. 'And every one of them wants to get to Keats, board a ship, and get the hell out. Some are waiting for the farcaster to be built, but most don't believe it'll happen in time. They're afraid.'

'Of the Ousters?'

'Them too,' said Theo, 'but mostly of the Shrike.'

The Consul turned his face from the coolness of the canopy. 'It's come south of the Bridle Range then?'

Theo laughed without humor. 'It's everywhere. Or *they're* everywhere. Most people are convinced that there are dozens or hundreds of the things now. Shrike deaths have been reported on all three continents. Everywhere except Keats, segments of the coast along the Mane, and a few of the big cities like Endymion.'

'How many casualties?' The Consul did not really want to know.

'At least twenty thousand dead or missing,' said Theo. 'There are a lot of injured people but that isn't the Shrike, is it?' Again came the dry laugh. 'The Shrike doesn't just *wound* people, does it? Uh-uh, people shoot each other by accident, fall down stairways or jump out windows in their panic, and trample each other in crowds. It's a fucking mess.'

In the eleven years the Consul had worked with Theo Lane, he had never heard the younger man use profanity of any sort. 'Is FORCE any help?' the Consul asked. 'Are they what's keeping the Shrike away from the big cities?'

Theo shook his head. 'FORCE hasn't done a damn thing except control the mobs. Oh, the Marines put on a

112

show of keeping the spaceport open here and the harbor landing zone at Port R secure, but they haven't even tried to confront the Shrike. They're waiting to fight the Ousters.'

'SDF?' asked the Consul, knowing even as he spoke that the poorly trained Self-defense Force would have been of little use.

Theo snorted. 'At least eight thousand of the casualties are SDF. General Braxton took the "Fighting Third" up the River Road to "strike at the Shrike menace in their lair" and that was the last we heard of them.'

'You're joking,' said the Consul, but one look at his friend's face told him that he wasn't. 'Theo,' he said, 'how in the world did you have time to meet us at the spaceport?'

'I didn't,' said the Governor-General. He glanced in the back. The others were sleeping or staring exhaustedly out windows. 'I needed to talk to you,' said Theo. 'Convince you not to go.'

The Consul started to shake his head but Theo grasped his arm, squeezed hard. 'Now listen to what I have to say, damn it. I know how hard it is for you to come back here after . . . what happened but, goddamn it, there's no sense in your throwing everything away for no reason. Abandon this stupid pilgrimage. Stay in Keats.'

'I can't . . .' began the Consul.

'*Listen* to me,' demanded Theo. 'Reason one: you're the finest diplomat and crisis manager I've ever seen and we need your skills.'

'It doesn't . . .'

'Shut up a minute. Reason two: you and the others won't get within two hundred klicks of the Time Tombs. This isn't like the old days when you were here and the goddamned suicides could get up there and even sit around for a week and maybe even change their minds and come home. The Shrike is on the *move*. It's like a plague.'

'I understand that but . . .'

'Reason three: *I* need you. I begged Tau Ceti Center to send someone else out. When I found that you were coming . . . well, hell, it got me through the last two years.'

The Consul shook his head, not understanding.

113

Theo started the turn toward the city center and then hovered, taking his eyes off the controls to look directly at the Consul. 'I want you to take over the governor-generalship. The Senate won't interfere – except perhaps for Gladstone – and by the time she finds out, it will be too late.'

The Consul felt as though someone had struck him below the third rib. He looked away, down at the maze of narrow streets and crooked buildings that was Jacktown, the Old City. When he could speak again, he said, 'I can't, Theo.'

'Listen, if you . . .'

'*No*. I mean I can*not*. It would be no good if I did accept it, but the simple truth is, I can't. I have to go on this pilgrimage.'

Theo straightened his glasses, stared straight ahead.

'Look, Theo, you're the most competent and capable Foreign Service professional I've ever worked with. I've been out of things for eight years. I think . . .'

Theo nodded tersely, interrupted. 'I suppose you want to go to the Shrike Temple.'

'Yes.'

The skimmer circled and settled. The Consul was staring at nothing, thinking, when the side doors of the skimmer raised and folded and Sol Weintraub said, 'Good God.'

The group stepped out and stared at the charred and toppled wreckage of what had been the Shrike Temple. Since the Time Tombs had been closed as too dangerous some twenty-five local years earlier, the Shrike Temple had become Hyperion's most popular tourist attraction. Filling three full city blocks, rising more than a hundred and fifty meters to its central, sharpened spire, the Shrike Church's central temple was part awe-inspiring cathedral, part Gothic joke with its fluid, buttressed curves of stone permabonded to its whiskered-alloy skeleton, part Escher print with its tricks of perspective and impossible angles, part Boschian nightmare with its tunnel entrances, hidden chambers, dark gardens, and forbidden sections, and – more than anything else – it had been part of Hyperion's past.

114

Now it was gone. Tall heaps of blackened stone were the only hint of the structure's former majesty. Melted alloy girders rose from the stones like the ribs of some giant carcass. Much of the rubble had tumbled into the pits, basements, and passages which had lain beneath the three-century-old landmark. The Consul walked close to the edge of a pit and wondered if the deep basements had – as legend decreed – actually connected to one of the planet's labyrinths.

'It looks as if they used a hellwhip on this place,' said Martin Silenus, using an archaic term for any high-energy laser weapon. The poet seemed suddenly sobered as he joined the Consul at the edge of the pit. 'I remember when the Temple and parts of the Old City were the only things here,' he said. 'After the disaster near the Tombs, Billy decided to relocate Jacktown here because of the Temple. Now it's gone. Christ.'

'No,' said Kassad.

The others looked at him.

The Colonel rose from where he had been examining the rubble. 'Not a hellwhip,' he said. 'Shaped plasma charges. Several of them.'

'Now do you want to stay here and go on this useless pilgrimage?' asked Theo. 'Come with me back to the consulate.' He was speaking to the Consul but extending the invitation to everyone.

The Consul turned away from the pit, looking at his former aide but now seeing, for the first time, the Governor-General of a besieged Hegemony world. 'We can't, Your Excellency,' said the Consul. 'At least I can't. I won't speak for the others.'

The four men and the woman shook their heads. Silenus and Kassad began unloading luggage. The rain returned as a light mist falling out of the darkness. At that second the Consul noticed the two FORCE attack skimmers hovering above the nearby rooftops. Darkness and chameleon-polymer hulls had hidden them well, but the rain now revealed their outlines. *Of course*, thought the Consul, *the Governor-General does not travel unescorted*.

'Did the priests escape? Were there survivors when the

Temple was destroyed?' asked Brawne Lamia.

'Yes,' said Theo. The de facto dictator of five million doomed souls removed his glasses and dried them on his shirttail. 'All of the Shrike Cult priests and acolytes escaped through tunnels. The mob had been surrounding this place for months. Their leader, a woman named Cammon from somewhere east of the Sea of Grass, gave everyone in the Temple plenty of warning before they set off the DL-20.'

'Where were the police?' asked the Consul. 'The SDF? FORCE?'

Theo Lane smiled and at that second he looked decades older than the young man the Consul had known. 'You folks have been in transit for three years,' he said. 'The universe has changed. Shrike cultists are being burned out and beaten up *in the Web*. You can imagine the attitude here. The Keats police have been absorbed under the martial law I declared fourteen months ago. They and the SDF watched while the mob torched the Temple. So did I. There were half a million people here that night.'

Sol Weintraub stepped closer. 'Do they know about us? About this final pilgrimage?'

'If they did,' said Theo, 'none of you would be alive. You'd think they'd welcome anything that might appease the Shrike, but the only thing the mob would notice is that you were chosen by the Shrike Church. As it was, I had to overrule my own Advisory Council. They were in favor of destroying your ship before it reached the atmosphere.'

'Why did you?' asked the Consul. 'Overrule them, I mean.'

Theo sighed and adjusted his glasses. 'Hyperion still needs the Hegemony, and Gladstone still has the vote of confidence of the All Thing, if not the Senate. And I still need you.'

The Consul looked at the rubble of the Shrike Temple.

'This pilgrimage was over before you got here,' said Governor-General Theo Lane. 'Will you come back to the consulate with me . . . at least in an advisory capacity?'

'I'm sorry,' said the Consul. 'I can't.'

Theo turned without a word, dropped into the skimmer, and lifted off. His military escort followed as a blur in the rain.

It was raining harder now. The group moved closer together in the growing darkness. Weintraub had rigged a makeshift hood over Rachel and the noise of the rain on plastic made the baby cry.

'What now?' said the Consul, looking around at the night and narrow streets. Their luggage lay heaped in a soggy pile. The world smelled of ashes.

Martin Silenus grinned. 'I know a bar.'

It turned out that the Consul also knew the bar; he had all but lived in Cicero's for most of his eleven-year assignment on Hyperion.

Unlike most things in Keats, on Hyperion, Cicero's was not named after some piece of pre-Hegira literary trivia. Rumor had it that the bar was named after a section of an Old Earth city – some said Chicago, USA, others were sure it was Calcutta, AIS – but only Stan Leweski, owner and great-grandson of the founder, knew for sure, and Stan had never revealed its secret. The bar itself had overflowed over the century and a half of its existence from a walkup loft in one of Jacktown's sagging older buildings along the Hoolie River to nine levels in *four* sagging old buildings along the Hoolie. The only consistent elements of decor at Cicero's over the decades were the low ceilings, thick smoke, and constant background babble which offered a sense of privacy in the midst of bustle.

There was no privacy this night. The Consul and the others paused as they carried their gear through the Marsh Lane entrance.

'Jesus wept,' muttered Martin Silenus

Cicero's looked as if it had been invaded by barbarian hordes. Every chair was filled, every table occupied, mostly by men, and the floors were littered with packs, weapons, bedrolls, antiquated comm equipment, ration boxes, and all of the other detritus of an army of refugees . . . or perhaps a refugee army. The heavy air of

Cicero's, which once had been filled with the blended scent of broiling steaks, wine, stim, ale, and T-free tobacco, was now laden with the overlapping smells of unwashed bodies, urine, and hopelessness.

At that moment the huge form of Stan Leweski materialized out of the gloom. The bar owner's forearms were as huge and heavy as ever, but his forehead had advanced more than a few centimeters against the receding tangle of black hair and there were more creases than the Consul remembered around the dark eyes. Those eyes were wide now as Leweski stared at the Consul. 'Ghost,' he said.

'No.'

'You are not dead?'

'No.'

'By damn!' declared Stan Leweski and, grasping the Consul by the upper arms, picked him up as easily as a man would lift a five-year-old. 'By damn! You *are* not dead. What are you doing here?'

'Checking your liquor license,' said the Consul. 'Put me down.'

Leweski carefully set the Consul down, tapped his shoulders, and grinned. He looked at Martin Silenus and the grin changed to a frown. 'You look familiar but I have never seen you before.'

'I knew your great-grandfather,' said Silenus. 'Which reminds me, do you have any of that pre-Hegira ale left? The warm, British stuff that tastes like recycled moose piss. I could never get enough of that.'

'Nothing left,' said Leweski. He pointed at the poet. 'By damn. Grandfather Jiri's trunk. That old holo of the satyr in the original Jacktown. Can it be?' He stared at Silenus and then at the Consul, touching them both gingerly with a massive forefinger. 'Two ghosts.'

'Six tired people,' said the Consul. The baby began crying again. 'Seven. Do you have space for us?'

Leweski turned in a half circle, hands spread, palms up. 'It is all like this. No space left. No food. No wine.' He squinted at Martin Silenus. 'No ale. Now we have become a big hotel with no beds. The SDF bastards stay here without paying and drink their own upcountry rotgut and wait for the world to end. That will happen soon enough, I think.'

The group was standing in what had once been the entrance mezzanine. Their heaped luggage joined a riot of gear already littering the floor. Small clusters of men shouldered their way through the throng and cast appraising glances at the newcomers – especially at Brawne Lamia. She returned their stares with a flat, cold glare.

Stan Leweski looked at the Consul for a moment. 'I have a balcony table. Five of those SDF Death Commandos have been parked there for a week, telling everyone and each other how they are going to wipe out the Ouster Legions with their bare hands. You want the table, I will throw the teat-suckers out.'

'Yes,' said the Consul.

Leweski had turned to leave when Lamia stopped him with a hand on his arm. 'Would you like a little help?' she asked.

Stan Leweski shrugged, grinned. 'I do not need it, but I might like it. Come.'

They disappeared into the crowd.

The third-floor balcony had just enough room for the splintered table and six chairs. Despite the insane crowding on the main floors, stairs, and landings, no one had challenged them for the space after Leweski and Lamia threw the protesting Death Commandos over the railing and into the river nine meters below. Somehow Leweski had managed to send up a tankard of beer and a basket of bread and cold beef.

The group ate in silence, obviously suffering more than the usual amount of postfugue hunger, fatigue, and depression. The darkness of the balcony was relieved only by dim, reflected light from deeper within Cicero's and by the lanterns on passing river barges. Most of the buildings along the Hoolie were dark but other city lights reflected from low clouds. The Consul could make out the ruins of the Shrike Temple half a kilometer upriver.

'Well,' said Father Hoyt, obviously recovered from the heavy dose of ultramorph and teetering on the

119

delicate balance between pain and sedation, 'what do we do next?'

When no one answered, the Consul closed his eyes. He refused to take the lead in anything. Sitting on the balcony at Cicero's, it was all too easy to fall back into the rhythms of a former life; he would drink until the early morning hours, watch the predawn meteor showers as the clouds cleared, and then stagger to his empty apartment near the market, going into the consulate four hours later showered, shaved, and seemingly human except for the blood in his eyes and the insane ache in his skull. Trusting in Theo – quiet, efficient Theo – to get him through the morning. Trusting in luck to get him through the day. Trusting in the drinking at Cicero's to get him through the night. Trusting in the unimportance of his posting to get him through life.

'You are all ready to leave for the pilgrimage?'

The Consul's eyes snapped open. A hooded figure stood in the doorway and for a second the Consul thought it was Het Masteen, but then he realized that this man was much shorter, his voice not accented with the stilted Templar consonants.

'If you are ready, we must go,' said the dark figure.

'Who are you?' asked Brawne Lamia.

'Come quickly,' was the shadow's only reply.

Fedmahn Kassad stood, bending to keep his head from striking the ceiling, and detained the robed figure, flipping back the man's hood with a flick of his left hand.

'An android!' said Lenar Hoyt, staring at the man's blue skin and blue-on-blue eyes.

The Consul was less surprised. For more than a century it had been illegal to own androids in the Hegemony, and none had been biofactured for almost that long, but they were still used for manual labor in remote parts of backwater, noncolony worlds – worlds like Hyperion. The Shrike Temple had used androids extensively, complying with the Church of the Shrike doctrine which proclaimed that androids were free from original sin, therefore spiritually superior to humankind and – incidentally – exempt from the Shrike's terrible and inevitable retribution.

'You must come quickly,' whispered the android, setting his hood in place.

'Are you from the Temple?' asked Lamia.

'Quiet!' snapped the android. He glanced into the hall, turned back, and nodded. 'We must hurry. Please follow me.'

All of them stood and then hesitated. The Consul watched as Kassad casually unsealed the long leather jacket he was wearing. He caught the briefest glimpse of a deathwand tucked in the Colonel's belt. Normally the Consul would have been appalled by even the thought of a deathwand nearby – the slightest mistaken touch could purée every synapse on the balcony – but at this moment he was oddly reassured by the sight of it.

'Our luggage . . .' began Weintraub.

'It has been seen to,' whispered the hooded man. 'Quickly now.'

The group followed the android down the stairs and into the night, their movement as tired and passive as a sigh.

—

The Consul slept late. Half an hour after sunrise a rectangle of light found its way between the porthole's shutters and fell across his pillow. The Consul rolled away and did not wake. An hour after that there came a loud clatter as the tired mantas which had pulled the barge all night were released and fresh ones harnessed. The Consul slept on. In the next hour the footsteps and cries of the crew on the deck outside his stateroom grew louder and more persistent, but it was the warning klaxon below the locks at Karla which finally brought him up out of his sleep.

Moving slowly in the druglike languor of fugue hangover, the Consul bathed as best he could with only basin and pump, dressed in loose cotton trousers, an old canvas shirt, and foam-soled walking shoes, and found his way to the mid-deck.

Breakfast had been set out on a long sideboard near a weathered table which could be retracted into the deck planking. An awning shaded the eating area and the crimson and gold canvas snapped to the breeze of their passage. It was a beautiful day, cloudless and bright, with Hyperion's sun making up in ferocity what it lacked in size.

M. Weintraub, Lamia, Kassad, and Silenus had been up for some time. Lenar Hoyt and Het Masteen joined the group a few minutes after the Consul arrived.

The Consul helped himself to toasted fish, fruit, and orange juice at the buffet and then moved to the railing. The water was wide here, at least a kilometer from shore to shore, and its green and lapis sheen echoed the sky. At first glance the Consul did not recognize the land on either side of the river. To the east, periscope-bean paddies stretched away into the haze of distance where the rising sun reflected on a thousand flooded surfaces. A few indigenie huts were visible at the junction of paddy dikes, their angled walls made of bleached weirwood or golden halfoak. To the west, the bottomland along the river was overgrown with low tangles of gissen, woman-grove root, and a flamboyant red fern the Consul did not recognize, all growing around mud marshes and miniature lagoons which stretched another kilometer or so to bluffs where scrub everblues clung to any bare spot between granite slabs.

For a second the Consul felt lost, disoriented on a world he thought he knew well, but then he remembered the klaxon at the Karla Locks and realized that they had entered a rarely used stretch of the Hoolie north of Doukhobor's Copse. The Consul had never seen this part of the river, having always traveled on or flown above the Royal Transport Canal which lay to the west of the bluffs. He could only surmise that some danger or disturbance along the main route to the Sea of Grass had sent them this back way along bypassed stretches of the Hoolie. He guessed that they were about a hundred and eighty kilometers northwest of Keats.

'It looks different in the daylight, doesn't it?' said Father Hoyt.

The Consul looked at the shore again, not sure what Hoyt was talking about; then he realized the priest meant the barge.

It had been strange – following the android messenger

122

in the rain, boarding the old barge, making their way through its maze of tessellated rooms and passages, picking up Het Masteen at the ruins of the Temple, and then watching the lights of Keats fall astern.

The Consul remembered those hours before and after midnight as from a fatigue-blurred dream, and he imagined the others must have been just as exhausted and disoriented. He vaguely remembered his surprise that the barge's crew were all android, but mostly he recalled his relief at finally closing the door of his stateroom and crawling into bed.

'I was talking to A. Bettik this morning,' said Weintraub, referring to the android who had been their guide. 'This old scow has quite a history.'

Martin Silenus moved to the sideboard to pour himself more tomato juice, added a dash of something from the flask he carried, and said, 'It's obviously been around a bit. The goddamn railings've been oiled by hands, the stairs worn by feet, the ceilings darkened by lamp soot, and the beds beaten saggy by generations of humping. I'd say it's several centuries old. The carvings and rococo finishes are fucking marvelous. Did you notice that under all the other scents the inlaid wood still smells of sandalwood? I wouldn't be surprised if this thing came from Old Earth.'

'It does,' said Sol Weintraub. The baby, Rachel, slept on his arm, softly blowing bubbles of saliva in her sleep. 'We're on the proud ship *Benares*, built in and named after the Old Earth city of the same name.'

'I don't remember hearing of any Old Earth city with that name,' said the Consul.

Brawne Lamia looked up from the last of her breakfast. '*Benares*, also known as Varanasi or Gandhipur, Hindi Free State. Part of the Second Asian Co-prosperity Sphere after the Third Sino-Japanese War. Destroyed in the Indo-Soviet Muslim Republic Limited Exchange.'

'Yes,' said Weintraub, 'the *Benares* was built quite some time before the Big Mistake. Mid-twenty-second century, I would guess. A. Bettik informs me that it was originally a levitation barge . . .'

'Are the EM generators still down there?' interrupted Colonel Kassad.

'I believe so,' said Weintraub. 'Next to the main salon on the lowest deck. The floor of the salon is clear lunar crystal. Quite nice if we were cruising at two thousand meters . . . quite useless now.'

'Benares,' mused Martin Silenus. He ran his hand lovingly across a time-darkened railing. 'I was robbed there once.'

Brawne Lamia put down her coffee mug. 'Old man, are you trying to tell us that you're ancient enough to remember *Old Earth*? We're not fools, you know.'

'My dear child,' beamed Martin Silenus, 'I am not trying to tell you anything. I just thought it might be entertaining – as well as edifying and enlightening – if at some point we exchanged lists of all the locations at which we have either robbed or been robbed. Since you have the unfair advantage of having been the daughter of a senator, I am sure that your list would be much more distinguished . . . and *much* longer.'

Lamia opened her mouth to retort, frowned, and said nothing.

'I wonder how this ship got to Hyperion?' murmured Father Hoyt. 'Why bring a levitation barge to a world where EM equipment doesn't work?'

'It would work,' said Colonel Kassad. 'Hyperion has *some* magnetic field. It just would not be reliable in holding anything airborne.'

Father Hoyt raised an eyebrow, obviously at a loss to see the distinction.

'Hey,' cried the poet from his place at the railing, 'the gang's all here!'

'So?' said Brawne Lamia. Her lips all but disappeared into a thin line whenever she spoke to Silenus.

'So we're all here,' he said. 'Let's get on with the storytelling.'

Het Masteen said, 'I thought it had been agreed that we would tell our respective stories after the dinner hour.'

Martin Silenus shrugged. 'Breakfast, dinner, who the

124

fuck cares? We're assembled. It's not going to take six or seven days to get to the Time Tombs, is it?'

The Consul considered. Less than two days to get as far as the river could take them. Two more days, or less if the winds were right, on the Sea of Grass. Certainly no more than one more day to cross the mountains. 'No,' he said. 'Not quite six days.

'All right,' said Silenus, 'then let's get on with the telling of tales. Besides, there's no guarantee that the Shrike won't come calling before we knock on his door. If these bedtime stories are supposed to be helpful to our survival chances in some way, then I say let's hear from everyone before the contributors start getting chopped and diced by that ambulatory food processor we're so eager to visit.'

'You're disgusting,' said Brawne Lamia.

'Ah, darling,' smiled Silenus, 'those are the same words you whispered last night after your second orgasm.'

Lamia looked away. Father Hoyt cleared his throat and said, 'Whose turn is it? To tell a story, I mean?' The silence stretched.

'Mine,' said Fedmahn Kassad. The tall man reached into the pocket of his white tunic and held up a slip of paper with a large 2 scribbled on it.

'Do you mind doing this now?' asked Sol Weintraub.

Kassad showed a hint of a smile. 'I wasn't in favor of doing it at all,' he said, 'but if it were done when 'tis done, then 'twere well it were done quickly.'

'Hey!' cried Martin Silenus. 'The man knows his pre-Hegira playwrights.'

'Shakespeare?' said Father Hoyt.

'No,' said Silenus. 'Lerner and fucking Lowe. Neil buggering Simon. Hamel fucking Posten.'

'Colonel,' Sol Weintraub said formally, 'the weather is nice, none of us seems to have anything pressing to do in the next hour or so, and we would be obliged if you would share the tale of what brings you to Hyperion on the Shrike's last pilgrimage.'

Kassad nodded. The day grew warmer as the canvas awning snapped, the decks creaked, and the levitation barge *Benares* worked its steady way upstream toward the mountains, the moors, and the Shrike.

THE SOLDIER'S TALE:
The War Lovers

It was during the Battle of Agincourt that Fedmahn Kassad encountered the woman he would spend the rest of his life seeking.

It was a wet and chilly late October morning in A.D. 1415. Kassad had been inserted as an archer into the army of Henry V of England. The English force had been on French soil since August 14 and had been retreating from superior French forces since October 8. Henry had convinced his War Council that the army could beat the French in a forced march to the safety of Calais. They had failed. Now, as October 25 dawned gray and drizzly, seven thousand Englishmen, mostly bowmen, faced a force of some twenty-eight thousand French men-at-arms across a kilometer of muddy field.

Kassad was cold, tired sick, and scared. He and the other archers had been surviving on little more than scavenged berries for the past week of the march and almost every man on the line that morning was suffering from diarrhea. The air temperature was in the low fifties Fahrenheit and Kassad had spent a long night trying to sleep on damp ground. He was impressed with the unbelievable realism of the experience – the Olympus Command School Historical Tactical Network was as far beyond regular stimsims as full-form holos were beyond tintypes – but the physical sensations were so convincing, so *real*, that Kassad did not relish the thought of being wounded. There were tales of cadets receiving fatal wounds in the OCS:HTN sims and being pulled dead from their immersion creches.

Kassad and the other bowmen on Henry's right flank had been staring at the larger French force for most of the morning when pennants waved, the fifteenth-century equivalent of sergeants brayed, and the archers obeyed the King's command and began marching against the

126

enemy. The ragged English line, stretching about seven hundred meters across the field from treeline to treeline, consisted of clusters of archers like Kassad's troop interspersed with smaller groups of men-at-arms. The English had no formal cavalry and most of the horses Kassad could see on his end of the field were carrying men clustered near the King's command group three hundred meters toward the center, or huddled around the Duke of York's position much closer to where Kassad and the other archers stood near the right flank. These command groups reminded Kassad of a FORCE:ground mobile staff HQ, only instead of the inevitable forest of comm antennae giving away their position, bright banners and pennants hung limp on pikes. An obvious artillery target, thought Kassad, and then reminded himself that this particular military nuance did not yet exist.

Kassad noticed that the French had plenty of horses. He estimated six or seven hundred mounted men formed in ranks on each of the French flanks and a long line of cavalry behind the main battle line. Kassad did not like horses. He had seen holos and pictures, of course, but he had not encountered the animals themselves until this exercise, and the size, smell, and sound of them tended to be unnerving – especially so when the damn quadrupeds were armored chest and head, shod in steel, and trained to carry armored men wielding four meters of lance.

The English advance halted. Kassad estimated that his battle line was about two hundred and fifty meters from the French. He knew from the experience of the past week that this was within longbow range, but he also knew that he would have to pull his arm half out of its socket to hold the pull.

The French were shouting what Kassad assumed were insults. He ignored them as he and his silent comrades stepped forward from where they had planted their long arrows and found soft ground in which to drive their stakes. The stakes were long and heavy and Kassad had been carrying his for a week. Almost a meter and a half long, the clumsy thing had been sharpened at both ends. When the order first came down for all archers to find saplings and cut stakes, somewhere in the deep woods just after they had crossed the Somme, Kassad had wondered idly what the things were for. Now he knew.

Every third archer carried a heavy mallet and now they took turns driving their stakes in at a careful angle. Kassad pulled out his long knife, resharpened the end which, even leaning, rose almost to his chest, and stepped back through the hedgehog of sharpened stakes to await the French charge.

The French did not charge.

Kassad waited with the others. His bow was strung, forty-eight arrows were planted in two clusters at his feet, and his feet were set properly.

The French did not charge.

The rain had stopped but a cool breeze had come up and what little body heat Kassad had generated by the short march and the task of driving stakes had been lost quickly. The only sounds were the metallic shufflings of men and horses, occasional mutterings or nervous laughs, and the heavier thud of hooves as the French cavalry rearranged itself but still refused to charge.

'Fuck this,' said a grizzled yeoman a few feet from Kassad. 'Those bastards've wasted our whole bleeding morning. They'd better piss or get off the pot.'

Kassad nodded. He was not sure if he was hearing and understanding Middle English or if the sentence had been in simple Standard. He had no idea if the grizzled archer was another Command School cadet, an instructor, or merely an artifact of the sim. He could not guess if the slang had been correct. He did not care. His heart was pounding and his palms were sweaty. He wiped his hands on his jerkin.

As if King Henry had taken his cue from the old man's muttering, command flags suddenly bobbed and rose, sergeants screamed, and row upon row of English archers raised their longbows, pulled when commands were shouted, released on the next command.

Four waves of arrows comprised of more than six thousand meter-long, chisel-pointed, clothyard missiles rose, seemed to hang in a cloud thirty meters up, and fell on the French.

There came the sound of horses screaming and a

thousand demented children pounding on ten thousand tin pots as the French men-at-arms leaned into the rain of arrows to let their steel helmets and their chest and shoulder armor take the brunt of the downpour. Kassad knew that in military terms little real damage had been done, but this was small solace to the occasional French soldier with ten inches of arrow through his eye, or to the scores of horses leaping, tumbling, and crashing into one another while their riders struggled to remove wooden shafts from the creatures' backs and flanks.

The French did not charge.

More commands were shouted. Kassad raised, readied, loosed his arrow. Again. And again. The sky darkened every ten seconds. Kassad's arm and back ached from the punishing rhythm. He found that he felt neither elation nor anger. He was doing his job. His forearm was raw. Again the arrows flew. And again. Fifteen of his first sheaf of twenty-four arrows were gone when a cry went up along the English line and Kassad paused and glanced down while holding full pull.

The French were charging.

A cavalry charge was something beyond Kassad's experience. Watching twelve hundred armored horses charging directly at him created internal sensations which Kassad found a bit unnerving. The charge took less than forty seconds but Kassad discovered that this was ample time for his mouth to go absolutely dry, his breathing to begin to have problems, and for his testicles to retreat completely into his body. If the rest of Kassad could have found a comparable hiding place, he would have seriously considered crawling into it.

As it was, he was too busy to run.

Firing on command, his line of archers got off five flat volleys at the attacking horsemen, managed one more shot in independent fire, and then they fell back five paces.

Horses, it turned out, were too smart to willingly impale themselves upon stakes – no matter how hard their human riders implored them to do so – but the second and third waves of cavalry did not stop as abruptly as the first, and in a single mad moment horses were down and screaming, riders were thrown and screaming, and Kassad was out and screaming, rushing at every downed Frenchman he could see, wielding a mallet on the prostrate form when he could, slashing through gaps in armor with his long knife when it was too crowded to swing the mallet. Soon he and the grizzled archer and a younger man who had lost his cap became an efficient killing team, closing in on a downed rider from three sides, Kassad using the mallet to knock the pleading horseman off his knees, then all three moving in with their blades.

Only one knight gained his feet and raised a sword to confront them. The Frenchman flipped up his visor and called out a clear request for honor and single combat. The old man and the youth circled like wolves. Kassad returned with his bow and put an arrow into the knight's left eye from ten paces.

The battle continued in the deadly comic-opera vein common to all armed combat since the first rock and thighbone duels on Old Earth. The French cavalry managed to turn and flee just as the first wave of ten thousand men-at-arms charged the English center on foot. The melee broke up the rhythm of the attack and, by the time the French had regained their initiative, Henry's own men-at-arms had braced to hold them at pike length while Kassad and several thousand other archers poured volley fire into the massed French infantry at close range.

That did not end the battle. It was not necessarily even the decisive moment. The turning point, when it came, was lost – as all such moments are – within the dust and turmoil of a thousand individual encounters where infantrymen faced infantrymen across the distance of their personal weapons. Before it was over some three hours later there would be minor variations on repeated themes, ineffective thrusts and clumsy counterthrusts, and a less than honorable moment when Henry would order prisoners killed rather than leave them in the rear when the English were confronted with a new threat. But the heralds and historians would later agree that the outcome had been sealed somewhere in the confusion during the first French infantry charge. The French died in their thousands. English dominion on that part of the Continent would continue for a while. The day of the armored man-at-arms, the knight, the embodiment of chivalry, was over – hammered into history's coffin by a few thousand ragtag peasant archers carrying longbows. The ultimate insult to the noble-born French dead – if the dead indeed could be further insulted – lay in the fact that the English archers were not only common men, common in the lowest, most flea-infested sense of the word, but that they were *draftees*. Doughboys. GIs. Grunts. AIPs. Spezzes. K-techs. Jump Rats.

But all that was in the lesson Kassad was supposed to have learned during the OCS:HTN exercise. He learned none of it. He was too busy having an encounter which would change his life.

The French man-at-arms went over the head of his falling horse, rolled once, and was up and running for the woods before the mud quit flying. Kassad followed. He was halfway to the tree line before he realized that the youth and the grizzled archer had not come with him. It did not matter. Kassad's adrenaline was flowing and the bloodlust had him in its grip.

The man-at-arms, who had just been thrown to the ground from a horse moving at full gallop and who was wearing sixty pounds of clumsy armor, should have been an easy prey to catch. He was not. The Frenchman glanced back once, saw Kassad coming on a full run with a mallet in his hand and his eye full of business, and then the man-at-arms shifted into a higher gear and reached the trees fifteen meters ahead of his pursuer.

Kassad was deep into the woods before he stopped, leaned on the mallet, gasped, and considered his position. Thuds, screams, and crashes from the battlefield behind him were muffled by distance and shrubbery. The trees were almost bare and still dripped from the rainstorm the night before; the floor of the forest was carpeted with a thick layer of old leaves and a snarl of shrubs and brambles. The man-at-arms had left a trail of broken branches and footprints for the first twenty meters or so, but now deer trails and overgrown paths made it difficult to see where he had passed.

Kassad moved slowly, stepping deeper into the woods, trying to be alert for any noise above the sound of his own panting and the insane pounding of his heart. It occurred to Kassad that, tactically speaking, this was not a brilliant move; the man-at-arms had been wearing full armor and carrying his sword when he disappeared in the bushes. At any moment the Frenchman might forget his panic, regret his temporary loss of honor, and remember his years of combat training. Kassad also had been trained. He looked down at his cloth shirt and leather vest. The mallet was still in his hands, the knife in his broad belt. He had been trained to use high-energy weapons with a killing range of a few meters to thousands of kilometers. He had been rated in plasma grenades, hell-whips, fleschette rifles, sonics, recoilless zero-gravity weapons, deathwands, kinetic assault guns, and beam gauntlets. He now had a working knowledge of an English longbow. None of these objects – including the longbow – was on his person at the moment.

'Ah, shit,' murmured Second Lieutenant Kassad.

The man-at-arms came out of the bushes like a charging bear, arms up, legs apart, the sword coming around in a flat arc meant to disembowel Kassad. The OCS cadet tried to leap back and raise his mallet at the same time. Neither effort was completely successful. The Frenchman's sword knocked the heavy mallet out of Kassad's grip while the dull point of the blade slashed through leather, shirt, and skin.

Kassad bellowed and stumbled backward again, tugging at the knife in his belt. His right heel caught the branch of a fallen tree and he went down backward, cursing and rolling deeper into the tangle of branches as the man-at-arms crashed forward, his heavy sword clearing limbs like an oversized machete. Kassad had his knife out by the time the man-at-arms had cleared a path through the deadfall, but the ten-inch blade was a pitiful thing against armor unless the knight was helpless. This knight was not helpless. Kassad knew that he would never get inside the arc of sword blade. His only hope was in running, but the tall trunk of the fallen tree behind him and the deadfall beyond eliminated that option. He did not wish to get cut down from behind as he turned. Nor from below as he climbed. Kassad did not wish to be cut down from any angle.

Kassad went into a knife fighter's crouch which he hadn't used since his street-fighting days in the Tharsis slums. He wondered how the simulation would deal with his death.

The figure appeared behind the man-at-arms like a sudden shadow. The noise of Kassad's mallet striking the knight's armored shoulder sounded precisely like someone bashing the hood of an EMV with a sledge-hammer.

The Frenchman staggered, turned to meet the new threat, and took a second mallet below in the chest. Kassad's savior was small; the man-at-arms did not go down. The French knight was raising his sword above his head when Kassad hit him behind and below the knees with a shoulder tackle.

Tree limbs snapped as the Frenchman went down. The small attacker stood astride the knight, pinning the armored man's sword arm with one foot while bringing the mallet down repeatedly onto helmet and visor. Kassad extricated himself from the tangle of legs and branches, sat on the downed man's knees, and began slashing through gaps in armor at groin, sides, and underarms. Kassad's rescuer jumped aside to plant both feet on the knight's wrist and Kassad scrambled forward, stabbing through crevices where the helmet met chest armor, finally slamming the blade through slits in the visor itself.

The knight screamed as the mallet came down a final time, almost catching Kassad's hand as the hammer drove the blade through the visor slit like a ten-inch tent peg. The man-at-arms arched, lifting Kassad and sixty pounds of armor clear of the ground in a final violent spasm and then fell back limply.

Kassad rolled onto his side. His rescuer collapsed beside him. Both were covered with sweat and the dead man's blood. Kassad looked at his savior. The woman was dressed in clothes not dissimilar to Kassad's. For a moment they merely lay there and gasped for air.

'Are you . . . all right?' Kassad managed after a while. He was suddenly struck by her appearance. Her brown hair was short by current Worldweb fashion, short and straight and cut so that the longest strands fell from the part, just a few centimeters left of the center of her forehead, to just above her right ear. It was a boy's haircut from some forgotten time, but she was no boy. Kassad thought that she was perhaps the most beautiful woman he had ever seen: bone structure so perfect that chin and cheekbones were shaped without being too sharp, large eyes glowing with life and intelligence, a gentle mouth with a soft underlip. Lying next to her, Kassad realized that she was tall – not so tall as he but obviously not a woman from the fifteenth century – and even under her loose tunic and baggy trousers he could see the soft swell of hips and breast. She appeared to be a few years older than Kassad, perhaps in her late twenties, but this fact barely registered as she continued staring into his face with those soft, beguiling, endlessly deep eyes.

'Are you all right?' he asked again. His voice sounded strange, even to himself.

She did not answer. Or, rather, she answered by sliding long fingers across Kassad's chest, ripping away the leather thongs which bound the rough vest. Her hands found his shirt. It was soaked with blood and ripped halfway down the front. The woman ripped it open the rest of the way. She moved against him now, her fingers and lips on his chest, hips already beginning to move. Her right hand found the cords to his trouser front, ripped them free.

Kassad helped her pull off the rest of his clothes, removed hers with three fluid movements. She wore nothing under her shirt and coarse-cloth trousers. Kassad's hand slid between her thighs, behind her, cupped her moving buttocks, pulled her closer, and slid to the moist roughness in front. She opened to him, her mouth closing on his. Somehow, with all of their motion and disrobing, their skin never lost contact. Kassad felt

134

his own excitement rubbing against the cusp of her belly.

She rolled above him then, her thighs astride his hips, her gaze still locked with his. Kassad had never been so excited. He gasped as her right hand went behind her, found him, guided him into her. When he opened his eyes again she was moving slowly, her head back, eyes closed. Kassad's hands moved up her sides to cup her perfect breasts. Nipples hardened against his palms.

They made love then. Kassad, at twenty-three standard years, had been in love once and had enjoyed sex many times. He thought he knew the way and the why of it. There was nothing in his experience to that moment which he could not have described with a phrase and a laugh to his squadmates in the hold of a troop transport. With the calm, sure cynicism of a twenty-three-year-old veteran he was sure that he would *never* experience anything that could not be so described, so dismissed. He was wrong. He could never adequately share the sense of the next few minutes with anyone else. He would never try.

They made love in a sudden shaft of late October light with a carpet of leaves and clothes beneath them and a film of blood and sweat oiling the sweet friction between them. Her green eyes stared down at Kassad, widening slightly when he began moving quickly, closing at the same second he closed his.

They moved together then in the sudden tide of sensation as old and inevitable as the movement of worlds: pulses racing, flesh quickening with its own moist purposes, a further, final rising together, the world receding to nothing at all – and then, still joined by touch and heartbeat and the fading thrill of passion, allowing consciousness to slide back to separate flesh while the world flowed in through forgotten senses.

They lay next to each other. The dead man's armor was cold against Kassad's left arm, her thigh warm against his right leg. The sunlight was a benediction. Hidden colors rose to the surface of things. Kassad turned his head and gazed at her as she rested her head on his shoulder. Her cheeks glowed with flush and autumn light and her hair lay like copper threads along the flesh of his arm. She curved her leg over his thigh and Kassad felt the clockwise stirring of renewed passion. The sun was warm on his face. He closed his eyes.

When he awoke she was gone. He was certain that only seconds had passed – no more than a minute, certainly – but the sunlight was gone, colors had flowed out of the forest, and a cool evening breeze moved bare branches.

Kassad dressed in torn clothes made stiff with blood. The French man-at-arms lay still and rigid in the unselfconscious attitude of death. He already seemed inanimate, a part of the forest. There was no sign whatsoever of the woman.

Fedmahn Kassad limped his way back through the woods, evening gloom, and a sudden, chilling drizzle.

The battlefield still held people, living and dead. The dead lay in heaps like the piles of toy soldiers Kassad had played with as a child. Wounded men moved slowly with the help of friends. Here and there furtive forms picked their way among the dead, and near the opposite tree line a lively group of heralds, both French and English, met in conclave with much pointing and animated conversation. Kassad knew that they had to decide upon a name for the battle so that their respective records would agree. He also knew that they would settle on the name of the nearest castle, Agincourt, even though it had figured in neither strategy nor battle.

Kassad was beginning to think that this was no simulation, that his life in the Worldweb was the dream and that this gray day had to be reality, when suddenly the entire scene froze with outlines of human figures, horses, and the darkening forest becoming as transparent as a fading holo. And then Kassad was being helped out of his simulation creche at the Olympus Command School and the other cadets and instructors were rising, talking, laughing with one another – all seemingly unaware that the world had changed forever.

For weeks Kassad spent every free hour wandering the Command School grounds, watching from the ramparts as the evening shadow of Mons Olympus covered first the Plateau forest, then the heavily settled highlands, then everything halfway to the horizon, and then all the world. And every second he thought about what had happened. He thought about her.

No one else had noticed anything strange in the simulation. No one else had left the battlefield. One instructor explained that nothing beyond the battlefield *existed* in that particular segment of the simulation. No one had missed Kassad. It was as if the incident in the forest – and the woman – had never happened.

Kassad knew better. He attended his classes on military history and mathematics. He put in his hours at the firing range and gym. He walked off barracks punishments on the Caldera Quadrangle, although these were rare. In general, young Kassad became an even more excellent officer cadet than he had been. But all the while he waited.

And then she came again.

Again it was in the final hours of an OCS:HTN simulation. By then Kassad had learned that the exercises were something more than mere simulations. The OCS:HTN was part of the Worldweb All Thing, the real-time network which governed Hegemony politics, fed information to tens of billions of data-hungry citizens, and had evolved a form of autonomy and consciousness all its own. More than a hundred and fifty planetary dataspheres mingled their resources within the framework created by six thousand omega-class AIs to allow the OCS:HTN to function.

'The HTN stuff doesn't simulate,' whined Cadet Radinski, the best AI expert Kassad could find and bribe to explain, 'it *dreams*, dreams with the best historical accuracy in the Web – way beyond the sum of its parts 'cause it plugs in holistic insight as well as facts – and when it dreams, it lets us dream with it.'

Kassad had not understood but he had believed. And then she came again.

In the First US–Vietnam War they made love in the aftermath of an ambush during the darkness and terror of a night patrol. Kassad wore rough camouflage

137

clothes – with no underwear because of the jungle crotch rot – and a steel helmet not much more advanced than those at Agincourt. She wore black pajamas and sandals, the universal garb of the Southeast Asian peasant. And the Viet Cong. Then neither of them wore anything as they made love standing in the night, her back against a tree and her legs wrapped around him, while beyond them the world exploded in the green glow of perimeter flares and the sputter-crack of claymores.

She came to him on the second day of Gettysburg and again at Borodino, where the clouds of powder smoke hung above the piles of bodies like a vapor congealed from departing souls.

They made love in the shattered hulk of an APC in Hellas Basin while the hovertank battle still raged and the red dust of the approaching simoon scraped and shrieked at the titanium hull. 'Tell me your name,' he had whispered in Standard. She shook her head. 'Are you real – outside the simulation?' he asked in the Japanese-English of that era. She had nodded and leaned closer to kiss him.

They lay together in a sheltered place among the ruins of Brasilia while deathbeams from Chinese EMVs played like blue searchlights on broken ceramic walls. During an unnamed battle after a siege of a forgotten tower city on the Russian steppes, he pulled her back into the shattered room where they had made love, and he whispered, 'I want to stay with you.' She touched his lips with a finger and shook her head. After the evacuation of New Chicago, as they lay on the hundredth-floor balcony where Kassad had set his sniper's nest for the last US President's hopeless rear-guard action, he placed his hand on the warm flesh between her breasts and said, 'Can you ever join me . . . out there?' She touched his cheek with her palm and smiled.

During the last year in Command School there were only five OCS:HTN sims as the cadets' training shifted to live field exercises. Sometimes, as when Kassad was strapped into the tactical command chair during a battalion-sized drop onto Ceres, he closed his eyes, looked between the primary-colored geographies of the cortically generated tactical/terrain matrix, and felt a sense of . . . someone? Of her? He was not sure.

And then she did not come again. Not in the final months of work. Not in the final simulation of the great Coal Sack Battle where General Horace Glennon-Height's mutiny was defeated. Not during the parades and parties of graduation, nor as the class marched in a final Olympian review before the Hegemony CEO, saluting from his red-lit levitation deck.

And there was no time even for dreaming as the young officers farcast to Earth's Moon for the Masada Ceremony, farcast again to Tau Ceti Center for their formal swearing-in to FORCE, and then they were finished.

Second Lieutenant Cadet Kassad became Lieutenant Kassad, spent three standard weeks free in the Web with a FORCE-issued universal card which allow him to farcast as far and as frequently as he wished, and then he was shipped out to the Hegemony Colonial Service training school on Lusus to prepare for active duty beyond the Web. He was sure that he would never see her again.

He was wrong.

Fedmahn Kassad had grown up in a culture of poverty and sudden death. As a member of the minority who still called themselves Palestinians, he and his family had lived in the slums of Tharsis, human testimony to the bitter legacy of the terminally dispossessed. Every Palestinian in the Worldweb and beyond carried the cultural memory of a century of struggle capped by a month of nationalist triumph before the Nuclear Jihad of 2038 wiped it all away. Then came their second Diaspora, this one lasting five centuries and leading to dead-end desert worlds like Mars, their dream buried with the death of Old Earth.

Kassad, like the other boys of the South Tharsis Relocation Camps, either ran with gangs or faced the option of being prey to every self-proclaimed predator in the camps. He chose to run with the gangs. Kassad had killed another youth by the time he was sixteen standard years old.

If Mars was known for anything in the Worldweb, it

was for hunting in the Mariner Valley, Schrauder's Zen Massif in Hellas Basin, and the Olympus Command School. Kassad did not have to travel to Mariner Valley to learn about hunting and being hunted, he had no interest in Zen Gnosticism, and as a teenager he felt nothing but contempt for the uniformed cadets who came from every part of the Web to train for FORCE. He joined with his peers in sneering at the New Bushido as a code for faggots, but an ancient vein of honor in the young Kassad's soul secretly resonated to the thought of a samurai class whose life and work revolved around duty, self-respect, and the ultimate value of one's word.

When Kassad was eighteen, a Tharsis Province higher circuit judge offered him the choice of a Martian year at polar work camp or volunteering for the John Carter Brigade then forming to help FORCE put down the resurgent Glennon-Height Rebellion in the Class Three colonies. Kassad volunteered and discovered that he enjoyed the discipline and cleanliness of military life, even though the John Carter Brigade saw only garrison duty within the Web and was dissolved shortly after Glennon-Height's cloned grandson died on Renaissance. Two days after his nineteenth birthday, Kassad applied to FORCE:ground and was turned down. He went on a nine-day drunk, awoke in one of the deeper hive tunnels of Lusus with his military comlog implant stolen – by someone who apparently had taken a correspondence course in surgery – his universal card and farcaster access revoked, and his head exploring new frontiers of pain.

Kassad worked on Lusus for a standard year, saving over six thousand marks and allowing physical labor in the 1.3-ES gravity to put an end to his Martian frailness. By the time he used his savings to ship out to Maui-Covenant on an ancient solar sail freighter with jury-rigged Hawking drives, Kassad was still lean and tall by Web standards, but what muscles there were worked wonderfully well by anyone's standards.

He arrived on Maui-Covenant three days before the vicious and unpopular Island War began there, and eventually the FORCE: combined commander at Firstsite got so tired of seeing the young Kassad waiting in his outer office that he allowed the boy to enlist in the 23rd Supply Regiment as an assistant hydrofoil driver. Eleven standard months later, Corporal Fedmahn Kassad of the Twelfth Mobile Infantry Battalion had received two Distinguished Service Clusters, a Senate Commendation for valor in the Equatorial Archipelago campaign, and two Purple Hearts. He was also tapped for FORCE command school and shipped Webward on the next convoy.

Kassad dreamed of her often. He had never learned her name, she had never spoken, but he could have recognized her touch and scent in total darkness among a thousand others. He thought of her as Mystery.

When other young officers went whoring or seeking girlfriends in the indigenie populations, Kassad would remain on base or take long walks through strange cities. He kept his obsession with Mystery secret, knowing full well how it would read on a psych report. Sometimes, on bivouac under multiple moons or in the womblike zero-g of a troop transport hold, Kassad would realize how insane his love affair with a phantom truly was. But then he would recall the small mole under her left breast which he had kissed one night, feeling her heartbeat under his lips as the ground itself shook from the firing of the big guns near Verdun. He would remember the impatient gesture with which she brushed back her hair as her cheek rested on his thigh. And the young officers would go to town or to the huts near the base, and Fedmahn Kassad would read another history book or jog along the perimeter or run tactical strategies on his comlog.

It was not long before Kassad came to the attention of his superiors.

During the undeclared war with the Free Miners in the Lambert Ring Territories, it was Lieutenant Kassad who led the surviving infantry troops and Marine guards in cutting through the bottom of the old asteroid bore shaft on Peregrine to evacuate the Hegemony consulate staff and citizens.

But it was during the short reign of the New Prophet

on Qom-Riyadh that Captain Fedmahn Kassad came to the attention of the entire Web.

The FORCE:space captain of the only Hegemony ship within two leap years of the colony world had been paying a courtesy call when the New Prophet chose to lead thirty million New Order Shi'ites against two continents of Suni shopkeepers and ninety thousand resident Hegemony infidels. The ship's captain and five of his executive officers were taken prisoner. Urgent fatline messages from Tau Ceti Center demanded that the ranking officer aboard the orbiting *HS Denieve* settle the situation on Qom-Riyadh, free all hostages, and depose the New Prophet . . . without resorting to the use of nuclear weapons within the planet's atmosphere. The *Denieve* was an aging orbital defense picket. It carried no nuclear weapons that could be used within an atmosphere. The ranking officer on board was FORCE:combined Captain Fedmahn Kassad.

On the third day of the revolution, Kassad landed the *Denieve*'s single assault boat in the main courtyard of the Grand Mosque at Mashhad. He and the other thirty-four FORCE troopers watched as the mob grew to three hundred thousand militants kept at bay only by the boat's containment field and the lack of an order to attack by the New Prophet. The New Prophet himself was no longer in the Grand Mosque; he had flown to the northern hemisphere of Riyadh to join in the victory celebrations there.

Two hours after he landed, Captain Kassad stepped out of his ship and broadcast a short announcement. He said that he had been raised as a Muslim. He also announced that interpretation of the Koran since the Shi'ites' seedship days had definitely shown that the God of Islam would neither condone nor allow the slaughter of the innocent, no matter how many jihads were proclaimed by tinhorn heretics like the New Prophet. Captain Kassad gave the leaders of the thirty million zealots three hours to surrender their hostages and return to their homes on the desert continent of Qom.

In the first three days of the revolution the armies of the New Prophet had occupied most of the cities on two continents and had taken more than twenty-seven thousand Hegemony hostages. Firing squads had been busy day and night settling ancient theological disputes and it was estimated that at least a quarter of a million Sunis had been slaughtered in the first two days of the New Prophet's occupation. In response to Kassad's ultimatum, the New Prophet announced that all of the infidels would be put to death immediately following his live television address that evening. He also ordered an attack on Kassad's assault boat.

Avoiding high explosives because of the Grand Mosque, the Revolutionary Guard used automatic weapons, crude energy cannon, plasma charges, and human wave attacks. The containment field held.

The New Prophet's televised address began fifteen minutes before Kassad's ultimatum ran out. The New Prophet agreed with Kassad's statement that Allah would horribly punish heretics but announced that it was the Hegemony infidels who would be so punished. It was the only time the New Prophet ever had been seen to lose his temper on camera. Screaming, saliva flying, he ordered the human wave attacks to be renewed on the grounded assault boat. He announced that at that moment a dozen fission bombs were being assembled at the occupied Power for Peace reactor in Ali. With these, the forces of Allah would be carried into space itself. The first fission bomb, he explained, would be used on the infidel Kassad's satanic assault boat that very afternoon. The New Prophet then began to explain exactly how the Hegemony hostages would be executed, but at that moment Kassad's deadline ran out.

Qom-Riyadh was, by its own choice and the accident of its distant location, a technically primitive world. But the inhabitants were not so primitive that they did not have an active datasphere. Nor were the revolutionary mullahs who had led the invasion so opposed to the 'Great Satan of Hegemony Science' that they refused to tie into the global data net with their personal comlogs.

The *HS Denieve* had seeded enough spysats so that by 1729 hours Qom-Riyadh Central Time, the datasphere had been tapped to the point that the Hegemony ship had identified sixteen thousand eight hundred and thirty revolutionary mullahs by their access codes. At 1729:30 hours the spysats began feeding their real-time targeting data to the twenty-one perimeter defense sats which Kassad's assault boat had left in low orbit. These orbital defense weapons were so old that the *Denieve*'s mission had been to return them to the Web for safe destruction. Kassad had suggested another use for them.

At precisely 1730 hours, nineteen of the small satellites detonated their fusion cores. In the nanoseconds before their self-destruction, the resulting X rays were focused, aimed, and released in sixteen thousand eight hundred and thirty invisible but very coherent beams. The ancient defense sats were not designed for atmospheric use and had an effective destructive radius of less than a millimeter. Luckily, that was all that was needed. Not all of the targeting beams penetrated whatever stood between the mullahs and the sky. Fifteen thousand seven hundred and eighty-four did.

The effect was immediate and dramatic. In each case the target's brain and cerebral fluid boiled, turned to vapor, and blew the encasing skull to bits. The New Prophet was in the middle of his live, planetwide broadcast – literally in the middle of pronouncing the word 'heretic' – when 1730 hours arrived.

For almost two minutes the TV screens and walls around the planet carried the image of the New Prophet's headless body slumped over the microphone. Then Fedmahn Kassad cut in on all bands to announce that his next deadline was one hour away and that any actions against the hostages would be met with a more dramatic demonstration of Allah's displeasure.

There were no reprisals.

That night, in orbit around Qom-Riyadh, Mystery visited Kassad for the first time since his cadet days. He was asleep but the visit was more than a dream and less than the alternative reality of the OCS:HTN sims. The woman and he were lying together under a light blanket beneath a broken roof. Her skin was warm and electric, her face little more than a pale outline against nighttime darkness. Overhead the stars had just begun to fade into the false light of predawn. Kassad realized that she was trying to speak to him; her soft lips formed words which were just below the threshold of Kassad's hearing. He pulled back a second in order to see her face better and, in so doing, lost contact completely. He awoke in his sleep webbing with moisture on his cheeks and the hum of the ship's systems sounding as strange to him as the breathing of some half-awakened beast.

Nine standard ship weeks later, Kassad stood before a FORCE court-martial review on Freeholm. He had known when he made his decision on Qom-Riyadh that his superiors would have no choice but to crucify or promote him.

FORCE prided itself on preparing itself for all contingencies in the Web or the colonial regions, but nothing had properly prepared it for the Battle of South Bressia and its implications for the New Bushido.

The New Bushido Code which governed Colonel Kassad's life had evolved out of the necessity for the military class to survive. After the obscenities of the late twentieth and early twenty-first centuries on Old Earth, when military leaders had committed their nations to strategies wherein entire civilian populations were legitimate targets while their uniformed executioners sat safe in self-contained bunkers fifty meters under the earth, the repugnance of the surviving civilians was so great that for more than a century the word 'military' was an invitation to a lynching.

As the New Bushido evolved it combined the age-old concepts of honor and individual courage with the need to spare civilians whenever possible. It also saw the wisdom of returning to the pre-Napoleonic concepts of small, 'nontotal' wars with defined goals and proscribed excesses. The Code demanded a forsaking of nuclear weapons and strategic bombing campaigns in all but the most extreme cases but, more than that, it demanded a return to Old Earth medieval concepts of set battles between small, professional forces at a mutually agreed-

145

upon time in a place where destruction of public and private property would be kept to a minimum.

This Code worked well for the first four centuries of post-Hegira expansion. The fact that essential technologies were essentially frozen in place for three of those centuries worked in the Hegemony's favor as its monopoly on the use of farcasters allowed it to apply the modest resources of FORCE at the right place in the required amount of time. Even when separated by the inevitable leap years of time-debt, no colonial or independent world could hope to match the power of the Hegemony. Incidents such as the political rebellion on Maui-Covenant, with its unique guerrilla warfare, or the religious insanity on Qom-Riyadh were put down quickly and firmly and any excesses in the campaigns merely pointed out the importance of returning to the strict Code of the New Bushido. But for all of FORCE's calculations and preparations, no one had adequately planned on the inevitable confrontation with the Ousters.

The Ousters had been the single external threat to the Hegemony for the four centuries since the forebears of the barbarian hordes had left Sol System in their crude fleet of leaking O'Neill cities, tumbling asteroids, and experimental comet farm clusters. Even after the Ousters acquired the Hawking drive, it remained official Hegemony policy to ignore them as long as their swarms stayed in the darkness between the stars and limited their in-system plunderings to scooping small amounts of hydrogen from gas giants and water ice from uninhabited moons.

The early Outback skirmishes such as Bent's World and GHC 2990 were considered aberrations, of little interest to the Hegemony. Even the pitched battle for Lee Three had been treated as a Colonial Service problem and when the FORCE task force arrived six local years after the attack, five years after the Ousters departed, any atrocities were conveniently forgotten in favor of the view that no barbarian raid would repeat itself when the Hegemony chose to flex its muscle.

In the decades which followed Lee Three, FORCE and Ouster space forces skirmished in a hundred border areas, but except for the odd Marine encounters in airless, weightless places, there were no infantry confrontations. Stories in the Worldweb proliferated: the Ousters would never be a threat to Earthlike worlds because of their three centuries of adaptation to weightlessness; the Ousters had evolved into something more – or less – than human; the Ousters did not have farcaster technology, would never have it, and thus never would be a threat to FORCE. Then came Bressia.

Bressia was one of those smug, independent worlds, pleased with both its convenient access to the Web and its eight-month separation from it, growing rich from the export of diamonds, burr root, and its unequaled coffee, coyly refusing to become a colony world but still dependent upon the Hegemony Protectorate and Common Market to meet its soaring economic goals. As with most such worlds, Bressia was proud of its Self-defense Force: twelve torchships, a refitted attack carrier which had been decommissioned by FORCE:space half a century earlier, twoscore or more of small, fast orbital patrol vessels, a standing army of ninety thousand volunteers, a respectable oceangoing navy, and a store of nuclear weapons stockpiled purely for symbolic purposes.

The Ouster Hawking wake had been noticed by Hegemony monitoring stations but was misinterpreted as merely another swarm migration which would pass no closer than half a light-year to the Bressian system. Instead, with a single course correction which was not detected until the swarm was within the Oört cloud radius, the Ousters fell on Bressia like some Old Testament plague. A minimum of seven standard months separated Bressia from any Hegemony rescue or response.

Bressia's space force was obliterated within the first twenty hours of fighting. The Ouster swarm then put more than three thousand ships into Bressia's cislunar space and began the systematic reduction of all planetary defenses.

The world had been settled by no-nonsense Central Europeans in the first wave of the Hegira, and its two continents bore the prosaic names of North Bressia and

South Bressia. North Bressia held desert, high tundra, and six major cities housing mostly burr-root harvesters and petroleum engineers. South Bressia, much more temperate in climate and geography, was the home for most of the world's four hundred million people and the huge coffee plantations.

As if to demonstrate what war had once been about, the Ousters scoured North Bressia – first with several hundred fallout-free nuclear weapons and tactical plasma bombs, then with deathbeams, and finally with tailored viruses. Only a handful of the fourteen million residents escaped. South Bressia received no bombardment except for the lancing of specific military targets, airports, and the large harbor at Solno.

FORCE doctrine held that, while a world could be reduced from orbit, actual military invasion of an industrialized planet was an impossibility; the problems with landing logistics, the immense area to be occupied, and the unwieldy size of the invading army were considered to be the ultimate arguments against invasion.

The Ousters obviously had not read the FORCE doctrine books. On the twenty-third day of the investiture, more than two thousand dropships and assault boats fell on South Bressia. What was left of the Bressian air force was destroyed in those first hours of the invasion. Two nuclear devices were actually detonated against Ouster staging areas: the first was deflected by energy fields and the second destroyed a single scoutship which may have been a decoy.

Ousters, it turned out, *had* changed physically in three centuries. They *did* prefer zero-gravity environments. But their mobile infantry's powered exoskeletons served very well and it was only a matter of days before the black-clad, long-limbed Ouster troops were swarming over South Bressia's cities like an infestation of giant spiders.

The last organized resistance collapsed on the nineteenth day of the invasion. Buckminster, the capital, fell the same day. The last fatline message from Bressia to the Hegemony was cut off in mid-transmission an hour after Ouster troops entered the city.

Colonel Fedmahn Kassad arrived with FORCE Fleet
One twenty-nine standard weeks later. Thirty omega-
class torchships protecting a single, farcaster-equipped
JumpShip penetrated the system at high speed. The singularity sphere was activated three hours after spin-
down and ten hours after that there were four hundred
FORCE ships of the line in system. The counterinvasion
began twenty-one hours later.

Those were the mathematics of the first minutes of the
Battle of Bressia. For Kassad, the memory of those days
and weeks held not mathematics but the terrible beauty
of combat. It was the first time JumpShips had been used
on anything above a division level and there was the
expected confusion. Kassad went through from five
light-minutes out and fell into gravel and yellow dust
because the assault boat farcaster portal was facing
down a steep incline made slick with mud and the blood
of the first squads through. Kassad lay in the mud and
looked down the hillside at madness. Ten of the seventeen farcaster assault boats were down and burning,
scattered across the foothills and plantation fields like
broken toys. The containment fields of the surviving
boats were shrinking under an onslaught of missile and
CPB fire that turned the landing areas into domes of
orange flame. Kassad's tactical display was a hopeless
mess; his visor showed a garble of impossible fire vectors, blinking red phosphors where FORCE troops lay
dying, and overlays of Ouster jamming ghosts. Someone
was screaming 'Oh, goddammit! Goddammit! Oh,
goddammit!' on his primary command circuit and the
implants registered a void where Command Group's
data should be.

An enlisted man helped him up, Kassad flicked mud
off his command wand and got out of the way of the next
squad farcasting through, and the war was on.

From his first minutes on South Bressia, Kassad
realized that the New Bushido was dead. Eighty thousand superbly armed and trained FORCE:ground troops
advanced from their staging areas, seeking battle in an
unpopulated place. Ouster forces retreated behind a line

of scorched earth, leaving only booby traps and dead civilians. FORCE used farcasters to outmaneuver the enemy, to force him to fight. The Ousters responded with a barrage of nuclear and plasma weapons, pinning the ground troops under forcefields while the Ouster infantry retreated to prepared defenses around cities and dropship staging areas.

There were no quick victories in space to shift the balance on South Bressia. Despite feints and occasional fierce battles, the Ousters retained complete control of everything within three AU of Bressia. FORCE:space units fell back and concentrated on keeping the fleet within farcaster range and protecting the primary JumpShip.

What had been forecast as a two-day battle ground on for thirty days, then sixty. Warfare had been thrown back to the twentieth or twenty-first century: long, grim campaigns fought through the brick dust of ruined cities over the corpses of civilians. The eighty thousand original FORCE troops were ground up, reinforced with a hundred thousand more, and were still being decimated when the call went out for two hundred thousand more. Only the grim resolve of Meina Gladstone and a dozen other determined senators kept the war alive and the troops dying while the billions of voices of the All Thing and the AI Advisory Council called for disengagement.

Kassad had understood the change of tactics almost at once. His street-fighting instincts had risen to the forefront even before most of his division was wiped out in the Battle of the Stoneheap. While other FORCE commanders were all but ceasing to function, frozen into indecision by this violation of the New Bushido, Kassad – in command of his regiment and in temporary command of his division after the nuking of Command Group Delta – was trading men for time and calling for the release of fusion weapons to spearhead his own counterattack. By the time the Ousters withdrew ninety-seven days after the FORCE 'rescue' of Bressia, Kassad had earned the double-edged nickname of the Butcher of South Bressia. It was rumored that even his own troops were afraid of him.

And Kassad dreamed of *her* with dreams that were more – and less – than dreams.

On the last night of the Battle for Stoneheap, in the maze of dark tunnels where Kassad and his hunter-killer groups used sonics and T-5 gas to flush out the last warrens of Ouster commandos, the Colonel fell asleep amid the flame and screams and felt the touch of her long fingers on his cheek and the soft compression of her breasts against him.

When they entered New Vienna on the morning after the space strike Kassad had called in, the troops following the glass-smooth, twenty-meter-wide burn grooves into the lanced city, Kassad had stared without blinking at the rows of human heads lying on the pavement, carefully lined up as if to welcome the rescuing FORCE troops with their accusatory stares. Kassad had returned to his command EMV, closed the hatches, and – curling up in the warm darkness smelling of rubber, heated plastics, charged ions – had heard *her* whispers over the babble of the C3 channels and implant coding.

On the night before the Ouster retreat, Kassad left the command conference on the *HS Brazil*, farcast to his HQ in the Indelibles north of the Hyne Valley, and took his command car to the summit to watch the final bombardment. The nearest of the tactical nuclear strikes was forty-five kilometers away. The plasma bombs blossomed like orange and blood-red flowers planted in a perfect grid. Kassad counted more than two hundred dancing columns of green light as the hellwhip lances ripped the broad plateau to shreds. And even before he slept, while he sat on the flare skirt of the EMV and shook pale afterimages from his eyes, she came. She wore a pale blue dress and walked lightly between the dead burr-root plants on the hillside. The breeze lifted the hem of the soft fabric of her dress. Her face and arms were pale, almost translucent. She called his name – he could almost hear the words – and then the second wave of bombardment rolled in across the plain below him and everything was lost in noise and flame.

As tends to be the case in a universe apparently ruled by irony, Fedmahn Kassad passed unscathed through ninety-seven days of the worst fighting the Hegemony had ever seen, only to be wounded two days after the last of the Ousters had retreated to their fleeing swarmships. He was in the Civic Center Building in Buckminster, one of only three buildings left standing in the city, giving curt answers to stupid questions from a Worldweb newsteep when a plasma booby trap no larger than a microswitch exploded fifteen floors above, blew the newsteep and two of Kassad's aides through a ventilator grille into the street beyond, and dropped the building on him.

Kassad was medevacked to division HQ and then far-cast to the JumpShip now in orbit around Bressia's second moon. There he was resuscitated and put on full life support while the military brass and Hegemony politicians decided what to do with him.

Because of the farcaster connection and the real-time media coverage of Bressia, Colonel Fedmahn Kassad had become somewhat of a *cause célèbre*. Those billions who had been appalled by the unprecedented savagery of the South Bressia campaign would have been pleased to see Kassad court-martialed or tried for war crimes. CEO Gladstone and many others considered Kassad and the other FORCE commanders as saviors.

In the end, Kassad was put on a hospital spinship for the slow trip back to the Web. Since most of the physical repair would be done in fugue anyway, it made some sense to let the old hospital ships work on the seriously wounded and the revivable dead. By the time Kassad and the other patients reached the Worldweb, they would be ready for active duty. More importantly, Kassad would have accrued a time-debt of at least eighteen standard months and whatever controversy surrounded him might well be over by that time.

Kassad awoke to see the dark shape of a woman bending over him. For a second he was sure that it was *her*, and then he realized that it was a FORCE medic.

'Am I dead?' he whispered.

'You were. You're on the *HS Merrick*. You've been through resuscitation and renewal several times but you probably don't remember because of the fugue hang-over. We're ready to start the next step in physical therapy. Do you feel like trying to walk?'

Kassad lifted his arm to cover his eyes. Even through the disorientation of fugue state, he now remembered the painful therapy sessions, the long hours in the RNA virus baths, and the surgery. Most of all the surgery. 'What's our route?' he asked, still shielding his eyes. 'I forget how we're getting back to the Web.'

The medic smiled as if this were a question he asked each time he came out of fugue. Perhaps it was. 'We'll be putting in at Hyperion and Garden,' she said. 'We're just entering the orbit of . . .'

The woman was interrupted by the sound of the end of the world – great brass trumpets blowing, metal ripping, furies screaming. Kassad rolled off the bed, wrapping the mattress around him as he fell in the one-sixth g. Hurricane winds slid him across the deck and hurled pitchers, trays, bedclothes, books, bodies, metal instruments, and countless other objects at him. Men and women were screaming, their voices rising through falsetto as the air rushed out of the ward. Kassad felt the mattress slam into the wall; he looked out between clenched fists.

A meter from him, a football-sized spider with wildly waving legs was trying to force itself into a crack which had suddenly appeared in the bulkhead. The thing's jointless legs seemed to be swatting at the paper and other detritus whirling around it. The spider rotated and Kassad realized that it was the head of the medic; she had been decapitated in the initial explosion. Her long hair writhed at Kassad's face. Then the crack widened to the width of a fist and the head disappeared through it.

Kassad pulled himself up just as the boom arm quit spinning and 'up' ceased to be. The only forces now in play were the hurricane winds still flinging everything in the ward toward the cracks and gaps in the bulkhead and the sickening lurch and tumble of the ship. Kassad swam against it all, pulling himself toward the door to the boom-arm corridor, using every handhold he could find, kicking free the last five meters. A metal tray struck him above the eye; a corpse with hemorrhaged eyes almost tumbled him back into the ward. The airtight emergency doors were slamming uselessly into a dead Marine whose spacesuited body blocked the seal from closing. Kassad rolled through into the boom-arm shaft and pulled the corpse after him. The door sealed behind him, but there was no more air in the shaft than there had been in the ward. Somewhere a klaxon's scream thinned to inaudibility.

Kassad also screamed, trying to relieve the pressure so that his lungs and eardrums would not burst. The boom arm was still draining air; he and the corpse were being sucked the hundred and thirty meters to the main body of the ship. He and the dead Marine tumbled along the boom-arm shaft in a grisly waltz.

It took Kassad twenty seconds to slap open the emergency releases on the Marine's suit, another minute to eject the man's corpse and to get his own body in. He was at least ten centimeters taller than the dead man, and although the suit was built to allow some expansion, it still pinched painfully at his neck and wrists and knees. The helmet squeezed his forehead like a cushioned vise. Gobbets of blood and a moist white material clung to the inside of the visor. The piece of shrapnel which had killed the Marine had left entrance and exit holes, but the suit had done its best to seal itself. Most of the chest lights were red and the suit did not respond when Kassad ordered it to give a status report, but the rebreather worked, although with a worrying rasp.

Kassad tried the suit radio. Nothing, not even background static. He found the comlog lead, jacked into a hull termex. Nothing. The ship pitched again then, metal reverberating to a succession of blows, and Kassad was thrown against the wall of the boom-arm shaft. One of the transport cages tumbled by, its severed cables whipping like the tentacles of an agitated sea anemone. There were corpses in the cage and more bodies tangled along the segments of spiral staircase still intact along the shaft wall. Kassad kicked the remaining distance to the end of the shaft and found all of the airtight doors there sealed, the boom-arm shaft itself irised shut, but there were holes in the primary bulkhead large enough to drive a commercial EMV through.

The ship lurched again and began to tumble more wildly, imparting complex new Coriolis forces to Kassad and everything else in the shaft. Kassad hung on torn metal and pulled himself through a rent in the triple hull of the *HS Merrick*.

He almost laughed when he saw the interior. Whoever had lanced the old hospital ship had done it right, chopping and stabbing the hull with CPBs until pressure seals failed, self-seal units ruptured, damage-control remotes overloaded, and the interior bulkheads collapsed. Then the enemy ship had put missiles into the guts of the hulk with warheads of what the FORCE:space people quaintly called canister shot. The effect had been quite similar to setting off an antipersonnel grenade in a crowded rat maze.

Lights shone through a thousand holes, here and there becoming colorful rays where they found a colloidal base in floating haze of dust or blood or lubricant. From where Kassad hung, twisting with the lurch and tumble of the ship, he could see a score or more of bodies, naked and torn, each moving with the deceptive underwater-ballet grace of the zero-gravity dead. Most of the corpses floated within their own small solar systems of blood and tissue. Several of them watched Kassad with the cartoon-character stares of their pressure-expanded eyes and seemed to beckon him closer with random, languid movements of arms and hands.

Kassad kicked through the wreckage to reach the main dropshaft to the command core. He had seen no weapons – it seemed that no one except the Marine had managed to suit up – but he knew that there would be a weapons locker in the command core or in the Marine quarters aft.

Kassad stopped at the last torn pressure seal and stared. He did laugh this time. Beyond this point there was no main dropshaft, no aft section. There was no ship. This section – a boom-arm and medical ward mod, a ragged chunk of the hull – had been ripped free of the ship as easily as Beowulf had torn the arm from Grendel's body. The final, unsealed doorway to the dropshaft led to open space. Some kilometers away,

Kassad could see a dozen other ravaged fragments of the *HS Merrick* tumbling in the glare of sunlight. A green and lapis planet loomed so close that Kassad felt a surge of acrophobia and clung more tightly to the doorframe. Even as he watched, a star moved above the limb of the planet, laser weapons winked their ruby morse, and a gutted ship section half a kilometer away across the gulf of vacuum from Kassad burst again in a gout of vaporized metal, freezing volatiles, and tumbling black specks which Kassad realized were bodies.

Kassad pulled himself deeper into the concealing tangle of wreckage and considered his situation. The Marine's suit could not last more than another hour – already Kassad could smell the rotten-eggs stench of the malfunctioning rebreather – and he had seen no airtight compartment or container during his struggle through the wreckage. And even if he found a closet or air-lock to shelter in, what then? Kassad did not know if the planet below was Hyperion or Garden, but he was sure that there was no FORCE presence on either world. He was also quite sure that no local defense forces would challenge an Ouster warship. It would be days before any patrol craft investigated the wreckage. It was quite possible, Kassad knew, that the orbit of the tumbling piece of junk he now inhabited would decay before they sent anyone up to check on it, sending thousands of tons of twisted metal burning through the atmosphere. The locals would not like that, Kassad knew, but from their point of view it might be preferable to let a bit of sky fall than to antagonize the Ousters. If the planet had primitive orbital defenses or ground-based CPBs, he realized with a grim smile, it would make more sense for them to blast the wreckage than to fire on the Ouster ship.

It would make no difference to Kassad. Unless he did something quickly, he would be dead long before the remnants of the ship entered atmosphere or the locals took action.

The Marine's amplification shield had been cracked by the shrapnel which had killed him, but now Kassad tugged what was left of the viewplate down over the visor. Telltales winked red but there was still enough suit power to show the amplified view glowing pale green through the spiderweb of cracks. Kassad watched as the Ouster torchship stood off a hundred klicks, its defense fields blurring background stars, and launched several objects. For an instant Kassad was sure that these were the *coup de grâce* missiles and he found himself grinning joylessly at the certainty of having only a few seconds to live. Then he noticed their low velocity and notched the amplification higher. The power lights blinked red and the amplifier failed, but not before Kassad had seen the tapering ovoid shapes, spotted with thrusters and cockpit blisters, each trailing a tangle of six jointless manipulator arms. 'Squids,' the FORCE:space people had called the Ouster boarding craft.

Kassad pulled himself farther back in the wreckage. He had only a few minutes before one or more of the squids reached his piece of the ship. How many Ousters would one of those things carry? Ten? Twenty? Kassad was sure that it would be no fewer than ten. And they would be well armed and rigged with infrared and motion sensors. The elite Ouster equivalent of Hegemony Space Marines, the commandos would not only have been trained for free-fall combat but had been born and bred to zero-g. Their long limbs, prehensile toes, and prosthetic tails would be added advantages for this environment, although Kassad doubted that they needed any more advantages than they already had.

He began to pull himself carefully back through the labyrinth of twisted metal, fighting the adrenaline fear-surge that made him want to kick off screaming through the darkness. *What did they want?* Prisoners. That would solve his immediate survival problem. All he had to do to survive was surrender. The difficulty with that solution was that Kassad had seen the FORCE:intelligence holos of the Ouster ship they had captured off Bressia. There had been more than two hundred prisoners in the storage bay of that ship. And the Ousters obviously had many questions for these Hegemony citizens. Perhaps they had found it inconvenient to feed and imprison so many – or perhaps it was their basic interrogation policy – but the fact was that the Bressian civilians and captured FORCE troops had been found flayed open and pinned down on steel trays like frogs in a biology lab, their organs bathed with nutrient fluids, arms and legs efficiently amputated, eyes removed, and their minds readied for interrogators' questions with crude cortical comtaps and shunt-plugs jacked directly through three-centimeter holes in the skulls.

Kassad pulled himself along, floating through debris and the tangled entrails of the ship's wiring. He felt no inclination whatsoever to surrender. The tumbling hulk vibrated and then steadied some as at least one of the squids attached itself to the hull or bulkhead. *Think*, Kassad commanded. He needed a weapon more than a hiding place. Had he seen anything during his crawl through the wreckage that would help him survive?

Kassad stopped moving and hung from an exposed section of fiberoptic cable while he thought. The medical ward where he had awakened, beds, fugue tanks, intensive care apparatus . . . most of it expelled through the breaches in the spinmod's hull. Boom-arm shaft, elevator cage, corpses on the stairs. No weapons. Most of the bodies had been stripped by the canister shot explosions or sudden decompression. The elevator cables? No, too long, impossible to sever without tools. Tools? He had seen none. The medical offices flayed open along the corridors beyond the main dropshaft. Medical imaging rooms, MRI tanks, and CPD bays flung open like looted sarcophagi. At least one operating room intact, its interior a maze of scattered instruments and floating cables. The solarium, scraped clean when the windows exploded outward. Patient lounges. Medics' lounges. The scrub rooms, corridors, and unidentifiable cubicles. The corpses.

Kassad hung there a second longer, oriented himself in the tumbling maze of light and shadow, and then kicked off.

He had hoped for ten minutes; he was given less than eight. He knew that the Ousters would be methodical and efficient but had underestimated how efficient they could be in zero-g. He gambled his life that there would

158

be at least two of them on each sweep – basic Space Marine procedure, much as FORCE:ground jump rats had learned to go door to door in city fighting, one to burst into each room, the other to provide cover fire. If there were more than two, if the Ousters worked in squads of four, Kassad almost certainly would be dead.

He was floating in the middle of Operating Room 3 when the Ouster came through the door. Kassad's rebreather had all but failed, he was floating immobile, gasping foul air, as the Ouster commando swung in, swung aside, and brought his two weapons to bear on the unarmed figure in a battered Marine spacesuit.

Kassad had bargained that the gruesome condition of his suit and visor would gain him a second or two. Behind his gore-smeared faceplate, Kassad's eyes stared sightlessly upward as the Ouster's chestlight swept across him. The commando carried two weapons – a sonic stunner in one hand and a smaller but much more lethal tightbeam pistol in the long toes of his left 'foot.' He raised the sonic. Kassad had time to notice the killing spike on the prosthetic tail and then he triggered the mouse in his gauntleted right hand.

It had taken Kassad most of his eight minutes to tie in the emergency generator to the operating-room circuits. Not all of the surgery lasers had survived, but six still worked. Kassad had positioned four of the smaller ones to cover the area just to the left of the doorway, the two bone-cutters to target the space to the right. The Ouster had moved to the right.

The Ouster's suit exploded. The lasers continued to slice away in their preprogrammed circles as Kassad propelled himself forward, ducking under the blue beams now swirling in a spreading mist of useless suit sealant and boiling blood. He wrested the sonic away just as the second Ouster swung into the room, agile as an Old Earth chimp.

Kassad pressed the sonic against the man's helmet and fired. The suited figure went limp. The prosthetic tail spasmed a few times from random nerve impulses. Triggering the sonic that close was no way to take a prisoner; a burst from that distance turned a human brain into something resembling oatmeal mush. Kassad did not want to take a prisoner.

He kicked free, grabbed a girder, swept the active sonic across the open doorway. No one else came through. A check twenty seconds later showed an empty corridor.

Kassad ignored the first body and stripped the man with the intact suit. The commando was naked under the spacesuit and it turned out not to be a man; the female commando had short-cropped blond hair, small breasts, and a tattoo just above her line of pubic hair. She was very pale and droplets of blood floated from her nose, ears, and eyes. Kassad made a note that the Ousters used women in their Marines. All of the Ouster bodies on Bressia had been male.

He kept his helmet and rebreather pack on as he kicked the body aside and tugged on the unfamiliar suit. Vacuum exploded blood vessels in his flesh. Deep cold nipped at him as he struggled with strange clasps and locks. Tall as he was, he was too short for the woman's suit. He could operate the hand gauntlets by stretching, but the foot gloves and tail connections were hopeless. He let them hang useless as he bailed out of his own helmet and wrestled the Ouster bubble into place.

Lights in the collar diskey glowed amber and violet. Kassad heard the rush of air through aching eardrums and almost gagged as a thick, rich stench assailed him. He assumed it was the sweet smell of home to an Ouster. Earphone patches in the bubble whispered coded commands in a language which sounded like an audio tape of Ancient English played backward at high speed. Kassad was gambling again, this time on the fact that Ouster ground units on Bressia had functioned as semi-independent teams united by voice radio and basic telemetry rather than a FORCE:ground type of tactical implant web. If they used the same system here, then the commando leader might know that two of his (or her) troops were missing, possibly even have medcom readings on them, but might *not* know exactly where they were.

Kassad decided that it was time to quit hypothesizing

and to get moving. He programmed the mouse to have the surgical lasers fire on anything entering the operating room, and then bounce-stumbled his way down the corridor. Moving in one of these damn suits, he thought, was like trying to walk in a gravity field while standing on your own trousers. He had brought along both energy pistols and – finding no belt, lockrings, hooks, Velcro pads, magclamps, or pockets to secure them with – now floated along like some drunken holodrama pirate, a weapon in each hand, bouncing from wall to wall. Reluctantly, he left one pistol floating behind him while he tried to hook himself along one-handed. The gauntlet fit like a size fifteen mitten on a size two hand. The damned tail wobbled, banged against his helmet bubble, and was a literal pain in the ass.

Twice he squeezed into crevices when he saw lights in the distance. He was just about to the deck opening where he had watched the squid approach when he rounded a corner and almost floated into three Ouster commandos.

The fact that he was wearing an Ouster suit gave him at least a two-second advantage. He shot the first suited figure in the helmet at point-blank range. The second man – or woman – fired a wild sonic burst past Kassad's left shoulder a second before he put three bolts into the Ouster's chestplate. The third commando flipped backward, found three handholds, and was out of sight around a broken bulkhead before Kassad could retarget. His headset rang with curses, commands, and questions. Kassad gave silent chase.

The third Ouster would have escaped if he had not rediscovered honor and turned to fight. Kassad felt an inexplicable sense of déjà vu as he put an energy bolt through the man's left eye from five meters away.

The corpse tumbled backward into sunlight. Kassad pulled himself to the opening and stared at the squid moored not twenty meters away. It was, he thought, the first undiluted piece of luck he had had in some time.

He kicked across the gap, knowing that if someone wanted to shoot him from the squid or the wreckage there was nothing he could do about it. He felt the scrotum-lifting tension he always experienced when he was an obvious target. No shots were fired. Commands and interrogatives squawked in his ears. He could not understand them, did not know where they originated, and, on the whole, thought it best if he stayed out of the dialogue.

The clumsiness of the suit almost caused him to miss the squid. He thought briefly that such an anticlimax would be the universe's fitting verdict on his martial pretensions: the brave warrior floating off into near-planet orbit, no maneuvering systems, no propellant, no reaction mass of any sort – even the pistol was non-recoil. He would end his life as useless and harmless as a child's runaway balloon.

Kassad stretched until his joints popped, caught a whip antenna, and pulled himself hand over hand to the squid's hull.

Where the hell was the airlock? The hull was relatively smooth for a spacefaring vessel but was decorated with a riot of designs, decals, and panels announcing what he assumed were the Ouster equivalents of NO STEP and DANGER: THRUSTER PORT. No entrances were visible. He guessed that there were Ousters on board, a pilot at least, and that they were probably wondering why their returning commando was crawling around the hull like a spavined crab rather than cycling the airlock. Or perhaps they knew why and were waiting inside with drawn pistols. At any rate, it was obvious that no one was going to open the door for him.

The hell with it, thought Kassad and shot out one of the observation blisters.

The Ousters kept a tidy ship. Not much more than the equivalent of a few lost paper clips and coins geysered out with the ship's air. Kassad waited until the eruption had died down and squeezed through the gap.

He was in the carrier section: a cushioned hold looking a lot like the jump rat bay of any dropship or APC. Kassad made a mental note that a squid probably held about twenty Ouster commandos in full vacuum combat gear. Now it was empty. An open hatch led to the cockpit.

Only the command pilot had remained on board and he was in the final process of unbelting when Kassad shot him. Kassad pushed the body into the carrier section and strapped himself into what he hoped was the command chair.

Warm sunlight came through the blister above him. Video monitors and console holos showed scenes from dead ahead, astern, and shoulder-camera glimpses of the search operation inside. Kassad caught a glimpse of the nude body in Operating Room 3 and several figures in a firefight with surgical lasers.

In the holodramas of Fedmahn Kassad's childhood, heroes always seemed to know how to operate skimmers, spacecraft, exotic EMVs, and other strange machinery whenever the need arose. Kassad had been trained to handle military transports, simple tanks and APCs, even an assault boat or dropship if he was desperate. If stranded on a runaway FORCE spacecraft, a remote possibility, he could find his way around the command core sufficiently to communicate with the primary computer or put out a distress call on a radio or fatline transmitter. Sitting in the command chair of an Ouster squid, Kassad did not have a clue.

That was not quite true. He immediately recognized the remote grip slots for the squid's tentacle manipulators, and given two or three hours of thought and inspection, he might have figured out several other controls. He did not have the time. The forward screen showed three spacesuited figures jumping for the squid, firing as they came. The pale, oddly alien head of an Ouster commander suddenly materialized on the holo console. Kassad heard shouts from his bubble earpatches.

Globules of sweat hung in front of his eyes and streaked the inside of his helmet. He shook them away as best he could, squinted at the control consoles, and pushed several likely-looking surfaces. If there were voice command circuits, override controls, or a suspicious ship's computer, Kassad knew, he was screwed. He had thought of all this in the second or two before he shot the pilot but had not been able to think of a way to coerce

163

or trust the man. No, this had to be the way, thought Kassad even as he tapped more control surfaces.

A thruster began firing.

The squid pulled and tugged at its moorings. Kassad bounced back and forth in his webbing. 'Shit,' he whispered, his first audible comment since he had asked the FORCE medic where the ship was putting in. He strained far enough forward to get his gauntleted fingers into the grip slots. Four of the six manipulators released. One ripped off. The final one tore away a chunk of bulkhead from the *HS Merrick*.

The squid tumbled free. Video cameras showed two of the space-suited figures missing their jumps, the third clutching at the same whip antenna which had saved Kassad. Knowing roughly where the thruster controls were now, Kassad tapped in a frenzy. An overhead light came on. All of the holo projectors went dead. The squid commenced a maneuver which incorporated all of the most violent elements of pitch, roll, and yaw. Kassad saw the spacesuited form tumble past the overhead blister, appear briefly on the forward video screen, become a speck on the aft screen. The Ouster was still firing energy bolts as he – or she – became too small to see.

Kassad struggled to stay conscious as the violent tumbling continued. Various voice and visual alarms were screaming for his attention. Kassad tapped at thruster controls, considered it a success, and pulled his hands away when he felt as if he were being pulled apart in only two directions rather than five.

A random camera shot showed him that the torchship was receding. Good. Kassad had no doubt that the Ouster warship could destroy him at any second, and that it *would* if he approached or threatened it in any way. He did not know if the squid was armed, personally doubted if it would carry anything larger than antipersonnel weapons, but he knew beyond a doubt that no torchship commander would allow an out-of-control shuttlecraft to come anywhere near his ship. Kassad assumed that the Ousters all knew by now that the squid had been hijacked by the enemy. He would not be surprised – disappointed, but not surprised – if the

torchship vaporized him at any second, but in the meantime he was counting on two emotions that were quint-
essentially human if not necessarily Ouster human:
curiosity and the desire for revenge.

Curiosity, he knew, could easily be overridden in times
of stress, but he counted on a paramilitary, semifeudal
culture like the Ousters' to be deeply involved with
revenge. Everything else being equal, with no chance to
hurt them further and almost no chance to escape, it
would seem that Colonel Fedmahn Kassad had become a
prime candidate for one of their dissection trays. He
hoped so.

Kassad looked at the forward video display, frowned,
and loosened his harness long enough to look out the
overhead blister. The ship was tumbling but not nearly
so violently as before. The planet seemed closer – one
hemisphere filled the view 'above' him – but he had no
idea how close the squid was to atmosphere. He could
read none of the data displays. He could only guess what
their orbital velocity had been and how violent a reentry
shock would be. His one long glimpse from the wreckage
of the *Merrick* had suggested to Kassad that they were
very close, perhaps only five or six hundred klicks above
the *surface*, and in the kind of parking orbit which he
knew preceded the launching of dropships.

Kassad tried to wipe his face and frowned when the
tips of loose gauntlet fingers tapped at his visor. He was
tired. Hell, only a few hours earlier he had been in fugue
and just a few ship-weeks before *that* he had almost
certainly been body-dead.

He wondered if the world below was Hyperion or Garden; he had been to neither but knew that Garden was
more widely settled, closer to becoming a Hegemony
colony. He hoped it was Garden.

The torchship launched three assault boats. Kassad
saw them clearly before the aft camera panned beyond
range. He tapped at the thruster controls until it felt
as though the ship was tumbling more quickly toward
the wall of planet above. There was little else he
could do.

* * *

The squid reached atmosphere before the three Ouster assault boats reached the squid. The boats undoubtedly were armed and well within range, but someone on the command circuit must have been curious. Or furious.

Kassad's squid was in no way aerodynamic. As with most ship-to-ship craft, the squid could flirt with planetary atmospheres but was doomed if it dove too deeply into the gravity well. Kassad saw the telltale red glow of reentry, heard the ion buildup on the active radio channels, and suddenly wondered if this had been such a good idea.

Atmospheric drag stabilized the squid and Kassad felt the first tentative tug of gravity as he searched the console and the command chair arms for the control circuit he prayed would be there. A static-filled video screen showed one of the dropships growing a blue-plasma tail as it decelerated. The illusion created was similar to that encountered when one skydiver watched another open his chute or activate his suspension rig; the assault boat seemed to climb suddenly.

Kassad had other things to worry about. There seemed to be no obvious bail-out control, no ejection apparatus. Every FORCE:space shuttle carried some sort of atmospheric egress device – it was a custom dating back almost eight centuries to when the entire realm of space flight consisted only of tentative excursions just above the skin of Old Earth's atmosphere. A ship-to-ship shuttle probably would never need a planetary bail-out device, but age-old fears written into ancient regulations tended to die hard.

Or so the theory went. Kassad could find nothing. The ship was quaking now, spinning, and beginning to heat up in earnest. Kassad slapped open his harness release and pulled himself toward the rear of the squid, not even sure what he was looking for. Suspension packs? Parachutes? A set of wings?

There was nothing in the troop carrier section except the corpse of the Ouster pilot and a few storage compartments not much larger than lunchboxes. Kassad tore through them, finding nothing bigger than a medkit. No miracle devices.

Kassad could *hear* the squid shaking and beginning to break up as he hung on a pivot ring and all but accepted the fact that the Ousters had not wasted money or space on such low-probability rescue devices for their squids. Why should they? Their lifetimes were spent in the darknesses between star systems; their concept of an atmosphere was the eight-klick pressurized tube of a can city. The external audio sensors on Kassad's bubble helmet began to pick up the raging hiss of air on the hull and through the broken blister in the aft section. Kassad shrugged. He had gambled too many times and lost.

The squid shuddered and bounced. Kassad could hear the manipulator tentacles tearing away from the bow. The Ouster's corpse suddenly was sucked up and out of the broken blister like an ant into a vacuum cleaner. Kassad clung to the pivot ring and stared through the open hatch at the control seats in the cockpit. It struck him that they were wonderfully archaic, like something out of a textbook of the earliest spacecraft. Parts of the ship's exterior were burning away now, roaring past the observation blisters like gobbets of lava. Kassad closed his eyes and tried to remember lectures from Olympus Command School on the structure and layout of ancient spacegoing craft. The squid began a terminal tumble. The noise was incredible.

'By Allah!' gasped Kassad, a cry he had not uttered since childhood. He began pulling himself forward into the cockpit, bracing himself on the open hatch, finding handholds on the deck as if he were climbing a vertical wall. He *was* climbing a wall. The squid had spun, stabilized in a stern-first death dive. Kassad climbed under a 3-g load, knowing that a single slip would break every bone in his body. Behind him, atmospheric hiss turned to a scream and then to a dragon roar. The troop carrier section was burning through in fierce, molten explosions.

Climbing into the command seat was like negotiating a rock overhang with the weight of two other climbers swinging from his back. The clumsy gauntlets made his grip on the headrest even less sure as Kassad hung over the vertical drop to the flaming cauldron of the carrier section. The ship lurched, Kassad swung his legs up, and he was in the command seat. The display videos were dead. Flame heated the overhead blister to a sick red. Kassad almost lost consciousness as he bent forward, his fingers feeling in the darkness below the command seat, between his knees. There was nothing. Wait . . . a handgrip. No, sweet Christ and Allah . . . a D-ring. Something out of the history books.

The squid began to break up. Overhead, the blister burned through and spattered liquid Perspex throughout the interior of the cockpit, splashing Kassad's suit and visor. He smelled plastic melting. The squid was spinning as it broke up. Kassad's sight turned pink, dimmed, was gone. He used numb fingers to tighten the harness . . . tighter . . . either it was cutting into his chest or the Perspex had burned through. His hand went back to the D-ring. Fingers too clumsy to close around it . . . no. *Pull*.

Too late. The squid flew apart in a final screech and explosion of flame, the control console tearing through the cockpit in ten thousand shrapnel-sized bits.

Kassad was slammed into his seat. Up. Out. Into the heart of the flame.

Tumbling.

Kassad was dimly aware that the seat was projecting its own containment field as it tumbled. Flame was centimeters from his face.

Pyrobolts fired, kicking the ejection seat out of the squid's blazing slipstream. The command seat made its own track of blue flame across the sky. Microprocessors spun the seat so that the disc of the forcefield was between Kassad and the furnace of friction. A giant sat on Kassad's chest as he decelerated across two thousand kilometers of sky at eight gravities.

Kassad forced his eyelids open once, noted that he lay curled in the belly of a long column of blue-white flame, and then he closed his eyes again. He saw no sign of a control for a parachute, suspension pack, or any other braking device. It didn't matter. He could not move his arms or hands in any case.

The giant shifted, grew heavier.

Kassad realized that part of his helmet bubble had melted or been blown away. The noise was indescribable. It didn't matter.

He closed his eyes more tightly. It was a good time to take a nap.

Kassad opened his eyes and saw the dark shape of a woman bending over him. For a second he thought it was *her*. He looked again and realized that it *was* her. She touched his cheek with cool fingers.

'Am I dead?' whispered Kassad, raising his own hand to grip her wrist.

'No.' Her voice was soft and throaty, burred with the hint of an accent he could not place. He had never heard her speak before.

'You're real?'

'Yes.'

Kassad sighed and looked around. He lay naked under a thin robe on some sort of couch or platform set in the middle of a dark, cavernous room. Overhead, starlight was visible through a broken roof. Kassad raised his other hand to touch her shoulder. Her hair was a dark nimbus above him. She wore a loose, thin gown which – even in the starlight – allowed him to see the outlines of her body. He caught her scent, the fragrant hint of soap and skin and *her* that he knew so well from their other times together.

'You must have questions,' she whispered as Kassad released the gold clasp which held her gown in place. The gown whispered to the floor. She wore nothing underneath. Above them, the band of the Milky Way was clearly visible.

'No,' said Kassad and pulled her to him.

Toward morning a breeze arose, and Kassad pulled the light cover over them. The thin material seemed to preserve all of their body heat and they lay together in perfect warmth. Somewhere sand or snow rasped at bare walls. The stars were very clear and very bright.

They awoke at the first hint of dawn, their faces close

169

together under the silken coverlet. She ran her hand down Kassad's side, finding old and recent scars.

'Your name?' whispered Kassad.

'Hush,' she whispered back, her hand sliding lower.

Kassad moved his face into the scented curve of her neck. Her breasts were soft against him. Night paled to morning. Somewhere sand or snow blew against bare walls.

They made love, slept, made love again. In full light they rose and dressed. She had laid out underwear, gray tunic and trousers for Kassad. They fit perfectly, as did the spongesocks and soft boots. The woman wore a similar outfit of navy blue.

'Your name?' Kassad asked as they left the building with the shattered dome and walked through a dead city.

'Moneta,' said his dream, 'or Mnemosyne, whichever name pleases you more.'

'Moneta,' whispered Kassad. He looked up at a small sun rising into a lapis sky. 'This is Hyperion?'

'Yes.'

'How did I land? Suspensor field? Parachute?'

'You descended under a wing of gold foil.'

'I don't hurt. There were no wounds?'

'They were tended to.'

'What is this place?'

'The City of Poets. Abandoned more than a hundred years ago. Beyond that hill lie the Time Tombs.'

'The Ouster assault boats that were following me?'

'One landed nearby. The Pain Lord took the crew unto himself. The other two set down some distance away.'

'Who is the Pain Lord?'

'Come,' said Moneta. The dead city ended in desert. Fine sand slid across white marble half buried in dunes. To the west an Ouster dropship sat with its portals irised open. Nearby, on a fallen column, a thermcube yielded hot coffee and fresh-baked rolls. They ate and drank in silence.

Kassad worked to recall the legends of Hyperion. 'The Pain Lord is the Shrike,' he said at last.

'Of course.'

'You're from here . . . from the City of Poets?'

Moneta smiled and slowly shook her head.

Kassad finished his coffee and set the cup down. The feeling that he was in a dream persisted, much stronger than during any sim he had ever participated in. But the coffee had tasted pleasantly bitter; the sun was warm on his face and hands.

'Come, Kassad,' said Moneta.

They crossed expanses of cold sand. Kassad found himself glancing skyward, knowing that the Ouster torchship could lance them from orbit . . . then knowing with a sudden certainty that it would not.

The Time Tombs lay in a valley. A low obelisk glowed softly. A stone sphinx seemed to absorb the light. A complex structure of twisted pylons threw shadows onto itself. Other tombs were silhouettes against the rising sun. Each of the tombs had a door and each door was open. Kassad knew that they had been open when the first explorers discovered the Tombs and that the structures were empty. More than three centuries of searching for hidden rooms, tombs, vaults, and passageways had been fruitless.

'This is as far as you can go,' Moneta said as they neared the cliff at the head of the valley. 'The time tides are strong today.'

Kassad's tactical implant was silent. He had no comlog. He searched his memory. 'There are anti-entropic forcefields around the Time Tombs,' he said.

'Yes.'

'The tombs are ancient. The anti-entropic fields keep them from aging.'

'No,' said Moneta. 'The time tides drive the Tombs backward through time.'

'Backward through time,' Kassad repeated stupidly.

'Look.'

Shimmering, miragelike, a tree of steel thorns appeared out of the haze and a sudden dust storm of ochre sand. The thing seemed to fill the valley, rising at least two hundred meters to the height of the cliffs. Branches shifted, dissolved, and reformed like elements of a poorly tuned hologram. Sunlight danced on five-meter-long thorns. Corpses of Ouster men and women, all naked, were impaled on at least a score of these thorns. Other branches held other bodies. Not all were human.

The dust storm obscured the view for a moment and when the winds subsided the vision was gone. 'Come,' said Moneta.

Kassad followed her through the fringes of the time tides, avoiding the ebb and flow of the anti-entropic field the way children would play tag with an ocean surf on a broad beach. Kassad felt the pull of the time tides like waves of *déjà vu* tugging at every cell of his body.

Just beyond the entrance to the valley, where hills opened to the dunes and low moors led to the City of Poets, Moneta touched a wall of blue slate and an entrance opened to a long, low room set into the cliff face.

'Is this where you live?' asked Kassad but saw immediately that there were no signs of habitation. The stone walls of the room were inset with shelves and crowded niches.

'We must ready ourselves,' whispered Moneta and the lighting shifted to a golden hue. A long rack lowered its wares. A wafer-thin strip of reflective polymer curtained from the ceiling to serve as a mirror.

Kassad watched with the calm passivity of a dreamer as Moneta stripped off her clothes and then his. Their nudity was no longer erotic, merely ceremonial.

'You have been in my dreams for years,' he told her.

'Yes. Your past. My future. The shock wave of events moves across time like ripples on a pond.'

Kassad blinked as she raised a gold ferule and touched his chest. He felt a slight shock and his flesh became a mirror, his head and face a featureless ovoid reflecting all the color tones and textures of the room. A second later Moneta joined him, her body becoming a cascade of reflections, water over quicksilver over chrome. Kassad saw his own reflecting reflection in every curve and muscle of her body. Moneta's breasts caught and bent the light; her nipples rose like small splashes on a mirrored pond. Kassad moved to embrace her and felt their surfaces flow together like magnetized fluid. Under the connected fields, his flesh touched hers.

'Your enemies await beyond the city,' she whispered. The chrome of her face flowed with light.

'Enemies?'

'The Ousters. The ones who followed you here.'

Kassad shook his head, saw the reflection do likewise. 'They're not important anymore.'

'Oh, yes,' whispered Moneta, 'the enemy is always important. You must arm yourself.'

'With what?' But even as he spoke, Kassad realized that she was touching him with a bronze sphere, a dull blue toroid. His altered body spoke to him now as clearly as troops reporting in on an implant command circuit. Kassad felt the bloodlust build in him with turgid strength.

'Come.' Moneta led the way into open desert again. The sunlight seemed polarized and heavy. Kassad felt that they were gliding across the dunes, flowing like liquid through the white marble streets of the dead city. Near the west end of town, near the shattered remnants of a structure still bearing the inscribed lintel of Poets' Amphitheatre, something stood waiting.

For a second Kassad thought it was another person wearing the chromium forcefields he and Moneta were draped in – but only for a second. There was nothing human about this particular quicksilver-over-chrome construct. Kassad dreamily noted the four arms, retractable fingerblades, the profusion of thornspikes on throat, forehead, wrists, knees, and body, but not once did his gaze leave the two thousand-faceted eyes which burned with a red flame that paled sunlight and dimmed the day to blood shadows.

The Shrike, thought Kassad.

'The Lord of Pain,' whispered Moneta.

The thing turned and led them out of the dead city.

Kassad approved of the way the Ousters had prepared their defenses. The two assault boats were grounded less than half a kilometer apart, their guns, projectors, and missile turrets covering each other and a full three hundred and sixty degrees of fire. Ouster ground troops had been busy digging revetments a hundred meters out from the boats and Kassad could see at least two EM tanks hull down, their projection arrays and launch tubes commanding the wide, empty moor between the Poets' City and the boats. Kassad's vision had been altered; he could see the overlapping ship containment fields as ribbons of yellow haze, the motion sensors and antipersonnel mines as eggs of pulsing red light.

He blinked, realizing that something was wrong with the image. Then it came to him: besides the thickness of the light and his enhanced perception of energy fields, nothing was moving. The Ouster troops, even those set in attitudes of motion, were as stiff as the toy soldiers he had played with as a boy in the Tharsis slums. The EM tanks were dug into their hull-down positions, but Kassad noticed that now even their acquisition radars – visible to him as concentric purple arcs – were motionless. He glanced skyward and saw some sort of large bird hanging in the sky, as unmoving as an insect frozen in amber. He passed a cloud of windblown dust hanging suspended, extended one chrome hand, and flicked spirals of particles to the ground.

Ahead of them, the Shrike strode casually through the red maze of sensor-mines, stepped over the blue lines of tripbeams, ducked under the violet pulses of the autofire scanners, passed through the yellow containment field and the green wall of the sonic defense perimeter, and walked into the assault boat's shadow. Moneta and Kassad followed.

— *How is this possible?* Kassad realized that he had posed the question through a medium that was something less than telepathy but something far more sophisticated than implant conduction.

— *He controls time.*

— *The Pain Lord?*

— *Of course.*

— *Why are we here?*

Moneta gestured toward the motionless Ousters.

— *They are your enemies.*

Kassad felt that he was finally awaking from a long

174

dream. This was *real*. The Ouster trooper's eyes, unblinking behind his helmet, were *real*. The Ouster assault boat, rising like a bronze tombstone to his left, was *real*.

Fedmahn Kassad realized that he could kill them all – commandos, assault boat crew, *all* of them – and they could do nothing about it. He knew that time had not stopped – any more than it stopped while a ship was under Hawking drive – it was merely a matter of varying rates. The bird frozen above them would complete the flap of its wings given enough minutes or hours. The Ouster in front of him would close his eyes in a blink if Kassad had the patience to watch long enough. Meanwhile, Kassad and Moneta and the Shrike could kill all of them without the Ousters realizing that they were under attack.

It was not fair, Kassad realized. It was wrong. It was the ultimate violation of the New Bushido, worse in its way than the wanton murder of civilians. The essence of honor lay in the moment of combat between equals. He was about to communicate this to Moneta when she said/thought —*Watch*.

Time began again with an explosion of sound not unlike the rush of air into an airlock. The bird soared and circled overhead. A desert breeze threw dust against the static-charged containment field. An Ouster commando rose from one knee, saw the Shrike and the two human shapes, screamed something over his tactical comm channel, and raised his energy weapon.

The Shrike did not seem to move – to Kassad it merely ceased being *here* and appeared *there*. The Ouster commando emitted a second, shorter scream, and then looked down in disbelief as the Shrike's arm withdrew with the man's heart in its bladed fist. The Ouster stared, opened his mouth as if to speak, and collapsed.

Kassad turned to his right and found himself face to face with an armored Ouster. The commando ponderously lifted a weapon. Kassad swung his arm, felt the chrome forcefield hum, and saw the flat of his hand cut through body armor, helmet, and neck. The Ouster's head rolled in the dust.

Kassad leaped into a low trench and saw several troopers begin to turn. Time was still out of joint; the enemy moved in extreme slow motion one second, jerked like a damaged holo to four-fifths speed in the next instant. They were never as quick as Kassad. Gone were his thoughts of the New Bushido. These were the barbarians who had tried to *kill* him. He broke one man's back, stepped aside, jabbed rigid, chrome fingers through the body armor of a second man, crushed the larynx of a third, dodged a knife blade moving in slow motion and kicked the spine out of the knife wielder. He leaped up out of the ditch.

—Kassad!

Kassad ducked as the laser beam crept past his shoulder, burning its way through the air like a slow fuse of ruby light. Kassad smelled ozone as it crackled past. *Impossible. I've dodged a laser!* He picked up a stone and flung it at the Ouster manning the tank-mounted hellwhip. A sonic boom cracked; the gunner exploded backward. Kassad pulled a plasma grenade from a corpse's bandolier, leaped to the tank hatch, was thirty meters away before the explosion geysered flame as high as the assault boat's bow.

Kassad paused in the eye of the storm to see Moneta in the center of her own circle of carnage. Blood splashed her but did not adhere, flowing like oil on water across the rainbow curves of chin, shoulder, breast, and belly. She looked at him across the battlefield and Kassad felt a renewed surge of bloodlust in himself.

Behind her, the Shrike moved slowly through the chaos, choosing victims as if he were harvesting. Kassad watched the creature wink in and out of existence and realized that to the Pain Lord he and Moneta would appear to be moving as slowly as the Ousters did to Kassad.

Time jumped, moved to four-fifths speed. The surviving troops were panicking now, firing into one another, deserting their posts, and fighting to get aboard the assault boat. Kassad tried to realize what the past minute or two had been like for them: blurs moving through their defensive positions, comrades dying in great gouts of blood. Kassad watched Moneta moving through their ranks, killing at her leisure. To his amazement, he discovered that he had some control of time: *blink* and his opponents slowed to one-third speed, *blink* and events moved at nearly their normal pace. Kassad's sense of honor and sanity called out for him to stop the slaughter but his almost sexual bloodlust overpowered any objections.

Someone in the assault boat had sealed the airlock and now a terrified commando used a shaped plasma charge to blow the portal open. The mob pressed in, trampling the wounded in their flight from unseen killers. Kassad followed them in.

The phrase 'fight like a cornered rat' is an extremely apt description. Throughout the history of military encounters, human combatants have been known to fight at their fiercest when challenged in enclosed places where flight is not an option. Whether in the passageways of La Haye Sainte and Hougoumont at Waterloo or in the Hive tunnels of Lusus, some of the most terrible hand-to-hand battles in history have been fought in cramped spaces where no retreat is possible. It was true this day. The Ousters fought . . . and died . . . like cornered rats.

The Shrike had disabled the assault boat. Moneta remained outside to kill the threescore commandos who had stayed at their posts. Kassad killed those within.

In the end, the final assault boat fired on its doomed counterpart. Kassad was outside by then and he watched the particle beams and high-intensity lasers creep toward him, followed an eternity later by missiles which seemed to move so slowly that he could have written his name on them in flight. By that time all of the Ousters were dead in and around the overrun boat, but its containment field held. Energy dispersion and impact explosions tossed corpses around on the outer perimeter, set fire to equipment, and glazed the sand to glass, but Kassad and Moneta watched from inside a dome of orange flame as the remaining assault boat retreated to space.

—*Can we stop them?* Kassad was panting, pouring sweat, and literally quivering from excitement.

—We could, replied Moneta, *but we do not want to. They will carry the message to the swarm.*

—What message?

'Come here, Kassad.'

He turned at the sound of her voice. The reflective forcefield was gone. Moneta's flesh was oiled with sweat; her dark hair was matted against her temples; her nipples were hard. 'Come here.'

Kassad glanced down at himself. His own forcefield was gone – he had *willed* it away – and he was more sexually excited than he could ever remember being.

'Come here.' Moneta whispered this time.

Kassad went to her, lifted her, felt the sweat-slick smoothness of her buttocks as he carried her to an empty stretch of grass atop a wind-carved hummock. He lowered her to the ground between piles of Ouster bodies, roughly opened her legs, took both her hands in the grasp of one of his, lifted her arms above her head, pinned them to the ground, and lowered his long body between her legs.

'Yes,' whispered Moneta as he kissed the lobe of her left ear, set his lips to the pulse at the hollow of her neck, licked the salt tang of sweat from her breasts. *Lying among the dead. More dead to come. The thousands. The millions. Laughter out of dead bellies. The long lines of troops emerging from JumpShips to enter the waiting flames.*

'Yes.' Her breath was hot in his ear. She freed her hands, slid them along Kassad's damp shoulders, trailed long nails down his back, grasped his buttocks to pull him closer. Kassad's erection scraped her pubic hair, throbbed against the cusp of her belly. *Farcaster portals opening to admit the cold lengths of attack carriers. The warmth of plasma explosions. Hundreds of ships, thousands, dancing and dying like dust motes in a whirlwind. Great columns of solid ruby light lancing across great distances, bathing targets in the ultimate surge of warmth, bodies boiling in red light.*

'Yes.' Moneta opened her mouth and body to him. Warmth above and below, her tongue in his mouth as he entered her, welcomed by warm friction. His body strained deep, pulled back slightly, allowed the moist warmth to engulf him further as they began to move together. *Heat on a hundred worlds. Continents burning in bright spasms, the roll of boiling seas. The air itself aflame. Oceans of superheated air swelling like warm skin rising to a lover's touch.*

'Yes . . . yes . . . yes.' Moneta breathes warmth against his lips. Her skin is oil and velvet. Kassad thrusts quickly now, the universe contracting as sensation expands, senses dwindling as she closes warm and wet and tight around him. Her hips thrust harshly in response now, as if sensing the terrible build in pressure at the base of his being. Demanding. Kassad grimaces, closes his eyes, sees . . .

. . . *fireballs expanding, stars dying, suns exploding in great pulses of flame, star systems perishing in an ecstasy of destruction* . . .

. . . he feels pain in his chest, his hips not stopping, moving faster, even as he opens his eyes and sees . . .

. . . the great thorn of steel rising from between Moneta's breasts, almost impaling him as he unconsciously pulls up and back, the thornblade drawing blood which drips on her flesh, her pale flesh, reflective now, flesh as cold as dead metal, his hips still moving even as he watches through passion-dimmed eyes as Moneta's lips wither and curl back, revealing rows of steel blades where teeth had been, metal blades slash at his buttocks where fingers had gripped, legs like powerful steel bands imprison his pumping hips, her eyes . . .

. . . in the last seconds before orgasm Kassad tries to pull away . . . his hands on her throat, pressing . . . she clings like a leech, a lamprey ready to drain him . . . they roll against dead bodies . . .

. . . her eyes like red jewels, blazing with a mad heat like that which fills his aching testicles, expanding like a flame, spilling over . . .

. . . Kassad slams both hands against the soil, lifts himself away from her . . . from it . . . his strength insane but not enough as terrible gravities press them together . . . sucking like a lamprey's mouth as he threatens to explode, looks in her eyes . . . the death of worlds . . . *the death of worlds!*

179

Kassad screams and pulls away. Strips of his flesh rip away as he lunges up and sideways. Metal teeth click shut in a steel vagina, missing his glans by a moist millimeter. Kassad slumps on his side, rolls away, hips moving, unable to stop his ejaculation. Semen explodes in streams, falls on the curled fist of a corpse. Kassad moans, rolls again, curls in a fetal position even as he comes again. And again.

He hears the hiss and rustle as she rises behind him. Kassad rolls on his back and squints up against sunlight and his own pain. She stands above him, legs apart, a silhouette of thorns. Kassad wipes sweat from his eyes, sees his wrist come away red with blood, and waits for the killing blow. His skin contracts in anticipation of the slash of blade into flesh. Panting, Kassad looks up to see Moneta above him, thighs flesh rather than steel, her groin matted from the moisture of their passion. Her face is dark, the sun behind her, but he sees red flames dying in the multifaceted pits of her eyes. She smiles and he sees sunlight glint on rows of metal teeth. 'Kassad . . .' she whispers and it is the sound of sand scraping against bone.

Kassad tears his gaze away, struggles to his feet, and stumbles across corpses and burning rubble in his terror to be free. He does not look back.

Scouting elements of Hyperion's Self-defense Force found Colonel Fedmahn Kassad almost two days later. He was discovered lying unconscious on one of the grassy moors which lead to the abandoned Chronos Keep, some twenty kilometers from the dead city and the wreckage of the Ouster ejection pod. Kassad was naked and almost dead from the effects of exposure and several serious wounds, but he responded well to emergency field treatment and was immediately airlifted south of the Bridle Range to a hospital at Keats. Reconnaissance squads from the SDF battalion moved northward carefully, cautious of the anti-entropic tides around the Time Tombs and wary of any booby traps left behind by the Ousters. There were none. The scouts found only the wreckage of Kassad's escape mechanism and the burned-out hulks of the two assault boats which the Ousters had lanced from orbit. There were no clues as to why they had slagged their own ships and the Ouster bodies – both in and around the boats – had been burned beyond any hope of autopsy or analysis.

Kassad regained consciousness three Hyperion days later, swore that he remembered nothing after stealing the squid, and was shipped out on a FORCE torchship two local weeks later.

Upon returning to the Web, Kassad resigned his commission. For a while he was active in antiwar movements, occasionally appearing on the All Thing net arguing disarmament. But the attack on Bressia had mobilized the Hegemony toward true interstellar war as had nothing else in three centuries, and Kassad's voice was either drowned out or dismissed as the guilty conscience of the Butcher of South Bressia.

In the sixteen years after Bressia, Colonel Kassad had disappeared from the Web and from the Web consciousness. Although there had been no more major battles, the Ousters remained the Hegemony's prime bogeymen. Fedmahn Kassad was only a fading memory.

It was late morning when Kassad finished his story. The Consul blinked and looked around him, noticing the ship and its surroundings for the first time in more than two hours. The *Benares* had come out into the main channel of the Hoolie. The Consul could hear the creaks of the chains and hawsers as the river mantas surged against their harnesses. The *Benares* appeared to be the only ship heading upriver, but now numerous small craft were visible going the other way. The Consul rubbed his forehead and was surprised to see his hand come away slick with sweat. The day had grown very warm and the shadow of the tarp had crept away from the Consul without his noticing. He blinked, wiped sweat from his eyes, and moved into the shade to get a drink from one of the liquor bottles the androids had set in a cabinet near the table.

'My God,' Father Hoyt was saying, 'so, according to this Moneta creature, the Time Tombs are moving *backward* in time?'

'Yes,' said Kassad.

'Is that possible?' asked Hoyt.

'Yes.' It was Sol Weintraub who answered.

'If that's true,' said Brawne Lamia, 'then you "met" this Moneta . . . or whatever her real name is . . . in her past but your future . . . in a meeting that's still to come.'

'Yes,' said Kassad.

Martin Silenus walked to the railing and spat into the river. 'Colonel, do you think the bitch *was* the Shrike?'

'I don't know.' Kassad's monotone was barely audible.

Silenus turned to Sol Weintraub. 'You're a scholar. Is there anything in the Shrike mythography that says the thing can change shape?'

'No,' said Weintraub. He was preparing a milk globe to feed his daughter. The infant made soft, mewling noises and moved tiny fingers.

'Colonel,' said Het Masteen, 'the forcefield . . . whatever the fighting suit was . . . did you bring it with you after the encounter with the Ousters and this . . . female?'

Kassad looked at the Templar a moment and then shook his head.

The Consul was staring into his drink but his head suddenly snapped upright with the force of a thought. 'Colonel, you said that you saw a vision of the Shrike's killing tree . . . the structure, the *thing* where it impales its victims.'

Kassad moved his basilisk stare from the Templar to the Consul. He slowly nodded.

'And there were bodies on it?'

Another nod.

The Consul wiped sweat from his upper lip. 'If the tree is traveling backward in time with the Time Tombs, then the victims are from *our* future.'

Kassad said nothing. The others also were staring at the Consul now but only Weintraub appeared to understand what the comment meant . . . and what the Consul's next question had to be.

The Consul resisted the urge to wipe the sweat from his

lips again. His voice was steady. 'Did you see any of us there?'

Kassad said nothing for more than a minute. The soft sounds of the river and the ship's rigging suddenly seemed very loud. Finally Kassad took a breath. 'Yes.'

Silence stretched again. Brawne Lamia broke it. 'Will you *tell* us who?'

'No.' Kassad rose and went to the stairway leading to the lower decks.

'Wait,' called Father Hoyt.

Kassad paused at the head of the stairway.

'Will you at least tell us two other things?'

'What?'

Father Hoyt grimaced from a wave of pain. His gaunt face went white under its film of perspiration. He took a breath and said, 'First, do you think the Shrike . . . the woman . . . somehow wants to use *you* to start this terrible interstellar war you foresaw?'

'Yes,' Kassad said softly.

'Second, will you tell us what you plan to petition the Shrike for . . . or this Moneta . . . when you meet them on the pilgrimage?'

Kassad smiled for the first time. It was a thin smile, and very, very cold. 'I will make no petition,' said Kassad. 'I will ask nothing of them. When I meet them this time, I will kill them.'

The other pilgrims did not speak or look at one another as Kassad went below. The *Benares* continued north-northeast into afternoon.

THREE

The barge *Benares* entered the river port of Naiad an hour before sunset. Crew and pilgrims pressed to the rail to stare at smoldering embers of what once had been a city of twenty thousand people. Little remained. The famous River Front Inn, built in the days of Sad King Billy, had burned to the foundations; its charred docks, piers, and screened balconies now collapsed into the shallows of the Hoolie. The customhouse was a burned-out shell. The airship terminal on the north end of town survived only as a blackened hulk, its mooring tower reduced to a spire of charcoal. There was no sign whatsoever of the small riverfront Shrike temple. Worst of all, from the pilgrims' point of view, was the destruction of the Naiad River Station – the harness dock lay burned and sagging, the manta holding pens open to the river.

'God *damn* it!' said Martin Silenus.

'Who did it?' asked Father Hoyt. 'The Shrike?'

'More likely the SDF,' said the Consul. 'Although they may have been fighting the Shrike.'

'I can't believe this,' snapped Brawne Lamia. She turned to A. Bettik, who had just joined them on the rear deck. 'Didn't you know this had happened?'

'No,' said the android. 'There has been no contact with any point north of the locks for more than a week.'

'Why the hell not?' asked Lamia. 'Even if this godforsaken world doesn't have a datasphere, don't you have radio?'

A. Bettik smiled slightly. 'Yes, M. Lamia, there is radio, but the comsats are down, the microwave repeater stations at the Karla Locks were destroyed, and we have no access to shortwave.'

'What about the mantas?' asked Kassad. 'Can we press on to Edge with the ones we have?'

Bettik frowned. 'We will have to, Colonel,' he said. 'But it is a crime. The two in harness will not recover from such a pull. With fresh mantas we would have put into Edge before dawn. With these two . . .' The android shrugged. 'With luck, if the beasts survive, we will arrive by early afternoon . . .'

'The windwagon will still be there, will it not?' asked Het Masteen.

'We must assume so,' said A. Bettik. 'If you will excuse me, I will see to feeding the poor beasts we have. We should be under way again within the hour.'

They saw no one in or near the ruins of Naiad. No river craft made their appearance above the city. An hour's pull northeast of the town they entered the region where the forests and farms of the lower Hoolie gave way to the undulating orange prairie south of the Sea of Grass. Occasionally the Consul would see the mud towers of architect ants, some of their serrated structures near the river reaching almost ten meters in height. There was no sign of intact human habitation. The ferry at Betty's Ford was totally gone, with not even a towrope or warming shack left to show where it had stood for almost two centuries. The River Runners Inn at Cave Point was dark and silent. A. Bettik and other crew members hallooed, but there was no response from the black cave mouth.

Sunset brought a sensuous stillness over the river, soon broken by a chorus of insect noises and night-bird calls. For a while the surface of the Hoolie became a mirror of the gray-green disk of twilight sky, disturbed only by the leap of dusk-feeding fish and the wake of the laboring mantas. As true darkness fell, innumerable prairie gossamers – much paler than their forest cousins, but also of greater wingspan, luminescent shades the size of small children – danced in the vales and valleys of the gently rolling hills. By the time the constellations emerged and the meteor trails began scarring the night sky, a brilliant display this far from all man-made light, the lanterns had been lit and dinner set out on the aft deck.

The Shrike pilgrims were subdued, as if still contemplating Colonel Kassad's grim and confusing tale. The Consul had been drinking steadily since before midday and now he felt the pleasant displacement – from reality, from the pain of memory – which allowed him to get through each day and night. Now he asked, his voice as careful and unslurred as only a true alcoholic's can be, whose turn it was to tell a tale.

'Mine,' said Martin Silenus. The poet also had been drinking steadily since early in the day. His voice was as carefully controlled as the Consul's but redness on his sharp cheeks and an almost manic brightness of eye gave the old poet away. 'At least I drew number three . . .' He held up his slip of paper. 'If you still want to hear the fucking thing.'

Brawne Lamia lifted her glass of wine, scowled, and set it down. 'Perhaps we should talk about what we have learned from the first two stories and how it might relate to our current . . . situation.'

'Not yet,' said Colonel Kassad. 'We don't have enough information.'

'Let M. Silenus speak,' said Sol Weintruab. 'Then we can begin discussing what we have heard.'

'I agree,' said Lenar Hoyt.

Het Masteen and the Consul nodded.

'Agreed!' cried Martin Silenus. 'I'll tell my story. Just let me finish my fucking glass of wine.'

THE POET'S TALE:
'Hyperion Cantos'

In the beginning was the Word. Then came the fucking word processor. Then came the thought processor. Then came the death of literature. And so it goes.

Francis Bacon once said, 'There arises from a bad and unapt formation of words a wonderful obstruction to the mind.' We have all contributed our wonderful obstructions to the mind, have we not? I more than most. One of the twentieth century's better, forgotten writers – that is better-comma-forgotten, once *bon* *mot*ed: 'I love being a writer. It's the paperwork I can't stand.' Get it? Well, amigos and amigette, I love being a poet. It's the goddamned words I can't stand.

Where to start?

Start with Hyperion perhaps?

(Fade in) Almost two standard centuries ago.

Sad King Billy's five seedships spin like gold dandelions above this all too familiar lapis sky. We land like conquistadors strutting to and fro; more than two thousand visual artists and writers and sculptors and poets and ARNists and vid makers and holie directors and composers and decomposers and God knows what all, supported by five times that many administrators and technicians and ecologists and supervisors and court chamberlains and professional ass kissers, not to mention the family of royal asses themselves, supported in turn by ten times *that* many androids willing to till the soil and stoke the reactors and raise the cities and lift that bale and tote that load . . . hell, you get the idea.

We landed on a world already seeded by the poor buggers who'd gone indigenie two centuries before and were living hand to mouth and cudgel to brain wherever they could. Naturally the noble descendants of these brave pioneers greeted us like gods – especially after a few of our security folk slagged a few of their more aggressive leaders – and naturally we accepted their worship as our due and put them to work next to our blueskins, plowing the south forty and working to build our shining city on the hill.

And it *was* a shining city on a hill. Seeing the ruins today can tell you nothing of the place. The desert had advanced in three centuries; the aqueducts from the mountains have fallen and shattered; the city itself is only bones. But in its day the City of Poets was fair indeed, a bit of Socrates's Athens with the intellectual excitement of Renaissance Venice, the artistic fervor of Paris in the days of the Impressionists, the true democracy of the first decade of Orbit City, and the unlimited future of Tau Ceti Center.

But, in the end, it was none of these things, of course. It was only Hrothgar's claustrophobic mead hall with the monster waiting in the darkness without. We had our Grendel, to be sure. We even had our Hrothgar if one squints a bit at Sad King Billy's poor slouched profile. We lacked only our Geats; our great, broad-shouldered, small-brained Beowulf with his band of merry psychopaths. So, lacking a Hero, we settled into the role of victims and composed our sonnets and rehearsed our ballets and unrolled our scrolls, while all the while our thorn-and-steel Grendel served the night with fear and harvested thighbones and gristle.

And this was when I – a satyr then, formed in flesh as mirror to my soul – came as close to completing my *Cantos*, my life's work, as I have come in five sad centuries of stubborn continuance.

(Fade to black)

It occurs to me that the Grendel tale is premature. The players have not been brought upon the stage. Dislinear plotting and non-contiguous prose have their adherents, not the least of which am I, but in the end, my friends, it is character which wins or loses immortality upon the vellum. Haven't you ever harbored the secret thought that somewhere Huck and Jim are – at this instant – poling their raft down some river just beyond our reach, so much more real are they than the shoe clerk who fitted us just a forgotten day ago? At any rate, if this fucking story's to be told, you should know who's in it. So – as much as it pains me – I'll back up to begin at the beginning.

In the beginning was the Word. And the Word was programmed in classic binary. And the Word said, 'Let there be life!' And so, somewhere in the TechnoCore vaults of my mother's estate, frozen sperm from my long-dead daddy was defrosted, set in suspension, shaken like the vanilla malts of yore, loaded into something part squirt gun and part dildo, and – at the magic touch of a trigger – ejaculated into Mother at a time when the moon was full and the egg was ripe.

Mother didn't have to be impregnated in this barbaric fashion, of course. She could have chosen *ex utero* fertilization, a male lover with a transplant of Daddy's

189

DNA, a clonal surrogate, a gene-spliced virgin birth, you name it . . . but, as she told me later, she opened her legs to tradition. My guess is that she preferred it that way.

Anyway, I was born.

I was born on Earth . . . *Old Earth* . . . and fuck you, Lamia, if you don't believe it. We lived on Mother's estate on an island not far from the North American Preserve.

Notes for sketch of home on Old Earth:

Fragile twilights fading from violet to fuchsia to purple above the crepe-paper silhouettes of trees beyond the southwest sweep of lawn. Skies as delicate as translucent china, unscarred by cloud or contrail. The presymphony hush of first light followed by the cymbal crash of sunrise. Oranges and russets igniting to gold, the long, cool descent to green: leaf shadow, shade, tendrils of cypress and weeping willow, the hushed green velvet of the glade.

Mother's estate – our estate – a thousand acres centered in a million more. Lawns the size of small prairies with grass so perfect it beckoned a body to lie on it, to nap on its soft perfection. Noble shade trees making sundials of the Earth, their shadows circling in stately procession; now mingling, now contracting to midday, finally stretching eastward with the dying of the day. Royal oak. Giant elms. Cottonwood and cypress and redwood and bonsai. Banyan trees lowering new trunks like smooth-sided columns in a temple roofed by sky. Willows lining carefully laid canals and haphazard streams, their hanging branches singing ancient dirges to the wind.

Our house rises on a low hill where, in the winter, the browning curves of lawn look like the smooth flank of some female beast, all thigh muscle and meant for speed. The house shows its centuries of accretion: a jade tower on the east courtyard catching the first light of dawn, a series of gables on the south wing throwing triangles of shadow on the crystal conservatory at teatime, the balconies and maze of exterior stairways along the east porticoes playing Escher games with afternoon's shadows.

It was after the Big Mistake but before everything grew uninhabitable. Mostly we occupied the estate during what we quaintly called 'periods of remission' – stretches of ten to eighteen quiet months between planet-wide spasms as the Kiev Team's goddamn little black hole digested bits of the Earth's center and waited for its next feast. During the 'Bad Times,' we vacationed at Uncle Kowa's place out beyond the moon, on a terraformed asteroid brought there before the Ouster migration.

You might already be able to tell that I was born with a silver spoon up my ass. I offer no apologies. After three thousand years of dabbling with democracy, the remaining Old Earth families had come to the realization that the only way to avoid such riffraff was not to allow them to breed. Or, rather, to sponsor seedship fleets; spinship explorations, new farcaster migrations . . . all of the panicked urgency of the Hegira . . . as long as they bred out there and left Old Earth alone. The fact that the homeworld was a diseased old bitch, gone in the teeth, didn't hurt the riffraff's urge to pioneer. No fools they.

And like the Buddha, I was almost grown before I saw my first hint of poverty. I was sixteen standard years old, on my *Wanderjahr*, and backpacking through India when I saw a beggar. The Hindu Old Families kept them around for religious reasons, but all I knew at the time was that here was a man in rags, ribs showing, holding out a wicker basket with an ancient credit diskey in it, begging for a touch of my universal card. My friends thought it was hysterical. I threw up. It was in Benares.

My childhood was privileged but not obnoxiously so. I have pleasant memories of Grande Dame Sybil's famous parties (she was a great-aunt on my mother's side). I remember one three-day affair she threw in the Manhattan Archipelago, guests ferried in by dropship from Orbit City and from the European arcologies. I remember the Empire State Building rising from the water, its many lights reflecting on the lagoons and fern canals; the EMVs unloading passengers on the observation deck while cooking fires burned on the overgrown island mounds of lower buildings all around.

The North American Preserve was our private playground in those days. It was said that about eight thousand people still resided in that mysterious continent, but half of these were rangers. The rest included the renegade ARNists who plied their trade by resurrecting species of plants and animals long absent from their antediluvian North American haunts, the ecology engineers, licensed primitives such as the Ogalalla Sioux or the Hell's Angel Guild, and the occasional tourist. I had a cousin who reportedly backpacked from one observation zone to the other in the Preserve, but he did so in the Midwest where the zones were relatively close together and where the dinosaur herds were much scarcer.

In the first century after the Big Mistake, Gaea was mortally injured but slow in the dying. The devastation was great during the Bad Times – and these came more often in precisely plotted spasms, shorter remissions, more terrible consequences after each attack – but the Earth abided and repaired itself as best it could.

The Preserve was, as I say, our playground but, in a real sense, so was all of the dying Earth. Mother let me have my own EMV when I was seven and there was no place on the globe farther than an hour's flight from home. My best friend, Amalfi Schwartz, lived in the Mount Erebus Estates in what had once been the Antarctic Republic. We saw each other daily. The fact that Old Earth law forbade farcasters did not bother us in the least; lying on some hillside at night looking up through the ten thousand Orbiting Lights and the twenty thousand beacons of the Ring, at the two or three thousand visible stars, we felt no jealousy, no urge to join the Hegira that even then was spinning the farcaster silk of the Worldweb. We were happy.

My memories of Mother are oddly stylized, as if she were another fictional construct from one of my Dying Earth novels. Perhaps she was. Perhaps I was raised by robots in the automated cities of Europe, suckled by androids in the Amazon Desert, or simply grown in a vat like brewer's yeast. What I recall is Mother's white gown sliding ghostlike through the shadowed rooms of the estate; infinitely delicate blue veins on the back of her thin-fingered hand as she poured tea in the damask and dust light of the conservatory; candlelight caught like a gold fly in the spiderweb sheen of her hair, hair done up in a bun in the style of the Grandes Dames. Sometimes I dream that I remember her voice, the lilt and tone and turn-in-the-womb *centerness* of it, but then I awake and it becomes only the wind moving lace curtains or the sound of some alien sea on stone.

From my earliest sense of *self*, I knew that I would be – should be – a poet. It was not as if I had a choice; more like the dying beauty all about breathed its last breath in me and commanded that I be doomed to play with words the rest of my days, as if in expiation for our race's thoughtless slaughter of its crib world. So what the hell; I became a poet.

I had a tutor whose name was Balthazar, human but ancient, a refugee from ancient Alexandria's flesh-scented alleys. Balthazar all but glowed blue-white from those crude, early Poulsen treatments; he was like an irradiated mummy of a man, sealed in liquid plastic. And randy as the proverbial goat. Centuries later, when I was in my satyr period, I felt that I finally understood poor don Balthazar's priapic compulsions, but in those days it was mostly a hindrance to keeping young girls on the estate's staff. Human or android, don Balthazar did not discriminate – he poinked them all.

Luckily for my education, there was nothing homo-sexual in don Balthazar's addiction to young flesh, so his escapades evidenced themselves either as absences from our tutorial sessions or an inordinate amount of attention lavished on memorizing verses from Ovid, Senesh, or Wu.

He was an excellent tutor. We studied the ancients and the late classical period, took field trips to the ruins of Athens, Rome, London, and Hannibal, Missouri, and never once had a quiz or test. Don Balthazar expected me to learn everything by heart at first encounter and I did not disappoint him. He convinced my mother that the pitfalls of 'progressive education' were not for an Old Earth family, so I never knew the mind-stunting shortcuts of RNA medication, datasphere immersion, systemic flashback training, stylized encounter groups, 'higher-level thinking skills' at the expense of facts, or preliterate programming. As a result of these deprivations, I was able to recite all of Fitzgerald's translation of the *Odyssey* by the time I was six, compose a sestina before I could dress myself, and think in spiral fugue-verse before I ever interfaced with an AI.

My scientific education, on the other hand, was something less than stringent. Don Balthazar had little interest in what he referred to as 'the mechanical side of the universe.' I was twenty-two before I realized that computers, RMUs, and Uncle Kowa's asteroidal life-support devices were *machines* and not some benevolent manifestations of the *animas* around us. I believed in fairies, woodsprites, numerology, astrology, and the magic of Midsummer's Eve deep in the primitive forests of the NAP. Like Keats and Lamb in Haydon's studio, don Balthazar and I drank toasts to 'the confusion of mathematics' and mourned the destruction of the poetry of the rainbow by M. Newton's prying prism. The early distrust and actual hatred of all things scientific and clinical served me well in later life. It is not difficult, I have learned, to remain a pre-Copernican pagan in the postscientific Hegemony.

My early poetry was execrable. As with most bad poets, I was unaware of this fact, secure in my arrogance that the very act of creating gave some worth to the worthless abortions I was spawning. My mother remained tolerant even as I left reeking little piles of doggerel lying around the house. She was indulgent of her only child even if he was as blithely incontinent as an unhousebroken llama. Don Balthazar never commented on my work; primarily, I assume, because I never showed him any of it. Don Balthazar thought that the venerable Daton was a fraud, that Salmud Brevy and Robert Frost should have hanged themselves with their own entrails, that Wordsworth was a fool, and that anything less than Shakespeare's sonnets was a profanation of the language. I saw no reason to bother don Balthazar with my verse, rife with budding genius though I knew it to be.

I published several of these little literary turds in the various hardcopy journals then in vogue in the various arcologies of the European Houses, the amateur editors of these crude journals being as indulgent of my mother as she was of me. Occasionally I would press Amalfi or one of my other playmates – less aristocratic than I and thus with access to the datasphere or fatline transmitters – to uplink some of my verses to the Ring or to Mars, and thus to the burgeoning farcaster colonies. They never replied. I assumed they were too busy.

Belief in one's identity as a poet or writer prior to the acid test of publication is as naive and harmless as the youthful belief in one's immortality . . . and the inevitable disillusionment is just as painful.

My mother died with Old Earth. About half the Old Families stayed during that last cataclysm; I was twenty years old then and had made my own romantic plans to die with the homeworld. Mother decided otherwise. What concerned her was not my premature demise – like me, she was far too self-centered to think of someone else at a time like *that* – nor even the fact that the death of my DNA would mark the end of a line of aristocrats which stretched back to the *Mayflower*; no, what bothered Mother was that the family was going to die out *in debt*. Our last hundred years of extravagance, it seems, had been financed through massive loans from the Ring Bank and other discreet extraterrestrial institutions. Now that the continents of Earth were crashing under the impact of contraction, the great forests aflame, the oceans heaving and heating themselves into a lifeless soup, the very air transforming itself into something too hot and thick to break and too thin to plow, *now* the banks wanted their money back. I was collateral.

Or, rather, Mother's plan was. She liquidated all available assets some weeks before that phrase became a literal reality, deposited a quarter of a million marks in long-term accounts in the fleeing Ring Bank, and dispatched me on a trip to the Rifkin Atmospheric Protectorate on Heaven's Gate, a minor world circling the star Vega. Even then, that poisonous world had a farcaster connection to Sol System, but I did not farcast. Nor was I a passenger on the single spinship with Hawking drive which put into Heaven's Gate each standard year. No, Mother sent me to this back end of the outback on a Phase Three ramship, *slower than light*, frozen with the cattle embryos and orange juice concentrate and feeder viruses, on a trip that took *one hundred and twenty-nine* shipboard years, with an objective time-debt of *one hundred and sixty-seven standard years*!

Mother figured that the accrued interest on the long-term accounts would be enough to pay off our family debt and perhaps allow me to survive comfortably for a while. For the first and last time in her life, Mother figured wrong.

Notes for a sketch of Heaven's Gate:

Mud lanes which run back from the station's conversion docks like a pattern of sores on a leper's back. Sufrus-brown clouds which hang in tatters from a rotten burlap sky. A tangle of shapeless wooden structures half decayed before they were ever fully constructed, their paneless windows now staring sightlessly into the gaping mouths of their neighbors. Indigenies breeding like . . . like humans, I suppose . . . eyeless cripples, lungs burned out with air rot, squiring a nest of a dozen offspring, the children's skin scabrous by age five-standard, their eyes watering incessantly from the sting of an atmosphere which will kill them before they're forty, their smiles carious, their oily hair rife with lice and the blood bags of dracula ticks. Proud parents beaming. Twenty million of these doomed schmucks, crowded into slums overflowing an island smaller than my family's west lawn on Old Earth, all of them fighting to breathe the only breathable air on a world where the standard is to inhale and die, crowding ever closer to the center of the sixty-mile radius of survivable atmosphere which the Atmospheric Generating Station had been able to provide *before* it began to malfunction.

Heaven's Gate: my new home.

Mother had not taken into account the possibility that all Old Earth accounts would be frozen – and then appropriated into the growing Worldweb economy. Nor had she remembered that the reason people had waited for the Hawking drive to see the spiral arm of the galaxy is that in long-term cryogenic sleep – as opposed to a few weeks or months of fugue – chances of terminal brain damage were one in six. I was lucky. When I was uncrated on Heaven's Gate and put to work digging out acid canals beyond the perimeter, I had suffered only a cerebral accident – a stroke. Physically, I was able to work in the mud pits within a few local weeks. Mentally, there was much left to be desired.

The left side of my brain had been shut down like a damaged section of a spinship being sealed off, air-tight doors leaving the doomed compartments open to vacuum. I could still think. Control of the right side of my body soon returned. Only the language centers had been damaged beyond simple repair. The marvelous organic computer wedged in my skull had dumped its language content like a flawed program. The right hemisphere was not without *some* language – but only the most emotionally charged units of communication could lodge in that affective hemisphere; my vocabulary was now down to nine words. (This, I learned later, was exceptional, many victims of CVAs retain only two or three.) For the record, here is my entire vocabulary of manageable words: fuck, shit, piss, cunt, goddamn, motherfucker, asshole, peepee, and poopoo.

A quick analysis will show some redundancy here. I had at my disposal eight nouns, which stood for six things; five of the eight nouns could double as verbs. I retained one indisputable noun and a single adjective which also could be used as a verb or expletive. My new language universe was comprised of four monosyllables, three compound words, and two baby-talk repetitions. My arena of literal expression offered four avenues to the topic of elimination, two references to human anatomy, one request for divine imprecation, one standard description of or request for coitus, and a coital variation which was no longer an option for me since my mother was deceased.

All in all, it was enough.

I will not say that I remember my three years in the mud pits and slime slums of Heaven's Gate with *fondness*, but it is true that these years were at least as formative as – and probably more so than – my previous two decades on Old Earth.

I soon found that among my intimate acquaintances – Old Sludge, the scoop-shovel foreman; Unk, the slumyard bully to whom I paid my protection bribes; Kiti, the lice-ridden crib doxy whom I slept with when I could afford it – my vocabulary served me well. 'Shit-fuck,' I would grunt, gesticulating. 'Asshole cunt peepee fuck.'

'Ah,' grinned Old Sludge, showing his one tooth, 'going to the company store to get some algae chewies, huh?'

'Goddamn poopoo,' I would grin back at him.

The life of a poet lies not merely in the finite language-dance of expression but in the nearly infinite combinations of perception and memory combined with the sensitivity to what is perceived and remembered. My three local years on Heaven's Gate, almost fifteen hundred standard days, allowed me to see, to feel, to hear – to remember, as if I literally had been born again. Little matter that I had been born again in hell; reworked experience is the stuff of all true poetry and raw experience was the birthing gift of my new life.

There was no problem adapting to a brave new world a century and a half beyond my own. For all of our talk of expansion and pioneering spirit these past five centuries, we all know how stultified and static our human universe has become. We are in a comfortable Dark Ages of the inventive mind; institutions change but little, and that by gradual evolution rather than revolution; scientific research creeps crablike in a lateral shuffle, where once it leaped in great intuitive bounds; devices change even less, plateau technologies common to us would be instantly identifiable – and operable! – to our great-grandfathers. So while I slept the Hegemony became a formal entity, the Worldweb was spun to something close to its final shape, the All Thing took its democratic place among the list of humanity's benevolent despots, the TechnoCore seceded from human service and then offered its help as an ally rather than a slave, and the Ousters retreated to darkness and the role of Nemesis . . . but all these things had been creeping toward critical mass even before I was frozen into my ice coffin between the pork bellies and sherbet, and such obvious extensions of old trends took little effort to understand. Besides, history viewed from the inside is always a dark, digestive mess, far different from the easily recognizable cow viewed from afar by historians.

My life was Heaven's Gate and the minute-to-minute demands of survival there. The sky was always an eternal yellow-brown sunset hanging like a collapsing ceiling mere meters above my shack. My shack was oddly comfortable: a table for eating, a cot for sleeping and fucking, a hole for pissing and shitting, and a window for silent staring. My environment mirrored my vocabulary.

Prison always has been a good place for writers, killing, as it does, the twin demons of mobility and diversion, and Heaven's Gate was no exception. The Atmospheric Protectorate owned my body but my mind – or what was left of it – was mine.

On Old Earth, my poetry was composed on a Sadu-Dekenar comlog thought processor while I lounged in a padded chaise longue or floated in my EM barge above dark lagoons or walked pensively through scented bowers. The execrable, undisciplined, limp-wristed flatulent products of those reveries already have been described. On Heaven's Gate, I discovered what a mental stimulant physical labor could be; not mere *physical* labor, I should add, but absolutely spine-bending, lung-racking, gut-ripping, ligament-tearing, and ball-breaking physical labor. But as long as the task is both onerous and repetitive, I discovered, the mind is not only *free* to wander to more imaginative climes, it actually *flees* to higher planes.

Thus, on Heaven's Gate, as I dredged bottom scum from the slop canals under the red gaze of Vega Primo or crawled on hands and knees through stalactites and stalagmites of rebreather bacteria in the station's labyrinthine lungpipes, I became a poet.

All I lacked were the words.

The twentieth century's most honored writer, William Gass, once said in an interview; 'Words are the supreme objects. They are *minded* things.'

And so they are. As pure and transcendent as any Idea which ever cast a shadow into Plato's dark cave of our perceptions. But they are also pitfalls of deceit and misperception. Words bend our thinking to infinite paths of self-delusion, and the fact that we spend most of our mental lives in brain mansions built of words means that we lack the objectivity necessary to see the terrible distortion of reality which language brings. Example: the Chinese pictogram for 'integrity' is a two-part symbol of a man literally standing next to his word. So far, so good. But what does the Late English word 'honesty' mean? Or 'Motherland'? Or 'progress'? Or 'democracy'? Or 'beauty'? But even in our self-deception, we become gods.

A philosopher/mathematician named Bertrand Russell, who lived and died in the same century as Gass, once wrote: 'Language serves not only to express thought but to make possible thoughts which could not exist without it.' Here is the essence of mankind's creative genius: not the edifices of civilization nor the bang-flash weapons which can end it, but the *words* which fertilize new concepts like spermatazoa attacking an ovum. It might be argued that the Siamese-twin infants of word/idea are the *only* contribution the human species can, will, or should make to the reveling cosmos. (Yes, our DNA is unique but so is a salamander's. Yes, we construct artifacts but so have species ranging from beavers to the architect ants whose crenellated towers are visible right now off the port bow. Yes, we weave real-fabric things from the dreamstuff of mathematics, but the universe is hardwired with arithmetic. Scratch a circle and π peeps out. Enter a new solar system and Tycho Brahe's formulae lie waiting under the black velvet cloak of space/time. But *where* has the universe hidden a *word* under its outer layer of biology, geometry, or insensate rock?) Even the traces of other intelligent life we have found – the blimps on Jove II, the Labyrinth Builders, the Seneschai empaths on Hebron, the Stick People of Durulis, the architects of the Time Tombs, the Shrike itself – have left us mysteries and obscure artifacts but no *language*. No *words*.

The poet John Keats once wrote to a friend of his named Bailey: 'I am certain of nothing but the holiness of the Heart's affections and the truth of Imagination – What the imagination seizes as Beauty must be truth – whether it existed before or not.'

The Chinese poet George Wu, who died in the Last Sino-Japanese War about three centuries before the Hegira, understood this when he recorded on his comlog: 'Poets are the mad midwives to reality. They see not what is, nor what can be, but what *must become*.' Later, on his last disk to his lover the week before he died, Wu said: 'Words are the only bullets in truth's bandolier. And poets are the snipers.'

You see, in the beginning was the Word. And the Word was made flesh in the weave of the human universe. And only the poet can expand this universe, finding shortcuts to new realities the way the Hawking drive tunnels under the barriers of Einsteinian space/time.

To be a poet, I realized, a *true poet*, was to become the Avatar of humanity incarnate; to accept the mantle of poet is to carry the cross of the Son of Man, to suffer the birth pangs of the Soul-Mother of Humanity.

To be a *true poet* is to become God.

I tried to explain this to my friends on Heaven's Gate. 'Piss, shit,' I said. 'Asshole motherfucker, goddamn shit goddamn. Cunt. Peepee cunt. Goddamn!'

They shook their heads and smiled, and walked away. Great poets are rarely understood in their own day.

The yellow-brown clouds rained acid on me. I waded in mud up to my thighs and cleaned leechweed from the city sewer pipes. Old Sludge died during my second year there when we were all working on a project extending the First Avenue Canal to the Midsump Mudflats. An accident. He was climbing a slime dune to rescue a single sulfur-rose from the advancing grouter when there was a mudquake. Kiti married shortly after that. She still worked part time as a crib doxy, but I saw less and less of her. She died in childbirth shortly after the green tsunami carried away Mudflat City. I continued to write poetry.

How is it, you might ask, that someone can write fine verse with a vocabulary of only nine right-hemisphere words?

The answer is that I used no words at all. Poetry is only secondarily about words. Primarily, it is about *truth*. I dealt with the *Ding an Sich*, the substance behind the shadow, weaving powerful concepts, similes, and connections the way an engineer would raise a skyscraper with the whiskered-alloy skeleton being constructed long before the glass and plastic and chromaluminum appears.

And slowly the words returned. The brain retrains and retools itself amazingly well. What had been lost in the left hemisphere found a home elsewhere or reasserted their primacy in the damaged regions like pioneers returning to a fire-damaged plain made more fertile by the flames. Where before a simple word like 'salt' would leave me stuttering and gasping, my mind probing emptiness like a tongue prodding the socket of a missing tooth, now the words and phrases flowed back slowly, like the names of forgotten playmates. During the day I labored in the slimefields, but at night I sat at my splintered table and wrote my *Cantos* by the light of a hissing ghee lamp. Mark Twain once opined in his homey way: 'The difference between the right word and the almost right word is the difference between lightning and the lightning bug.' He was droll but incomplete. During those long months of beginning my *Cantos* on Heaven's Gate, I discovered that the difference between finding the right word as opposed to accepting the almost right word was the difference between being *struck* by lightning and merely watching a lightning display.

So my *Cantos* began and grew. Written on the flimsy sheets of recycled leechweed fiber which they issued by the ton for use as toilet paper, scribbled by one of the cheap felt-tip pens sold at the Company Store, the *Cantos* took shape. As the words returned, slipping into place like once scattered pieces of a 3-D puzzle, I needed a form. Returning to don Balthazar's teachings, I tried on the measured nobility of Milton's epic verse. Gaining confidence, I added the romantic sensuality of a Byron matured by a Keatsish celebration of the language. Stirring all this, I seasoned the mixture with a dash of Yeats's brilliant cynicism and a pinch of Pound's obscure, scholastic arrogance. I chopped, diced, and added such ingredients as Eliot's control of imagery, Dylan Thomas's feel for place, Delmore Schwartz's sense of doom, Steve Tem's touch of horror, Salmud Brevy's plea for innocence, Daton's love of the convoluted rhyme scheme, Wu's worship of the physical, and Edmond Ki Fererra's radical playfulness.

In the end, of course, I threw this entire mixture out and wrote the *Cantos* in a style all my own.

If it had not been for Unk the slumyard bully, I probably still would be on Heaven's Gate, digging acid canals by day and writing *Cantos* by night.

It was my day off and I was carrying my *Cantos* – the only copy of my manuscript! – to the Company Library in the Common Hall to do some research when Unk and two of his cronies appeared from an alley and demanded immediate payment of the next month's protection money. We had no universal cards in the Heaven's Gate Atmospheric Protectorate; we paid our debts in company scrip or bootleg marks. I had neither. Unk demanded to see what was in my plastic shoulder bag. Without thinking, I refused. It was a mistake. If I'd shown Unk the manuscript, he most probably would have scattered it in the mud and slapped me around after making threats. As it was, my refusal angered him so he and his two Neanderthal companions tore open the bag, scattered the manuscript in the mud, and beat me within the proverbial inch of my life.

It so happened that on this day an EMV belonging to a Protectorate air quality control manager was passing low above and the wife of the manager, traveling alone to the arc's Company Residential Store, ordered the EMV down, had her android servant retrieve me and what was left of my *Cantos*, and then personally drove me to the Company Hospital. Normally, the members of the bonded work force received medical aid, if any, at the walk-in Bio Clinic, but the hospital did not want to refuse the wife of a manager so I was admitted – still unconscious – and watched over by a human doctor and the manager's wife while I recovered in a healing tank.

All right, to make a banal long story into a banal short story, I'll cut to the uplink. Helenda – that was the manager's wife – read my manuscript while I was floating in renewal nutrient. She liked it. On the same day I was being decanted in the Company Hospital, Helenda farcast to Renaissance where she showed my *Cantos* to her sister Felia, who had a friend whose lover knew an editor at Transline Publishing. When I awoke the next day, my broken ribs had been set, my shattered cheekbone had been healed, my bruises were gone, and I'd received five new teeth, a new cornea for my left eye, and a contract with Transline.

My book came out five weeks later. A week after that, Helenda divorced her manager and married me. It was her seventh marriage, my first. We honeymooned on the Concourse and, when we returned a month later, my book had sold more than a billion copies – the first book of verse to hit the bestseller lists in four centuries – and I was a millionaire many times over.

Tyrena Wingreen-Feif was my first editor at Transline. It was her idea to title the book *The Dying Earth* (a records search showed a novel by that name five hundred years earlier, but the copyright had lapsed and the book was out of print). It was her idea to publish just the sections of the *Cantos* which dealt with the nostalgic final days of Old Earth. And it was her idea to remove the sections which she thought would bore the readers – the philosophical passages, the descriptions of my mother, the sections which paid homage to earlier poets, the places where I played with experimental verse, the more personal passages – everything, in fact, except the descriptions of the idyllic final days which, emptied of all heavier freight, came across as sentimental and insipid. Four months after publication *The Dying Earth* had sold two and a half billion hardfax copies, an abridged and digitalized version was available on the See Thing datasphere, and it had been optioned for the holies. Tyrena pointed out that the timing had been perfect . . . that the original trauma shock of the death of Old Earth had meant a century of denial, almost as if Earth had never existed, followed by a period of revived interest culminating in the Old Earth nostalgia cults which could now be found on every world in the Web. A book – even a book of verse – dealing with the final days had struck at precisely the right moment.

For me, the first few months of life as a celebrity in the Hegemony were far more disorienting than my earlier transition from spoiled son of Old Earth to enslaved stroke victim on Heaven's Gate. During those first months I did book and fax signing on more than a hundred worlds; I appeared on 'The AllNet Now!' show with Marmon Hamlit; I met CEO Senister Perót and All Thing Speaker Drury Fein as well as a score of senators; I spoke to the Interplanetary Society of PEN Women and to the Lusus Writers' Union; I was given honorary degrees at the University of New Earth and at Cambridge Two; I was feted, interviewed, imaged, reviewed (favorably), bioed (unauthorized), lionized, serialized, and swindled. It was a busy time.

Notes for a sketch of life in the Hegemony:

My home has thirty-eight rooms on thirty-six worlds. No doors: the arched entrances are farcaster portals, a few opaqued with privacy curtains, most open to observation and entry. Each room has windows everywhere and at least two walls with portals. From the grand dining hall on Renaissance Vector, I can see the bronze skies and the verdigris towers of Keep Enable in the valley below my volcanic peak, and by turning my head I can look through the farcaster portal and across the expense of white carpet in the formal living area to see the Edgar Allan Sea crash against the spires of Point Prospero on Nevermore. My library looks out on the glaciers and green skies of Nordholm while a walk of ten paces allows me to *descend* a short stairway to my tower study, a comfortable, open room encircled by polarized glass which offers a three-hundred-sixty-degree view of the highest peaks of the Kushpat Karakoram, a mountain range two thousand kilometers from the nearest settlement in the easternmost reaches of the Jamnu Republic on Deneb Drei.

The huge sleeping room Helenda and I share rocks gently in the boughs of a three-hundred-meter Worldtree on the Templar world of God's Grove and connects to a solarium which sits alone on the arid saltflats of Hebron. Not all of our views are of wilderness: the media room opens to a skimmer pad on the hundred and thirty-eighth floor of a Tau Ceti Center arctower and our patio lies on a terrace overlooking the market in the Old Section of bustling New Jerusalem. The architect, a student of the legendary Millon DeHaVre, has incorporated several small jokes into the house's design: the steps *go down* to the tower room, of course, but equally droll is the exit from the eyrie which leads to the exercise room on the lowest level of Lusus's deepest Hive, or perhaps the guest bathroom which consists of toilet, bidet, sink and shower stall on an open, wall-less raft afloat on the violet seaworld of Mare Infinitus.

At first the shifts in gravity from room to room were disturbing, but I soon adapted, subconsciously bracing myself for the drag of Lusus and Hebron and Sol Draconi Septem, unconsciously anticipating the less than l-standard-g freedom of the majority of the rooms.

In the ten standard months Helenda and I are together we spend little time in our home, preferring instead to move with friends among the resorts and vacation arcologies and night spots of the Worldweb. Our 'friends' are the former farcaster set, now calling themselves the Caribou Herd after an extinct, Old Earth migratory mammal. This herd consists of other writers, a few successful visual artists, Concourse intellectuals, All Thing media representatives, a few radical ARNists and cosmetic gene splicers, Web aristocrats, wealthy farcaster freaks and Flashback addicts, a few holie and stage directors, a scattering of actors and performance artists, several Mafia dons gone straight, and a revolving list of recent celebrities . . . myself included.

Everyone drinks, uses stims and autoimplants, takes the wire, and can afford the best drugs. The drug of choice is Flashback. It is definitely an upper-class vice: one needs the full range of expensive implants to fully experience it. Helenda has seen to it that I have been so fitted: biomonitors, sensory extenders, and internal comlog, neural shunts, kickers, metacortex processors, blood chips, RNA tapeworms . . . my mother wouldn't have recognized my insides.

I try Flashback twice. The first time is a glide – I target my ninth birthday party and hit it with the first salvo. It is all there: the servants singing on the north lawn at day-break, don Balthazar grudgingly canceling classes so I can spend the day with Amalfi in my EMV, streaking across the gray dunes of the Amazon Basin in gay abandon; the torchlight procession that evening as representatives of the other Old Families arrive at dusk, their brightly wrapped presents gleaming under the moon and the Ten Thousand Lights. I rise from nine hours in Flashback with a smile on my face. The second trip almost kills me.

I am four and crying, seeking my mother through end-less rooms smelling of dust and old furniture. Android servants seek to console me but I shake off their hands, running down hallways soiled with shadows and the soot of too many generations. Breaking the first rule I ever learned, I throw open the doors to Mother's sewing room, her sanctum sanctorum to which she retires for three hours every afternoon and from which she emerges with her soft smile, the hem of her pale dress whispering across the carpet like the echo of a ghost's sigh.

Mother is sitting there in the shadows. I am four and my finger has been hurt and I rush to her, throwing myself into her arms.

She does not respond. One of her elegant arms remains reclined along the back of the chaise longue, the other remains limp on the cushion.

I pull back, shocked by her cool plasticity. I tug open the heavy velvet drapes without rising from her lap.

Mother's eyes are white, rolled back in her head. Her lips are slightly open. Drool moistens the corners of her mouth and glints on her perfect chin. From the gold threads of her hair – done up in the Grande Dame style she favors – I see the cold steel gleam of the stim wire and the duller sheen of the skull socket she has plugged it into. The patch of bone on either side is very white. On the table near her left hand lies the empty Flashback syringe.

The servants arrive and pull me away. Mother never blinks. I am pulled screaming from the room.

I wake screaming.

Perhaps it was my refusal to use Flashback again which hastened Helenda's departure, but I doubt it. I was a toy to her – a primitive who amused her by my innocence about a life she had taken for granted for many decades. Whatever the case, my refusal to Flashback left me with many days without her; the time spent in replay is real time and Flashback users often die having spent more days of their lives under the drug than they ever experienced conscious.

At first I entertained myself with the implants and technotoys which had been denied to me as a member of an Old Earth Family. The datasphere was a constant delight that first year – I called up information almost continually, living in a frenzy of full interface. I was as addicted to raw data as the Caribou Herd were to their stims and drugs. I could imagine don Balthazar spinning in his molten grave as I gave up long-term memory for the transient satisfaction of implant omniscience. It was only later that I felt the loss – Fitzgerald's *Odyssey*, Wu's *Final March*, and a score of other epics which had survived my stroke now were shredded like cloud fragments in a high wind. Much later, freed of implants, I painstakingly learned them all again.

For the first and only time in my life I became political. Days and nights would pass with me monitoring the Senate on farcaster cable or lying tapped into the All

Thing. Someone once estimated that the All Thing deals with about a hundred active pieces of Hegemony legislation per day, and during my months spent screwed into the sensorium I missed none of them. My voice and name became well known on the debate channels. No bill was too small, no issue too simple or too complex for my input. The simple act of voting every few minutes gave me a false sense of having *accomplished* something. I finally gave up the political obsession only after I realized that accessing the All Thing regularly meant either staying home or turning into a walking zombie. A person constantly busy accessing on his implants makes a pitiful sight in public and it didn't take Helenda's derision to make me realize that if I stayed home I would turn into an All Thing sponge like so many millions of other slugs around the Web. So I gave up politics. But by then I had found a new passion: religion.

I joined religions. Hell, I helped *create* religions. The Zen Gnostic Church was expanding exponentially and I became a true believer, appearing on HTV talk shows and searching for my Places of Power with all of the devoutness of a pre-Hegira Muslim pilgrimaging to Mecca. Besides, I loved farcasting. I had earned almost a hundred million marks from royalties for *The Dying Earth*, and Helenda had invested well, but someone once figured that a farcaster home such as mine cost more than fifty thousand marks a day just to keep in the Web and I did not limit my farcasting to the thirty-six worlds of my home. Transline Publishing had qualified me for a gold universal card and I used it liberally, farcasting to unlikely corners of the Web and then spending weeks staying in luxury accommodations and leasing EMVs to find my Places of Power in remote areas of backwater worlds.

I found none. I renounced Zen Gnosticism about the same time Helenda divorced me. By that time the bills were piling up and I had to liquidate most of the stocks and long-term investments remaining to me after Helenda had taken her share. (I was not only naive and in love when she had had her attorneys draw up the marriage contract . . . I was stupid.)

Eventually, even with such economies as cutting down my farcasting and dismissing the android servants, I was facing financial disaster.

I went to see Tyrena Wingreen-Feif.

'No one wants to read poetry,' she said, leafing through the thin stack of *Cantos* I had written in the past year and a half.

'What do you mean?' I said. '*The Dying Earth* was poetry.'

'*The Dying Earth* was a fluke,' said Tyrena. Her nails were long and green and curved in the latest mandarin fashion; they curled around my manuscript like the claws of some chlorophyll beast. 'It sold because the mass subconscious was ready for it.'

'Maybe the mass subconscious is ready for this,' I said. I was beginning to get angry.

Tyrena laughed. It was not an altogether pleasant sound. 'Martin, Martin, Martin,' she said. 'This is *poetry*. You're writing about Heaven's Gate and the Caribou Herd, but what comes across is loneliness, displacement, angst, and a cynical look at humanity.'

'So?'

'So no one wants to *pay* for a look at another person's angst,' laughed Tyrena.

I turned away from her desk and walked to the far side of the room. Her office took up the entire four hundred and thirty-fifth floor of the Transline Spire in the Babel section of Tau Ceti Center. There were no windows; the circular room was open from floor to ceiling, shielded by a solar-generated containment field which showed no shimmer whatsoever. It was like standing between two gray plates suspended halfway between the sky and earth. I watched crimson clouds move between the lesser spires half a kilometer below and I thought about hubris. Tyrena's office had no doorways, stairways, elevators, field lifts, or trapdoors: no connection to the other levels at all. One entered Tyrena's office through the five-faceted farcaster which shimmered in midair like an abstract holosculpture. I found myself thinking about tower fires and power failures as well as hubris. I said,

'Are you saying that you won't publish it?'

'Not at all,' smiled my editor. 'You've earned Transline several billion marks, Martin. We will publish it. All I am saying is that no one will buy it.'

'You're wrong!' I shouted. 'Not everyone recognizes fine poetry, but there are still enough people who read to make it a bestseller.'

Tyrena did not laugh again but her smile slashed upward in a twist of green lips. 'Martin, Martin, Martin,' she said, 'the population of literate people has been declining steadily since Gutenberg's day. By the twentieth century, less than two percent of the people in the so-called industrialized democracies read even one book a year. And that was *before* the smart machines, dataspheres, and user-friendly environments. By the Hegira, ninety-eight percent of the Hegemony's population had no reason to read anything. So they didn't bother learning how to. It's worse today. There are more than a hundred billion human beings in the Worldweb and less than one percent of them bothers to hardfax any printed material, much less *read a book*.'

'*The Dying Earth* sold almost three billion copies,' I reminded her.

'Mm-hmm,' said Tyrena. 'It was the Pilgrim's Progress Effect.'

'The what?'

'Pilgrim's Progress Effect. In the Massachusetts Colony of . . . what was it! – seventeenth-century Old Earth, every decent family had to have a copy in the household. But, my heavens, no one had to *read* it. It was the same with Hitler's *Mein Kampf* or Stukatsky's *Visions in the Eye of a Decapitated Child*.'

'Who was Hitler?' I said.

Tyrena smiled slightly. 'An Old Earth politician who did some writing. *Mein Kampf* is still in print . . . Transline renews the copyright every hundred and thirty-eight years.'

'Well, look,' I said, 'I'm going to take a few weeks to polish up the *Cantos* and give it my best shot.'

'Fine,' smiled Tyrena.

'I suppose you'll want to edit it the way you did last time?'

'Not at all,' said Tyrena. 'Since there's no core of nostalgia this time, you might as well write it the way you want.'

I blinked. 'You mean I can keep in the blank verse this time?'

'Of course.'

'And the philosophy?'

'Please do.'

'And the experimental sections?'

'Yes.'

'And you'll print it the way I write it?'

'Absolutely.'

'Is there a *chance* it'll sell?'

'Not a hope in hell.'

My 'few weeks to polish up the *Cantos*' turned into ten months of obsessive labor. I shut off most of the rooms in the house, keeping only the tower room on Deneb Drei, the exercise room on Lusus, the kitchen, and the bathroom raft on Mare Infinitus. I worked a straight ten hours a day, took a break for some vigorous exercise followed by a meal and a nap, and then returned to my writing table for another eight-hour stint. It was similar to the time five years before when I was recovering from my stroke and it sometimes took an hour or a day for a word to come to me, for a concept to sink its roots into the firm soil of language. Now it was an even slower process as I agonized over the perfect word, the precise rhyme scheme, the most playful image, and the most ineffable analog to the most elusive emotion.

After ten standard months I was done, acknowledging the ancient aphorism to the effect that no book or poem is ever finished, merely abandoned.

'What do you think?' I asked Tyrena as she read through the first copy.

Her eyes were blank, bronze disks in that week's fashion, but this did not hide the fact that there were tears there. She brushed one away. 'It's beautiful,' she said.

212

'I tried to discover the voice of some of the Ancients,' I said, suddenly shy.

'You succeeded brilliantly.'

'The Heaven's Gate Interlude is still rough,' I said.

'It's perfect.'

'It's about loneliness,' I said.

'It is loneliness.'

'Do you think it's ready?' I asked.

'It's perfect . . . a masterpiece.'

'Do you think it'll sell?' I asked.

'No fucking way.'

They planned an initial run of seventy million hardfax copies of *Cantos*. Transline ran ads throughout the datasphere, placed HTV commercials, transmitted software inserts, successfully solicited blurbs from best-selling authors, made sure it was reviewed in the *New New York Times Book Section* and the *TC² Review*, and generally spent a fortune on advertising.

The *Cantos* sold twenty-three thousand hardfax copies during the first year it was in print. At ten percent royalties of the 12MK cover price, I had earned back 13,800MK of my 2,000,000MK advance from Transline. The second year saw a sale of 638 hardfax copies; there were no datasphere rights sold, no holie options, and no book tours.

What the *Cantos* lacked in sales it made up for in negative reviews: 'Indecipherable . . . archaic . . . irrelevant to all current concerns,' said the *Times Book Section*. 'M. Silenus has committed the ultimate act of non-communication,' wrote Urban Kapry in the *TC² Review*, 'by indulging himself in an orgy of pretentious obfuscation.' Marmon Hamlit on 'AllNet Now!' issued the final deathblow: 'Oh, the poetry thing from Whatshisname – couldn't read it. Didn't try.'

Tyrena Wingreen-Feif did not seem concerned. Two weeks after the first reviews and hardfax returns came in, a day after my thirteen-day binge ended, I farcast to her office and threw myself into the black flowfoam chair which crouched in the center of the room like a velvet panther. One of Tau Ceti Center's legendary thunderstorms was going on and Jovian-sized lightning crashes were rending the blood-tinged air just beyond the invisible containment field.

'Don't sweat it,' said Tyrena. This week's fashions included a hairdo which sent black spikes thrusting half a meter above her forehead and a body field opaciter which left shifting currents of color concealing – and revealing – the nudity beneath. 'The first run only amounted to sixty thousand fax transmits so we're not out much there.'

'You said seventy million were planned,' I said.

'Yeah, well, we changed our minds after Transline's resident AI read it.'

I slumped lower in the flowfoam. 'Even the AI hated it?'

'The AI *loved* it,' said Tyrena. 'That's when we knew for sure that *people* were going to hate it.'

I sat up. 'Couldn't we have sold copies to the TechnoCore?'

'We did,' said Tyrena. 'One. The millions of AIs there probably real-time-shared it the minute it came in over fatline. Interstellar copyright doesn't mean shit when you're dealing with silicon.'

'All right,' I said, slumping. 'What next?' Outside, lightning bolts the size of Old Earth's ancient superhighways danced between the corporate spires and cloud towers.

Tyrena rose from her desk and walked to the edge of the carpeted circle. Her body field flickered like electrically charged oil on water. 'Next,' she said, 'you decide if you want to be a writer or the Worldweb's biggest jerk-off.'

'What?'

'You heard me.' Tyrena turned and smiled. Her teeth had been capped to gold points. 'The contract allows us to recover the advance in any way we have to. Seizing your assets at Interbank, recovering the gold coins you've got hidden on Homefree, and selling that gaudy farcaster house would about do it. And then you can go join the other artistic dilettantes and dropouts and

214

mental cases that Sad King Billy collects on whatever Outback world he lives on.'

I stared.

'Then again,' she said and smiled her cannibal smile, 'we can just forget this temporary setback and you can get to work on your next book.'

My next book appeared five standard months later. *The Dying Earth II* picked up where *The Dying Earth* left off, in plain prose this time, the sentence length and chapter content carefully guided by neuro-bio-monitored responses on a test group of 638 average hardfax readers. The book was in novel form, short enough not to intimidate the potential buyer at Food Mart checkout stands, and the cover was a twenty-second interactive holo wherein the tall, swarthy stranger – Amalfi Schwartz, I suppose, although Amalfi was short and pale and wore corrective lenses – rips the bodice of the struggling female just to the nipple line before the protesting blonde turns toward the viewer and cries for help in a breathless whisper provided by porn holie star Leeda Swann.

Dying Earth II sold nineteen million copies.

'Not bad,' said Tyrena. 'It takes awhile to build an audience.'

'The first *Dying Earth* sold three billion copies,' I said.

'*Pilgrim's Progress*,' she said. '*Mein Kampf*. Once in a century. Maybe less.'

'But it sold three *billion* . . .'

'Look,' said Tyrena. 'In twentieth-century Old Earth, a fast food chain took dead cow meat, fried it in grease, added carcinogens, wrapped it in petroleum-based foam, and sold nine hundred billion units. Human beings. Go figure.'

Dying Earth III introduced the characters of Winona, the escaped slave girl who rose to the ownership of her own fiberplastic plantation (never mind that fiberplastic never grew on Old Earth), Arturo Redgrave, the dashing blockade runner (what blockade?!), and Innocence Sperry, the nine-year-old telepath dying of an unspecified Little Nell disease. Innocence lasted until

Dying Earth IX, and on the day Transline allowed me to kill the little shit off, I went out to celebrate with a six-day, twenty-world binge. I awoke in a lungpipe on Heaven's Gate, covered with vomit and rebreather mold, nursing the Web's biggest headache and the sure knowledge that I soon would have to start on Volume X of *The Chronicles of the Dying Earth*.

It isn't hard being a hack writer. Between *Dying Earth II* and *Dying Earth IX*, six standard years had passed relatively painlessly. My research was meager, my plots formulaic, my characters cardboard, my prose preliterate, and my free time was my own. I traveled. I married twice more; each wife left me with no hard feelings but with a sizable portion of the royalties from my next *Dying Earth*. I explored religions and serious drinking, finding more hope of lasting solace in the latter.

I kept my home, adding six rooms on five worlds, and filled it with fine art. I entertained. Writers were among my acquaintances but, as in all times, we tended to mistrust and badmouth each other, secretly resenting the other's successes and finding fault in their work. Each of us knew in his or her heart that he or she was a true artist of the word who merely happened to be commercial; the others were hacks.

Then, on a cool morning with my sleeping room rocking slightly in the upper branches of my tree on the Templar world, I awoke to a gray sky and the realization that my muse had fled.

It had been five years since I had written any poetry. The *Cantos* lay open in the Deneb Drei tower, only a few pages finished beyond what had been published. I had been using thought processors to write my novels and one of these activated as I entered the study. SHIT, it printed out, WHAT DID I DO WITH MY MUSE?

It says something about the type of writing I had been doing that my muse could flee without my noticing. For those who do not write and who never have been stirred by the creative urge, talk of muses seems a figure of speech, a quaint conceit, but for those of us who live by the Word, our muses are as real and necessary as the soft clay of language which they help to sculpt. When one is writing – *really* writing – it is as if one is given a fatline to the gods. No true poet has been able to explain the exhilaration one feels when the mind becomes an *instrument* as surely as does the pen or thought processor, ordering and expressing the revelations flowing in *from somewhere else*.

My muse had fled. I sought her in the other worlds of my house but only silence echoed back from the art-bedecked walls and empty spaces. I farcast and flew to my favorite places, watching the suns set on the windblown prairies of Grass and the night fogs obscure the ebony crags of Nevermore, but although I emptied my mind of the trash-prose of the endless *Dying Earth*, there came no whispers from my muse.

I sought her in alcohol and Flashback, returning to the productive days on Heaven's Gate when her inspiration was a constant buzzing in my ears, interrupting my work, waking me from sleep, but in the relived hours and days her voice was as muted and garbled as a damaged audio disk from some forgotten century.

My muse had fled.

I farcast to Tyrena Wingreen-Feif's office at the precise moment of my appointment. Tyrena had been promoted from editor-in-chief of the hardfax division to publisher. Her new office occupied the highest level of the Tau Ceti Center Transline Spire and standing there was like perching on the carpeted summit of the galaxy's tallest, thinnest peak; only the invisible dome of the slightly polarized containment field arched overhead and the edge of the carpet ended in a six-kilometer drop. I wondered if other authors felt the urge to jump.

'The new opus?' said Tyrena. Lusus was dominating the fashion universe this week and 'dominate' was the right word; my editor was dressed in leather and iron, rusted spikes on her wrists and neck and a massive bandolier across her shoulder and left breast. The cartridges looked real.

'Yeah,' I said and tossed the manuscript box on her desk.

'Martin, Martin, Martin,' she sighed, 'when are you going to transmit your books rather than going to all the trouble of printing them out and bringing them here in person?'

'There's a strange satisfaction in delivering them,' I said. 'Especially this one.'

'Oh?'

'Yes,' I said. 'Why don't you read some of it?'

Tyrena smiled and clicked black fingernails along the cartridges in her bandolier. 'I'm sure it's up to your usual high standards, Martin,' she said. 'I don't have to look at it.'

'Please do,' I said.

'Really,' said Tyrena, 'there's no reason. It always makes me nervous to read a new work while the author is present.'

'This one won't,' I said. 'Read just the first few pages.'

She must have heard something in my voice because she frowned slightly and opened the box. The frown deepened as she read the first page and flipped through the rest of the manuscript.

Page one had a single sentence: 'And then, one fine morning in October, the Dying Earth swallowed its own bowels, spasmed its final spasm and died.' The other two hundred and ninety-nine pages were blank.

'A joke, Martin?'.

'Nope.'

'A subtle hint then? You would like to begin a new series?'

'Nope.'

'It's not as if we hadn't expected it, Martin. Our story-liners have come up with several exciting series ideas for you. M. Subwaizee thinks that you would be perfect for the novelizations of the Crimson Avenger holies.'

'You can stick the Crimson Avenger up your corporate ass, Tyrena,' I said cordially. 'I'm finished with Transline and this premasticated gruel you call fiction.'

Tyrena's expression did not flicker. Her teeth were not pointed; today they were rusted iron to match the spikes on her wrists and the collar around her neck. 'Martin,

Martin, Martin,' she sighed, 'you have no idea how finished you will be if you don't apologize, straighten up, and fly right. But that can wait until tomorrow. Why don't you step home, sober up, and think about this?'

I laughed. 'I'm as sober as I've been in eight years, lady. It just took me awhile to realize that it wasn't just *me* who's writing crap . . . there's not a book published in the Web this year that hasn't been total garbage. Well, I'm getting off the scow.'

Tyrena rose. For the first time I noticed that on her simulated canvas web belt there hung a FORCE deathwand. I hoped that it was a designer-fake as the rest of her costume.

'Listen, you miserable, no-talent hack,' she hissed. 'Transline owns you from the balls up. If you give us any more trouble we'll have you working in the Gothic Romance factory under the name Rosemary Titmouse. Now go home, sober up, and get to work on *Dying Earth X*.'

I smiled and shook my head.

Tyrena squinted slightly. 'You're still into us for almost a million-mark advance,' she said. 'One word to Collections and we'll seize every room of your house except that goddamn raft you use as an outhouse. You can sit on it until the oceans fill up with crap.'

I laughed a final time. 'It's a self-contained disposal unit,' I said. 'Besides, I sold the house yesterday. The check for the balance of the advance should have been transmitted by now.'

Tyrena tapped the plastic grip of her deathwand. 'Transline's copyrighted the Dying Earth concept, you know. We'll just have someone else write the books.'

I nodded. 'They're welcome to it.'

Something in my ex-editor's voice changed when she realized that I was serious. Somewhere, I sensed, there was an advantage to her if I stayed. 'Listen,' she said, 'I'm sure we can work this out, Martin. I was saying to the director the other day that your advances were too small and that Transline should let you develop a new story line . . .'

'Tyrena, Tyrena, Tyrena,' I sighed. 'Goodbye.'

I farcast to Renaissance Vector and then to Parsimony, where I boarded a spinship for the three-week voyage to Asquith and the crowded kingdom of Sad King Billy.

Notes for a sketch of Sad King Billy:

His Royal Highness King William XXIII, sovereign lord of the Kingdom of Windsor-in-Exile, looks a bit like a wax candle of a man who has been left on a hot stove. His long hair runs in limp rivulets to slumped shoulders while the furrows on his brow trickle downward to the tributaries of wrinkles around the basset-hound eyes, and then run southward again through folds and frown lines to the maze of wattles in neck and jowls. King Billy is said to remind anthropologists of the worry dolls of the Outback Kinshasa, to make Zen Gnostics recall the Pitiful Buddha after the temple fire on Tai Zhin, and to send media historians rushing to their archives to check photos of an ancient flat-film movie actor named Charles Laughton. None of these references mean anything to me; I look at King Billy and think of my long-dead tutor don Balthazar after a week-long binge.

Sad King Billy's reputation for gloominess is exaggerated. He often laughs; it is merely his misfortune that his peculiar form of laughter makes most people think he is sobbing.

A man cannot help his physiognomy, but in His Highness's case, the entire persona tends to suggest either 'buffoon' or 'victim.' He dresses, if that can be the word, in something approaching a constant state of anarchy, defying the taste and color sense of his android servants, so that on some days he clashes with himself and his environment simultaneously. Nor is his appearance limited to sartorial chaos – King William moves in a permanent sphere of dishabille, his fly unsealed, his velvet cape torn and tattered and drawing crumbs magnetically from the floor, his left sleeve ruffle twice as long as the right, which – in turn – looks as if it has been dipped in jam.

You get the idea.

For all this, Sad King Billy has an insightful mind and

a passion for the arts and literature which has not been equaled since the true Renaissance days on old Old Earth.

In some ways King Billy is the fat child with his face eternally pressed to the candy store window. He loves and appreciates fine music but cannot produce it. A connoisseur of ballet and all things graceful, His Highness is a klutz, a moving series of pratfalls and comic bits of clumsiness. A passionate reader, unerring poetry critic, and patron of forensics, King Billy combines a stutter in his verbal expression with a shyness which will not allow him to show his verse or prose to anyone else.

A lifelong bachelor now entering his sixtieth year, King Billy inhabits the tumbledown palace and two-thousand-square-mile kingdom as if it were another suit of rumpled, royal clothes. Anecdotes abound: one of the famous oil painters whom King Billy supports finds His Majesty walking head down, hands clasped behind him, one foot on the garden path and one in the mud, obviously lost in thought. The artist hails his patron. Sad King Billy looks up, blinks, looks around as if awakening from a long nap. 'Excuse me,' His Highness says to the bemused painter, 'b-b-but could you p-p-please tell me – was I headed *toward* the palace or *away* from the p-p-palace?' 'Toward the palace, Your Majesty,' replies the artist. 'Oh, g-g-good,' sighs the King, 'then I've had lunch.'

General Horace Glennon-Height had begun his rebellion and the Outback world of Asquith lay directly in his path of conquest. Asquith was not worried – the Hegemony had offered a FORCE:space fleet as a shield – but the royal ruler of the Kingdom of Monaco-in-Exile seemed more melted than ever when he called me in.

'Martin,' said His Majesty, 'you've h-h-heard about the b-battle for Fomalhaut?'

'Yeah,' I said. 'It doesn't sound like anything to worry about. Fomalhaut was just the kind of place Glennon-Height's been hitting . . . small, no more than a few thousand colonists, rich in minerals, and with a time-debt of at least – what was it? – twenty standard months from the Web.'

'Twenty-three,' said Sad King Billy. 'So you d-d-don't think that w-we are in d-d-d-jeopardy?'

'Uh-uh,' I said. 'With only a three-week real-transit time and a time-debt of less than a year, the Hegemony can always get forces here from the Web faster than the General can spin up from Fomalhaut.'

'Perhaps,' mused King Billy, beginning to lean on a globe and then jumping upright as it started to turn under his weight. 'But none-the-the less I've decided to start our own m-m-modest Hegira.'

I blinked, surprised. Billy had been talking about relocating the kingdom in exile for almost two years, but I had never thought he would go through with it.

'The sp-sp-sp . . . the ships are ready on Parvati,' he said. 'Asquith has agreed to su-su-su . . . to provide the transport we need to the Web.'

'But the palace?' I said. 'The library? The farms and grounds?'

'Donated, of course,' said King Billy, 'but the contents of the library will travel with us.'

I sat on the arm of the horsehair divan and rubbed my cheek. In the ten years I had been in the kingdom, I had progressed from Billy's subject of patronage to tutor, to confidant, to friend, but never did I pretend to understand this disheveled enigma. Upon my arrival he had granted me an immediate audience. 'D-d-do you w-w-wish to j-j-join the other t-t-talented people in our little colony?' he had asked.

'Yes, Your Majesty.'

'And w-w-will you wr-wr-write more books like the *D-D-Dying Earth*?'

'Not if I can help it, Your Majesty.'

'I r-r-read it, you know,' the little man had said. 'It was v-v-very interesting.'

'You're most kind, Sir.'

'B-b-b-bullshit, M. Silenus. It w-w-was interesting because someone had obviously b-b-bowdlerized it and left in all the *bad* parts.'

I had grinned, surprised by the sudden revelation that I was going to like Sad King Billy.

'B-b-but the *Cantos*,' he sighed, 'th-th-that was a

222

book. Probably the finest volume of v-v . . . poetry published in the Web in the last two centuries. How you managed to get that by the mediocrity police I will never know. I ordered twenty thousand copies for the k-k-kingdom.'

I bowed my head slightly, at a loss for words for the first time since my poststroke days two decades before.

'Will you write more p-p-poetry like the *Cantos*?'

'I came here to try, Your Majesty.'

'Then welcome,' said Sad King Billy. 'You will stay in the west wing of the p-p-p . . . castle, near my offices, and my door will always be open to you.'

Now I glanced at the closed door and at the little sovereign who – even when smiling – looked as if he were on the verge of tears. 'Hyperion?' I asked. He had mentioned the colony world-gone-primitive many times.

'Precisely. The android seedships have been there for some years, M-M-Martin. Preparing the way, as it were.'

I raised an eyebrow. King Billy's wealth came not from the assets of the kingdom but from major investments in the Web economy. Even so, if he had been carrying on a surreptitious recolonization effort for years, the cost must have been staggering.

'D-d-do you remember why the original colonists named the pluh-pluh-pluh . . . the world Hyperion, Martin?'

'Sure. Before the Hegira they were a tiny freehold on one of the moons of Saturn. They couldn't last without terrestrial resupply, so they emigrated to the Outback and named the survey world after their moon.'

King Billy smiled sadly. 'And do you know why the name is p-p-propitious for *our* endeavor?'

It took me about ten seconds to make the connection. 'Keats,' I said.

Several years earlier, near the end of a long discussion about the essence of poetry, King Billy had asked me who was the purest poet who had ever lived.

'The purest?' I had said. 'Don't you mean the greatest?'

'No, no,' said Billy, 'that's absurd t-t-to argue over who is the *greatest*. I'm curious about your opinion of the p-p-purest . . . the closest to the essence you describe.'

I had thought about it a few days and then brought my answer to King Billy as we watched the setting suns from the top of the bluff near the palace. Red and blue shadows stretched across the amber lawn toward us. 'Keats,' I said.

'John Keats,' whispered Sad King Billy. 'Ahh.' And then a moment later: 'Why?'

So I had told him what I knew about the nineteenth-century Old Earth poet; about his upbringing, training, and early death . . . but mostly about a life dedicated almost totally to the mysteries and beauties of poetic creation.

Billy had seemed interested then; he seemed obsessed now as he waved his hand and brought into existence a holo model which all but filled the room. I moved backward, stepping through hills and buildings and grazing animals to get a better view.

'Behold Hyperion,' whispered my patron. As was usually the case when he was totally absorbed, King Billy forgot to stutter. The holo shifted through a series of views: river cities, port cities, mountain eyries, a city on a hill filled with monuments to match the strange buildings in a nearby valley.

'The Time Tombs?' I said.

'Precisely. The greatest mystery in the known universe.'

I frowned at the hyperbole. 'They're fucking empty,' I said. 'They've *been* empty since they were discovered.'

'They are the source of a strange, anti-entropic force-field which lingers still,' said King Billy. 'One of the few phenomena outside singularities which dares to tamper with time itself.'

'It's no big deal,' I said. 'It must've been like painting rust preventative on metal. They were made to last but they're *empty*. And since when do we go bugfuck about technology?'

'Not technology,' sighed King Billy, his face melting into deeper grooves. '*Mystery*. The strangeness of place so necessary to some creative spirits. A perfect mixture of the classical utopia and the pagan mystery.'

I shrugged, not impressed.

Sad King Billy waved the holo away. 'Has your p-p-poetry improved?'

I crossed my arms and glared at the regal dwarf-slob. 'No.'

'Has your m-m-muse returned?'

I said nothing. If looks could have killed, we would all be crying 'The King is dead, long live the King!' before nightfall.

'Very w-w-well,' he said, showing that he could look insufferably smug as well as sad. 'P-p-pack your bags, my boy. We're going to Hyperion.'

(Fade in)

Sad King Billy's five seedships floating like golden dandelions above a lapis sky. White cities rising on three continents: Keats, Endymion, Port Romance . . . the Poets' City itself. More than eight thousand of Art's pilgrims seeking escape from the tyranny of mediocrity and searching for a renewal of vision on this rough-hewn world.

Asquith and Windsor-in-Exile had been a center for android biofacture in the century following the Hegira, and now these blueskinned friends-of-man labored and tilled with the understanding that once these final labors were finished they were free at last. The white cities rose. The indigenies, tired of playing native, came out of their villages and forests and helped us rebuild the colony to more human specifications. The technocats and bureaucrats and ecocrats were thawed and let loose upon the unsuspecting world and Sad King Billy's dream came one step closer to reality.

By the time we arrived at Hyperion, General Horace Glennon-Height was dead, his brief but brutal mutiny already crushed, but there was no turning back.

Some of the more rugged artists and artisans spurned the Poets' City and eked out rugged but creative lives in Jacktown or Port Romance, or even in the expanding frontiers beyond, but I stayed.

I found no muse on Hyperion during those first years. For many, the expansion of distance because of limited transportation – EMVs were unreliable, skimmers scarce – and the contraction of artificial consciousness due to absence of datasphere, no access to the All Thing, and only one fatline transmitter – all led to a renewal of creative energies, a new realization of what it meant to be human and an artist.

Or so I heard.

No muse appeared. My verse continued to be technically proficient and dead as Huck Finn's cat.

I decided to kill myself.

But first I spent some time, nine years at least, carrying out a community service by providing the one thing new Hyperion lacked: decadence.

From a biosculptor aptly named Graumann Hacket, I obtained the hairy flanks, hooves, and goat legs of a satyr. I cultivated my beard and extended my ears. Graumann made interesting alterations to my sexual apparatus. Word got around. Peasant girls, indigenies, the wives of our true-blue city planners and pioneers – all awaited a visit from Hyperion's only resident satyr or arranged one themselves. I learned what 'priapic' and 'satyriasis' really mean. Besides the unending series of sexual contests, I allowed my drinking bouts to become legendary and my vocabulary to return to something approaching the old poststroke days.

It was fucking wonderful. It was fucking hell.

And then on the night I had set aside to blow my brains out, Grendel appeared.

Notes for a sketch of our visiting monster:

Our worst dreams have come alive. Something wicked shuns the light. Shades of Morbius and the Krell. Keep the fires high, Mother, Grendel comes tonight.

At first we think the missing are merely absent; there are no watchers on the walls of our city, no walls actually, no warriors at the door of our mead hall. Then a husband reports a wife who disappears between the evening meal and the tucking in of their two children. Then Hoban Kristus, the abstract implosionist, fails to appear at midweek performance at Poets' Amphitheatre, his first missed cue in eighty-two years of treading the boards. Concern rises. Sad King Billy returns from his labors as overseer on the Jacktown restoration and promises that security will be tightened. A sensor net is woven around the town. ShipSecurity officers sweep the Time Tombs and report that all remains empty. Mechs are sent into the labyrinth entrance at the base of the Jade Tomb and report nothing in a six-thousand-kilometer probe. Skimmers, automated and manned, sweep the area between the city and the Bridle Range and sense nothing larger than the heat signature of a rock eel. For a local week there are no more disappearances.

Then the deaths begin.

The sculptor Pete Garcia is found in his studio . . . and in his bedroom . . . and in the yard beyond. Ship-Security Manager Truin Hines is foolish enough to tell a newsteep: 'It's like he was mauled by some vicious animal. But no animal I've ever seen could do that to a man.'

We are all secretly thrilled and titillated. True, the dialogue is bad, straight out of a million movies and holies we've scared ourselves with, but *now we are part of the show*.

Suspicion turns toward the obvious: a psychopath is loose among us, probably killing with a pulse-blade or hellwhip. This time he (or she) had not found time to dispose of the body. Poor Pete.

ShipSecurity Manager Hines is sacked and City Manager Pruett receives permission from His Majesty to hire, train, and arm a city police force of approximately twenty officers. There is talk of truth-testing the entire Poets' City population of six thousand. Sidewalk cafes buzz with conversation on civil rights . . . we were technically out of the Hegemony – did we have any rights? . . . and harebrained schemes are hatched to catch the murderer.

Then the slaughter begins.

There was no pattern to the murders. Bodies were found in twos and threes, or alone, or not at all. Some of the disappearances were bloodless; others left gallons of gore. There were no witnesses, no survivors of attacks. Location did not seem to matter: the Weimont family

227

lived in one of the outlying villas but Sira Rob never stirred from her tower studio near the center of town; two of the victims disappeared alone, at night, apparently while walking in the Zen Garden, but Chancellor Lehman's daughter had private bodyguards yet vanished while alone in a bathroom on the seventh floor of Sad King Billy's palace.

On Lusus or Tau Ceti Center or a dozen other of the old Web worlds, the deaths of a thousand people add up to minor news – items for datasphere short-term or the inside pages of the morning paper – but in a city of six thousand on a colony of fifty thousand, a dozen murders – like the proverbial sentence to be hanged in the morning – tend to focus one's attention wonderfully well.

I knew one of the first victims. Sissipriss Harris had been one of my first conquests as a satyr – and one of my most enthusiastic – a beautiful girl, long blond hair too soft to be real, a fresh-picked-peach complexion too virginal to dream of touching, a beauty too perfect to believe: precisely the sort that even the most timid male dreams of violating, Sissipriss now had been violated in earnest. They found only her head, lying upright in the center of Lord Byron's Plaza as if she had been buried to her neck in pourable marble. I knew when I heard these details precisely what kind of creature we were dealing with, for a cat I had owned on Mother's estate had left similar offerings on the south patio most summer mornings – the head of a mouse staring up from the sandstone in pure rodent amazement, or perhaps a ground squirrel's toothy grin – killing trophies from a proud but hungry predator.

Sad King Billy came to visit me while I was working on my *Cantos*.

'Good morning, Billy,' I said.

'It's *Your Majesty*,' grumped His Majesty in a rare show of royal pique. His stutter had disappeared the day the royal dropship landed on Hyperion.

'Good morning, Billy, Your Majesty.'

'Hnnrh,' growled my liege lord, moving some papers

and managing to sit in the only puddle of spilled coffee on an otherwise dry bench. 'You're writing again, Silenus.'

I saw no reason to acknowledge an acknowledgment of the obvious.

'Have you always used a pen?'

'No,' I said, 'only when I want to write something worth reading.'

'Is that worth reading?' He gestured toward the small heap of manuscript I had accrued in two local weeks of work.

'Yes.'

'Yes? Just *yes*?'

'Yes.'

'Will I get to read it soon?'

'No.'

King Billy looked down and noticed that his leg was in a puddle of coffee. He frowned, moved, and mopped at the shrinking pool with the hem of his cape. 'Never?' he said.

'Not unless you outlive me.'

'Which I plan to do,' said the King. 'While you expire from playing goat to the kingdom's ewes.'

'Is that an attempt at a metaphor?'

'Not in the least,' said King Billy. 'Merely an observation.'

'I haven't forced my attentions on a ewe since my boyhood days on the farm,' I said. 'I promised my mother in song that I wouldn't indulge in sheep fucking again without asking her permission.' While King Billy looked on mournfully, I sang a few bars of an ancient ditty called 'There'll Never Be Another Ewe.'

'Martin,' he said, 'someone or something is killing my people.'

I set aside my paper and pen. 'I know,' I said.

'I need your help.'

'How, for Christ's sake? Am I supposed to track down the killer like some HTV detective? Have a fight to the fucking death on Reichenbach fucking Falls?'

'That would be satisfactory, Martin. But in the meantime a few opinions and words of advice would suffice.'

'Opinion One,' I said, 'it was stupid to come here. Opinion Two, it's stupid to stay. Advice Alpha/Omega: leave.'

King Billy nodded dolefully. 'Leave this city or all of Hyperion?'

I shrugged.

His Majesty rose and walked to the window of my small study. It looked out across a three-meter alley to the brick wall of the automated recycling plant next door. King Billy studied the view. 'You're aware,' he said, 'of the ancient legend of the Shrike?'

'I've heard bits of it.'

'The indigenies associate the monster with the Time Tombs,' he said.

'The indigenies smear paint on their bellies for the harvest celebration and smoke unrecombinant tobacco,' I said.

King Billy nodded at the wisdom of this. He said: 'The Hegemony Firstdown Team was wary of this area. They set up the multichannel recorders and kept their bases south of the Bridle.'

'Look,' I said, 'Your Majesty . . . what do you want? Absolution for screwing up and building the city here? You're absolved. Go and sin no more, my son. Now, if you don't mind, Your Royalship, *adiós*. I've got dirty limericks to write here.'

King Billy did not turn away from the window. 'You recommend that we evacuate the city, Martin?'

I hesitated only a second. 'Sure.'

'And would you leave with the rest?'

'Why wouldn't I?'

King Billy turned and looked me in the eye. '*Would* you?'

I said nothing. After a minute I looked away.

'I thought so,' said the ruler of the planet. He clasped his pudgy hands behind his back and stared at the wall again. 'If I were a detective,' he said, 'I would be suspicious. The city's least productive citizen starts writing again after a decade of silence only . . . what, Martin? . . . two days after the first murders happened. Now he's disappeared from the social life he once dominated and

230

spends his time composing an epic poem . . . why, even the young girls are safe from his goatish ardor.'

I sighed. 'Goatish ardor, m'lord?'

King Billy glanced over his shoulder at me.

'All right,' I said. 'You've got me. I confess. I've been murdering them and bathing in their blood. It works as a fucking literary aphrodisiac. I figure two . . . three hundred more victims, tops . . . and I'll have my next book ready for publication.'

King Billy turned back to the window.

'What's the matter,' I said, 'don't you believe me?'

'No.'

'Why not?'

'Because,' said the King, 'I know who the murderer is.'

We sat in the darkened holopit and watched the Shrike kill novelist Sira Rob and her lover. The light level was very low; Sira's middle-aged flesh seemed to glow with a pale phosphorescence while her much younger boyfriend's white buttocks gave the illusion in the dim light of floating separately from the rest of his tanned body. Their lovemaking was reaching its frenzied peak when the inexplicable occurred. Rather than the final thrusts and sudden pause of orgasm, the young man seemed to levitate up and backward, rising into the air as if Sira had somehow forcefully ejected him from her body. The sound track on the disk, previously consisting of the usual banal pants, gasps, exhortations, and instructions one would expect from such activity, suddenly filled the holopit with screams – first the young man's, then Sira's.

There was a thud as the boy's body struck a wall off camera. Sira's body lay waiting in tragically comic vulnerability, her legs wide, arms open, breasts flattened, thighs pale. Her head had been thrown back in ecstasy but now she had time to raise it, shock and anger already replacing the oddly similar expression of imminent orgasm. She opened her mouth to shout something.

No words. There came the watermelon-carving sound of blades piercing flesh, of hooks being pulled free of tendon and bone. Sira's head went back, her mouth opened impossibly wide, and her body exploded from the breastbone down. Flesh separated as if an invisible ax were chopping Sira Rob for kindling. Unseen scalpels completed the job of opening her, lateral incisions appearing like obscene time-lapse footage of a mad surgeon's favorite operation. It was a brutal autopsy performed on a living person. On a once living person, rather, for when the blood stopped flying and the body ceased spasming, Sira's limbs relaxed in death, legs opening again in an echo of the obscene display of viscera above. And then – for the briefest second – there was a blur of red and chrome near the bed.

'Freeze, expand, and augment,' King Billy told the house computer.

The blur resolved itself into a head out of a jolt addict's nightmare: a face part steel, part chrome, and part skull, teeth like a mechanized wolf's crossed with a steam shovel, eyes like ruby lasers burning through blood-filled gems, forehead penetrated by a curved spike-blade rising thirty centimeters from a quicksilver skull, and a neck ringed with similar thorns.

'The Shrike?' I asked.

King Billy nodded – the merest movement of chin and jowls.

'What happened to the boy?' I asked.

'There was no sign of him when Sira's body was discovered,' said the King. 'No one knew he was missing until this disk was discovered. He has been identified as a young recreation specialist from Endymion.'

'You just found the holo?'

'Yesterday,' said King Billy. 'The security people found the imager on the ceiling. Less than a millimeter across. Sira had a library of such disks. The camera apparently was there only to record . . . ah . . .'

'The bedroom follies,' I said.

'Precisely.'

I stood up and approached the floating image of the creature. My hand passed through forehead, spike, and jaws. The computer had calculated its size and represented it properly. Judging from the thing's head, our local Grendel stood more than three meters tall. 'Shrike,' I muttered, more in greeting than in identification.

'What can you tell me about it, Martin?'

'Why ask me?' I snapped. 'I'm a poet, not a mythohistorian.'

'You accessed the seedship computer with a query about the Shrike's nature and origins.'

I raised an eyebrow. Computer access was supposed to be as private and anonymous as datasphere entry in the Hegemony. 'So what?' I said. 'Hundreds of people must have checked out the Shrike legend since the killings began. Maybe thousands. It's the only fucking monster legend we've *got*.'

King Billy moved his wrinkles and folds up and down. 'Yes,' he said, 'but you searched the files three months before the first disappearance.'

I sighed and slumped into the holopit cushions. 'All right,' I said, 'I did. So what? I wanted to use the fucking legend in the fucking poem I'm writing, so I researched it. Arrest me.'

'What did you learn?'

I was very angry now. I stamped satyr hooves into the soft carpet. 'Just the stuff in the fucking file,' I snapped. 'What in the hell do you want from me, Billy?'

The King rubbed his brow and winced as he accidentally stuck his little finger in his eye. 'I don't know,' he said. 'The security people wanted to take you up to the ship and put you on full interrogative interface. I chose to talk to you instead.'

I blinked, feeling a strange zero-g sensation in my stomach. Full interrogative meant cortical shunts and sockets in the skull. Most people interrogated that way recovered fully. Most.

'Can you tell me what aspect of the Shrike legend you planned to use in your poem?' King Billy asked softly.

'Sure,' I said. 'According to the Shrike Cult gospel that the indigenies started, the Shrike is the Lord of Pain and the Angel of Final Atonement, come from a place beyond time to announce the end of the human race. I liked that conceit.'

'The end of the human race,' repeated King Billy.

'Yeah. He's Michael the Archangel and Moroni and Satan and Masked Entropy and the Frankenstein monster all rolled into one package,' I said. 'He hangs around the Time Tombs waiting to come out and wreak havoc when it's mankind's time to join the dodo and the gorilla and the sperm whale on the extinction Hit Parade list.'

'The Frankenstein monster,' mused the short little fat man in the wrinkled cape. 'Why him?'

I took a breath. 'Because the Shrike Cult believes that mankind somehow *created* the thing,' I said, although I knew that King Billy knew everything I knew and more.

'Do they know how to *kill* it?' he asked.

'Not that I know of. He's supposed to be immortal, beyond time.'

'A god?'

I hesitated. 'Not really,' I said at last. 'More like one of the universe's worst nightmares come to life. Sort of like the Grim Reaper, but with a penchant for sticking souls on a giant thorn tree . . . while the people's souls are still in their bodies.'

King Billy nodded.

'Look,' I said, 'if you insist on splitting hairs from back-world theologies, why don't you fly to Jacktown and ask a few of the Cult priests?'

'Yes,' said the King, chin on his pudgy fist, obviously distracted, 'they're already on the seedship being interrogated. It's all most confusing.'

I rose to leave, not sure if I would be allowed to.

'Martin?'

'Yeah.'

'Before you go, can you think of anything else that could help us understand this thing?'

I paused in the doorway, feeling my heart batting at my ribs to get out. 'Yeah,' I said, my voice only marginally steady. 'I can tell you who and what the Shrike really is.'

'Oh?'

'It's my muse,' I said, and turned, and went back to my room to write.

Of course I had summoned the Shrike. I knew that. I had summoned it by beginning my epic poem about it. In the beginning was the Word.

I retitled my poem *The Hyperion Cantos*. It was not about the planet but about the passing of the self-styled Titans called humans. It was about the unthinking hubris of a race which dared to murder its homeworld through sheer carelessness and then carried that dangerous arrogance to the stars, only to meet the wrath of a god which humanity had helped to sire. *Hyperion* was the first serious work I had done in many years and it was the best I would ever do. What began as a comic-serious homage to the ghost of John Keats became my last reason for existence, an epic tour de force in an age of mediocre farce. *Hyperion Cantos* was written with a skill I could never have attained, with a mastery I could never have gained, and sung in a voice which was not mine. The passing of humankind was my topic. The Shrike was my muse.

A score more people died before King Billy evacuated the City of Poets. Some of the evacuees went to Endymion or Keats or one of the other new cities, but most voted to take the seedships back to the Web. King Billy's dream of a creative utopia died, although the King himself lived on in the gloomy palace at Keats. Leadership of the colony passed to the Home Rule Council, which petitioned the Hegemony for membership and immediately established a Self-defense Force. The SDF – made up primarily of the same indigenies who had been cudgeling each other a decade before, but commanded now by self-styled officers from our new colony – succeeded only in disturbing the peacefulness of the night with their automated skimmer patrols and marring the beauty of the returning desert with their mobile surveillance mechs.

Surprisingly, I was not the only one to stay behind; at least two hundred remained, although most of us avoided social contact, smiling politely when we passed on Poets' Walk or while we ate apart in the echoing emptiness of the dining dome.

The murders and disappearances continued, averaging about one a local fortnight, although they were usually discovered not by us but by the regional SDF commander, who demanded a head count of citizens every few weeks.

The image that remains in my mind from that first year is an unusually communal one: the night we gathered on the Commons to watch the seedship leave. It was at the height of the autumn meteor season and Hyperion's night skies were already ablaze with gold streaks and red crisscrosses of flame when the seedship's engines fired, a small sun flared, and for an hour we watched as friends and fellow artists receded as a streak of fusion flame. Sad King Billy joined us that night and I remember that he looked at me before he solemnly reentered his ornate coach to return to the safety of Keats.

In the dozen years which followed I left the city half a dozen times; once to find a biosculptor who could rid me of my satyr affectation, the other times to buy food and supplies. The Shrike Temple had renewed the Shrike pilgrimages by this time, and on my trips I would use their elaborate avenue to death in reverse – the walk to Chronos Keep, the aerial tram across the Bridle Range, the windwagons, and the Charon barge down the Hoolie. Coming back, I would stare at the pilgrims and wonder who would survive.

Few visited the City of Poets. Our half-finished towers began to look like tumbled ruins. The gallerias with their splendid metal-glass domes and covered arcades grew heavy with vines; pyreweed and scargrass poked up between the flagstones. The SDF added to the chaos, setting mines and booby traps to kill the Shrike, but only succeeding in devastating once beautiful sections of the city. Irrigation broke down. The aqueduct collapsed. The desert encroached. I moved from room to room in King Billy's abandoned palace, working on my poem, waiting for my muse.

When you think about it, the cause-effect begins to resemble some mad logic-loop by the data artist Carolus or perhaps a print by Escher: the Shrike had come into existence because of the incantatory powers of my poem but the poem could not have existed without the threat/presence of the Shrike as muse. Perhaps I was a bit mad in those days.

In a dozen years sudden death culled the city of dilettantes until only the Shrike and I remained. The annual passage of the Shrike Pilgrimage was a minor irritation, a distant caravan crossing the desert to the Time Tombs. Sometimes a few figures returned, fleeing across vermilion sands to the refuge of Chronos Keep twenty kilometers to the southwest. More often, no one emerged.

I watched from the shadows of the city. My hair and beard had grown until they covered some of the rags I wore. I came out mostly at night, moving through the ruins like a furtive shadow, sometimes gazing at my lighted palace tower like David Hume peering in his own windows and solemnly deciding that he wasn't home. I never moved the food synthesizer from the dining dome to my apartments, preferring instead to eat in the echoing silence under that cracked *duomo* like some addled Eloi fattening himself up for the inevitable Morlock.

I never saw the Shrike. Many nights, just before dawn, I would awaken from a nap at a sudden sound – the scratch of metal on stone, the rasp of sand under something's foot – but although I was often sure that I was being watched, I never saw the watcher.

Occasionally I made the short trip to the Time Tombs, especially at night, avoiding the soft, disconcerting tugs of the anti-entropic time tides while I moved through complicated shadows under the wings of the Sphinx or stared at stars through the emerald wall of the Jade Tomb. It was upon my return from one of these nocturnal pilgrimages that I found an intruder in my study.

'Impressive, M-M-M-Martin,' said King Billy, tapping one of several heaps of manuscript which lay about the room. Seated in the oversized chair at the long table, the failed monarch looked old, more melted than ever. It was obvious that he had been reading for several hours. 'Do you r-r-really think that mankind d-d-d-deserves

237

such an end?' he asked softly. It had been a dozen years since I had heard the stutter.

I moved away from the door but did not answer. Billy had been a friend and patron for more than twenty standard years, but at that moment I could have killed him. The thought of someone reading *Hyperion* without permission filled me with rage.

'You d-d-date your p-p-p . . . cantos?' said King Billy, riffling through the most recent stack of completed pages.

'How did you get here?' I snapped. It was not an idle question. Skimmers, dropships, and helicopters had not had much luck flying to the Time Tombs region in recent years. The machines arrived *sans* passengers. It had done wonders in fueling the Shrike myth.

The little man in the rumpled cape shrugged. His uniform was meant to be brilliant and regal but merely made him look like an overweight Harlequin. 'I followed the last batch of pilgrims,' he said. 'And then c-c-came down from Keep Chronos to visit. I notice that you've written nothing in many months, M-M-Martin. Can you explain that?'

I glowered in silence while sidling closer.

'Perhaps I can explain it,' said King Billy. He looked at the last completed page of *Hyperion Cantos* as if it had the answer to a long-puzzled riddle. 'The last stanzas were written the same week last year that J.T. Telio disappeared.'

'So?' I had moved to the far edge of the table now. Feigning a casual attitude, I pulled a short stack of manuscript pages closer and moved them out of Billy's reach.

'So that w-w-w-was . . . according to the SDF monitors . . . the d-d-date of the death of the last remaining Poets' City dweller,' he said. 'The last except for y-y-you, that is, Martin.'

I shrugged and began moving around the table. I needed to get to Billy without getting the manuscript in the way.

'You know, you haven't f-f-f-finished it, Martin,' he said in his deep, sad voice. 'There is still some chance that humanity s-s-s-survives the Fall.'

'No,' I said and sidled closer.

238

'But you can't write it, can you, Martin? You can't c-c-c-compose this poetry unless your m-m-muse is shedding blood, can you?'

'Bullshit,' I said.

'Perhaps. But a fascinating coincidence. Have you ever wondered why *you* have been spared, Martin?'

I shrugged again and slid another stack of papers out of his reach. I was taller, stronger, and meaner than Billy, but I had to be sure that none of the manuscript would be damaged if he struggled as I lifted him out of his seat and threw him out.

'It's t-t-t-time we did something about this problem,' said my patron.

'No,' I said, 'it's time you left.' I shoved the last stacks of poetry aside and raised my arms, surprised to see a brass candlestick in one hand.

'Stop right there, please,' King Billy said softly and lifted a neural stunner from his lap.

I paused only a second. Then I laughed. 'You miserable little hangdog fraud,' I said. 'You couldn't use a fucking weapon if your life depended on it.'

I stepped forward to beat him up and throw him out.

My cheek was against the stone of the courtyard but one eye was open enough for me to see that stars still shone through the broken latticework of the galleria dome. I could not blink. My limbs and torso tingled with the pinpricks of returning sensation, as if my entire body had fallen asleep and was now coming painfully awake. It made me want to scream, but my jaw and tongue refused to work. Suddenly I was lifted and propped against a stone bench so that I could see the courtyard and the dry fountain which Rithmet Corbet had designed. The bronze Laocoön wrestled with bronze snakes in the flickering illumination of the predawn meteor showers.

'I'm s-s-sorry, Martin,' came a familiar voice, 'b-b-but this m-m-madness has to end.' King Billy came into my field of view carrying a tall stack of manuscript. Other heaps of pages lay on the shell of the fountain at the foot of the metal Trojan. An open bucket of kerosene sat nearby.

I managed to blink. My eyelids moved like rusted iron.

'The stun should w-w-wear off any s-s-s . . . any minute,' said King Billy. He reached into the fountain, raised a sheaf of manuscript, and ignited it with a flick of his cigarette lighter.

'No!' I managed to scream through clenched jaws.

The flames danced and died. King Billy let the ashes drop into the fountain and lifted another stack of pages, rolling them into a cylinder. Tears glistened on lined cheeks illuminated by flame. 'You c-c-called it f-f-forth,' gasped the little man. 'It must be f-f-finished.'

I struggled to rise. My arms and legs jerked like a marionette's mishandled limbs. The pain was incredible. I screamed again and the agonized sound echoed from marble and granite.

King Billy lifted a fat sheaf of papers and paused to read from the top page:

> *'Without story or prop*
> *But my own weak mortality, I bore*
> *The load of this eternal quietude,*
> *The unchanging gloom, and the three fixed shapes*
> *Ponderous upon my senses a whole moon.*
> *For by my burning brain I measured sure*
> *Her silver seasons shedded on the night*
> *And ever day by day I thought I grew*
> *More gaunt and ghostly – Oftentimes I prayed,*
> *Intense, that Death would take me from the vale*
> *And all its burdens – Gasping with despair*
> *Of change, hour after hour I cursed myself.'*

King Billy raised his face to the stars and consigned this page to flame.

'No!' I cried again and forced my legs to bend. I got to one knee, tried to steady myself with an arm ablaze with pinpricks, and fell on my side.

The shadow in the cape lifted a stack too thick to roll and peered at it in the dim light.

> *'Then I saw a wan face*
> *Not pinned by human sorrows, but bright blanched*
> *By an immortal sickness which kills not;*

240

> *It works a constant change, which happy death*
> *Can put no end to; deathwards progressing*
> *To no death was that visage; it had passed*
> *The lily and the snow; and beyond these*
> *I must not think now, though I saw that face . . .'*

King Billy moved his lighter and this and fifty other pages burst into flame. He dropped the burning papers into the fountain and reached for more.

'Please!' I cried and pulled myself up, stiffening my legs against the twitches of random nerve impulses while leaning against the stone bench. 'Please.'

The third figure did not actually appear so much as allow its presence to impinge upon my consciousness; it was as if it always had been there and King Billy and I had failed to notice it until the flames grew bright enough. Impossibly tall, four-armed, molded in chrome and cartilage, the Shrike turned its red gaze on us.

King Billy gasped, stepped back, and then moved forward to feed more cantos to the fire. Embers rose on warm drafts. A flight of doves burst from the vine-choked girders of the broken dome with an explosion of wing sound.

I moved forward in a motion more lurch than step. The Shrike did not move, did not shift its bloody gaze.

'Go!' cried King Billy, stutter forgotten, voice exalted, a blazing mass of poetry in each hand. 'Return to the pit whence you came!'

The Shrike seemed to incline its head ever so slightly. Red light gleamed on sharp surfaces.

'My lord!' I cried, although to King Billy or the apparition from hell I did not know then and know not now. I staggered the last few paces and reached for Billy's arm.

He was not there. One second the aging King was a hand's length from me and in the next instant he was ten meters away, raised high above the courtyard stones. Fingers like steel thorns pierced his arms and chest and thighs, but he still writhed and my *Cantos* burned in his fists. The Shrike held him out like a father offering his son for baptism.

'Destroy it!' Billy cried, his pinned arms making pitiful gestures. 'Destroy it!'

241

I stopped at the fountain's edge, tottered weakly against the rim. At first I thought he meant destroy the Shrike . . . and then I thought he meant the poem . . . and then I realized that he meant both. A thousand pages and more of manuscript lay tumbled in the dry fountain. I picked up the bucket of kerosene.

The Shrike did not move except to pull King Billy slowly back against his chest in an oddly affectionate motion. Billy writhed and screamed silently as a long steel thorn emerged from his harlequin silk just above the breastbone. I stood there stupidly and thought of butterfly collections I had displayed as a child. Slowly, mechanically, I sloshed kerosene on the scattered pages.

'End it!' gasped King Billy. 'Martin, for the love of God!'

I picked up the lighter from where he had dropped it. The Shrike made no move. Blood soaked the black patches of Billy's tunic until they blended with the crimson squares already here. I thumbed the antique lighter once, twice, a third time; sparks only. Through my tears I could see my life's work lying in the dusty fountain. I dropped the lighter.

Billy screamed. Dimly, I heard blades rubbing bone as he twisted in the Shrike's embrace. 'Finish it!' he cried. 'Martin . . . oh, God!'

I turned then, took five fast paces, and threw the half-full bucket of kerosene. Fumes blurred my already blurred vision. Billy and the impossible creature that held him were soaked like two comics in a slapstick holie. I saw Billy blink and splutter, I saw the slickness on the Shrike's chiseled muzzle reflect the meteor-brightened sky, and then the dying embers of burned pages in Billy's still clenched fists ignited the kerosene.

I raised my hands to protect my face – too late, beard and eyebrows singed and smoldered – and staggered backward until the rim of the fountain stopped me.

For a second the pyre was a perfect sculpture of flame, a blue and yellow *Pietà* with a four-armed madonna holding a blazing Christ figure. Then the burning figure writhed and arched, still pinned by steel thorns and a score of scalpeled talons, and a cry went up which to this day I cannot believe emanated from the human half of that death-embraced pair. The scream knocked me to my knees, echoed from every hard surface in the city, and drove the pigeons into wheeling panic. And the scream continued for minutes after the flaming vision simply ceased to be, leaving behind neither ashes nor retinal image. It was another minute or two before I realized that the scream I now heard was mine.

Anticlimax is, of course, the warp and way of things. Real life seldom structures a decent denouement.

It took me several months, perhaps a year, to recopy the kerosene-damaged pages and to rewrite the burned *Cantos*. It will be no surprise to learn that I did not finish the poem. It was not by choice. My muse had fled.

The City of Poets decayed in peace. I stayed another year or two – perhaps five, I do not know; I was quite mad by then. To this day records of early Shrike pilgrims tell of the gaunt figure, all hair and rags and bulging eyes, who would wake them from their Gethsemane sleep by screaming obscenities and shaking his fist at the silent Time Tombs, daring the coward within to show itself.

Eventually the madness burned itself out – although the embers will always glow – and I hiked the fifteen hundred kilometers to civilization, my backpack weighted down with just manuscript, surviving on rock eels and snow and on nothing at all for the last ten days.

The two and a half centuries since are not worth telling, much less reliving. The Poulsen treatments to keep the instrument alive and waiting. Two long, cold sleeps in illegal, sublight, cryogenic voyages; each swallowing a century or more; each taking its toll in brain cells and memory.

I waited then. I will still. The poem must be finished. It *will* be finished.

In the beginning was the Word.

In the end . . . past honor, past life, past caring . . .

In the end will be the Word.

FOUR

The *Benares* put into Edge a little after noon on the next day. One of the mantas had died in harness only twenty kilometers downriver from their destination and A. Bettik had cut it loose. The other had lasted until they tied up to the bleached pier and then it rolled over in total exhaustion, bubbles rising from its twin airholes. Bettik ordered this manta cut loose as well, explaining that it had a slim chance of surviving if it drifted along in the more rapid current.

The pilgrims had been awake and watching the scenery roll by since before sunrise. They spoke little and none had found anything to say to Martin Silenus. The poet did not appear to mind . . . he drank wine with his breakfast and sang bawdy songs as the sun rose.

The river had widened during the night and by morning it was a two-kilometer-wide highway of blue gray cutting through the low green hills south of the Sea of Grass. There were no trees this close to the Sea, and the browns and golds and heather tones of the Mane shrubs had gradually brightened to the bold greens of the two-meter-tall northern grasses. All morning the hills had been pressed lower until now they were compressed into low bands of grassy bluffs on either side of the river. An almost invisible darkening hung above the horizon to the north and east, and those pilgrims who had lived on ocean worlds and knew it as a promise of the approaching sea had to remind themselves that the only sea now near was comprised of several billion acres of grass.

Edge never had been a large outpost and now it was totally deserted. The score of buildings lining the rutted lane from the dock had the vacant gaze of all abandoned structures and there were signs on the riverfront that the population had fled weeks earlier. The Pilgrims' Rest, a three-century-old inn just below the crest of the hill, had been burned.

A. Bettik accompanied them to the summit of the low bluff. 'What will you do now?' Colonel Kassad asked the android.

'According to the terms of the Temple bonditure, we are free after this trip,' said Bettik. 'We shall leave the *Benares* here for your return and take the launch downriver. And then we go on our way.'

'With the general evacuations?' asked Brawne Lamia.

'No.' Bettik smiled. 'We have our own purposes and pilgrimages on Hyperion.'

The group reached the rounded crest of the bluff. Behind them, the *Benares* seemed a small thing tied to a sagging dock; the Hoolie ran southwest into the blue haze of distance below the town and curved west above it, narrowing toward the impassable Lower Cataracts a dozen kilometers upriver from Edge. To their north and east lay the Sea of Grass.

'My God,' breathed Brawne Lamia.

It was as if they had climbed the last hill in creation. Below them, a scattering of docks, wharves, and sheds marked the end of Edge and the beginning of the Sea. Grass stretched away forever, rippling sensuously in the slight breeze and seeming to lap like a green surf at the base of the bluffs. The grass seemed infinite and seamless, stretching to all horizons and apparently rising to precisely the same height as far as the eye could see. There was not the slightest hint of the snowy peaks of the Bridle Range, which they knew lay some eight hundred kilometers to the northwest. The illusion that they were gazing at a great green sea was nearly perfect, down to the wind-ruffled shimmers of stalks looking like whitecaps far from shore.

'It's beautiful,' said Lamia, who had never seen it before.

'It's striking at sunset and sunrise,' said the Consul.

'Fascinating,' murmured Sol Weintraub, lifting his infant so that she could see. She wiggled in happiness and concentrated on watching her fingers.

246

'A well-preserved ecosystem,' Het Masteen said approvingly. 'The Muir would be pleased.'

'Shit,' said Martin Silenus.

The others turned to stare.

'There's no fucking windwagon,' said the poet.

The four other men, woman, and android stared silently at the abandoned wharves and empty plain of grass.

'It's been delayed,' said the Consul.

Martin Silenus barked a laugh. 'Or it's left already. We were supposed to be here last night.'

Colonel Kassad raised his powered binoculars and swept the horizon. 'I find it unlikely that they would have left without us,' he said. 'The wagon was to have been sent by the Shrike Temple priests themselves. They have a vested interest in our pilgrimage.'

'We could walk,' said Lenar Hoyt. The priest looked pale and weak, obviously in the grip of both pain and drugs, and barely able to stand, much less walk.

'No,' said Kassad. 'It's hundreds of klicks and the grass is over our heads.'

'Compasses,' said the priest.

'Compasses don't work on Hyperion,' said Kassad, still watching through his binoculars.

'Direction finders then,' said Hoyt.

'We have an IDF, but that isn't the point,' said the Consul. 'The grass is sharp. Half a klick out and we'd be nothing but tatters.'

'And there are the grass serpents,' said Kassad, lowering the glasses. 'It's a well-preserved ecosystem but not one to take a stroll in.'

Father Hoyt sighed and half collapsed into the short grass of the hilltop. There was something close to relief in his voice when he said. 'All right, we go back.'

A. Bettik stepped forward. 'The crew will be happy to wait and ferry you back to Keats in the *Benares* should the windwagon not appear.'

'No,' said the Consul, 'take the launch and go.'

'Hey, just a fucking minute!' cried Martin Silenus. 'I don't remember electing you dictator, amigo. *We need to get there*. If the fucking windwagon doesn't show, we'll have to find another way.'

The Consul wheeled to face the smaller man. 'How? By boat? It takes two weeks to sail up the Mane and around the North Littoral to Otho or one of the other staging areas. And that's when there are ships available. Every seagoing vessel on Hyperion is probably involved in the evacuation effort.'

'Dirigible then,' growled the poet.

Brawne Lamia laughed. 'Oh, yes. We've seen so *many* in the two days we've been on the river.'

Martin Silenus whirled and clenched his fists as if to strike the woman. Then he smiled. 'All right then, lady, what do we do? Maybe if we sacrifice someone to a grass serpent the transportation gods will smile on us.'

Brawne Lamia's stare was arctic. 'I thought burned offerings were more your style, little man.'

Colonel Kassad stepped between the two. His voice barked command. 'Enough. The Consul's right. We stay here until the wagon arrives. M. Masteen, M. Lamia, go with A. Bettik to supervise the unloading of our gear. Father Hoyt and M. Silenus will bring some wood up for a bonfire.'

'A bonfire?' said the priest. It was hot on the hillside.

'After dark,' said Kassad. 'We want the windwagon to know we're here. Now let's *move*.'

It was a quiet group that watched the powered launch move downriver at sunset. Even from two kilometers away the Consul could see the blue skins of the crew. The *Benares* looked old and abandoned at its wharf, already a part of the deserted city. When the launch was lost in the distance, the group turned to watch the Sea of Grass. Long shadows from the river bluffs crept out across what the Consul already found himself thinking of as the surf and shallows. Farther out, the sea seemed to shift in color, the grass mellowing to an aquamarine shimmer before darkening to a hint of verdurous depths. The lapis sky melted into the reds and golds of sunset, illuminating their hilltop and setting the pilgrims' skins aglow with liquid light. The only sound was the whisper of wind in grass.

'We've got a fucking huge heap of baggage,' Martin Silenus said loudly. 'For a bunch of folks on a one-way trip.'

It was true, thought the Consul. Their luggage made a small mountain on the grassy hilltop.

'Somewhere in there,' came the quiet voice of Het Masteen, 'may lie our salvation.'

'What do you mean?' asked Brawne Lamia.

'Yeah,' said Martin Silenus, lying back, putting his hands under his head, and staring at the sky. 'Did you bring a pair of undershorts that are Shrikeproof?'

The Templar shook his head slowly. The sudden twilight cast his face in shadow under the cowl of the robe. 'Let us not trivialize or dissemble,' he said. 'It is time to admit that each of us has brought on this pilgrimage something which he or she hopes will alter the inevitable outcome when the moment arrives that we must face the Lord of Pain.'

The poet laughed. 'I didn't bring even my lucky fucking rabbit's foot.'

The Templar's hood moved slightly. 'But your manuscript perhaps?'

The poet said nothing.

Het Masteen moved his invisible gaze to the tall man on his left. 'And you, Colonel, there are several trunks which bear your name. Weapons, perhaps?'

Kassad raised his head but did not speak.

'Of course,' said Het Masteen, 'it would be foolish to go hunting without a weapon.'

'What about me?' asked Brawne Lamia, folding her arms. 'Do you know what secret weapon I've smuggled along?'

The Templar's oddly accented voice was calm. 'We have not yet heard your tale, M. Lamia. It would be premature to speculate.'

'What about the Consul?' asked Lamia.

'Oh, yes, it is obvious what weapon our diplomatic friend has in store.'

The Consul turned from his contemplation of the sunset. 'I brought only some clothes and two books to read,' he said truthfully.

'Ah,' sighed the Templar, 'but what a beautiful space-craft you left behind.'

Martin Silenus jumped to his feet. 'The fucking ship!' he cried. 'You can call it, can't you? Well, goddammit, get your dog whistle out, I'm tired of sitting here.'

The Consul pulled a strand of grass and stripped it. After a minute he said:

'Even if I could call it . . . and you heard A. Bettik say that the comsats and repeater stations were down . . . even if I could call it, we couldn't land north of the Bridle Range. That meant instant disaster even *before* the Shrike began ranging south of the mountains.'

'Yeah,' said Silenus, waving his arms in agitation, 'but we could get across this fucking . . . *lawn*! Call the ship.'

'Wait until morning,' said the Consul. 'If the wind-wagon's not here, we will discuss alternatives.'

'Fuck that . . .' began the poet, but Kassad stepped forward with his back to him, effectively removing Silenus from the circle.

'M. Masteen,' said the Colonel, 'what is *your* secret?'

There was enough light from the dying sky to show a slight smile on the Templar's thin lips. He gestured toward the mound of baggage. 'As you see, my trunk is the heaviest and most mysterious of all.'

'It's a Möbius cube,' said Father Hoyt. 'I've seen ancient artifacts transported that way.'

'Or fusion bombs,' said Kassad.

Het Masteen shook his head. 'Nothing so crude,' he said.

'Are you going to tell us?' demanded Lamia.

'When it is my turn to speak,' said the Templar.

'Are you next?' asked the Consul. 'We can listen while we wait.'

Sol Weintraub cleared his throat. 'I have number four,' he said, showing the slip of paper. 'But I would be more than pleased to trade with the True Voice of the Tree.' Weintraub lifted Rachel from his left shoulder to his right, patting her gently on the back.

Het Masteen shook his head. 'No, there is time. I meant only to point out that in hopelessness there is always hope. We have learned much from the stories so

250

far. Yet each of us has some seed of promise buried even deeper than we have admitted.'

'I don't see . . .' began Father Hoyt but was interrupted by Martin Silenus's sudden shout.

'It's the wagon! The fucking windwagon. Here at last!'

It was another twenty minutes before the windwagon tied up to one of the wharves. The craft came out of the north, its sails white squares against a dark plain draining of color. The last light had faded by the time the large ship had tacked close to the low bluff, folded its main sails, and rolled to a stop.

The Consul was impressed. The thing was wooden, handcrafted, and huge – curved in the pregnant lines of some seagoing galleon out of Old Earth's ancient history. The single gigantic wheel, set in the center of the curving hull, normally would have been invisible in the two-meter-tall grass, but the Consul caught a glimpse of the underside as he carried luggage onto the wharf. From the ground it would be six or seven meters to the railing, and more than five times that height to the tip of the mainmast. From where he stood, panting from exertion, the Consul could hear the snap of pennants far above and a steady, almost subsonic hum that would be coming from either the ship's interior flywheel or its massive gyroscopes.

A gangplank extruded from the upper hull and lowered itself to the wharf. Father Hoyt and Brawne Lamia had to step back quickly or be crushed.

The windwagon was less well lighted than the *Benares*; illumination appeared to consist of several lanterns hanging from spars. No crew had been visible during the approach of the ship and no one came into view now.

'Hallo!' called the Consul from the base of the gangplank. No one answered.

'Wait here a minute, please,' said Kassad and mounted the long ramp in five strides.

The others watched while Kassad paused at the top, touched his belt where the small deathwand was tucked, and then disappeared amidships. Several minutes later a light flared through broad windows at the stern, casting trapezoids of yellow on the grass below.

'Come up,' called Kassad from the head of the ramp. 'It's empty.'

The group struggled with their luggage, making several trips. The Consul helped Het Masteen with the heavy Möbius cube and through his fingertips he could feel a faint but intense vibration.

'So where the fuck is the crew?' asked Martin Silenus when they were assembled on the foredeck. They had taken their single-file tour through the narrow corridors and cabins, down stairways more ladder than stairs, and through cabins not much bigger than the built-in bunks they contained. Only the rearmost cabin – the captain's cabin, if that is what it was – approached the size and comfort of standard accommodations on the *Benares*.

'It's obviously automated,' said Kassad. The FORCE officer pointed to halyards which disappeared into slots in the deck, manipulators all but invisible among the rigging and spars, and the subtle hint of gears halfway up the lateen-rigged rear mast.

'I didn't see a control center,' said Lamia. 'Not so much as a diskey or C-spot nexus.' She slipped her comlog from a breast pocket and tried to interface on standard data, comm, and biomed frequencies. There was no response from the ship.

'The ships used to be crewed,' said the Consul. 'Temple initiates used to accompany the pilgrims to the mountains.'

'Well, they're not here now,' said Hoyt. 'But I guess we can assume that *someone* is still alive at the tram station or Keep Chronos. They sent the wagon for us.'

'Or everyone's dead and the windwagon is running on an automatic schedule,' said Lamia. She looked over her shoulders as rigging and canvas creaked in a sudden gust of wind. 'Damn, it's weird to be cut off from everybody and everything like this. It's like being blind and deaf. I don't know how colonials stand it.'

Martin Silenus approached the group and sat on the railing. He drank from a long green bottle and said:

'Where's the Poet? Show him! Show him,
Muses mine, that I may know him!
'Tis the man who with a man
    Is an equal, be he king,
Or poorest of the beggar-class,
    Or any other wondrous thing
A man may be 'twixt ape and Plato.
'Tis the man who with a bird,
Wren or eagle, finds his way to
    All its instincts. He hath heard
The lion's roaring, and can tell
    What his horny throat expresseth,
And to him the tiger's yell
    Comes articulate and presseth
On his ear like mother-tongue.'

'Where did you get that wine bottle?' asked Kassad.

Martin Silenus smiled. His eyes were small and bright in the lantern glow. 'The gallery's fully stocked and there's a bar. I declared it open.'

'We should fix some dinner,' said the Consul although all he wanted at the moment was some wine. It had been more than ten hours since they had last eaten.

There came a clank and whir and all six of them moved to the starboard rail. The gangplank had drawn itself in. They whirled again as canvas unfurled, lines grew taut, and somewhere a flywheel hummed into the ultrasonic. Sails filled, the deck tilted slightly, and the windwagon moved away from the wharf and into the darkness. The only sounds were the flap and creak of the ship, the distant rumble of the wheel, and the rasp of grass on the hull bottom.

The six of them watched as the shadow of the bluff fell behind, the unlighted beacon pyre receding as a faint gleam of starlight on pale wood, and then there were only the sky and night and swaying circles of lantern light.

'I'll go below,' said the Consul, 'and see if I can get a meal together.'

The others stayed awhile, feeling the slight surge and rumble through the soles of their feet and watching darkness pass. The Sea of Grass was visible only as the place where stars ended and flat blackness began. Kassad used a handbeam to illuminate glimpses of canvas and rigging, lines being pulled tight by invisible hands, and then he checked all the corners and shadowed places from stern to bow. The others watched in silence. When he clicked the light off, the darkness seemed less oppressive, the starlight brighter. A rich, fertile smell – more of a farm in springtime than of the sea – came to them on a breeze which had swept across a thousand kilometers of grass.

Sometime later the Consul called to them and they went below to eat.

The galley was cramped and there was no mess table, so they used the large cabin in the stern as their common room, pushing three of the trunks together as a makeshift table. Four lanterns swinging from low beams made the room bright. A breeze blew in when Het Masteen opened one of the tall windows above the bed.

The Consul set plates piled high with sandwiches on the largest trunk and returned again with thick white cups and a coffee therm. He poured while the others ate.

'This is quite good,' said Fedmahn Kassad. 'Where did you get the roast beef?'

'The cold box is fully stocked. There's another large freezer in the aft pantry.'

'Electrical?' asked Het Masteen.

'No. Double insulated.'

Martin Silenus sniffed a jar, found a knife on the sandwich plate, and added great dollops of horseradish to his sandwiches. His eyes sparkled with tears as he ate.

'How long does this crossing generally take?' Lamia asked the Consul.

He looked up from his study of the circle of hot black coffee in his cup. 'I'm sorry, what?'

'Crossing the Sea of Grass. How long?'

'A night and half a day to the mountains,' said the Consul. 'If the winds are with us.'

'And then . . . how long to cross the mountains?' asked Father Hoyt.

'Less than a day,' said the Consul.

'If the tramway is running,' added Kassad.

The Consul sipped the hot coffee and made a face. 'We have to assume it is. Otherwise . . .'

'Otherwise what?' demanded Lamia.

'Otherwise,' said Colonel Kassad, moving to the open window and putting his hands on his hips, 'we will be stranded six hundred klicks from the Time Tombs and a thousand from the southern cities.'

The Consul shook his head. 'No,' he said. 'The Temple priests or whoever are behind this pilgrimage have seen to it that we've gotten this far. They'll make sure we go all the way.'

Brawne Lamia crossed her arms and frowned. 'As what . . . sacrifices?'

Martin Silenus whooped a laugh and brought out his bottle:

> *'Who are these coming to the sacrifice?*
> *To what green altar, O mysterious priest,*
> *Lead'st thou that heifer lowing at the skies,*
> *And all her silken flanks with garlands dressed?*
> *What little town by river or sea-shore,*
> *Or mountain-built with peaceful citadel,*
> *Is emptied of its folk, this pious morn?*
> *And, little town, thy streets for evermore*
> *Will silent be; and not a soul, to tell*
> *Why thou art desolate, can e'er return.'*

Brawne Lamia reached under her tunic and brought out a cutting laser no larger than her little finger. She aimed it at the poet's head. 'You miserable little shit. One more word out of you and . . . I swear . . . I'll slag you where you stand.'

The silence was suddenly absolute except for the background rumble-groan of the ship. The Consul moved toward Martin Silenus. Colonel Kassad took two steps behind Lamia.

The poet took a long drink and smiled at the dark-haired woman. His lips were moist. 'Oh build your ship of death,' he whispered. 'Oh build it!'

255

Lamia's fingers were white on the pencil laser. The Consul edged closer to Silenus, not knowing what to do, imagining the whipping beam of light fusing his own eyes. Kassad leaned toward Lamia like two meters of tensed shadow.

'Madam,' said Sol Weintraub from where he sat on the bunk against the far wall, 'need I remind you that there is a child present?'

Lamia glanced to her right. Weintraub had removed a deep drawer from a ship's cupboard and had set it on the bed as a cradle. He had bathed the infant and come in silently just before the poet's recitation. Now he set the baby softly in the padded nest.

'I'm sorry,' said Brawne Lamia and lowered the small laser. 'It's just that he makes me so . . . angry.'

Weintraub nodded, rocking the drawer slightly. The gentle roll of the windwagon combined with the incessant rumble of the great wheel appeared to have already put the child to sleep. 'We're all tired and tense,' said the scholar. 'Perhaps we should find our lodgings for the night and turn in.'

The woman sighed and tucked the weapon in her belt. 'I won't sleep,' she said. 'Things are too . . . strange.'

Others nodded. Martin Silenus was sitting on the broad ledge below the stern windows. Now he pulled up his legs, took a drink, and said to Weintraub, 'Tell your story, old man.'

'Yes,' said Father Hoyt. The priest looked exhausted to the point of being cadaverous, but his feverish eyes burned. 'Tell us. We need to have the stories told and time to think about them before we arrive.'

Weintraub passed a hand across his bald scalp. 'It's a dull tale,' he said. 'I've been to Hyperion before. There are no confrontations with monsters, no acts of heroism. It's a tale by a man whose idea of epic adventure is speaking to a class without his notes.'

'All the better,' said Martin Silenus. 'We need a soporific.'

Sol Weintraub sighed, adjusted his glasses, and nodded. There were a few streaks of dark in his beard, but most of it had gone gray. He turned the lantern low over the baby's bed and moved to a chair in the center of the room.

The Consul turned down the other lamps and poured more coffee for those who wanted it. Sol Weintraub's voice was slow, careful in phrase and precise in wording, and before long the gentle cadence of his story blended with the soft rumble and slow pitchings of the windwagon's progress north.

THE SCHOLAR'S TALE:
The River Lethe's Taste is Bitter

Sol Weintraub and his wife Sarai had enjoyed their life even before the birth of their daughter; Rachel made things as close to perfect as the couple could imagine.

Sarai was twenty-seven when the child was conceived, Sol was twenty-nine. Neither of them had considered Poulsen treatments because neither of them could afford it, but even without such care they looked forward to another fifty years of health.

Both had lived their entire lives on Barnard's World, one of the oldest but least exciting members of the Hegemony. Barnard's was in the Web, but it made little difference to Sol and Sarai since they could not afford frequent farcaster travel and had little wish to go at any rate. Sol had recently celebrated his tenth year with Nightenhelser College, where he taught history and classical studies and did his own research on ethical evolution. Nightenhelser was a small school, fewer than three thousand students, but its academic reputation was outstanding and it attracted young people from all over the Web. The primary complaint of these students was that Nightenhelser and its surrounding community of Crawford constituted an island of civilization in an ocean of corn. It was true; the college was three thousand flat kilometers away from the capital of Bussard and the terraformed land in between was given over to farming. There had been no forests to fell, no hills to deal with, and no mountains to break the flat monotony of cornfields, bean-fields, cornfields, wheatfields, cornfields, rice paddies, and cornfields. The radical poet Salmud

Brevy had taught briefly at Nightenhelser before the Glennon-Height Mutiny, had been fired, and upon far-casting to Renaissance Vector had told his friends that Crawford County on South Sinzer on Barnard's World constituted the Eighth Circle of Desolation on the smallest pimple on the absolute ass-end of Creation.

Sol and Sarai Weintraub liked it. Crawford, a town of twenty-five thousand, might have been reconstructed from some nineteenth-century mid-American template. The streets were wide and over-arched with elms and oaks. (Barnard's had been the second extrasolar Earth colony, centuries before the Hawking drive and Hegira, and the seedships then had been huge.) Homes in Crawford reflected styles ranging from early Victorian to Canadian Revival, but they all seemed to be white and set far back on well-trimmed lawns.

The college itself was Georgian, an assemblage of red brick and white pillars surrounding the oval common. Sol's office was on the third floor of Placher Hall, the oldest building on campus, and in the winter he could look out on bare branches which carved the common into complex geometries. Sol loved the chalk-dust and old-wood smell of the place, a smell which had not changed since he was a freshman there, and each day climbing to his office he treasured the deeply worn grooves in the steps, a legacy of twenty generations of Nightenhelser students.

Sarai had been born on a farm halfway between Bussard and Crawford and had received her PhD in music theory a year before Sol earned his doctorate. She had been a happy and energetic young woman, making up in personality what she lacked in accepted norms of physical beauty, and she carried this attractiveness of person into later life. Sarai had studied offworld for two years at the University of New Lyons on Deneb Drei, but she was homesick there: the sunsets were abrupt, the much-vaunted mountains slicing off the sunlight like a ragged scythe, and she longed for the hours-long sunsets of home where Barnard's Star hung on the horizon like a great, tethered, red balloon while the sky congealed to evening. She missed the perfect flatness where – peering

258

from her third-floor room under the steep gables – a little girl could look fifty kilometers across tasseled fields to watch a storm approach like a bruise-black curtain lit within by lightning bolts. And Sarai missed her family.

She and Sol met a week after she transferred to Nightenhelser; it was another three years before he proposed marriage and she accepted. At first she saw nothing in the short graduate student. She was still wearing Web fashions then, involved in Post-Destructionist music theories, reading *Obit* and *Nihil* and the most avant-garde magazines from Renaissance Vector and TC², feigning sophisticated weariness with life and a rebel's vocabulary – and none of this jelled with the undersized but earnest history major who spilled fruit cocktail on her at Dean Moore's honors party. Any exotic qualities which might have come from Sol Weintraub's Jewish legacy were instantly negated by his BW accent, his Crawford Squire Shop wardrobe, and the fact that he had come to the party with a copy of Detresque's *Solitudes in Variance* absentmindedly tucked under his arm.

For Sol it was love at first sight. He stared at the laughing, red-cheeked girl and ignored the expensive dress and affected mandarin nails in favor of the personality which blazed like a beacon to the lonely junior. Sol had not known he was lonely until he met Sarai, but after the first time he shook her hand and spilled fruit salad down the front of her dress he knew that his life would be empty forever if they did not marry.

They married the week after the announcement of Sol's teaching appointment at the college. Their honeymoon was on Maui-Covenant, his first farcast trip abroad, and for three weeks they rented a mobile isle and sailed alone on it through the wonders of the Equatorial Archipelago. Sol never forgot the images from those sun-drenched and wind-filled days, and the secret image he would always most cherish was of Sarai rising nude from a nighttime swim, the Core stars blazing above while her own body glowed constellations from the phosphorescence of the island's wake.

They had wanted a child immediately but it was to be five years before nature agreed.

Sol remembered cradling Sarai in his arms as she curled in pain, a difficult delivery, until finally, incredibly, Rachel Sarah Weintraub was born at 2:01 A.M. in Crawford County Med Center.

The presence of an infant intruded upon Sol's solipsistic life as a serious academic and Sarai's profession as music critic for Barnard's datasphere, but neither minded. The first months were a blend of constant fatigue and joy. Late at night, between feedings, Sol would tiptoe into the nursery just to check on Rachel and to stand and gaze at the baby. More often than not he would find Sarai already there and the two would watch, arm in arm, at the miracle of a baby sleeping on its stomach, rump in the air, head burrowed into the bumper pad at the head of the crib.

Rachel was one of those rare children who managed to be cute without becoming self-consciously precious; by the time she was two standard years old her appearance and personality were striking – her mother's light brown hair, red cheeks, and broad smile, her father's large brown eyes. Friends said that the child combined the best portions of Sarai's sensitivity and Sol's intellect. Another friend, a child psychologist from the college, once commented that Rachel at age five showed the most reliable indicators of true giftedness in a young person: structured curiosity, empathy for others, compassion, and a fierce sense of fair play.

One day in his office, studying ancient files from Old Earth, Sol was reading about the effect of Beatrice on the world view of Dante Alighieri when he was struck by a passage written by a critic from the twentieth or twenty-first century:

> She [Beatrice] alone was still real for him, still implied meaning in the world, and beauty. Her nature became his landmark – what Melville would call, with more sobriety than we can now muster, his Greenwich Standard . . .

Sol paused to access the definition of Greenwich Standard, and then he read on. The critic had added a personal note:

Most of us, I hope, have had some child or spouse or friend like Beatrice, someone who by his very nature, his seemingly innate goodness and intelligence, makes us uncomfortably conscious of our lies when we lie.

Sol had shut off the display and gazed out at the black geometries of branches above the common.

Rachel was not insufferably perfect. When she was five standard, she carefully cut the hair of her five favorite dolls and then cut her own hair shortest of all. When she was seven, she decided that the migrant workers staying in their run-down houses on the south end of town lacked a nutritious diet, so she emptied the house's pantries, cold boxes, freezers, and synthesizer banks, talked three friends into accompanying her, and distributed several hundred marks' worth of the family's monthly food budget.

When she was ten, Rachel responded to a dare from Stubby Berkowitz and tried to climb to the top of Crawford's oldest elm. She was forty meters up, less than five meters from the top, when a branch broke and she fell two thirds of the way to the ground. Sol was paged on his comlog while discussing the moral implications of Earth's first nuclear disarmament era and he left the class without a word and ran the twelve blocks to the Med Center.

Rachel had broken her left leg, two ribs, punctured a lung, and fractured her jaw. She was floating in a bath of recovery nutrient when Sol burst in, but she managed to look over her mother's shoulder, smile slightly, and say through the wire cast on her jaw: 'Dad, I was fifteen feet from the *top*. Maybe closer. I'll make it next time.'

Rachel graduated with honors from secondary tutorials and received scholarship offers from corporate academies on five worlds and three universities, including Harvard on New Earth. She chose Nightenhelser.

It was little surprise to Sol that his daughter chose

archaeology as a major. One of his fondest memories of her was the long afternoons she had spent under the front porch when she was about two, digging in the loam, ignoring spiders and googlepeds, rushing into the house to show off every plastic plate and tarnished pfennig she had excavated, demanding to know where it had come from, what were the people like who had left it there?'

Rachel received her undergraduate degree when she was nineteen standard, worked that summer on her grandmother's farm, and farcast away the next fall. She was at Reichs University on Freeholm for twenty-eight local months, and when she returned it was as if color had flowed back into Sol and Sarai's world.

For two weeks their daughter – an adult now, self-aware and secure in some ways that grown-ups twice her age often failed to be – rested and reveled in being home. One evening, walking across the campus just after sunset, she pressed her father on details of his heritage. 'Dad, do you still consider yourself a Jew?'

Sol had run his hand over his thinning hair, surprised by the question. 'A Jew? Yes, I suppose so. It doesn't mean what it once did, though.'

'Am I a Jew?' asked Rachel. Her cheeks glowed in the fragile light.

'If you want to be,' said Sol. 'It doesn't have the same significance with Old Earth gone.'

'If I'd been a boy, would you have had me circumcised?'

Sol had laughed, delighted and embarrassed by the question.

'I'm serious,' said Rachel.

Sol adjusted his glasses. 'I guess I would have, kiddo. I never thought about it.'

'Have you been to the synagogue in Bussard?'

'Not since my bar mitzvah,' said Sol, thinking back to the day fifty years earlier when his father had borrowed Uncle Richard's Vikken and had flown the family to the capital for the ritual.

'Dad, why do Jews feel that things are . . . less important now than before the Hegira?'

Sol spread his hands – strong hands, more those of a stoneworker than an academic. 'That's a good question, Rachel. Probably because so much of the dream is dead. Israel is gone. The New Temple lasted less time than the first and second. God broke His word by destroying the Earth a second time in the way He did. And this Diaspora is . . . forever.'

'But Jews maintain their ethnic and religious identity in some places,' his daughter insisted.

'Oh, sure. On Hebron and isolated areas of the Concourse you can find entire communities . . . Hasidic, Orthodox, Hasmonean, you name it . . . but they tend to be . . . nonvital, picturesque . . . tourist-oriented.'

'Like a theme park?'

'Yes.'

'Could you take me to Temple Beth-el tomorrow? I can borrow Khaki's strat.'

'No need,' said Sol. 'We'll use the college's shuttle.' He paused. 'Yes,' he said at last, 'I would like to take you to the synagogue tomorrow.'

It was getting dark under the old elms. Streetlights came on up and down the wide lane which led to their home.

'Dad,' said Rachel, 'I'm going to ask you a question I've asked about a million times since I was two. Do you believe in God?'

Sol had not smiled. He had no choice but to give her the answer he had given her a million times. 'I'm waiting to,' he said.

Rachel's postgraduate work dealt with alien and pre-Hegira artifacts. For three standard years Sol and Sarai would receive occasional visits followed by fatline flimsies from exotic worlds near but not within the Web. They all knew that her field work in quest of dissertation would soon take her beyond the Web, into the Outback where time-debt ate away at the lives and memories of those left behind.

'Where the hell is Hyperion?' Sarai had asked during Rachel's last vacation before the expedition left. 'It sounds like a brand name for some new household product.'

'It's a great place, Mom. There are more nonhuman artifacts there than any place except Armaghast.'

'Then why not go to Armaghast?' said Sarai. 'It's only a few months from the Web. Why settle for second best?'

'Hyperion hasn't become the big tourist attraction yet,' said Rachel. 'Although they're beginning to become a problem. People with money are more willing to travel outside the Web now.'

Sol had found his voice suddenly husky. 'Will you be going to the labyrinth or the artifacts called the Time Tombs?'

'The Time Tombs, Dad. I'll be working with Dr Melio Arundez and he knows more about the Tombs than anyone alive.'

'Aren't they dangerous?' asked Sol, framing the question as casually as he could but hearing the edge in his voice.

Rachel smiled. 'Because of the Shrike legend? No. Nobody's been bothered by that particular legend for two standard centuries.'

'But I've seen documents about the trouble there during the second colonization . . .' began Sol.

'Me too, Dad. But they didn't know about the big rock eels that came down into the desert to hunt. They probably lost a few people to those things and panicked. *You* know how legends begin. Besides, the rock eels have been hunted to extinction.'

'Spacecraft don't land there,' persisted Sol. 'You have to sail to the Tombs. Or hike. Or some damn thing.'

Rachel laughed. 'In the early days, people flying in underestimated the effects of the anti-entropic fields and there were some accidents. But there's dirigible service now. They have a big hotel called Keep Chronos at the north edge of the mountains where hundreds of tourists a year stay.'

'Will you be staying there?' asked Sarai.

'Part of the time. It'll be *exciting*, Mom.'

'Not too exciting, I hope,' said Sarai and all of them had smiled.

* * *

264

During the four years that Rachel was in transit – a few weeks of cryogenic fugue for her – Sol found that he missed his daughter much more than if she had been out of touch but busy somewhere in the Web. The thought that she was flying away from him faster than the speed of light, wrapped in the artificial quantum cocoon of the Hawking effect, seemed unnatural and ominous to him.

They kept busy. Sarai retired from the critic business to devote more time to local environmental issues, but for Sol it was one of the most hectic times of his life. His second and third books came out and the second one – *Moral Turning Points* – caused such a stir that he was in constant demand at offworld conferences and symposia. He traveled to a few alone, to a few more with Sarai, but although both of them enjoyed the *idea* of traveling, the actual experience of facing strange foods, different gravities, and the light from strange suns all paled after a while and Sol found himself spending more time at home researching his next book, attending conferences, if he had to, via interactive holo from the college.

It was almost five years after Rachel left on her expedition that Sol had a dream which would change his life.

Sol dreamed that he was wandering through a great structure with columns the size of small redwood trees and a ceiling lost to sight far above him, through which red light fell in solid shafts. At times he caught glimpses of things far off in the gloom to his left or right: once he made out a pair of stone legs rising like massive buildings through the darkness; another time he spied what appeared to be a crystal scarab rotating far above him, its insides ablaze with cool lights.

Finally Sol stopped to rest. Far behind him he could hear what sounded like a great conflagration, entire cities and forests burning. Ahead of him glowed the lights he had been walking toward, two ovals of deepest red.

He was mopping sweat from his brow when an immense voice said to him:

'Sol! Take your daughter, your only daughter
Rachel, whom you love, and go to the world called
Hyperion and offer her there as a burnt offering
at one of the places of which I shall tell you.'

And in his dream Sol had stood and said, 'You can't be
serious.' And he had walked on through darkness, the
red orbs glowing now like bloody moons hanging above
an indistinct plain, and when he stopped to rest the
immense voice said:

'Sol! Take your daughter, your only daughter
Rachel, whom you love, and go to the world called
Hyperion and offer her there as a burnt offering at
one of the places of which I shall tell you.'

And Sol had shrugged off the weight of the voice and had
said distinctly into the darkness, 'I heard you the first
time . . . the answer is still no.'

Sol knew he was dreaming then, and part of his mind
enjoyed the irony of the script, but another part wanted
only to waken. Instead, he found himself on a low balcony looking down on a room where Rachel lay naked on
a broad block of stone. The scene was illuminated by the
glow of the twin red orbs. Sol looked down at his right
hand and found a long, curved knife there. The blade
and handle appeared to be made of bone.

The voice, sounding more than ever to Sol like some
cut-rate holie director's shallow idea of what God's voice
should sound like, came again:

'Sol! You must listen well. The future of humankind depends upon your obedience in this matter.
You must take your daughter, your daughter Rachel whom you love, and go to the world called
Hyperion and offer her there as a burnt offering at
one of the places of which I shall tell you.'

And Sol, sick of the whole dream yet somehow alarmed
by it, had turned and thrown the knife far into the darkness. When he turned back to find his daughter, the

266

scene had faded. The red orbs hung closer than ever, and now Sol could see that they were multifaceted gems the size of small worlds.

The amplified voice came again:

'So? You have had your chance, Sol Weintraub. If you change your mind, you know where to find me.'

And Sol awakened half laughing, half chilled by the dream. Amused by the thought that the entire Talmud and the Old Testament might be nothing more than a cosmic shaggy-dog story.

About the time Sol was having his dream, Rachel was on Hyperion finishing her first year of research there. The team of nine archaeologists and six physicists had found Keep Chronos fascinating but far too crowded with tourists and would-be Shrike pilgrims, so after the first month spent commuting from the hotel, they had set up a permanent camp between the ruined city and the small canyon holding the Time Tombs.

While half the team excavated the more recent site of the unfinished city, two of Rachel's colleagues helped her catalogue every aspect of the Tombs. The physicists were finished with the anti-entropic fields and spent much of their time setting small flags of different colors to mark the limits of the so-called time tides.

Rachel's team concentrated their work in the structure called the Sphinx, although the creature represented in stone was neither human nor lion; it may not have been a creature at all, although the smooth lines atop the stone monolith suggested curves of a living thing, and the sweeping appendages made everyone think of wings. Unlike the other Tombs, which lay open and were easily inspected, the Sphinx was a mass of heavy blocks honeycombed with narrow corridors, some of which tightened to impossibility, some of which widened to auditorium-sized proportions, but none of which led anywhere but back on themselves. There were no crypts, treasure rooms, plundered sarcophogi, wall murals, or secret passages, merely a maze of senseless corridors through sweating stone.

Rachel and her lover, Melio Arundez, began mapping the Sphinx, using a method which had been in use for at least seven hundred years, having been pioneered in the Egyptian pyramids sometime in the twentieth century. Arranging sensitive radiation and cosmic ray detectors at the lowest point in the Sphinx, they recorded arrival times and deflection patterns of the particles passing through the mass of stone above them, watching for hidden rooms or passages which would not show up even on deep imaging radar. Because of the busy tourist season and the concern of the Hyperion Home Rule Council that the Tombs might be damaged by such research, Rachel and Melio went out to their site every night at midnight, making the half-hour walk and crawl through the corridor maze which they had rigged with blue glow-globes. There, sitting under hundreds of thousands of tons of stone, they would watch their instruments until morning, listening to their earphones ping with the sound of particles born in the belly of dying stars.

The time tides had not been a problem with the Sphinx. Of all the Tombs, it seemed the least protected by the anti-entropic fields and the physicists had carefully mapped the times when the tide surges might pose a threat. High tide was at 1000 hours, receding only twenty minutes later back toward the Jade Tomb half a kilometer to the south. Tourists were not allowed near the Sphinx until after 1200 hours, and to leave a margin of safety, the site made sure they were out by 0900. The physics team had planted chronotropic sensors at various points along the paths and walkways between the Tombs, both to alert the monitors to variations of the tides and to warn the visitors.

With only three weeks to go of her year of research on Hyperion, Rachel awoke one night, left her sleeping lover, and took a ground effect jeep from the camp to the Tombs. She and Melio had decided that it was foolish for both of them to monitor the equipment every night; now they alternated, one working at the site while the other collated data and prepared for the final project – a radar mapping of the dunes between the Jade Tomb and the Obelisk.

The night was cool and beautiful. A profusion of stars stretched from horizon to horizon, four or five times the number Rachel had grown up looking at from Barnard's World. The low dunes whispered and shifted in the strong breeze blowing from the mountains in the south.

Rachel found lights still burning at the site. The physics team was just calling it a day loading their own jeep. She chatted with them, had a cup of coffee as they drove away, and then took her backpack and made the twenty-five-minute trip into the basement of the Sphinx.

For the hundredth time Rachel wondered who had built the Tombs and for what purpose. Dating of the construction materials had been useless because of the effect of the anti-entropic field. Only analysis of the Tombs in relation to the erosion of the canyon and other surrounding geological features had suggested an age of at least half a million years. The feeling was that the architects of the Time Tombs had been humanoid, even though nothing but the gross scale of the structures suggested such a thing. Certainly the passageways in the Sphinx revealed little: some were human enough in size and shape, but then meters farther along the same corridor might dwindle to a tube the size of a sewer pipe and then transform itself into something larger and more random than a natural cavern. Doorways, if they could be called such since they opened to nothing in particular, might be triangular or trapezoidal or ten-sided as commonly as rectangular.

Rachel crawled the last twenty meters down a steep slope, sliding her backpack ahead of her. The heatless glow-globes gave the rock and her flesh a bluish, bloodless cast. The 'basement,' when she reached it, seemed a haven of human clutter and smells. Several folding chairs filled the center of the small space while detectors, oscilloscopes, and other paraphernalia lined the narrow table against the north wall. A plank on sawhorses along the opposite wall held coffee cups, a chess set, a half-eaten doughnut, two paperbacks, and a plastic toy of some sort of dog in a grass skirt.

Rachel settled in, set her coffee therm next to the toy, and checked the cosmic ray detectors. The data appeared to be the same: no hidden rooms or passages, just a few niches even the deep radar had missed. In the morning Melio and Stefan would set a deep probe working, getting an imager filament in and sampling the air before digging further with a micro-manipulator. So far a dozen such niches had turned up nothing of interest. The joke at camp was that the next hole, no bigger than a fist, would reveal miniature sarcophagi, undersized urns, a petite mummy, or – as Melio put it – 'a teeny-tiny Tutankhamen.'

Out of habit, Rachel tried the comm links on her comlog. Nothing. Forty meters of stone tended to do that. They had talked of stringing telephone wire from the basement to the surface, but there had been no pressing need and now their time was almost up. Rachel adjusted the input channels on her comlog to monitor the detector data and then settled back for a long, boring night.

There was the wonderful story of the Old Earth pharaoh – was it Cheops? – who authorized his huge pyramid, agreed to the burial chamber being deep under the center of the thing, and then lay awake nights for years in a claustrophobic panic, thinking of all those tons of stone above him for all eternity. Eventually the pharaoh ordered the burial chamber repositioned two thirds the way up the great pyramid. Most unorthodox. Rachel could understand the king's position. She hoped that – wherever he was – he slept better now.

Rachel was almost dozing herself when – at 0215 – her comlog chirped, the detectors screamed, and she jumped to her feet. According to the sensors, the Sphinx had suddenly grown a dozen new chambers, some larger than the total structure. Rachel keyed displays and the air misted with models that changed as she watched. Corridor schematics twisted back on themselves like rotating Möbius strips. The external sensors indicated the upper structure twisting and bending like polyflex in the wind – or like wings.

Rachel knew that it was some type of multiple

malfunction, but even as she tried to recalibrate she called data and impressions into her comlog. Then several things happened at once.

She heard the drag of feet in the corridor above her.

All of the displays went dead simultaneously.

Somewhere in the maze of corridors a time-tide alarm began to blare.

All of the lights went off.

This final event made no sense. The instrument packages held their own power supplies and would have stayed lit through a nuclear attack. The lamp they used in the basement had a new ten-year power cell. The glowglobes in the corridors were bioluminescent and needed no power.

Nonetheless, the lights were out. Rachel pulled a flashlight laser out of the knee pocket of her jumpsuit and triggered it. Nothing happened.

For the first time in her life, terror closed on Rachel Weintraub like a hand on her heart. She could not breathe. For ten seconds she willed herself to be absolutely still, not even listening, merely waiting for the panic to recede. When it had subsided enough for her to breathe without gasping, she felt her way to the instruments and keyed them. They did not respond. She lifted her comlog and thumbed the diskey. Nothing . . . which was impossible, of course, given the solid-state invulnerability and power-cell reliability of the thing. Still, nothing.

Rachel could hear her pulse pounding now but she again fought back the panic and began feeling her way toward the only exit. The thought of finding her way through the maze in absolute darkness made her want to scream but she could think of no other alternatives.

Wait. There had been old lights throughout the Sphinx maze but the research team had strung the glow-globes. *Strung* them. There was a perlon line connecting them all the way to the surface.

Fine. Rachel groped her way toward the exit, feeling the cold stone under her fingers. Was it this cold before?

There came the clear sound of something sharp scraping its way down the access shaft.

'Melio?' called Rachel into the blackness. 'Tanya? Kurt?'

The scraping sounded very close. Rachel backed away, knocking over an instrument and chair in the blackness. Something touched her hair and she gasped, raised her hand.

The ceiling was lower. The solid block of stone, five meters square, slid lower even as she raised her other hand to touch it. The opening to the corridor was half-way up the wall. Rachel staggered toward it, swinging her hands in front of her like a blind person. She tripped over a folding chair, found the instrument table, fol-lowed it to the far wall, felt the bottom of the corridor shaft disappearing as the ceiling came lower. She pulled back her fingers a second before they were sliced off.

Rachel sat down in the darkness. An oscilloscope scraped against the ceiling until the table cracked and collapsed under it. Rachel moved her head in short, des-perate arcs. There was a metallic rasp – almost a breath-ing sound – less than a meter from her. She began to back away, sliding across a floor suddenly filled with broken equipment. The breathing grew louder.

Something sharp and infinitely cold grasped her wrist. Rachel screamed at last.

There was no fatline transmitter on Hyperion in those days. Nor did the spinship *HS Farraux City* have FTL-comm capability. So the first Sol and Sarai heard of their daughter's accident was when the Hegemony consulate on Parvati fatlined the college that Rachel had been injured, that she was stable but unconscious, and that she was being transferred from Parvati to the Web world of Renaissance Vector via medical torchship. The trip would take a little over ten days' shiptime with a five-month time-debt. Those five months were agony for Sol and his wife, and by the time the medical ship put in at the Renaissance farcaster nexus, they had imagined the worst a thousand times. It had been eight years since they had last seen Rachel.

The Med Center in DaVinci was a floating tower sus-tained by direct broadcast power. The view over the

Como Sea was breathtaking but neither Sol nor Sarai had time for it as they went from level to level in search of their daughter. Dr Singh and Melio Arundez met them in the hub of Intensive Care. Introductions were rushed.

'Rachel?' asked Sarai.

'Asleep,' said Dr Singh. She was a tall woman, aristocratic but with kind eyes. 'As far as we can tell, Rachel has suffered no physical . . . ah . . . injury. But she has been unconscious now for some seventeen standard weeks, her time. Only in the past ten days have her brain waves registered deep sleep rather than coma.'

'I don't understand,' said Sol. 'Was there an accident at the site? A concussion?'

'Something happened,' said Melio Arundez, 'but we're not sure what. Rachel was in one of the artifacts . . . alone . . . her comlog and other instruments recorded nothing out of the ordinary. But there was a surge in a phenomenon there known as anti-entropic fields . . .'

'The time tides,' said Sol. 'We know about them. Go on.'

Arundez nodded and opened his hands as if molding air. 'There was a . . . field surge . . . more like a tsunami than a tide . . . the Sphinx . . . the artifact Rachel was in . . . was totally inundated. I mean, there was no *physical* damage but Rachel was unconscious when we found her . . .' He turned to Dr Singh for help.

'Your daughter was in a coma,' said the doctor. 'It was not possible to put her into cryogenic fugue in that condition . . .'

'So she came through quantum leap without fugue?' demanded Sol. He had read about the psychological damage to travelers who had experienced the Hawking effect directly.

'No, no,' soothed Singh. 'She was unconscious in a way which shielded her quite as well as fugue state.'

'Is she *hurt*?' demanded Sarai.

'We don't know,' said Singh. 'All life signs have returned to near normal. Brain-wave activity is nearing a conscious state. The problem is that her body appears to have absorbed . . . that is, the anti-entropic field appears to have contaminated her.'

Sol rubbed his forehead. 'Like radiation sickness?'

Dr Singh hesitated. 'Not precisely . . . ah . . . this case is quite unprecedented. Specialists in aging diseases are due in this afternoon from Tau Ceti Center, Lusus, and Metaxas.'

Sol met the woman's gaze. 'Doctor, are you saying that Rachel contracted some aging disease on Hyperion?' He paused a second to search his memory. 'Something like Methuselah syndrome or early Alzheimer's disease?'

'No,' said Singh, 'in fact your daughter's illness has no name. The medics here are calling it Merlin's sickness. You see . . . your daughter is aging at a normal rate . . . but as far as we can tell, she is aging backward.'

Sarai pulled away from the group and stared at Singh as if the doctor were insane. 'I want to see my daughter,' she said, quietly but very firmly. 'I want to see Rachel *now*.'

Rachel awakened less than forty hours after Sol and Sarai arrived. Within minutes she was sitting up in bed, talking even while the medics and technicians bustled around her. '*Mom! Dad!* What are you doing here?' Before either could answer, she looked around her and blinked. 'Wait a minute, where's *here*? Are we in Keats?'

Her mother took her hand. 'We're in a hospital in DaVinci, dear. On Renaissance Vector.'

Rachel's eyes widened almost comically. 'Renaissance. We're in the *Web*?' She looked around her in total bewilderment.

'Rachel, what is the last thing you remember?' asked Dr Singh.

The young woman looked uncomprehendingly at the medic. 'The last thing I . . . I remember going to sleep next to Melio after . . .' She glanced at her parents and touched her cheeks with the tips of her fingers. 'Melio? The others? Are they . . .'

'Everyone on the expedition is all right,' soothed Dr Singh. 'You had a slight accident. About seventeen weeks have passed. You're back in the Web. Safe. Everyone in your party is all right.'

274

'Seventeen *weeks* . . .' Under the fading remnant of her tan, Rachel went very pale.

Sol took her hand. 'How do you feel, kiddo?' The return pressure on his fingers was heartbreakingly weak.

'I don't know, Daddy,' she managed. 'Tired. Dizzy. *Confused.*'

Sarai sat on the bed and put her arms around her. 'It's all right, baby. Everything's going to be all right.'

Melio entered the room, unshaven, his hair rumpled from the nap he had been taking in the outer lounge. 'Rache?'

Rachel looked at him from the safety of her mother's arm. 'Hi,' she said, almost shyly. 'I'm back.'

Sol's opinion had been and continued to be that medicine hadn't really changed much since the days of leeches and poultices; nowadays they whirred one in centrifuges, realigned the body's magnetic field; bombarded the victim with sonic waves, tapped into the cells to interrogate the RNA, and then admitted their ignorance without actually coming out and saying so. The only thing that had changed was that the bills were bigger.

He was dozing in a chair when Rachel's voice awoke him.

'Daddy?'

He sat up, reached for her hand. 'Here, kiddo.'

'Where am I, Dad? What's happened?'

'You're in a hospital on Renaissance, baby. There was an accident on Hyperion. You're all right now except it's affecting your memory a bit.'

Rachel clung to his hand. 'A hospital? In the Web? How'd I get here? How long have I been here?'

'About five weeks,' whispered Sol. 'What's the last thing you remember, Rachel?'

She sat back on her pillows and touched her forehead, feeling the tiny sensors there. 'Melio and I had been at the meeting. Talking with the team about setting up the search equipment in the Sphinx. Oh . . . Dad . . . I haven't told you about Melio . . . he's . . .'

'Yes,' said Sol and handed Rachel her comlog. 'Here, kiddo. Listen to this.' He left the room.

Rachel touched the diskey and blinked as her own voice began talking to her. 'OK, Rache, you just woke up. You're confused. You don't know how you got here. Well, something's happened to you, kid. Listen up.

'I'm recording this on the twelfth day of Tenmonth, year 457 of the Hegira, A.D. 2739 old reckoning. Yes, I *know* that's half a standard year from the last thing you remember. Listen.

'Something happened in the Sphinx. You got caught up in the time tide. It changed you. You're aging backward, as dumb as that sounds. Your body's getting younger every minute, although that's not the important part right now. When you sleep . . . when *we* sleep . . . you forget. You lose another day from your memory *before* the accident, and you lose everything since. Don't ask me why. The doctors don't know. The experts don't know. If you want an analogy, just think of a tapeworm virus . . . one of the old kind . . . that's chewing up the data in your comlog . . . *backward* from the last entry.

'They don't know why the memory loss hits you when you sleep, either. They tried stay-awakes, but after about thirty hours you just go catatonic for a while and the virus does its thing anyway. So what the hell.

'You know something? This talking about yourself in the third person is sort of therapeutic. Actually, I'm lying here waiting for them to take me up to imaging, knowing I'll fall asleep when I get back . . . knowing I'll forget *everything* again . . . and it scares the shit out of me.

'OK, key the diskey for short-term and you get a prepared spiel here that should catch you up on everything since the accident. Oh . . . Mom and Dad are both here and they know about Melio. But *I* don't know as much as I used to. When did we first make love with him, mmm? The second month on Hyperion? Then we have just a few weeks left, Rachel, and then we'll be just acquaintances. Enjoy your memories while you can, girl.

'This is yesterday's Rachel, signing off.'

Sol came in to find his daughter sitting upright in the bed, still grasping the comlog tightly, her face pale and terrified. 'Daddy . . .'

He went to sit next to her and let her cry . . . for the twentieth night in a row.

Eight standard weeks after she arrived on Renaissance, Sol and Sarai waved goodbye to Rachel and Melio at the Da Vinci farcaster multiport and then farcast home to Barnard's World.

'I don't think she should have left the hospital,' muttered Sarai as they took the evening shuttle to Crawford. The continent was a patchwork of harvest-ready right angles below them.

'Mother,' said Sol, touching her knee, 'the doctors would have kept her there forever. But they're doing it for their own curiosity now. They've done everything they can to help her . . . nothing. She has a life to live.'

'But why go away with . . . with him?' said Sarai. 'She barely knows him.'

Sol sighed and leaned back against the cushions of his seat. 'In two weeks she won't remember him at all,' he said. 'At least in the way they share now. Look at it from her position, Mother. Fighting every day to reorient herself in a world gone mad. She's twenty-five years old and in love. Let her be happy.'

Sarai turned her face to the window and together, not speaking, they watched the red sun hang like a tethered balloon on the edge of evening.

Sol was well into the second semester when Rachel called. It was a one-way message via farcaster cable from Freeholm and her image hung in the center of the old holopit like a familiar ghost.

'Hi, Mom. Hi, Dad. Sorry I haven't written or called the past few weeks. I guess you know that I've left the university. And Melio. It was dumb to try to take new graduate-level stuff. I'd just forget Tuesday whatever was discussed Monday. Even with disks and comlog prompts it was a losing battle. I may enroll in the under-graduate program again . . . I remember *all* of it! Just kidding.

'It was just too hard with Melio, too. Or so my notes tell me. It wasn't *his* fault, I'm sure of that. He was

277

gentle and patient and loving to the end. It's just that . . . well, you can't start from scratch on a relationship every *day*. Our apartment was filled with photos of us, notes I wrote to myself about us, holos of us on Hyperion, but . . . you know. In the morning he would be an absolute stranger. By afternoon I began to believe what we'd had, even if I couldn't remember. By evening I'd be crying in his arms . . . then, sooner or later, I'd go to sleep. It's better this way.'

Rachel's image paused, turned as if she was going to break contact, and then steadied. She smiled at them. 'So anyway, I've left school for a while. The Freeholm Med Center wants me full time but they'd have to get in line . . . I got an offer from the Tau Ceti Research Institute that's hard to turn down. They offer a . . . I think they call it a "research honorarium" . . . that's bigger than what we paid for four years at Nightenhelser and all of Reichs combined.

'I turned them down. I'm still going in as an out-patient, but the RNA transplant series just leaves me with bruises and a depressed feeling. Of course, I could just be depressed because every morning I can't remember where the bruises came from. Ha-ha.

'Anyway, I'll be staying with Tanya for a while and then maybe . . . I thought maybe I'd come home for a while. Secondmonth's my birthday . . . I'll be twenty-two again. Weird, huh? At any rate, it's a lot easier being around people I know and I met Tanya just after I trans-ferred here when I was twenty-two . . . I think you understand.

'So . . . is my old room still here, Mom, or have you turned it into a mah-jongg parlor like you've always threatened? So write or give me a call. Next time I'll shell out the money for two-way so we can really talk. I just . . . I guess I thought . . .'

Rachel waved. 'Gottago. See you later, alligators. I love you both.'

Sol flew to Bussard City the week before Rachel's birth-day to pick her up at the world's only public farcaster terminex. He saw her first, standing with her luggage

278

near the floral clock. She looked young but not noticeably younger than when they had waved goodbye on Renaissance Vector. No, Sol realized, there was something less *confident* about her posture. He shook his head to rid himself of such thoughts, called to her, and ran to hug her.

The look of shock on her face when he released her was so profound that he could not ignore it. 'What is it, sweetie? What's wrong?'

It was one of the few times he had ever seen his daughter totally at a loss for words.

'I . . . you . . . I forgot,' she stammered. She shook her head in a familiar way and managed to laugh and cry at the same instant. 'You look a little different is all, Dad. I *remember* leaving here like it was . . . literally . . . yesterday. When I saw . . . your hair . . .' Rachel covered her mouth.

Sol ran his hand across his scalp. 'Ah, yes,' he said, suddenly close to laughing and crying himself. 'With your school and travels, it's been more than eleven years. I'm old. And bald.' He opened his arms again. 'Welcome back, little one.'

Rachel moved into the protective circle of his embrace.

For several months things went well. Rachel felt more secure with familiar things around, and for Sarai the heartbreak of their daughter's illness was temporarily offset by the pleasure of having her home again.

Rachel rose early every morning and viewed her private 'orientation show' which, Sol knew, contained images of him and Sarai a dozen years older than she remembered. He tried to imagine what it was like for Rachel: she awoke in her own bed, memory fresh, twenty-two years old, home on vacation before going offworld to graduate school, only to find her parents suddenly aged, a hundred small changes in the house and town, the news different . . . years of history having passed her by.

Sol could not imagine it.

Their first mistake was acceding to Rachel's wishes in inviting her old friends to her twenty-second birthday party: the same crew who had celebrated the first time – irrepressible Niki, Don Stewart and his friend Howard, Kathi Obeg and Marta Tyn, her best friend Linna McKyler – all of them then just out of college, shucking off cocoons of childhood for new lives.

Rachel had seen them all since her return. But she had slept . . . and forgotten. And Sol and Sarai this one time did not remember that she had forgotten.

Niki was thirty-four standard, with two children of her own – still energetic, still irrepressible, but ancient by Rachel's standards. Don and Howard talked about their investments, their children's sports accomplishments, and their upcoming vacations. Kathi was confused, speaking only twice to Rachel and then as if she was speaking to an impostor. Marta was openly jealous of Rachel's youth. Linna, who had become an ardent Zen Gnostic in the years between, cried and left early.

When they had gone, Rachel sat in the postparty ruin of the living room and stared at the half-eaten cake. She did not cry. Before going upstairs she hugged her mother and whispered to her father, 'Dad, please don't let me do anything like that again.'

Then she went upstairs to sleep.

It was that spring when Sol again had the dream. He was lost in a great, dark place, lighted only by two red orbs. It was not absurd when the flat voice said:

'Sol. Take your daughter, your only Rachel, whom you love, and go to the world called Hyperion and offer her there as a burnt offering at one of the places of which I shall tell you.'

And Sol had screamed into the darkness:

'You already have her, you son of a bitch! What do I have to do to get her back? Tell me! Tell me, goddamn you!'

And Sol Weintraub woke sweating with tears in his eyes and anger in his heart. In the other room he could feel his daughter sleeping while the great worm devoured her.

*   *   *

In the months which followed Sol became obsessive about obtaining information on Hyperion, the Time Tombs, and the Shrike. As a trained researcher, he was astounded that there were so little hard data on so provocative a topic. There was the Church of the Shrike, of course – there were no temples on Barnard's World but many in the Web – but he soon found that seeking hard information in Shrike cult literature was like trying to map the geography of Sarnath by visiting a Buddhist monastery. Time was mentioned in Shrike Church dogma, but only in the sense that the Shrike was supposed to be '. . . the Angel of Retribution from Beyond Time' and that true time had ended for the human race when Old Earth died and that the four centuries since had been 'false time.' Sol found their tracts the usual combination of double talk and navel lint-gathering common to most religions. Still, he planned to visit a Shrike Church temple as soon as he had explored more serious avenues of research.

Melio Arundez launched another Hyperion expedition, also sponsored by Reichs University, this one with the stated goal of isolating and understanding the time-tide phenomenon which had inflicted the Merlin sickness on Rachel. A major development was the Hegemony Protectorate's decision to send along on that expedition a fatline transmitter for installation at the Hegemony consulate in Keats. Even so, it would be more than three years' Web time before the expedition arrived on Hyperion. Sol's first instinct was to go with Arundez and his team – certainly any holodrama would have the primary characters returning to the scene of the action. But Sol overrode the instinctive urge within minutes. He was a historian and philosopher; any contribution he might make to the expedition's success would be minute, at best. Rachel still retained the interest and skills of a well-trained undergraduate archaeologist-to-be, but those skills dwindled a bit each day and Sol could see no benefit to her returning to the site of the accident. Each day would be a shock to her, awakening on a strange world, on a mission which would require skills unknown to her. Sarai would not allow such a thing.

Sol set aside the book he was working on – an analysis of Kierkegaard's theories of ethics as compromise morality as applied to the legal machinery of the Hegemony – and concentrated on collecting arcane data on time, on Hyperion, and on the story of Abraham.

Months spent carrying on business as usual and collecting information did little to satisfy his need for action. Occasionally he vented his frustration on the medical and scientific specialists who came to examine Rachel like streams of pilgrims to a holy shrine.

'How the hell can this be happening!' he screamed at one little specialist who had made the mistake of being both smug and condescending to the patient's father. The doctor had a head so hairless, his face looked like lines painted on a billiard ball. 'She's begun growing smaller!' Sol shouted, literally buttonholing the retreating expert. 'Not so one can see, but bone mass is decreasing. How can she even *begin* to become a child again? What the *hell* does that do to the law of conservation of mass?'

The expert had moved his mouth but had been too rattled to speak. His bearded colleague answered for him. 'M. Weintraub,' he said, 'sir. You have to understand that your daughter is currently inhabiting . . . ah . . . think of it as a localized region of reversed entropy.'

Sol wheeled on the other man. 'Are you saying that she is merely stuck in a bubble of backwardness?'

'Ah . . . no,' said the colleague, massaging his chin nervously. 'Perhaps a better analogy is that . . . biologically at least . . . the life/metabolism mechanism has been reversed . . . ah . . .'

'Nonsense,' snapped Sol. 'She doesn't excrete for nutrition or regurgitate her food. And what about all the neurological activity? Reverse the electrochemical impulses and you get nonsense. Her brain *works*, gentlemen . . . it's her memory that is disappearing. Why, gentlemen? Why?'

The specialist finally found his voice. 'We don't know why, M. Weintraub. Mathematically, your daughter's body resembles a time-reversed equation . . . or perhaps an object which has passed through a rapidly spinning black hole. We don't know *how* this has happened or *why* the physically impossible is occurring in this instance, M. Weintraub. We just don't know enough.'

Sol shook each man's hand. 'Fine. That's all I wanted to know, gentlemen. Have a good trip back.'

On Rachel's twenty-first birthday she came to Sol's door an hour after they had all turned in. 'Daddy?'

'What is it, kiddo?' Sol pulled on his robe and joined her in the doorway. 'Can't sleep?'

'I haven't slept for two days,' she whispered. 'Been taking stay-awakes so I can get through all of the briefing stuff I left in the Wanta Know? file.'

Sol nodded.

'Daddy, would you come downstairs and have a drink with me? I've got some things I want to talk about.'

Sol got his glasses from the nightstand and joined her downstairs.

It proved to be the first and only time that Sol would get drunk with his daughter. It was not a boisterous drunk – for a while they chatted, then began telling jokes and making puns, until each was giggling too hard to continue. Rachel started to tell another story, sipped her drink just at the funniest part, and almost snorted whiskey out her nose, she was laughing so hard. Each of them thought it was the funniest thing that had ever happened.

'I'll get another bottle,' said Sol when the tears had ceased. 'Dean Moore gave me some Scotch last Christmas . . . I think.'

When he returned, walking carefully, Rachel had sat up on the couch and brushed her hair with her fingers. He poured her a small amount and the two drank in silence for a while.

'Daddy?'

'Yes?'

'I went through the whole thing. Saw myself, listened to myself, saw the holos of Linna and the others all middle-aged . . .'

'Hardly middle-aged,' said Sol. 'Linna will be thirty-five next month . . .'

'Well, *old*, you know what I mean. Anyway, I read the medical briefs, saw the photos from Hyperion, and you know what?'

'What?'

'I don't believe any of it, Dad.'

Sol put down his drink and looked at his daughter. Her face was fuller than before, less sophisticated. And even more beautiful.

'I mean, I *do* believe it,' she said with a small, scared laugh. 'It's not like you and Mom would put on such a cruel joke. Plus there's your . . . your age . . . and the news and all. I know it's *real*, but I don't *believe* it. Do you know what I mean, Dad?'

'Yes,' said Sol.

'I mean I woke up this morning and I thought, *Great . . . tomorrow's the paleontology exam and I've hardly studied.* I was looking forward to showing Roger Sherman a thing or two . . . he thinks he's so *smart*.'

Sol took a drink. 'Roger died three years ago in a plane crash south of Bussard,' he said. He would not have spoken without the whiskey in him, but he had to find out if there was a Rachel hiding within the Rachel.

'I know,' said Rachel and pulled her knees up to her chin. 'I accessed everybody I knew. Gram's dead. Professor Eikhardt isn't teaching anymore. Niki married some . . . *salesman*. A lot happens in four years.'

'More than eleven years,' said Sol. 'The trip to and from Hyperion left you six years behind us stay-at-homes.'

'But that's normal,' cried Rachel. 'People travel outside the Web all the time. *They* cope.'

Sol nodded. 'But this is different, kiddo.'

Rachel managed a smile and drained the last of her whiskey. 'Boy, what an understatement.' She set the glass down with a sharp, final sound. 'Look, here's what I've decided. I've spent two and a half days going through all of the stuff she . . . I . . . prepared to let me know what's happened, what's going on . . . and *it just doesn't help.*'

Sol sat perfectly still, not even daring to breathe.

'I mean,' said Rachel, 'knowing that I'm getting

younger every day, losing the memory of people I haven't even *met* yet . . . I mean, what happens next? I just keep getting younger and smaller and less capable until I just *disappear* someday? Jesus, Dad.' Rachel wrapped her arms more tightly around her knees. 'It's sort of funny in a weird way, isn't it?'

'No,' Sol said quietly.

'No, I'm sure it's not,' said Rachel. Her eyes, always large and dark, were moist. 'It must be the worst nightmare in the world for you and Mom. Every day you have to watch me come down the stairs . . . confused . . . waking up with yesterday's memories but hearing my own voice tell me that yesterday was *years* ago. That I had a love affair with some guy named Amelio . . .'

'Melio,' whispered Sol.

'Whatever. It just doesn't *help*, Dad. By the time I can even begin to absorb it, I'm so worn out that I have to sleep. Then . . . well, you know what happens then.'

'What . . .' began Sol and had to clear his throat. 'What do you want us to do, little one?'

Rachel looked him in the eye and smiled. It was the same smile she had gifted him with since her fifth week of life. 'Don't tell me, Dad,' she said firmly. 'Don't let *me* tell me. It just hurts. I mean, I didn't *live* those times . . .' She paused and touched her forehead. 'You know what I mean, Dad. The Rachel who went to another planet and fell in love and got hurt . . . that was *a different Rachel*! I shouldn't have to suffer her pain.' She was crying now. 'Do you understand? Do you?'

'Yes,' said Sol. He opened his arms and felt her warmth and tears against his chest. 'Yes, I understand.'

Fatline messages from Hyperion came frequently the next year but they were all negative. The nature and source of the anti-entropic fields had not been found. No unusual time-tide activity had been measured around the Sphinx. Experiments with laboratory animals in and around the tidal regions had resulted in sudden death for some animals, but the Merlin sickness had not been replicated. Melio ended every message with 'My love to Rachel.'

*   *   *

Sol and Sarai used money loaned from Reichs University to receive limited Poulsen treatments in Bussard City. They were already too old for the process to extend their lives for another century, but it restored the look of a couple approaching fifty standard rather than seventy. They studied old family photos and found that it was not too difficult to dress the way they had a decade and a half before.

Sixteen-year-old Rachel tripped down the stairs with her comlog tuned to the college radio station. 'Can I have rice cereal?'

'Don't you have it every morning?' smiled Sarai.

'Yes,' grinned Rachel. 'I just thought we might be out or something. I heard the phone. Was that Niki?'

'No,' said Sol.

'Damn,' said Rachel and glanced at them. 'Sorry. But she *promised* she'd call as soon as the standardized scores came in. Three weeks since tutorials. You'd think I'd have heard *some*thing.'

'Don't worry,' said Sarai. She brought the coffeepot to the table, started to pour Rachel a cup, poured it for herself. 'Don't worry, honey. I promise you that your scores will be good enough to get you into any school you want.'

'*Mom*,' sighed Rachel. 'You don't *know*. It's a dog-eat-dog world out there.' She frowned. 'Have you seen my math ansible? My room was all messed around. I couldn't find *any*thing.'

Sol cleared his throat. 'No classes today, kiddo.'

Rachel stared. 'No classes? On a Tuesday? Six weeks from graduation? What's up?'

'You've been sick,' Sarai said firmly. 'You can stay home one day. Just today.'

Rachel's frown deepened. 'Sick? I don't feel sick. Just sort of *weird*. Like things aren't . . . aren't right somehow. Like why's the couch moved around in the media room? And where's Chips? I called and called but he didn't come.'

Sol touched his daughter's wrist. 'You've been sick for a while,' he said. 'The doctor said you might wake up with a few gaps. Let's talk while we walk over to the campus. Want to?'

Rachel brightened. 'Skip classes and go to the college? Sure.' She faked a look of consternation. 'As long as we don't run into Roger Sherman. He's taking freshman calculus up there and he's such a *pain*.'

'We won't see Roger,' said Sol. 'Ready to go?'

'Almost.' Rachel leaned over and gave her mother a huge hug. ' 'Later alligator.'

' 'While, crocodile,' said Sarai.

'Okay,' grinned Rachel, her long hair bouncing. 'I'm ready.'

The constant trips to Bussard City had required the purchase of an EMV and on a cool day in autumn Sol took the slowest route, far below the traffic lanes, enjoying the sight and smell of the harvested fields below. More than a few men and women working in the fields waved to him.

Bussard had grown impressively since Sol's childhood, but the synagogue was still there on the edge of one of the oldest neighborhoods in the city. The temple was old, Sol felt old, even the yarmulke he put on as he entered seemed ancient, worn thin by decades of use, but the rabbi was young. Sol realized that the man was at least forty – his hair was thinning on either side of the dark skullcap – but to Sol's eyes he was little more than a boy. Sol was relieved when the younger man suggested that they finish their conversation in the park across the street.

They sat on a park bench. Sol was surprised to find himself still carrying the yarmulke, passing the cloth from hand to hand. The day smelled of burning leaves and the previous night's rain.

'I don't quite understand, M. Weintraub,' said the rabbi. 'Is it the dream you're disturbed about or the fact that your daughter has become ill since you began the dream?'

Sol raised his head to feel the sunlight on his face. 'Neither, exactly,' he said. 'I just can't help but feel that the two are connected somehow.'

287

The rabbi ran a finger over his lower lip. 'How old is your daughter?'

'Thirteen,' said Sol after an imperceptible pause.

'And is the illness . . . serious? Life threatening?'

'Not life threatening,' said Sol. 'Not yet.'

The rabbi folded his arms across an ample belly. 'You don't believe . . . may I call you Sol?'

'Of course.'

'Sol, you don't believe that by having this dream . . . that somehow you've caused your little girl's illness. Do you?'

'No,' said Sol and sat a moment, wondering deep within if he was telling the truth. 'No, Rabbi, I don't think . . .'

'Call me Mort, Sol.'

'All right, Mort. I didn't come because I believe that I – or the dream – am causing Rachel's illness. But I believe my subconscious might be trying to tell me something.'

Mort rocked back and forth slightly. 'Perhaps a neuro-specialist or psychologist could help you more there, Sol. I'm not sure what I . . .'

'I'm interested in the story of Abraham,' interrupted Sol. 'I mean, I've had some experience with different ethical systems, but it's hard for me to understand one which began with the order to a father to slay his son.'

'No, no, no!' cried the rabbi, waving oddly childlike fingers in front of him. 'When the time came, God stayed Abraham's hand. He would not have allowed a human sacrifice in His name. It was the *obedience* to the will of the Lord that . . .'

'Yes,' said Sol. 'Obedience. But it says, "Then Abraham put forth his hand, and took the knife to slay his son." God must have looked into his soul and seen that Abraham *was* ready to slay Isaac. A mere show of obedience without inner commitment would not have appeased the God of Genesis. What would have happened if Abraham had loved his son more than he loved God?'

Mort drummed his fingers on his knee a moment and then reached out to grasp Sol's upper arm. 'Sol, I can see you're upset about your daughter's illness. Don't get it mixed up with a document written eight thousand years ago. Tell me more about your little girl. I mean, children don't *die* of diseases anymore. Not in the Web.'

Sol rose, smiled, and stepped back to free his arm. 'I'd like to talk more, Mort. I want to. But I have to get back. I have a class this evening.'

'Will you come to temple this Sabbath?' asked the rabbi, extending stubby fingers for a final human contact.

Sol dropped the yarmulke into the younger man's hands. 'Perhaps one of these days, Mort. One of these days I will.'

Later the same autumn Sol looked out the window of his study to see the dark figure of a man standing under the bare elm in front of the house. *The media*, thought Sol, his heart sinking. For a decade he had been dreading the day the secret got out, knowing it would mean the end of their simple life in Crawford. He walked out into the evening chill. 'Melio!' he said when he saw the tall man's face.

The archaeologist stood with his hands in the pockets of his long blue coat. Despite the ten standard years since their last contact, Arundez had aged but little – Sol guessed that he was still in his late twenties. But the younger man's heavily tanned face was lined with worry. 'Sol,' he said and extended his hand almost shyly.

Sol shook his hand warmly. 'I didn't know you were back. Come into the house.'

'No.' The archaeologist took a half step back. 'I've been out here for an hour, Sol. I didn't have the courage to come to the door.'

Sol started to speak but then merely nodded. He put his hands in his own pockets against the chill. The first stars were becoming visible above the dark gables of the house. 'Rachel's not home right now,' he said at last. 'She went to the library. She . . . she thinks she has a history paper due.'

Melio took a ragged breath and nodded in return.

'Sol,' he said, his voice thick, 'you and Sarai need to understand that we did everything we could. The team was on Hyperion for almost three standard years. We would have stayed if the university hadn't cut our funds. There was *nothing* . . .'

'We know,' said Sol. 'We appreciated the fatline messages.'

'I spent months alone in the Sphinx myself,' said Melio. 'According to the instruments, it was just an inert pile of stones, but sometimes I thought I felt . . . *something*. . .' He shook his head again. 'I failed her, Sol.'

'No,' said Sol and gripped the younger man's shoulder through the wool coat. 'But I have a question. We've been in touch with our senators . . . even talked to the Science Council directors : . . but no one can explain to me why the Hegemony hasn't spent more time and money investigating the phenomena on Hyperion. It seems to me that they should have invested that world into the Web long ago, if only for its scientific potential. How can they ignore an enigma like the Tombs?'

'I know what you mean, Sol. Even the early cutoff of our funds was suspicious. It's as if the Hegemony had a policy to keep Hyperion at arm's length.'

'Do you think . . .' began Sol but at the moment Rachel approached them in the autumn twilight. Her hands were thrust deep in her red jacket, her hair was cut short in the decades-old style of adolescents everywhere, and her full cheeks were flushed with the cold. Rachel was teetering on the brink of childhood and young adulthood; her long legs in jeans, sports shoes, and bulky jacket might have been the silhouette of a boy.

She grinned at them. 'Hi, Dad.' Stepping closer in the dim light, she nodded at Melio shyly. 'Sorry, didn't mean to interrupt your conversation.'

Sol took a breath. 'That's all right, kiddo. Rachel, this is Dr Arundez from Reichs University on Freeholm. Dr Arundez, my daughter Rachel.'

'Pleased to meet you,' said Rachel, beaming in earnest now. 'Wow, Reichs. I've read their catalogues. I'd *love* to go there someday.'

Melio nodded rigidly. Sol could see the stiffness in his

shoulders and torso. 'Do you . . .' began Melio. 'That is, what would you like to study there?'

Sol thought the pain in the man's voice must be audible to Rachel but she only shrugged and laughed. 'Oh, jeez, *everything*. Old Mr Eikhardt – he's the paleontology/archaeology tute in the advanced class I take up at the Ed Center – he says they have a *great* classics and ancient artifacts department.'

'They do,' managed Melio.

Rachel glanced shyly from her father to the stranger, apparently sensing the tension there but not knowing the source. 'Well, I'm just interrupting your conversation more here. I've got to get in and get to bed. I guess I've had this strange virus . . . sort of like meningitis, Mom says, only it must make me sort of goofy. Anyway, nice to meet you, Dr Arundez. I hope I'll see you at Reichs someday.'

'I hope that too,' said Melio, staring at her so intensely in the gloom that Sol had the feeling he was trying to memorize everything about the instant.

'Okay, well . . .' said Rachel and stepped back, her rubber-soled shoes squeaking on the sidewalk, 'good night, then. See you in the morning, Dad.'

'Good night, Rachel.'

She paused at the doorway. The gaslight on the lawn made her look much younger than thirteen. ' 'Later, alligators.'

' 'While, crocodile,' said Sol and heard Melio whisper it in unison.

They stood awhile in silence, feeling the night settle on the small town. A boy on a bicycle rode by, leaves crackling under his wheels, spokes gleaming in the pools of light under the old streetlamps. 'Come in the house,' Sol said to the silent man. 'Sarai will be very pleased to see you. Rachel will be asleep.'

'Not now,' said Melio. He was a shadow there, his hands still in his pockets. 'I need to . . . it was a mistake, Sol.' He started to turn away, looked back. 'I'll phone when I get to Freeholm,' he said. 'We'll get another expedition put together.'

Sol nodded. *Three years transit*, he thought. *If they*

left tonight she would be . . . not quite ten before they arrive. 'Good,' he said.

Melio paused, raised a hand in farewell, and walked away along the curb, ignoring the leaves that crunched underfoot.

Sol never saw him in person again.

The largest Church of the Shrike in the Web was on Lusus and Sol farcast there a few weeks before Rachel's tenth birthday. The building itself was not much larger than an Old Earth cathedral, but it seemed gigantic with its effect of flying buttresses in search of a church, twisted upper stories, and support walls of stained glass. Sol's mood was low and the brutal Lusian gravity did nothing to lighten it. Despite his appointment with the bishop, Sol had to wait more than five hours before he was allowed into the inner sanctum. He spent most of the time staring at the slowly rotating twenty-meter, steel and polychrome sculpture which might have been of the legendary Shrike . . . and might have been an abstract homage to every edged weapon ever invented. What interested Sol the most were the two red orbs floating within the nightmare space which might have been a skull.

'M. Weintraub?'

'Your Excellency,' said Sol. He noticed that the acolytes, exorcists, lectors, and ostiaries who had kept him company during the long wait had prostrated themselves on the dark tiles at the high priest's entry. Sol managed a formal bow.

'Please, please, do come in, M. Weintraub,' said the priest. He indicated the doorway to the Shrike sanctuary with a sweep of his robed arm.

Sol passed through, found himself in a dark and echoing place not too dissimilar from the setting of his recurrent dream, and took a seat where the bishop indicated. As the cleric moved to his own place at what looked like a small throne behind an intricately carved but thoroughly modern desk, Sol noticed that the high priest was a native Lusian, gone to fat and heavy in the jowls, but formidable in the way all Lusus residents seemed to be. His robe was striking in its redness . . . a bright, arterial red, flowing more like a contained liquid than like silk or velvet, trimmed in onyx ermine. The bishop wore a large ring on each finger and they alternated red and black, producing a disturbing effect in Sol.

'Your Excellency,' began Sol, 'I apologize in advance for any breach in church protocol which I have committed . . . or may commit. I confess I know little about the Church of the Shrike, but what I do know has brought me here. Please forgive me if I inadvertently display my ignorance by my clumsy use of titles or terms.'

The bishop wiggled his fingers at Sol. Red and black stones flashed in the weak light. 'Titles are unimportant, M. Weintraub. Addressing us as "Your Excellency" is quite acceptable for a nonbeliever. We must advise you, however, that the formal name of our modest group is the Church of the Final Atonement and the entity whom the world so blithely calls . . . the Shrike . . . we refer to . . . if we take His name at all . . . as the Lord of Pain or, more commonly, the Avatar. Please proceed with the important query you said you had for us.'

Sol bowed slightly. 'Your Excellency, I am a teacher . . .'

'Excuse us for interrupting, M. Weintraub, but you are much more than a teacher. You are a scholar. We are very familiar with your writings on moral hermeneutics. The reasoning therein is flawed but quite challenging. We use it regularly in our courses in doctrinal apologetics. Please proceed.'

Sol blinked. His work was almost unknown outside the most rarefied academic circles and this recognition had thrown him. In the five seconds it took him to recover, Sol found it preferable to believe that the Shrike bishop wanted to know with whom he spoke and had an excellent staff. 'Your Excellency, my background is immaterial. I asked to see you because my child . . . my daughter . . . has taken ill as a possible result of research she was carrying out in an area which is of some importance to your Church. I speak, of course, of the so-called Time Tombs on the world of Hyperion.'

The bishop nodded slowly. Sol wondered if he knew about Rachel.

'You are aware, M. Weintraub, that the area you referred to . . . what we call the Covenant Arks . . . has recently been declared off limits to so-called researchers by the Home Rule Council of Hyperion?'

'Yes, Your Excellency. I have heard that. I understand that your Church was instrumental in that legislation being passed.'

The bishop showed no response to this. Far off in the incense-layered gloom, small chimes sounded.

'At any rate, Your Excellency, I hoped that some aspect of your Church's doctrine might shed light on my daughter's illness.'

The bishop inclined his head forward so that the single shaft of light which illuminated him gleamed on his forehead and cast his eyes into shadow. 'Do you wish to receive religious instruction in the mysteries of the Church, M. Weintraub?'

Sol touched his beard with a finger. 'No, Your Excellency, unless in so doing I might improve the wellbeing of my daughter.'

'And does your daughter wish to be initiated into the Church of the Final Atonement?'

Sol hesitated a beat. 'Again, Your Excellency, she wishes to be well. If joining the Church would heal or help her, it would be a very serious consideration.'

The bishop sat back in a rustle of robes. Redness seemed to flow from him into the gloom. 'You speak of *physical* wellbeing, M. Weintraub. Our Church is the final arbiter of *spiritual* salvation. Are you aware that the former invariably flows from the latter?'

'I am aware that this is an old and widely respected proposition,' said Sol. 'The total wellbeing of our daughter is the concern of my wife and myself.'

The bishop rested his massive head on his fist. 'What is the nature of your daughter's illness, M. Weintraub?'

'It is . . . a time-related illness, Your Excellency.'

The bishop sat forward, suddenly tense. 'And at which of the holy sites did you say your daughter contracted this malady, M. Weintraub?'

'The artifact called the Sphinx, Your Excellency.'

The bishop stood so quickly that papers on his desk-top were knocked to the floor. Even without the robes, the man would have massed twice Sol's weight. In the fluttering red robes, stretched to his full height, the Shrike priest now towered over Sol like crimson death incarnate. 'You can go!' bellowed the big man. 'Your daughter is the most blessed and cursed of individuals. There is nothing that you or the Church . . . or any agent in this life . . . can do for her.'

Sol stood . . . or, rather, sat . . . his ground. 'Your Excellency, if there is any possibility . . .'

'NO!' cried the bishop, red in the face now, a consummately consistent apparition. He tapped at his desk. Exorcists and lectors appeared in the doorway, their black robes with red trim an ominous echo of the bishop. The all-black ostiaries blended with the shadows. 'The audience is at an end,' said the bishop with less volume but infinite finality. 'Your daughter has been chosen by the Avatar to atone in a way which all sinners and nonbelievers must someday suffer. Someday very soon.'

'Your Excellency, if I can have just five minutes more of your time . . .'

The bishop snapped his fingers and the exorcists came forward to escort Sol out. The men were Lusian. One of them could have handled five scholars Sol's size.

'Your Excellency . . .' cried Sol after he had shrugged off the first man's hands. The three other exorcists came to assist with the equally brawny lectors hovering nearby. The bishop had turned his back and seemed to be staring into the darkness.

The outer sanctuary echoed to grunts and the scraping of Sol's heels and to at least one loud gasp as Sol's foot made contact with the least priestly parts of the lead exorcist. The outcome of the debate was not affected. Sol landed in the street. The last ostiary to turn away tossed Sol's battered hat to him.

Ten more days on Lusus achieved nothing but more gravity fatigue for Sol. The Temple bureaucracy would not answer his calls. The courts could offer him no wedge. The exorcists waited just within the doors of the vestibule.

Sol farcast to New Earth and Renaissance Vector, to Fuji and TC², to Deneb Drei and Deneb Vier, but everywhere the Shrike temples were closed to him.

Exhausted, frustrated, out of money, Sol 'cast home to Barnard's World, got the EMV out of the long-term lot, and arrived home an hour before Rachel's birthday.

'Did you bring me anything, Daddy?' asked the excited ten-year-old. Sarai had told her that day that Sol had been gone.

Sol brought out the wrapped package. It was the collected *Anne of Green Gables* series. It was not what he had wanted to bring her.

'Can I open it?'

'Later, little one. With the other things.'

'Oh, *please*, Dad. Just one thing now. Before Niki and the other kids get here?'

Sol caught Sarai's eye. She shook her head. Rachel remembered inviting Niki and Linna and her other friends to the party only days before. Sarai had not yet come up with an excuse.

'All right, Rachel,' he said. 'Just this one before the party.'

While Rachel ripped into the small package, Sol saw the giant package in the living room, secured with red ribbon. The new bike, of course. Rachel had asked for the new bike for a year before her tenth birthday. Sol tiredly wondered if she would be surprised tomorrow to find the new bike here the day *before* her tenth birthday. Or perhaps they would get rid of the bike that night, while Rachel slept.

Sol collapsed onto the couch. The red ribbon reminded him of the bishop's robes.

Sarai had never had an easy time of surrendering the past. Every time she cleaned and folded and put away a set of Rachel's outgrown baby clothes, she had shed secret tears that Sol somehow knew about. Sarai had treasured every stage of Rachel's childhood, enjoying the day-to-day *normalcy* of things; a normalcy which she quietly accepted as the best of life. She had always felt that the essence of human experience lay not primarily in the peak experiences, the wedding days and triumphs which stood out in the memory like dates circled in red on old calendars, but, rather, in the unselfconscious flow of little things – the weekend afternoon with each member of the family engaged in his or her own pursuit, their crossings and connections casual, dialogues imminently forgettable, but the *sum* of such hours creating a synergy which was important and eternal.

Sol found Sarai in the attic, weeping softly as she went through boxes. These were not the gentle tears once shed for the ending of small things. Sarai Weintraub was *angry*.

'What are you doing, Mother?'

'Rachel needs clothes. Everything is too big. What fit on an eight-year-old won't fit a seven-year-old. I have some more of her things here somewhere.'

'Leave it,' said Sol. 'We'll buy something new.'

Sarai shook her head. 'And have her wonder every day where all of her favorite clothes have gone? No. I've saved some things. They're here somewhere.'

'Do it later.'

'Damn it, there *is* no later!' shouted Sarai and then turned away from Sol and raised her hands to her face. 'I'm sorry.'

Sol put his arms around her. Despite the limited Poulsen treatments, her bare arms were much thinner than he remembered. Knots and cords under rough skin. He hugged her tightly.

'I'm sorry,' she repeated, sobbing openly now. 'It's just not *fair*.'

'No,' agreed Sol. 'It's not fair.' The sunlight coming through the dusty attic panes had a sad, cathedral quality to it. Sol had always loved the smell of an attic – the hot and stale *promise* of a place so underused and filled with future treasures. Today it was ruined.

He crouched next to a box. 'Come, dear,' he said, 'we'll look together.'

* * *

Rachel continued to be happy, involved with life, only slightly confused by the incongruities which faced her each morning when she awoke. As she grew younger it became easier to explain away the changes that appeared to have occurred overnight – the old elm out front gone, the new apartment building on the corner where M. Nesbitt used to live in a colonial-era home, the absence of her friends – and Sol began to see as never before the flexibility of children. He now imagined Rachel living on the breaking crest of the wave of time, not seeing the murky depths of the sea beyond, keeping her balance with her small store of memories and a total commitment to the twelve to fifteen hours of *now* allowed her each day.

Neither Sol nor Sarai wanted their daughter isolated from other children and it was difficult to find ways to make contact. Rachel was delighted to play with the 'new girl' or 'new boy' in the neighborhood – children of other instructors, the grandchildren of friends, for a while with Niki's daughter – but the other children had to grow accustomed to Rachel greeting them anew each day, remembering nothing of their common past, and only a few had the sensitivity to continue such a charade for the sake of a playmate.

The story of Rachel's unique illness was no secret in Crawford, of course. The fact of it had spread through the college the first year of Rachel's return and the entire town knew soon after. Crawford reacted in the fashion of small towns immemorial – some tongues wagged constantly, some people could not keep the pity and pleasure at someone else's misfortune out of their voices and gazes – but mostly the community folded its protective wings around the Weintraub family like an awkward mother bird shielding its young.

Still, they were allowed to live their lives, and even when Sol had to cut back classes and then take an early retirement because of trips seeking medical treatment for Rachel, the real reason was mentioned by no one.

But it could not last, of course, and on the spring day when Sol stepped onto the porch and saw his weeping seven-year-old daughter coming back from the park surrounded and followed by a pack of newsteeps, their camera implants gleaming and comlogs extended, he knew that a phase of their life was over forever. Sol jumped from the porch and ran to Rachel's side.

'M. Weintraub, is it true that your daughter contracted a terminal time illness? What's going to happen in seven years? Will she just disappear?'

'M. Weintraub! M. Weintraub! Rachel says that she thinks Raben Dowell is Senate CEO and this is the year A.D. 2711. Has she lost those thirty-four years completely or is this a delusion caused by the Merlin sickness?'

'Rachel! Do you remember being a grown woman? What's it feel like to be a kid again?'

'M. Weintraub! M. Weintraub! Just one still image, please. How about you get a picture of Rachel when she was older and you and the kid stand looking at it?'

'M. Weintraub! Is it true that this is the curse of the Time Tombs? Did Rachel see the Shrike monster?'

'Hey, Weintraub! Sol! Hey, Solly! What're you and the little woman going to do when the kid's gone?'

There was a newsteep blocking Sol's way to the front door. The man leaned forward, the stereo lenses of his eyes elongating as they zoomed in for a close-up of Rachel. Sol grabbed the man's long hair – which was conveniently tied in a queue – and flung him aside.

The pack brayed and bellowed outside the house for seven weeks. Sol realized what he had known and forgotten about very small communities: they were frequently annoying, always parochial, sometimes prying on a one-to-one level, but never had they subscribed to the vicious legacy of the so-called 'public's right to know.'

The Web did. Rather than have his family become permanent prisoners to the besieging reporters, Sol went on the offensive. He arranged interviews on the most pervasive farcaster cable news programs, participated in All Thing discussions, and personally attended the Concourse Medical Research Conclave. In ten standard months he asked for help for his daughter on eighty worlds.

Offers poured in from ten thousand sources but the bulk of the communications were from faith healers, project promoters, institutes and free-lance researchers offering their services in exchange for the publicity, Shrike cultists and other religious zealots pointing out that Rachel deserved the punishment, requests from various advertising agencies for product endorsements, offers from media agents to 'handle' Rachel for such endorsements, offers of sympathy from common people – frequently enclosing credit chips, expressions of disbelief from scientists, offers from holie producers and book publishers for exclusive rights to Rachel's life, and a barrage of real estate offers.

Reichs University paid for a team of evaluators to sort the offers and see if anything might benefit Rachel. Most of the communications were discarded. A few medical or research offers were seriously considered. In the end, none seemed to offer any avenue of research or experimental therapy which Reichs had not already tried. One fatline flimsy came to Sol's attention. It was from the Chairman of Kibbutz K'far Shalom on Hebron and read simply:

IF IT BECOMES TOO MUCH, COME.

It soon became too much. After the first few months of publicity the siege seemed to lift, but this was only the prelude to the second act. Faxsimmed tabloids referred to Sol as the 'Wandering Jew,' the desperate father wandering afar in search of a cure for his child's bizarre illness – an ironic title given Sol's lifelong dislike of travel. Sarai inevitably was 'the grieving mother.' Rachel was 'the doomed child' or, in one inspired headline, 'Virgin Victim of the Time Tombs' Curse.' None of the family could go outside without finding a newsteep or imager hiding behind a tree.

Crawford discovered that there was money to be found in the Weintraubs' misfortune. At first the town held the line, but when entrepreneurs from Bussard City moved in with gift shops, T-shirt concessions, tours, and datachip booths for the tourists who were coming in larger and larger numbers, the local business people first dithered, then wavered, then decided unanimously that, if there was commerce to be carried on, the profits should not go to outsiders.

After four hundred and thirty-eight standard years of comparative solitude, the town of Crawford received a farcaster terminex. No longer did visitors have to suffer the twenty-minute flight from Bussard City. The crowds grew.

On the day they moved it rained heavily and the streets were empty. Rachel did not cry, but her eyes were very wide all day and she spoke in subdued tones. It was ten days before her sixth birthday. 'But, Daddy, *why* do we have to move?'

'We just do, honey.'

'But *why*?'

'It's something we have to do, little one. You'll like Hebron. There are lots of parks there.'

'But how come you never *said* we were going to move?'

'We did, sweetie. You must have forgotten.'

'But what about Gram and Grams and Uncle Richard and Aunt Tetha and Uncle Saul and everybody?'

'They can come visit us any time.'

'But what about Niki and Linna and my *friends*?'

Sol said nothing but carried the last of the luggage to the EMV. The house was sold and empty; furniture had been sold or sent ahead to Hebron. For a week there had been a steady stream of family and old friends, college associates, and even some of the Reichs med team who had worked with Rachel for eighteen years, but now the street was empty. Rain streaked the Perspex canopy of the old EMV and ran in complex rivulets. The three of them sat in the vehicle for a moment, staring at the house. The interior smelled of wet wool and wet hair.

Rachel clutched the teddy bear Sarai had resurrected from the attic six months earlier. She said, 'It's not fair.'

'No,' agreed Sol. 'It's not fair.'

Hebron was a desert world. Four centuries of terraforming had made the atmosphere breathable and a few million acres of land arable. The creatures which had lived there before were small and tough and infinitely wary, and so were the creatures imported from Old Earth, including the human kind.

'Ahh,' gasped Sol the day they arrived in the sun-baked village of Dan above the sun-baked kibbutz of K'far Shalom, 'what masochists we Jews are. Twenty thousand surveyed worlds fit for our kind when the Hegira began, and those schmucks came here.'

But it was not masochism which brought either the first colonists or Sol and his family. Hebron was mostly desert, but the fertile areas were almost frighteningly fertile. Sinai University was respected throughout the Web and its Med Center brought in wealthy patients and a healthy income for the cooperative. Hebron had a single farcaster terminex in New Jerusalem and allowed portals nowhere else. Belonging to neither the Hegemony nor Protectorate, Hebron taxed travelers heavily for farcaster privilege and allowed no tourists outside New Jerusalem. For a Jew seeking privacy, it was perhaps the safest place in three hundred worlds trod by man.

The kibbutz was more a cooperative by tradition than in operation. The Weintraubs were welcomed to their own home – a modest place offering sun-dried adobe, curves instead of right angles, and bare wood floors, but also offering a view from the hill which showed an infinite expanse of desert beyond the orange and olive groves. The sun seemed to dry up everything, thought Sol, even worries and bad dreams. The light was a physical thing. In the evening their house glowed pink for an hour after the sun had set.

Each morning Sol sat by his daughter's bed until she awoke. The first minutes of her confusion were always painful to him, but he made sure that he was the first thing Rachel saw each day. He held her while she asked her questions.

'Where are we, Daddy?'

'In a wonderful place, little one. I'll tell you all about it over breakfast.'

'How did we get here?'

'By 'casting and flying and walking a bit,' he would say. 'It's not so far away . . . but far enough to make it an adventure.'

'But my bed's here . . . my stuffed animals . . . why don't I remember coming?'

And Sol would hold her gently by the shoulders and look into her brown eyes and say, 'You had an accident, Rachel. Remember in *The Homesick Toad* where Terrence hits his head and forgets where he lives for a few days? It was sort of like that.'

'Am I better?'

'Yes,' Sol would say, 'you're all better now.' And the house would fill with the smell of breakfast and they would go out to the terrace where Sarai waited.

Rachel had more playmates than ever. The kibbutz cooperative had a school where she was always the welcomed visitor, greeted anew each day. In the long afternoons the children played in the orchards and explored along the cliffs.

Avner, Robert, and Ephraim, the Council elders, urged Sol to work on his book. Hebron prided itself on the number of scholars, artists, musicians, philosophers, writers and composers it sheltered as citizens and long-term residents. The house, they pointed out, was a gift of the state. Sol's pension, though small by Web standards, was more than adequate for their modest needs in K'far Shalom. To Sol's surprise, however, he found that he enjoyed physical labor. Whether working in the orchards or clearing stones in the unclaimed fields or repairing a wall above the city, Sol found that his mind and spirit were freer than they had been in many years. He discovered that he could wrestle with Kierkegaard while he waited for mortar to dry and find new insights in Kant and Vandeur while carefully checking the apples for worms. At the age of seventy-three standard, Sol earned his first calluses.

In the evenings he would play with Rachel and then take a walk in the foothills with Sarai as Judy or one of the other neighbor girls watched their sleeping child. One weekend they went away to New Jerusalem, just Sol

303

and Sarai, the first time they had been alone together for that long since Rachel returned to live with them seventeen standard years before.

But everything was not idyllic. Too frequent were the nights when Sol awoke alone and walked barefoot down the hall to see Sarai watching over Rachel in her sleep. And often at the end of a long day, bathing Rachel in the old ceramic tub or tucking her in as the walls glowed pinkly, the child would say, 'I like it here, Daddy, but can we go home tomorrow?' And Sol would nod. And after the good-night story, and the lullaby, and the good-night kiss, sure that she was asleep, he would begin to tiptoe out of the room only to hear the muffled ' 'Later, alligator' from the blanketed form on the bed, to which he had to reply ' 'While, crocodile.' And lying in bed himself, next to the softly breathing and possibly sleeping length of the woman he loved, Sol would watch the strips of pale light from one or both of Hebron's small moons move across the rough walls and he would talk to God.

Sol had been talking to God for some months before he realized what he was doing. The idea amused him. The dialogues were in no way prayers but took the form of angry monologues which – just short of the point where they became diatribes – became vigorous arguments with himself. Only not just with himself. Sol realized one day that the topics of the heated debates were so profound, the stakes to be settled so serious, the ground covered so broad, that the only person he could possibly be berating for such shortcomings was God Himself. Since the concept of a personal God, lying awake at night worrying about human beings, intervening in the lives of individuals, always had been totally absurd to Sol, the thought of such dialogues made him doubt his sanity.

But the dialogues continued.

Sol wanted to know how any ethical system – much less a religion so indomitable that it had survived every evil mankind could throw at it – could flow from a command from God for a man to slaughter his son. It did not matter to Sol that the command had been rescinded at the last moment. It did not matter that the command was a test of obedience. In fact, the idea that it was the *obedience* of Abraham which allowed him to become the father of all the tribes of Israel was precisely what drove Sol into fits of fury.

After fifty-five years of dedicating his life and work to the story of ethical systems, Sol Weintraub had come to a single, unshakable conclusion: any allegiance to a deity or concept or universal principle which put *obedience* above decent behavior toward an innocent human being was evil.

> — *So define 'innocent'?* came the vaguely amused, faintly querulous voice which Sol associated with these arguments.
> — A child is innocent, thought Sol. Isaac was. Rachel is.
> — *'Innocent' by the mere fact of being a child?*
> — Yes.
> — *And there is no situation where the blood of the innocent must be shed for a greater cause?*
> — No, thought Sol. None.
> — *But the 'innocent' are not restricted to children, I presume.*
> — Sol hesitated, sensing a trap, trying to see where his subconscious interlocutor was heading. He could not. No, he thought, the 'innocent' include others as well as children.
> — *Such as Rachel? At age twenty-four? The innocent should not be sacrificed at any age?*
> — That's right.
> — *Perhaps this is part of the lesson which Abraham needed to learn before he could be father to the blessed of the nations of the earth.*
> — What lesson? thought Sol. What lesson? But the voice in his mind had faded and now there were only the sounds of night birds outside and the soft breathing of his wife beside him.

Rachel could still read at age five. Sol had trouble remembering when she had learned to read – it seemed she always had been able to. 'Four standard,' said Sarai. 'It was early summer . . . three months after her birthday. We were picnicking in the field above the college, Rachel was looking at her *Winnie-the-Pooh* book, and suddenly she said, "I hear a voice in my head".'

Sol remembered then.

He also remembered the joy he and Sarai had felt at the rapid acquisition of new skills Rachel had shown at that age. He remembered because now they were confronted with the reverse of that process.

'Dad,' said Rachel from where she lay on the floor of his study, carefully coloring, 'how long has it been since Mom's birthday?'

'It was on Monday,' said Sol, preoccupied with something he was reading. Sarai's birthday had not yet come but Rachel remembered it.

'I *know*. But how long has it been since then?'

'Today is Thursday,' said Sol. He was reading a long Talmudic treatise on obedience.

'I *know*. But how many *days*?'

Sol put down the hard copy. 'Can you name the days of the week?' Barnard's World had used the old calendar.

'Sure,' said Rachel. 'Saturday, Sunday, Monday, Tuesday, Wednesday, Thursday, Friday, Saturday . . .'

'You said Saturday already.'

'Yeah. But how many *days* ago?'

'Can you count from Monday to Thursday?'

Rachel frowned, moved her lips. She tried again, counting on her fingers this time. 'Four days?'

'Good,' said Sol. 'Can you tell me what ten minus four is, kiddo?'

'What does minus mean?'

Sol forced himself to look at his papers again. 'Nothing,' he said. 'Something you'll learn at school.'

'When we go home tomorrow?'

'Yes.'

One morning when Rachel went off with Judy to play with the other children – she was too young to attend

306

school any longer – Sarai said: 'Sol, we have to take her to Hyperion.'

Sol stared at her. 'What?'

'You heard me. We can't wait until she is too young to walk . . . to talk. Also, we're not getting any younger.' Sarai barked a mirthless laugh. 'That sounds strange, doesn't it? But we're not. The Poulsen treatments will be wearing off in a year or two.'

'Sarai, did you forget? The doctors all say that Rachel could not survive cryogenic fugue. No one experiences FTL travel without fugue state. The Hawking effect can drive one mad . . . or worse.'

'It doesn't matter,' said Sarai. 'Rachel has to return to Hyperion.'

'What on earth are you talking about?' said Sol, angered.

Sarai gripped his hand. 'Do you think you're the only one who has had the dream?'

'Dream?' managed Sol.

She sighed and sat at the white kitchen table. Morning light struck the plants on the sill like a yellow spotlight. 'The dark place,' she said. 'The red lights above. The voice. Telling us to . . . telling us to take . . . to go to Hyperion. To make . . . an offering.'

Sol licked his lips but there was no moisture there. His heart pounded. 'Whose name . . . whose name is called?'

Sarai looked at him strangely. 'Both of our names. If you weren't there . . . in the dream with me . . . I could never have borne it all these years.'

Sol collapsed into his chair. He looked down at the strange hand and forearm lying on the table. The knuckles of the hand were beginning to enlarge with arthritis; the forearm was heavily veined, marked with liver spots. It was his hand, of course. He heard himself say: 'You never mentioned it. Never said a word . . .'

This time Sarai's laugh was without bitterness. 'As if I had to! All those times both of us coming awake in the dark. And you covered with sweat. I knew from the first time that it was not merely a dream. We have to go, Father. Go to Hyperion.'

Sol moved the hand. It still did not feel a part of him. 'Why? For God's sake, why, Sarai? We can't . . . *offer* Rachel . . .'

'Of course not, Father. Haven't you thought about this? We have to go to Hyperion . . . to wherever the dream tells us to go . . . and offer ourselves instead.'

'Offer ourselves,' repeated Sol. He wondered if he was having a heart attack. His chest ached so terribly that he could not take in a breath. He sat for a full minute in silence, convinced that if he attempted to utter a word only a sob would escape. After another minute he said: 'How long have you . . . thought about this, Mother?'

'Do you mean *known* what we must do? A year. A little more. Just after her fifth birthday.'

'A year! Why haven't you said something?'

'I was waiting for you. To realize. To *know*.'

Sol shook his head. The room seemed far away and slightly tilted. 'No. I mean, it doesn't seem . . . I have to *think*, Mother.' Sol watched as the strange hand patted Sarai's familiar hand.

She nodded.

Sol spent three days and nights in the arid mountains, eating only the thick-crusted bread he had brought and drinking from his condenser therm.

Ten thousand times in the past twenty years he had wished that *he* could take Rachel's illness; that if anyone had to suffer it should be the father, not the child. Any parent would feel that way – *did* feel that way every time his child lay injured or racked with fever. Surely it could not be that simple.

In the heat of the third afternoon, as he lay half dozing in the shade of a thin tablet of rock, Sol learned that it was *not* that simple.

— Can that be Abraham's answer to God? That *he* would be the offering, not Isaac?
— *It could have been Abraham's. It cannot be yours.*
— Why?

308

As if in answer, Sol had the fever-vision of naked adults filing toward the ovens past armed men, mothers hiding their children under piles of coats. He saw men and women with flesh hanging in burned strips carrying the dazed children from the ashes of what once had been a city. Sol knew that these images were no dreams, were the very stuff of the First and Second Holocausts, and in his understanding knew before the voice spoke in his mind what the answer was. What it must be.

— *The parents have offered themselves. That sacrifice already has been accepted. We are beyond that.*
— Then what? What!

Silence answered him. Sol stood in the full glare of the sun, almost fell. A black bird wheeled overhead or in his vision. Sol shook his fist at the gunmetal sky.

— You use Nazis as your instruments. Madmen. Monsters. You're a goddamn monster yourself.
— *No.*

The earth tilted and Sol fell on his side against sharp rocks. He thought that it was not unlike leaning against a rough wall. A rock the size of his fist burned his cheek.

— The correct answer for Abraham was obedience, thought Sol. Ethically, Abraham was a child himself. All men were at that time. The correct answer for Abraham's children was to become adults and to offer themselves instead. What is the correct answer for *us*?

There was no answer. The ground and sky quit spinning. After a while Sol rose shakily, rubbed the blood and grit from his cheek, and walked down to the town in the valley below.

'No,' Sol told Sarai, 'we will not go to Hyperion. It is not the correct solution.'

309

'You would have us do nothing then.' Sarai's lips were white with anger but her voice was firmly in control.

'No. I would have us not to do the *wrong* thing.'

Sarai expelled her breath in a hiss. She waved toward the window where their four-year-old was visible playing with her toy horses in the backyard. 'Do you think *she* has time for us to do the wrong thing . . . or anything . . . indefinitely?'

'Sit down, Mother.'

Sarai remained standing. There was the faintest sprinkling of spilled sugar on the front of her tan cotton dress. Sol remembered the young woman rising nude from the phosphorescent wake of the motile isle on Maui-Covenant.

'We have to do something,' she said.

'We've seen over a hundred medical and scientific experts. She's been tested, prodded, probed, and tortured by two dozen research centers. I've been to the Shrike Church on every world in this Web; they won't see me. Melio and the other Hyperion experts at Reichs say that the Shrike Cult has nothing like the Merlin sickness in their doctrine and the indigenies on Hyperion have no legends of the malady or clues to its cure. Research during the three years the team was on Hyperion showed nothing. Now research there is illegal. Access to the Time Tombs is granted only to the so-called pilgrims. Even getting a travel visa to Hyperion is becoming almost impossible. And if we take Rachel, the trip may kill her.'

Sol paused for breath, touched Sarai's arm again. 'I'm sorry to repeat all this, Mother. But we have done something.'

'Not enough,' said Sarai. 'What if we go as pilgrims?'

Sol folded his arms in frustration. 'The Church of the Shrike chooses its sacrificial victims from thousands of volunteers. The Web is full of stupid, depressed people. Few of these return.'

'Doesn't that prove something?' Sarai whispered quickly, urgently. 'Somebody or something is preying on these people.'

'Bandits,' said Sol.

Sarai shook her head. 'The golem.'

'You mean the Shrike.'

'It's the golem,' insisted Sarai. 'The same one we see in the dream.'

Sol was uneasy. 'I don't see a golem in the dream. What golem?'

'The red eyes that watch,' said Sarai. 'It's the same golem that Rachel heard that night in the Sphinx.'

'How do you know that she heard anything?'

'It's in the *dream*,' said Sarai. 'Before we enter the place where the golem waits.'

'We haven't dreamed the same dream,' said Sol. 'Mother, Mother . . . why haven't you told me this before?'

'I thought I was going mad,' whispered Sarai.

Sol thought of his secret conversations with God and put his arm around his wife.

'Oh, Sol,' she whispered against him, 'it hurts so much to watch. And it's so lonely here.'

Sol held her. They had tried to go home – home would always be Barnard's World – half a dozen times to visit family and friends, but each time the visits were ruined by an invasion of newsteeps and tourists. It was no one's fault. News traveled almost instantaneously through the megadatasphere of a hundred and sixty Web worlds. To scratch the curiosity itch one had only to pass a universal card across a terminex diskey and step through a farcaster. They had tried arriving unannounced and traveling incognito but they were not spies and the efforts were pitiful. Within twenty-four standard hours of their reentry to the Web, they were besieged. Research institutes and large med centers easily provided the security screen for such a visit, but friends and family suffered. Rachel was NEWS.

'Perhaps we could invite Tetha and Richard again . . .' began Sarai.

'I have a better idea,' said Sol. 'Go yourself, Mother. You want to see your sister but you also want to see, hear, and *smell* home . . . watch a sunset where there are no iguanas . . . walk in the fields. Go.'

'Go? Just me? I couldn't be away from Rachel . . .'

'Nonsense,' said Sol. 'Twice in twenty years – almost forty if we count the good days before . . . anyway, twice in twenty years doesn't constitute child neglect. It's a wonder that this family can stand one another, we've been cooped up together so long.'

Sarai looked at the tabletop, lost in thought. 'But wouldn't the news people find me?'

'I bet not,' said Sol. 'It's Rachel they seem to key on. If they do hound you, come home. But I bet you can have a week visiting everyone at home before the teeps catch on.'

'A week,' gasped Sarai. 'I couldn't . . .'

'Of course you can. In fact, you *must*. It will give me a few days to spend more time with Rachel and then when you come back refreshed I'll spend some days selfishly working on the book.'

'The Kierkegaard one?'

'No. Something I've been playing with called *The Abraham Problem*.'

'Clumsy title,' said Sarai.

'It's a clumsy problem,' said Sol. 'Now go get packed. We'll fly you to New Jerusalem tomorrow so you can 'cast out before the Sabbath begins.'

'I'll think about it,' she said, sounding unconvinced.

'You'll *pack*,' said Sol, hugging her again. When the hug was completed he had turned her away from the window so that she faced the hallway and the bedroom door. 'Go. When you return from home I'll have thought of something we *can* do.'

Sarai paused. 'Do you promise?'

Sol looked at her. 'I promise I will before time destroys everything. I swear as Rachel's father that I'll find a way.'

Sarai nodded, more relaxed than he had seen her in months. 'I'll go pack,' she said.

When he and the child returned from New Jerusalem the next day, Sol went out to water the meager lawn while Rachel played quietly inside. When he came in, the pink glow of sunset infusing the walls with a sense of sea warmth and quiet, Rachel was not in her bedroom or the other usual places. 'Rachel?'

When there was no answer he checked the backyard again, the empty street.

'Rachel!' Sol ran in to call the neighbors but suddenly there was the slightest of sounds from the deep closet Sarai used for storage. Sol quietly opened the screen panel.

Rachel sat beneath the hanging clothes, Sarai's antique pine box open between her legs. The floor was littered with photos and holochips of Rachel as a high school student, Rachel on the day she set off for college, Rachel standing in front of a carved mountainside on Hyperion. Rachel's research comlog lay whispering on the four-year-old Rachel's lap. Sol's heart seized at the familiar sound of the confident young woman's voice.

'Daddy,' said the child on the floor, her own voice a tiny frightened echo of the voice on the comlog, 'you never told me that I had a sister.'

'You don't, little one.'

Rachel frowned. 'Is this Mommy when she was . . . not so big? Uh-uh, it can't be. *Her* name's Rachel, too, she says. How can . . .'

'It's all right,' he said. 'I'll explain . . .' Sol realized that the phone was ringing in the living room, had been ringing. 'Just a moment, sweetie. I'll be right back.'

The holo that formed above the pit was of a man Sol had never seen before. Sol did not activate his own imager, eager to get rid of the caller. 'Yes?' he said abruptly.

'M. Weintraub? M. Weintraub who used to live on Barnard's World, currently in the village of Dan on Hebron?'

Sol started to disconnect and then paused. Their access code was unfiled. Occasionally a salesperson called from New Jerusalem, but offworld calls were rare. And, Sol suddenly realized, his stomach feeling a stab of cold, *it was past sundown on the Sabbath*. Only emergency holo calls were allowed.

'Yes?' said Sol.

'M. Weintraub,' said the man, staring blindly past Sol, 'there's been a terrible accident.'

When Rachel awoke her father was sitting by the side of her bed. He looked tired. His eyes were red and his cheeks were gray with stubble above the line of his beard.

'Good morning, Daddy.'

'Good morning, sweetheart.'

Rachel looked around and blinked. Some of her dolls and toys and things were there, but the room was not hers. The light was different. The air felt different. Her daddy looked different. 'Where are we, Daddy?'

'We've gone on a trip, little one.'

'Where to?'

'It doesn't matter right now. Hop out, sweetie. Your bath is ready and then we have to get dressed.'

A dark dress she had never seen before lay at the base of her bed. Rachel looked at the dress and then back at her father. 'Daddy, what's the matter? Where's Mommy?'

Sol rubbed his cheek. It was the third morning since the accident. It was the day of the funeral. He had told her each of the preceding days because he could not imagine lying to her then; it seemed the ultimate betrayal – of both Sarai and Rachel. But he did not think he could do it again. 'There's been an accident, Rachel,' he said, his voice a pained rasp. 'Mommy died. We're going to go say goodbye to her today.' Sol paused. He knew by now that it would take a minute for the fact of her mother's death to become real for Rachel. On the first day he had not known if a four-year-old could truly comprehend the concept of death. He knew now that Rachel could.

Later, as he held the sobbing child, Sol tried to understand the accident he had described so briefly to her. EMVs were by far the safest form of personal transportation mankind had ever designed. Their lifters could fail but, even so, the residual charge in the EM generators would allow the aircar to descend safely from any altitude. The basic, failsafe design of an EMV's

314

collision-avoidance equipment had not changed in centuries. But everything failed. In this case it was a joy-riding teenage couple in a stolen EMV outside the traffic lanes, accelerating to Mach 1.5 with all lights and transponders off to avoid detection, who defied all odds by colliding with Aunt Tetha's ancient Vikken as it descended toward the Bussard City Opera House landing apron. Besides Tetha and Sarai and the teenagers, three others died in the crash as pieces of falling vehicles cartwheeled into the crowded atrium of the Opera House itself.

Sarai.

'Will we ever see Mommy again?' Rachel asked between sobs. She had asked this each time.

'I don't know, sweetheart,' responded Sol truthfully.

The funeral was at the family cemetery in Kates County on Barnard's World. The press did not invade the graveyard itself but teeps hovered beyond the trees and pressed against the black iron gate like an angry storm tide.

Richard wanted Sol and Rachel to stay a few days, but Sol knew what pain would be inflicted on the quiet farmer if the press continued their assault. Instead, he hugged Richard, spoke briefly to the clamoring reporters beyond the fence, and fled to Hebron with a stunned and silent Rachel in tow.

Newsteeps followed to New Jerusalem and then attempted to follow to Dan, but military police overrode their chartered EMVs, threw a dozen in jail as an example, and revoked the farcaster visas of the rest.

In the evening Sol walked the ridge lines above the village while Judy watched his sleeping child. He found that his dialogue with God was audible now and he resisted the urge to shake his fist at the sky, to shout obscenities, to throw stones. Instead he asked questions, always ending with – Why?

There was no answer. Hebron's sun set behind distant ridges and the rocks glowed as they gave up their heat. Sol sat on a boulder and rubbed his temples with his palms.

Sarai.

They had lived a full life, even with the tragedy of Rachel's illness hanging over them. It was too ironic that in Sarai's first hour of relaxation with her sister . . . Sol moaned aloud.

The trap, of course, had been in their total absorption with Rachel's illness. Neither had been able to face the future beyond Rachel's . . . death? Disappearance? The world had hinged upon each day their child lived and no thought had been given to the chance of accident, the perverse antilogic of a sharp-edged universe. Sol was sure that Sarai had considered suicide just as he had, but neither of them could ever have abandoned the other. Or Rachel. He had never considered the possibility of being alone with Rachel when . . .

Sarai!

At that moment Sol realized that the often angry dialogue which his people had been having with God for so many millennia had not ended with the death of Old Earth . . . nor with the new Diaspora . . . but continued still. He and Rachel and Sarai had been part of it, were part of it now. He let the pain come. It filled him with the sharp-edged agony of resolve.

Sol stood on the ridge line and wept as darkness fell.

In the morning he was next to Rachel's bed when sunlight filled the room.

'Good morning, Daddy.'

'Good morning, sweetheart.'

'Where are we, Daddy?'

'We've gone on a trip. It's a pretty place.'

'Where's Mommy?'

'She's with Aunt Tetha today.'

'Will we see her tomorrow?'

'Yes,' said Sol. 'Now let's get you dressed and I'll make breakfast.'

Sol began to petition the Church of the Shrike when Rachel turned three. Travel to Hyperion was severely limited and access to the Time Tombs had become all but impossible. Only the occasional Shrike Pilgrimage sent people to that region.

Rachel was sad that she had to be away from her

mother on her birthday but the visit of several children from the kibbutz distracted her a bit. Her big present was an illustrated book of fairy tales which Sarai had picked out in New Jerusalem months before.

Sol read some of the stories to Rachel before bedtime. It had been seven months since she could read any of the words herself. But she loved the stories – especially 'Sleeping Beauty' – and made her father read it to her twice.

'I'm gonna show Mommy it when we get home,' she said through a yawn as Sol turned out the overhead light.

'Good night, kiddo,' he said softly, pausing at the door.

'Hey, Daddy?'

'Yes?'

' 'Later, alligator.'

' 'While, crocodile.'

Rachel giggled into her pillow.

It was, Sol thought during the final two years, not so much different from watching a loved one falling into old age. Only worse. A thousand times worse.

Rachel's permanent teeth had fallen out over intervals between her eighth and second birthdays. Baby teeth replaced them but by her eighteenth month half of these had receded into her jaw.

Rachel's hair, always her one vanity, grew shorter and thinner. Her face lost its familiar structure as baby fat obscured the cheekbones and firm chin. Her coordination failed by degrees, noticeable at first in a sudden clumsiness as she handled a fork or pencil. On the day she could no longer walk, Sol put her down in her crib early and then went into his study to get thoroughly and quietly drunk.

Language was the hardest for him. Her vocabulary loss was like the burning of a bridge between them, the severing of a final line of hope. It was sometime after her second birthday receded that Sol tucked her in and, pausing in the doorway, said, ' 'Later, alligator.'

'Huh?'

'See you later, alligator.

Rachel giggled.

'You say – "In a while, crocodile," ' said Sol. He told her what an alligator and crocodile were.

'In a while, 'acadile,' giggled Rachel.

In the morning she had forgotten.

Sol took Rachel with him as he traveled the Web – no longer caring about the newsteeps – petitioning the Shrike Church for pilgrimage rights, lobbying the Senate for a visa and access to forbidden areas on Hyperion, and visiting any research institute or clinic which might offer a cure. Months were lost while more medics admitted failure. When he fled back to Hebron, Rachel was fifteen standard months old; in the ancient units used on Hebron she weighed twenty-five pounds and measured thirty inches tall. She could no longer dress herself. Her vocabulary consisted of twenty-five words, of which her favorites were 'Mommy' and 'Daddy.'

Sol loved carrying his daughter. There were times when the curve of her head against his cheek, her warmth against his chest, the smell of her skin – all worked to allow him to forget the fierce injustice of it all. At those times Sol would have been temporarily at peace with the universe if only Sarai had been there. As it was, there were temporary cease-fires in his angry dialogue with a God in Whom he did not believe.

— What possible reason can there be for this?

— *What reason has been visible for all of the forms of pain suffered by humankind?*

— Precisely, thought Sol, wondering if he had just won a point for the first time. He doubted it.

— *The fact of a thing not being visible does not mean it does not exist.*

— That's clumsy. It shouldn't take three negatives to make a statement. Especially to state something as nonprofound as that.

318

— *Precisely, Sol. You're beginning to get the drift
  of all this.*
— What?

There was no answer to his thoughts. Sol lay in his
house and listened to the desert wind blow.

.

Rachel's last word was 'Mamma,' uttered when she was
just over five months old.

She awoke in her crib and did not – could not – ask
where she was. Her world was one of mealtimes, naps,
and toys. Sometimes when she cried Sol wondered if she
was crying for her mother.

Sol shopped in the small stores in Dan, taking the
infant with him as he selected diapers, nursing paks, and
the occasional new toy.

The week before Sol left for Tau Ceti Center,
Ephraim and the two other elders came to talk. It was
evening and the fading light glowed on Ephraim's bald
scalp. 'Sol, we're worried about you. The next few
weeks will be hard. The women want to help. We want
to help.'

Sol laid his hand on the older man's forearm. 'It's
appreciated, Ephraim. Everything the last few years is
appreciated. This is our home now, too. Sarai would
have . . . would have wanted me to say thank you. But
we're leaving on Sunday. Rachel is going to get better.'

The three men on the long bench looked at one another. Avner said, 'They've found a cure?'

'No,' said Sol, 'but I've found a reason to hope.'

'Hope is good,' Robert said in cautious tones.

Sol grinned, his teeth white against the gray of his
beard. 'It had better be,' he said. 'Sometimes it is all
we're given.'

The studio holo camera zoomed in for a close-up of
Rachel as the infant sat cradled in Sol's arm on the set
of 'Common Talk.' 'So you're saying,' said Devon
Whiteshire, the show's host and the third-best-known
face in the Web datasphere, 'that the Shrike Church's
refusal to allow you to return to the Time Tombs . . .

319

and the Hegemony's tardiness in processing a visa . . . these things will doom your child to this . . . *extinction*?'

'Precisely,' said Sol. 'The voyage to Hyperion cannot be made in under six weeks. Rachel is now twelve weeks old. Any further delay by either the Shrike Church or the Web bureaucracy will kill this child.'

The studio audience stirred. Devon Whiteshire turned toward the nearest imaging remote. His craggy, friendly visage filled the monitor frame. 'This man doesn't know if he can save his child,' said Whiteshire, his voice powerful with subtle feeling, 'but all he asks is a chance. Do you think he . . . and the baby . . . deserve one? If so, access your planetary representatives and your nearest Church of the Shrike temple. The number of your nearest temple should be appearing now.' He turned back to Sol. 'We wish you luck, M. Weintraub. And' – Whiteshire's large hand touched Rachel's cheek – 'we wish you Godspeed, our young friend.'

The monitor image held on Rachel until it faded to black.

The Hawking effect caused nausea, vertigo, headache, and hallucinations. The first leg of the voyage was the ten-day transit to Parvati on the Hegemony torchship *HS Intrepid*.

Sol held Rachel and endured. They were the only people fully conscious aboard the warship. At first Rachel cried, but after some hours she lay quietly in Sol's arms and stared up at him with large, dark eyes. Sol remembered the day she was born – the medics had taken the infant from atop Sarai's warm stomach and handed her to Sol. Rachel's dark hair was not much shorter then, her gaze no less profound.

Eventually they slept from sheer exhaustion.

Sol dreamed that he was wandering through a structure with columns the size of redwood trees and a ceiling lost to sight far above him. Red light bathed cool emptiness. Sol was surprised to find that he still carried Rachel in his arms. Rachel as a child had never been in his dream before. The infant looked up at him and Sol felt the *contact* of her consciousness as surely as if she had spoken aloud.

320

Suddenly a different voice, immense and cold, echoed through the void:

'Sol! Take your daughter, your only daughter Rachel, Whom you love, and go to the world called Hyperion and offer her there as a burnt offering at one of the places of which I shall tell you.'

Sol hesitated and looked back to Rachel. The baby's eyes were deep and luminous as she looked up at her father. Sol felt the unspoken *yes*. Holding her tightly, he stepped forward into the darkness and raised his voice against the silence:

'Listen! There will be no more offerings, neither child nor parent. There will be no more sacrifices for anyone other than our fellow human. The time of obedience and atonement is past.'

Sol listened. He could feel the pounding of his heart and Rachel's warmth against his arm. From somewhere high above there came the cold sound of wind through unseen fissures. Sol cupped his hand to his mouth and shouted:

'That's all! Now either leave us alone or join us as a father rather than a receiver of sacrifices. You have the choice of Abraham!'

Rachel stirred in his arms as a rumble grew out of the stone floor. Columns vibrated. The red gloom deepened and then winked out, leaving only darkness. From far away there came the boom of huge footsteps. Sol hugged Rachel to him as a violent wind roared past.

There was a glimmer of light as both he and Rachel awoke on the *HS Intrepid* outward bound for Parvati to transfer to the treeship *Yggdrasill* for the planet Hyperion. Sol smiled at his seven-week-old daughter. She smiled back.

It was her last and her first smile.

The main cabin of the windwagon was silent when the old scholar finished his story. Sol cleared his throat and took a drink of water from a crystal goblet. Rachel slept on in the makeshift cradle of the open drawer. The windwagon rocked gently on its way, the rumble of the great wheel and the hum of the main gyroscope a lulling background noise.

'My God,' Brawne Lamia said softly. She started to speak again and then merely shook her head.

Martin Silenus closed his eyes and said:

> *'Considering that, all hatred driven hence,*
> *The soul recovers radical innocence*
> *And learns at last that it is self-delighting,*
> *Self-appeasing, self-affrighting,*
> *And that its own sweet will is Heaven's will;*
> *She can, though every face will scowl*
> *And every windy quarter howl*
> *Or every bellows burst, be happy still.'*

Sol Weintraub asked, 'William Butler Yeats?'

Silenus nodded. ' "A Prayer for My Daughter." '

'I think I'm going up on deck for a breath of air before turning in,' said the Consul. 'Would anyone care to join me?'

Everyone did. The breeze of their passage was refreshing as the group stood on the quarterdeck and watched the darkened Sea of Grass rumble by. The sky was a great, star-splashed bowl above them, scarred by meteor trails. The sails and rigging creaked with a sound as old as human travel.

'I think we should post guards tonight,' said Colonel Kassad. 'One person on watch while the others sleep. Two-hours intervals.'

'I agree,' said the Consul. 'I'll take the first watch.'

'In the morning . . .' began Kassad.

'Look!' cried Father Hoyt.

They followed his pointing arm. Between the blaze of constellations, colored fireballs flared – green, violet, orange, green again – illuminating the great plain of grass around them like flashes of heat lightning. The stars and meteor trails paled to insignificance beside the sudden display.

'Explosions?' ventured the priest.

'Space battle,' said Kassad. 'Cislunar. Fusion weapons.' He went below quickly.

'The Tree,' said Het Masteen, pointing to a speck of light which moved among the explosions like an ember floating through a fireworks display.

Kassad returned with his powered binoculars and handed them around.

'Ousters?' asked Lamia. 'Is it the invasion?'

'Ousters, almost certainly,' said Kassad. 'But almost as certainly just a scouting raid. See the clusters? Those are Hegemony missiles being exploded by the Ouster ramscouts' countermeasures.'

The binoculars came to the Consul. The flashes were quite clear now, an expanding cumulus of flame. He could see the speck and long blue tail of at least two scoutships fleeing from the Hegemony pursuers.

'I don't think . . .' began Kassad and then stopped as the ship and sails and Sea of Grass glowed bright orange in reflected glare.

'Dear Christ,' whispered Father Hoyt. 'They've hit the treeship.'

The Consult swept the glass left. The growing nimbus of flames could be seen with the naked eye but in the binoculars the kilometer-long trunk and branch array of the *Yggdrasill* was visible for an instant as it burned and flared, long tendrils of flame arcing away into space as the containment fields failed and the oxygen burned. The orange cloud pulsed, faded, and fell back on itself as the trunk became visible for a final second even as it glowed and broke up like the last long ember in a dying fire. Nothing could have survived. The treeship *Yggdrasill* with its crew and complement of clones and semisentient erg drivers was dead.

The Consul turned toward Het Masteen and belatedly held out the binoculars. 'I'm so . . . sorry,' he whispered.

The tall Templar did not take the glasses. Slowly he lowered his gaze from the skies, pulled forward his cowl, and went below without a word.

The death of the treeship was the final explosion. When ten minutes had passed and no more flares had disturbed the night, Brawne Lamia spoke. 'Do you think they got them?'

'The Ousters?' said Kassad. 'Probably not. The scoutships are built for speed and defense. They're light-minutes away by now.'

'Did they go after the treeship on purpose?' asked Silenus. The poet sounded very sober.

'I think not,' said Kassad. 'Merely a target of opportunity.'

'Target of opportunity,' echoed Sol Weintraub. The scholar shook his head. 'I'm going to get a few hours' sleep before sunrise.'

One by one the others went below. When only Kassad and the Consul were left on deck, the Consul said, 'Where should I stand watch?'

'Make a circuit,' said the Colonel. 'From the main corridor at the base of the ladder you can see all of the stateroom doors and the entrance to the mess and galley. Come above and check the gangway and decks. Keep the lanterns lit. Do you have a weapon?'

The Consul shook his head.

Kassad handed over his deathwand. 'It's on tight beam – about half a meter at ten meters' range. Don't use it unless you're sure that there's an intruder. The rough plate that slides forward is the safety. It's on.'

The Consul nodded, making sure that his finger stayed away from the firing stud.

'I'll relieve you in two hours,' said Kassad. He checked his comlog. 'It'll be sunrise before my watch is over.' Kassad looked at the sky as if expecting the *Yggdrasill* to reappear and continue its firefly path across the sky. Only the stars glowed back. On the northeastern horizon a moving mass of black promised a storm.

Kassad shook his head. 'A waste,' he said and went below.

The Consul stood there awhile and listened to the wind in the canvas, the creek of rigging, and the rumble of the wheel. After a while he went to the railing and stared at darkness while he thought.

FIVE

Sunrise over the Sea of Grass was a thing of beauty. The Consul watched from the highest point on the aft deck. After his watch he had tried to sleep, given it up, and come up onto deck to watch the night fade into day. The stormfront had covered the sky with low clouds and the rising sun lit the world with brilliant gold reflected from above and below. The windwagon's sails and lines and weathered planks glowed in the brief benediction of light in the few minutes before the sun was blocked by the ceiling of clouds and color flowed out of the world once again. The wind which followed this curtain closing was chill, as if it had blown down from the snowy peaks of the Bridle Range just visible as a dark blur on the northeastern horizon.

Brawne Lamia and Martin Silenus joined the Consul on the aft deck, each nursing a cup of coffee from the galley. The wind whipped and tugged at the rigging. Brawne Lamia's thick mass of curls fluttered around her face like a dark nimbus.

'Morning,' muttered Silenus, squinting out over his coffee cup at the wind-rippled Sea of Grass.

'Good morning,' replied the Consul, amazed at how alert and refreshed he felt for not having slept at all the night before. 'We have a headwind, but the wagon still seems to be making decent time. We'll definitely be to the mountains before nightfall.'

'Hrrgnn,' commented Silenus and buried his nose in the coffee cup.

'I didn't sleep at all last night,' said Brawne Lamia, 'just for thinking about M. Weintraub's story.'

'I don't think . . .' began the poet and then broke off

as Weintraub came onto deck, his baby peering over the lip of an infant carrier sling on his chest.

'Good morning, everyone,' said Weintraub, looking around and taking a deep breath. 'Mmm, brisk, isn't it?'

'Fucking freezing,' said Silenus. 'North of the mountains it'll be even worse.'

'I think I'll go down to get a jacket,' said Lamia, but before she could move there came a single shrill cry from the deck below.

'*Blood!*'

There was, indeed, blood everywhere. Het Masteen's cabin was strangely neat – bed unslept in, travel trunk and other boxes stacked precisely in one corner, robe folded over a chair – except for the blood which covered great sections of the deck, bulkhead, and overhead. The six pilgrims crowded just inside the entrance, reluctant to go farther in.

'I was passing on my way to the upper deck,' said Father Hoyt, his voice a strange monotone. 'The door was slightly ajar. I caught a glimpse of . . . the blood on the wall.'

'*Is* it blood?' demanded Martin Silenus.

Brawne Lamia stepped into the room, ran a hand through a thick smear on the bulkhead, and raised her fingers to her lips. 'It's blood.' She looked around, walked to the wardrobe, looked briefly among the empty shelves and hangers, and then went to the small porthole. It was latched and bolted from the inside.

Lenar Hoyt looked more ill than usual and staggered to a chair. 'Is he dead then?'

'We don't know a damn thing except that Captain Masteen isn't in his room and a lot of blood *is*,' said Lamia. She wiped her hand on her pant leg. 'The thing to do now is search the ship thoroughly.'

'Precisely,' said Colonel Kassad, 'and if we do not find the Captain?'

Brawne Lamia opened the porthole. Fresh air dissipated the slaughterhouse smell of blood and brought in the rumble of the wheel and the rustle of grass under the hull. 'If we don't find Captain Masteen,' she said, 'then we assume that he either left the ship under his own will or was taken off.'

'But the *blood* . . .' began Father Hoyt.

'Doesn't prove anything,' finished Kassad. 'M. Lamia's correct. We don't know Masteen's blood type or genotype. Did anyone see or hear *anything*?'

There was silence except for negative grunts and the shaking of heads.

Martin Silenus looked around. 'Don't you people recognize the work of our friend the Shrike when you see it?'

'We don't know that,' snapped Lamia. 'Maybe someone *wanted* us to think that it was the Shrike's doing.'

'That doesn't make sense,' said Hoyt, still gasping for air.

'Nonetheless,' said Lamia, 'we'll search in twos. Who has weapons besides myself?'

'I do,' said Colonel Kassad. 'I have extras if needed.'

'No,' said Hoyt.

The poet shook his head.

Sol Weintraub had returned to the corridor with his child. Now he looked in again. 'I have nothing,' he said.

'No,' said the Consul. He had returned the deathwand to Kassad when his shift ended two hours before first light.

'All right,' said Lamia, 'the priest will come with me on the lower deck. Silenus, go with the Colonel. Search the mid-deck. M. Weintraub, you and the Consul check everything above. Look for *anything* out of the ordinary. Any sign of struggle.'

'One question,' said Silenus.

'What?'

'Who the hell elected you queen of the prom?'

'I'm a private investigator,' said Lamia, leveling her gaze on the poet.

Martin Silenus shrugged. 'Hoyt here is a priest of some forgotten religion. That doesn't mean we have to genuflect when he says Mass.'

'All right,' sighed Brawne Lamia. 'I'll give you a better reason.' The woman moved so fast that the Consul almost missed the action in a blink. One second she was standing by the open port and in the next she was half-way across the stateroom, lifting Martin Silenus off the deck with one arm, her massive hand around the poet's thin neck. 'How about,' she said, 'that you do the logical thing because it's the logical thing to do?'

'Gkkrgghh,' managed Martin Silenus.

'Good,' said Lamia without emotion and dropped the poet to the deck. Silenus staggered a meter and almost sat on Father Hoyt.

'Here,' said Kassad, returning with two small neural stunners. He handed one to Sol Weintraub. 'What do you have?' Kassad asked Lamia.

The woman reached into a pocket of her loose tunic and produced an ancient pistol.

Kassad looked at the relic for a moment and then nodded. 'Stay with your partner,' he said. 'Don't shoot at anything unless it's positively identified and unquestionably threatening.'

'That describes the bitch I plan to shoot,' said Silenus, still massaging his throat.

Brawne Lamia took a half step toward the poet. Fedmahn Kassad said, 'Shut up. Let's get this over with.' Silenus followed the Colonel out of the stateroom.

Sol Weintraub approached the Consul, handed him the stunner. 'I don't want to hold this thing with Rachel. Shall we go up?'

The Consul took the weapon and nodded.

The windwagon held no further sign of Templar Voice of the Tree Het Masteen. After an hour of searching, the group met in the stateroom of the missing man. The blood there seemed darker and drier.

'Is there a chance that we missed something?' said Father Hoyt. 'Secret passages? Hidden compartments?'

'There's a chance,' said Kassad, 'but I swept the ship with heat and motion sensors. If there's anything else on board larger than a mouse, I can't find it.'

'If you had these sensors,' said Silenus, 'why the fuck did you have us crawling through bilge and byways for an hour?'

'Because the right equipment or apparel can hide a man from a heat-'n'-beat search.'

'So, in answer to my question,' said Hoyt, pausing a second as a visible wave of pain passed through him, 'with the right equipment or apparel, Captain Masteen might be hiding in a secret compartment somewhere.'

'Possible but improbable,' said Brawne Lamia. 'My guess is that he's no longer aboard.'

'The Shrike,' said Martin Silenus in a disgusted tone. It was not a question.

'Perhaps,' said Lamia. 'Colonel, you and the Consul were on watch through those four hours. Are you sure that you heard and saw nothing?'

Both men nodded.

'The ship was quiet,' said Kassad. 'I would have heard a struggle even before I went on watch.'

'And I didn't sleep after my watch,' said the Consul. 'My room shared a bulkhead with Masteen's. I heard nothing.'

'Well,' said Silenus, 'we've heard from the two men who were creeping around in the dark with weapons when the poor shit was killed. They say they're innocent. Next case!'

'If Masteen was killed,' said Kassad, 'it was with no deathwand. No silent modern weapon I know throws that much blood around. There were no gunshots heard – no bullet holes found – so I presume M. Lamia's automatic pistol is not suspect. *If* this is Captain Masteen's blood, then I would guess an edged weapon was used.'

'The Shrike *is* an edged weapon,' said Martin Silenus.

Lamia moved to the small stack of luggage. 'Debating isn't going to solve anything. Let's see if there's anything in Masteen's belongings.'

Father Hoyt raised a hesitant hand. 'That's . . . well, *private*, isn't it? I don't think we have the right.'

Brawne Lamia crossed her arms. 'Look, Father, if Masteen's dead, it doesn't matter to him. If he's still alive, looking through this stuff might give us some idea where he was taken. Either way, we have to try to find a clue.'

Hoyt looked dubious but nodded. In the end, there was little invasion of privacy. Masteen's first trunk held only a few changes of linen and a copy of *Muir's Book of Life*. The second bag held a hundred separately wrapped seedlings, flash-dried and nestled in moist soil.

'Templars must plant at least a hundred offspring of the Eternal Tree on whatever world they visit,' explained the Consul. 'The shoots rarely take, but it's a ritual.'

Brawne Lamia moved toward the large metal box which had sat at the bottom of the pile.

'Don't touch that!' snapped the Consul.

'Why not?'

'It's a Möbius cube,' responded Colonel Kassad for the Consul. 'A carbon-carbon-shell set around a zero impedance containment field folded back on itself.'

'So?' said Lamia. 'Möbius cubes seal artifacts and stuff in. They don't explode or anything.'

'No,' agreed the Consul, 'but what they *contain* may explode. May already *have* exploded, for that matter.'

'A cube that size could hold a kiloton nuclear explosion in check as long as it was boxed during the nanosecond of ignition,' added Fedmahn Kassad.

Lamia scowled at the trunk. 'Then how do we know that something in there didn't kill Masteen?'

Kassad pointed to a faintly glowing green strip along the trunk's only seam. 'It's sealed. Once unsealed, a Möbius cube has to be reactivated at a place where containment fields can be generated. Whatever's in there didn't harm Captain Masteen.'

'So there's no way to tell?' mused Lamia.

'I have a good guess,' said the Consul.

The others looked at him. Rachel began to cry and Sol pulled a heating strip on a nursing pak.

'Remember,' said the Consul, 'at Edge yesterday when M. Masteen made a big deal out of the cube? He talked about it as if it were a secret weapon?'

'A weapon?' said Lamia.

'Of course!' Kassad said suddenly. 'An erg!'

'Erg?' Martin Silenus stared at the small crate. 'I thought ergs were those forcefield critters that Templars use on their treeships.'

'They are,' said the Consul. 'The things were found about three centuries ago living on asteroids around Aldebaran. Bodies about as big as a cat's spine, mostly a piezoelectric nervous system sheathed in silicon gristle, but they feed on . . . and manipulate . . . forcefields as large as those generated by small spinships.'

'So how do you get all that into such a little box?' asked Silenus, staring at the Möbius cube. 'Mirrors?'

'In a sense,' said Kassad. 'The thing's field would be damped . . . neither starving nor feeding. Rather like cryogenic fugue for us. Plus this must be a small one. A cub, so to speak.'

Lamia ran her hand along the metal sheath. 'Templars control these things? Communicate with them?'

'Yes,' said Kassad. 'No one is quite sure how. It's one of the Brotherhood secrets. But Het Masteen must have been confident that the erg would help him with . . .'

'The Shrike,' finished Martin Silenus. 'The Templar thought that this energy imp would be his secret weapon when he faced the Lord of Pain.' The poet laughed.

Father Hoyt cleared his throat. 'The Church has accepted the Hegemony's ruling that . . . these creatures . . . ergs . . . are not sentient beings . . . and thus not candidates for salvation.'

'Oh, they're sentient, all right, Father,' said the Consul. 'They *perceive* things far better than we could ever imagine. But if you meant intelligent . . . self-aware . . . then you're dealing with something along the lines of a smart grasshopper. Are grasshoppers candidates for salvation?'

Hoyt said nothing. Brawne Lamia said, 'Well, evidently Captain Masteen thought this thing was going to be *his* salvation. Something went wrong.' She looked around at the bloodstained bulkheads and at the drying stains on the deck. 'Let's get out of here.'

The windwagon tacked into increasingly strong winds as the storm approached from the northeast. Ragged banners of clouds raced white beneath the low, gray ceiling of stormfront. Grasses whipped and bent under gusts of cold wind. Ripples of lightning illuminated the horizon and were followed by rolls of thunder sounding like warning shots across the windwagon's bow. The pilgrims watched in silence until the first icy raindrops drove them below to the large stateroom in the stern.

'This was in his robe pocket,' said Brawne Lamia, holding up a slip of paper with the number 5 on it.

'So Masteen would have told his story next,' muttered the Consul.

Martin Silenus tilted his chair until his back touched the tall windows. Storm light made his satyr's features appear slightly demonic. 'There's another possibility,' he said. 'Perhaps someone who hasn't spoken yet had the fifth spot and killed the Templar to trade places.'

Lamia stared at the poet. 'That would have to be the Consul or me,' she said, her voice flat.

Silenus shrugged.

Brawne Lamia pulled another piece of paper from her tunic. 'I have number six. What would I have achieved? I go next anyway.'

'Then perhaps it's what Masteen would have *said* that needed to be silenced,' said the poet. He shrugged again. 'Personally, I think the Shrike has begun harvesting us. Why did we think we'd be allowed to get to the Tombs when the thing's been slaughtering people halfway from here to Keats?'

'This is different,' said Sol Weintraub. 'This is the Shrike Pilgrimage.'

'So?'

In the silence that followed, the Consul walked to the windows. Wind-driven torrents of rain obscured the Sea and rattled the leaded panes. The wagon creaked and leaned heavily to starboard as it began another leg of its tack.

'M. Lamia,' asked Colonel Kassad, 'do you want to tell your story now?'

Lamia folded her arms and looked at the rain-streaked glass. 'No. Let's wait until we get off this damned ship. It stinks of death.'

The windwagon reached the port of Pilgrims' Rest in midafternoon but the storm and tired light made it feel like late evening to the weary passengers. The Consul had expected representatives from the Shrike Temple to meet them here at the beginning of the penultimate stage of their journey but Pilgrims' Rest appeared to the Consul to be as empty as Edge had been.

The approach to the foothills and the first sight of the Bridle Range was as exciting as any landfall and brought all six of the would-be pilgrims on deck despite the cold rain which continued to fall. The foothills were sere and sensuous, their brown curves and sudden upthrustings contrasting strongly with the verdant monochrome of the Sea of Grass. The nine-thousand-meter peaks beyond were only hinted at by gray and white planes soon intersected by low clouds, but even so truncated were powerful to behold. The snow line came down to a point just above the collection of burned-out hovels and cheap hotels which had been Pilgrims' Rest.

'If they destroyed the tramway, we're finished,' muttered the Consul. The thought of it, forbidden until now, made his stomach turn over.

'I see the first five towers,' said Colonel Kassad, using his powered glasses. 'They seem intact.'

'Any sign of a car?'

'No . . . wait, yes. There's one in the gate at the station platform.'

'Any moving?' asked Martin Silenus, who obviously understood how desperate their situation would be if the tramway was not intact.

'No.'

The Consul shook his head. Even in the worst weather with no passengers, the cars had been kept moving to keep the great cables flexed and free of ice.

The six of them had their luggage on deck even before the windwagon reefed its sails and extended a gangplank. Each now wore a heavy coat against the elements – Kassad in FORCE-issue thermouflage cape, Brawne Lamia in a long garment called a trenchcoat for reasons long forgotten, Martin Silenus in thick furs which rippled now sable, now gray with the vagaries of wind, Father Hoyt in long black which made him more of a scarecrow figure than ever, Sol Weintraub in a thick goosedown jacket which covered him and the child, and the Consul in the thinning but serviceable greatcoat his wife had given him some decades before.

'What about Captain Masteen's things?' asked Sol as they stood at the head of the gangplank. Kassad had gone ahead to reconnoiter the village.

'I brought them up,' said Lamia. 'We'll take them with us.'

'It doesn't seem right somehow,' said Father Hoyt. 'Just going on, I mean. There should be some . . . service. Some recognition that a man has died.'

'*May* have died,' reminded Lamia, easily lifting a forty-kilo backpack with one hand.

Hoyt looked incredulous. 'Do you really believe that M. Masteen might be alive?'

'No,' said Lamia. Snowflakes settled on her black hair.

Kassad waved to them from the end of the dock and they carried their luggage off the silent windwagon. No one looked back.

'Empty?' called Lamia as they approached the Colonel. The tall man's cloak was still fading from its gray and black chameleon mode.

'Empty.'

'Bodies?'

'No,' said Kassad. He turned toward Sol and the Consul. 'Did you get the things from the galley?'

Both men nodded.

'What things?' asked Silenus.

'A week's worth of food,' said Kassad, turning to look up the hill toward the tramway station. For the first time the Consul noticed the long assault weapon in the crook of the Colonel's arm, barely visible under the cloak. 'We're not sure if there are any provisions beyond this point.'

Will we be alive a week from now? thought the Consul. He said nothing.

They ferried the gear to the station in two trips. Wind whistled through the open windows and shattered domes of the dark buildings. On the second trip, the Consul carried one end of Masteen's Möbius cube while Lenar Hoyt puffed and panted under the other end.

336

'Why are we taking the erg thing with us?' gasped Hoyt as they reached the base of the metal stairway leading to the station. Rust streaked and spotted the platform like orange lichen.

'I don't know,' said the Consul, gasping for breath himself.

From the terminal platform they could see far out over the Sea of Grass. The windwagon sat where they had left it, sails reefed, a dark and lifeless thing. Snow squalls moved across the prairie and gave the illusion of whitecaps on the numberless stalks of high grass.

'Get the material aboard,' called Kassad. 'I'll see if the running gear can be reset from the operator's cabin up there.'

'Isn't it automatic?' asked Martin Silenus, his small head almost lost in thick furs. 'Like the windwagon?'

'I don't think so,' said Kassad. 'Go on, I'll see if I can get it started up.'

'What if it leaves without you?' called Lamia at the Colonel's retreating back.

'It won't.'

The interior of the tramcar was cold and bare except for metal benches in the forward compartment and a dozen rough bunks in the smaller, rear area. The car was big – at least eight meters long by five wide. The rear compartment was partitioned from the front cabin by a thin metal bulkhead with an opening but no door. A small commode took up a closet-sized corner of this aft compartment. Windows rising from waist height to the roofline lined the forward compartment.

The pilgrims heaped their luggage in the center of the wide floor and stomped around, waved their arms, or otherwise worked to stay warm. Martin Silenus lay full length on one of the benches, with only his feet and the top of his head emerging from fur. 'I forgot,' he said, 'how the fuck do you turn on the heat in this thing?'

The Consul glanced at the dark lighting panels. 'It's electrical. It'll come on when the Colonel gets us moving.'

'*If* the Colonel gets us moving,' said Silenus.

Sol Weintraub had changed Rachel's diaper. Now he bundled her up again in an infant's thermsuit and rocked her in his arms. 'Obviously I've never been here before,' he said. 'Both of you gentlemen have?'

'Yeah,' said the poet.

'No,' said the Consul. 'But I've seen pictures of the tramway.'

'Kassad said he *returned* to Keats once this way,' called Brawne Lamia from the other room.

'I think . . .' began Sol Weintraub and was interrupted by a great grinding of gears and a wild lurch as the long car rocked sickeningly and then swung forward under the suddenly moving cable. Everyone rushed to the window on the platform side.

Kassad had thrown his gear aboard before climbing the long ladder to the operator's cabin. Now he appeared in the cabin's doorway, slid down the long ladder, and ran toward the car. The car was already passing beyond the loading area of the platform.

'He isn't going to make it,' whispered Father Hoyt.

Kassad sprinted the last ten meters with legs that looked impossibly long, a cartoon stick figure of a man.

The tramcar slid out of the loading notch, swung free of the station. Space opened between the car and the station. It was eight meters to the rocks below. The platform deck was streaked with ice. Kassad ran full speed ahead even as the car pulled away.

'Come on!' screamed Brawne Lamia. The others picked up the cry.

The Consul looked up at sheaths of ice cracking and dropping away from the cable as the tramcar moved up and forward. He looked back. There was too much space. Kassad could never make it.

Fedmahn Kassad was moving at an incredible speed when he reached the edge of the platform. The Consul was reminded for the second time of the Old Earth jaguar he had seen in a Lusus zoo. He half expected to see the Colonel's feet slip on a patch of ice, the long legs flying out horizontal, the man falling silently to the snowy boulders below. Instead, Kassad seemed to fly for an endless moment, long arms extended, cape flying out behind. He disappeared behind the car.

There came a thud, followed by a long minute when no one spoke or moved. They were forty meters high now, climbing toward the first tower. A second later Kassad became visible at the corner of the car, pulling himself along a series of icy niches and handholds in the metal. Brawne Lamia flung open the cabin door. Ten hands helped pull Kassad inside.

'Thank God,' said Father Hoyt.

The Colonel took a deep breath and smiled grimly. 'There was a dead man's brake. I had to rig the lever with a sandbag. I didn't want to bring the car back for a second try.'

Martin Silenus pointed to the rapidly approaching support tower and the ceiling of clouds just beyond. The cable stretched upward into oblivion. 'I guess we're crossing the mountains now whether we want to or not.'

'How long to make the crossing?' asked Hoyt.

'Twelve hours. A little less perhaps. Sometimes the operators would stop the cars if the wind rose too high or the ice got too bad.'

'We won't be stopping on this trip,' said Kassad.

'Unless the cable's breached somewhere,' said the poet. 'Or we hit a snag.'

'Shut up,' said Lamia. 'Who's interested in heating some dinner?'

'Look,' said the Consul.

They moved to the forward windows. The tram rose a hundred meters above the last brown curve of foothills. Kilometers below and behind they caught a final glimpse of the station, the haunted hovels of Pilgrims' Rest, and the motionless windwagon.

Then snow and thick cloud enveloped them.

The tramcar had no real cooking facilities but the aft bulkhead offered a cold box and a microwave for reheating. Lamia and Weintraub combined various meats and vegetables from the windwagon's galley to produce a passable stew. Martin Silenus had brought along wine bottles from the *Benares* and the windwagon and he chose a Hyperion burgundy to go with the stew.

They were nearly finished with their dinner when the gloom pressing against the windows lightened and then lifted altogether. The Consul turned on his bench to see the sun suddenly reappear, filling the tramcar with a transcendent golden light.

There was a collective sigh from the group. It had seemed that darkness had fallen hours before, but now, as they rose above a sea of clouds from which rose an island chain of mountains, they were treated to a brilliant sunset. Hyperion's sky had deepened from its daytime glaucous glare to the bottomless lapis lazuli of evening while a red-gold sun ignited cloud towers and great summits of ice and rock. The Consul looked around. His fellow pilgrims, who had seemed gray and small in the dim light of half a minute earlier, now glowed in the gold of sunset.

Martin Silenus raised his glass. 'That's better, by God.'

The Consul looked up at their line of travel, the massive cable dwindling to threadlike thinness far ahead and then to nothing at all. On a summit several kilometers beyond, gold light glinted on the next support tower.

'One hundred and ninety-two pylons,' said Silenus in a singsong tour guide's bored tones. 'Each pylon is constructed of duralloy and whiskered carbon and stands eighty-three meters high.'

'We must be high,' said Brawne Lamia in a low voice.

'The high point of the ninety-six-kilometer tramcar voyage lies above the summit of Mount Dryden, the fifth highest peak in the Bridle Range, at nine thousand two hundred forty-six meters,' droned on Martin Silenus.

Colonel Kassad looked around. 'The cabin's pressurized. I felt the change-over some time ago.'

'Look,' said Brawne Lamia.

The sun had been resting on the horizon line of clouds for a long moment. Now it dipped below, seemingly igniting the depths of storm cloud from beneath and casting a panoply of colors along the entire western edge of the world. Snow cornices and glaze ice still glowed along the western side of the peaks, which rose a

340

kilometer or more above the rising tramcar. A few brighter stars appeared in the deepening dome of sky.

The Consul turned to Brawne Lamia. 'Why don't you tell your story now, M. Lamia? We'll want to sleep later, before arriving at the Keep.'

Lamia sipped the last of her wine. 'Does everyone want to hear it now?'

Heads nodded in the roseate twilight. Martin Silenus shrugged.

'All right,' said Brawne Lamia. She set down her empty glass, pulled her feet up on the bench so that her elbows rested on her knees, and began her tale.

THE DETECTIVE'S TALE: The Long Good-Bye

I knew the case was going to be special the minute that he walked into my office. He was beautiful. By that I don't mean effeminate or 'pretty' in the male-model, HTV-star mode, merely . . . beautiful.

He was a short man, no taller than I, and I was born and raised in Lusus's 1.3-g field. It was apparent in a second that my visitor was not from Lusus – his compact form was well proportioned by Web standards, athletic but thin. His face was a study in purposeful energy: low brow, sharp cheekbones, compact nose, solid jaw, and a wide mouth that suggested both a sensuous side and a stubborn streak. His eyes were large and hazel-colored. He looked to be in his late twenties standard.

Understand, I didn't itemize all this the moment he walked in. My first thought was, *Is this a client*? My second thought was, *Shit, this guy's beautiful*.

'M. Lamia?'

'Yeah.'

'M. Brawne Lamia of AllWeb Investigations?'

'Yeah.'

He looked around as if he didn't quite believe it. I understood the look. My office is on the twenty-third level of an old industrial hive in the Old Digs section of Iron Pig on Lusus. I have three big windows that look out on Service Trench 9 where it's always dark and always drizzling thanks to a massive filter drip from the Hive above. The view is mostly of abandoned automated loading docks and rusted girders.

What the hell, it's cheap. And most of my clients call rather than show up in person.

'May I sit down?' he asked, evidently satisfied that a bona fide investigatory agency would operate out of such a slum.

'Sure,' I said and waved him to a chair. 'M . . . ah?'

'Johnny,' he said.

He didn't look like a first-name type to me. Something about him breathed *money*. It wasn't his clothes – common enough casuals in black and gray, although the fabric was better than average – it was just a sense that the guy had class. There was something about his accent. I'm good at placing dialects – it helps in this profession – but I couldn't place this guy's homeworld, much less local region.

'How can I help you, Johnny?' I held out the bottle of Scotch I had been ready to put away as he entered.

Johnny-boy shook his head. Maybe he thought I wanted him to drink from the bottle. Hell, I have more class than that. There are paper cups over by the water cooler. 'M. Lamia,' he said, the cultivated accent still bugging me by its elusiveness, 'I need an investigator.'

'That's what I do.'

He paused. Shy. A lot of my clients are hesitant to tell me what the job is. No wonder, since ninety-five percent of my work is divorce and domestic stuff. I waited him out.

'It's a somewhat sensitive matter,' he said at last.

'Yeah, M . . . ah, Johnny, most of my work falls under that category. I'm bonded with UniWeb and everything having to do with a client falls under the Privacy Protection Act. *Everything* is confidential, even the fact that we're talking now. Even if you decide not to hire me.' That was basic bullshit since the authorities could get at my files in a moment if they ever wanted to, but I sensed that I had to put this guy at ease somehow. God, he was beautiful.

342

'Uh-huh,' he said and glanced around again. He leaned forward. 'M. Lamia, I would want you to investigate a murder.'

This got my attention. I'd been reclining with my feet on the desk; now I sat up and leaned forward. 'A *murder*? Are you sure? What about the cops?'

'They aren't involved.'

'That's not possible,' I said with the sinking feeling that I was dealing with a loony rather than a client. 'It's a crime to conceal a murder from the authorities.' What I thought was: *Are you the murderer, Johnny*?

He smiled and shook his head. 'Not in this case.'

'What do you mean?'

'I mean, M. Lamia, that a murder *was* committed but that the police – local and Hegemony – have neither knowledge of it nor jurisdiction over it.'

'Not possible,' I said again. Outside, sparks from an industrial welder's torch cascaded into the trench along with the rusty drizzle. 'Explain.'

'A murder was committed outside of the Web. Outside of the Protectorate. There were no local authorities.'

That made sense. Sort of. For the life of me, though, I couldn't figure where he was talking about. Even the Outback settlements and colonial worlds have cops. On board some sort of spaceship? Uh-uh. The Interstellar Transit Authority has jurisdiction there.

'I see,' I said. It'd been some weeks since I'd had a case. 'All right, tell me the details.'

'And the conversation will be confidential even if you do not take the case?'

'Absolutely.'

'And if you do take the case, you will report only to me?'

'Of course.'

My prospective client hesitated, rubbing his fingers against his chin. His hands were exquisite. 'All right,' he said at last.

'Start at the beginning,' I said. 'Who was murdered?'

Johnny sat up straight, an attentive schoolboy. There was no doubting his sincerity. He said, 'I was.'

It took ten minutes to get the story out of him. When he was finished, I no longer thought he was crazy. I was. Or I would be if I took the job.

Johnny – his real name was a code of digits, letters, and cipher bands longer than my arm – was a cybrid.

I'd heard about cybrids. Who hasn't? I once accused my first husband of being one. But I never expected to be sitting in the same room with one. Or to find it so damned attractive.

Johnny was an AI. His consciousness or ego or whatever you want to call it floated somewhere in the megadatasphere datumplane of TechnoCore. Like everyone else except maybe the current Senate CEO or the AIs' garbage removers, I had no idea where the TechnoCore was. The AIs had peacefully seceded from human control more than three centuries ago – before my time – and while they continued to serve the Hegemony as allies by advising the All Thing, monitoring the dataspheres, occasionally using their predictive abilities to help us avoid major mistakes or natural disasters, the TechnoCore generally went about its own indecipherable and distinctly nonhuman business in privacy.

Fair enough, it seemed to me.

Usually AIs do business with humans and human machines via the datasphere. They can manufacture an interactive holo if they need to – I remembered during the Maui-Covenant incorporation, the TechnoCore ambassadors at the treaty signing looked suspiciously like the old holo star Tyrone Bathwaite.

Cybrids are a whole different matter. Tailored from human genetic stock, they are far more human in appearance and outward behavior than androids are allowed to be. Agreements between the TechnoCore and the Hegemony allow only a handful of cybrids to be in existence.

I looked at Johnny. From an AI's perspective, the beautiful body and intriguing personality sitting across the desk from me must be merely another appendage, a remote, somewhat more complex but otherwise no more important than any one of ten thousand such sensors, manipulators, autonomous units, or other remotes that an AI might use in a day's work. Discarding 'Johnny' probably would create no more concern in an AI than clipping a fingernail would bother me.

What a waste, I thought.

'A cybrid,' I said.

'Yes. Licensed. I have a Worldweb user's visa.'

'Good,' I heard myself say. 'And someone . . . murdered your cybrid and you want me to find out who?'

'No,' said the young man. He had brownish-red curls. Like his accent, the hairstyle eluded me. It seemed archaic somehow, but I had seen it *somewhere*. 'It was not merely this body that was murdered. My assailant murdered *me*.'

'You?'

'Yes.'

'You as in the . . . ah . . . AI itself?'

'Precisely.'

I didn't get it. AIs can't die. Not as far as anyone in the Web knew. 'I don't get it,' I said.

Johnny nodded, 'Unlike a human personality which can . . . I believe the consensus is . . . be destroyed at death, my own consciousness cannot be terminated. There was, however, as a result of the assault, an . . . interruption. Although I possessed . . . ah . . . shall we say duplicate recordings of memories, personality, et cetera, there was a loss. Some data were destroyed in the attack. In that sense, the assailant committed murder.'

'I see,' I lied. I took a breath. 'What about the AI authorities . . . if there are such things . . . or the Hegemony cybercops? Wouldn't they be the ones to go to?'

'For personal reasons,' said the attractive young man whom I was trying to see as a cybrid, 'it is important – even necessary – that I do not consult these sources.'

I raised an eyebrow. This sounded more like one of my regular clients.

'I assure you,' he said, 'it is nothing illegal. Nor unethical. Merely . . . embarrassing to me on a level which I cannot explain.'

I folded my arms across my chest. 'Look, Johnny. This is a pretty half-assed story. I mean, I only have your word that you're a cybrid. You might be a scam artist for all I know.'

He looked surprised. 'I had not thought of that. How would you like me to show you that I am what I say I am?'

I did not hesitate a second. 'Transfer a million marks to my checking account in TransWeb,' I said.

Johnny smiled. At the same instant my phone rang and the image of a harried man with the TransWeb code block floating behind him said, 'Excuse me, M. Lamia, but we wondered with a . . . ah . . . deposit of this size if you would be interested in investigating our long-term savings options or our mutual assured market possibilities?'

'Later,' I said.

The bank manager nodded and vanished.

'That could've been a simulation,' I said.

Johnny's smile was pleasant. 'Yes, but even that would be a satisfactory demonstration, would it not?'

'Not necessarily.'

He shrugged. 'Assuming I am what I say I am, will you take the case?'

'Yeah.' I sighed. 'One thing though. My fee isn't a million marks. I get five hundred a day plus expenses.'

The cybrid nodded. 'Does that mean you will take the case?'

I stood up, put on my hat, and pulled an old coat from a rack by the window. I bent over the lower desk drawer, smoothly sliding my father's pistol into a coat pocket. 'Let's go,' I said.

'Yes,' said Johnny. 'Go where?'

'I want to see where you were murdered.'

Stereotype has it that someone born on Lusus hates to leave the Hive and suffers from instant agoraphobia if we visit anything more open to the elements that a shopping mall. The truth of it is, most of my business comes from . . . and leads to . . . offworld. Skiptracing deadbeats who use the farcaster system and a change of identity to try to start over. Finding philandering spouses who think rendezvousing on a different planet will keep them safe from discovery. Tracking down missing kids and absent parents.

Still, I was surprised to the point of hesitating a second when we stepped through the Iron Pig Concourse farcaster onto an empty stone plateau which seemed to stretch to infinity. Except for the bronze rectangle of the farcaster portal behind us, there was no sign of civilization anywhere. The air smelled like rotten eggs. The sky was a yellow-brown cauldron of sick-looking clouds. The ground around us was gray and scaled and held no visible life, not even lichen. I had no idea how far away the horizon really was, but we felt *high* and it looked *far*, and there was no hint of trees, shrubs, or animal life in the distance either.

'Where the hell are we?' I asked. I had been sure that I knew all of the worlds in the Web.

'Madhya,' said Johnny, pronouncing it something like 'Mudye.'

'I never heard of it,' I said, putting one hand in my pocket and finding the pearl-handled grip of Dad's automatic.

'It's not officially in the Web yet,' said the cybrid. 'Officially it's a colony of Parvati. But it's only light-minutes from the FORCE base there and the farcaster connections have been set up before Madhya joins the Protectorate.'

I looked at the desolation. The hydrogen-sulfide stench was making me ill and I was afraid it was going to ruin my suit. 'Colonies? Nearby?'

'No. There are several small cities on the other side of the planet.'

'What's the nearest inhabited area?'

'Nanda Devi. A town of about three hundred people. It's more than two thousand kilometers to the south.'

'Then why put a farcaster portal here?'

'Potential mining sites,' said Johnny. He gestured toward the gray plateau. 'Heavy metals. The consortium authorized over a hundred farcaster portals in this hemisphere for easy access once the development began.'

'Okay,' I said. 'It's a good place for a murder. Why'd you come here?'

'I don't know. It was part of the memory section lost.'

'Who'd you come with?'

'I don't know that either.'

'What do you know?'

The young man put his graceful hands in his pockets. 'Whoever . . . whatever . . . attacked me used a type of weapon known in the Core as an AIDS II virus.'

'What's that?'

'AIDS II was a human plague disease back long before the Hegira,' said Johnny. 'It disabled the immune system. This. . . virus. . . works the same with an AI. In less than a second it infiltrates security systems and turns lethal phagocyte programs against the host . . . against the AI itself. Against *me*.'

'So you couldn't have contracted this virus naturally?'

Johnny smiled. 'Impossible. It's comparable to asking a shooting victim if he might not have fallen on the bullets.'

I shrugged. 'Look, if you want a datumnet or AI expert, you've come to the wrong woman. Other than accessing the sphere like twenty billion other chumps, I know zilch about the ghost world.' I used the old term to see if it would get a rise out of him.

'I know,' said Johnny, still equable. 'That's not what I want you to do.'

'What *do* you want me to do?'

'Find out who brought me here and killed me. And why.'

'All right. Why do you think this is where the murder took place?'

'Because this is where I regained control of my cybrid when I was . . . reconstituted.'

'You mean your cybrid was incapacitated while the virus destroyed you?'

'Yes.'

'And how long did that last?'

'My death? Almost a minute before my reserve persona could be activated.'

I laughed. I couldn't help myself.

'What is amusing, M. Lamia?'

348

'Your concept of death,' I said.

The hazel eyes looked sad. 'Perhaps it is amusing to you, but you have no idea what a minute of . . . disconnection . . . means to an element of the TechnoCore. It is eons of time and information. Millennia of non-communication.'

'Yeah,' I said, able to hold back my own tears without too much effort. 'So what did your body, your cybrid do while you were changing personae tapes or whatever?'

'I presume it was comatose.'

'It can't handle itself autonomously?'

'Oh, yes, but not when there's a general systems failure.'

'So where did you come to?'

'Pardon me?'

'When you reactivated the cybrid, where was it?'

Johnny nodded in understanding. He pointed to a boulder less than five meters from the farcaster. 'Lying there.'

'Oh this side or the other side?'

'The other side.'

I went over and examined the spot. No blood. No notes. No murder weapons left lying about. Not even a footprint or indication that Johnny's body had lain there for that eternity of a minute. A police forensics team might have read volumes into the microscopic and biotic clues left there, but all I could see was hard rock.

'If your memory's really gone,' I said, 'how do you know someone else came here with you?'

'I accessed the farcaster records.'

'Did you bother to check the mystery person or person's name on the universal card charge?'

'We both farcast on my card,' said Johnny.

'Just one other person?'

'Yes.'

I nodded. Farcaster records would solve *every* inter-world crime if the portals were true teleportation; the transport data record could have re-created the subject down to the last gram and follicle. Instead, a farcaster essentially is just a crude hole ripped in space/time by a phased singularity. If the farcaster criminal doesn't use

349

his or her own card, the only data we get are origination and destination.

'Where'd you two farcast from?' I asked.

'Tau Ceti Center.'

'You have the portal code?'

'Of course.'

'Let's go there and finish this conversation,' I said. 'This place stinks to high heaven.'

TC^2, the age-old nickname for Tau Ceti Center, is certainly the most crowded world in the Web. Besides its population of five billion people scrabbling for room on less than half the land area of Old Earth, it has an orbital ring ecology that is home for half a billion more. In addition to being the capital of the Hegemony and home of the Senate, TC^2 is the business nexus for Webtrade. Naturally the portal number Johnny had found brought us to a six-hundred-portal terminex in one of the biggest spires in New London, one of the oldest and largest city sections.

'Hell,' I said, 'let's get a drink.'

There was a choice of bars near the terminex and I picked one that was relatively quiet: a simulated ship's tavern, dark, cool, with plenty of fake wood and brass. I ordered a beer. I never drink the hard stuff or use Flashback when on a case. Sometimes I think that need for self-discipline is what keeps me in the business.

Johnny also ordered a beer, a dark, German brew bottled on Renaissance Vector. I found myself wondering what vices a cybrid might have. I said:

'What else did you find out before coming to see me?'

The young man opened his hands. 'Nothing.'

'Shit,' I said reverently. 'This is a joke. With all the powers of an AI at your disposal, you can't trace your cybrid's whereabouts and actions for a few days prior to your . . . accident?'

'No.' Johnny sipped his beer. 'Rather, I could but there are important reasons why I do not want my fellow AIs to find me investigating.'

'You suspect one of them?'

Instead of answering, Johnny handed me a flimsy of

350

his universal card purchases. 'The blackout caused by my murder left five standard days unaccounted for. Here are the card charges for that time.'

'I thought you said you were only disconnected for a minute.'

Johnny scratched his cheek with one finger. 'I was lucky to lose only five days' worth of data,' he said.

I waved over the human waiter and ordered another beer. 'Look,' I said, 'Johnny . . . whoever you are, I'll never be able to get an angle on this case unless I know more about you and your situation. Why would someone want to kill you if they know you'll be reconstituted or whatever the hell it is?'

'I see two possible motives,' said Johnny over his beer.

I nodded. 'One would be to create just the memory loss they succeeded in getting,' I said. 'That would suggest that, whatever it was they wanted you to forget, it'd occurred or come to your attention in the past week or so. What's the second motive?'

'To send me a message,' said Johnny. 'I just don't know what it is. Or from whom.'

'Do you know who would want to kill you?'

'No.'

'No guesses at all?'

'None.'

'Most murders,' I said, 'are acts of sudden, mindless rage committed by someone the victim knows well. Family. A friend or lover. A majority of the premeditated ones are usually carried out by someone close to the victim.'

Johnny said nothing. There was something about his face that I found incredibly attractive – a sort of masculine strength combined with a feminine sense of awareness. Perhaps it was the eyes.

'Do AIs have families?' I asked. 'Feuds? Squabbles? Lovers' spats?'

'No.' He smiled slightly. 'There *are* quasi-family arrangements, but they share none of the requirements of emotion or responsibility that human families exhibit. AI "families" are primarily convenient code groups for showing where certain processing trends originated.'

'So you don't think another AI attacked you?'

'It's possible.' Johnny rotated his glass in his hands. 'I just do not see why they would attack me through my cybrid.'

'Easier access?'

'Perhaps. But it complicates things for the assailant. An attack in datumplane would have been infinitely more lethal. Also, I do fail to see any motive for another AI. It makes no sense. I'm a threat to no one.'

'Why do you have a cybrid, Johnny? Maybe if I understood your role in things, I could get a motive.'

He picked up a pretzel and played with it. 'I have a cybrid . . . in some ways I *am* a cybrid, because my . . . function . . . is to observe and react to human beings. In a sense, I was human once myself.'

I frowned and shook my head. So far nothing he'd said had made sense.

'You've heard of personality retrieval projects?' he asked.

'No.'

'A standard year ago, when the FORCE sims re-created the personality of General Horace Glennon-Height to see what made him such a brilliant general? It was in all the news.'

'Yeah.'

'Well, I am . . . or was . . . an earlier and much more complicated retrieval project. My core persona was based on a pre-Hegira Old Earth poet. Ancient. Born late eighteenth century Old Calendar.'

'How the hell can they reconstruct a personality that lost in time?'

'Writings,' said Johnny. 'His letters. Diaries. Critical biographies. Testimony of friends. But mostly through his verse. The sim re-creates the environment, plugs in the known factors, and works backward from the creative products. *Voilà* – a persona core. Crude at first but, by the time I came into being, relatively refined. Our first attempt was a twentieth-century poet named Ezra Pound. Our persona was opinionated to the point of absurdity, prejudiced beyond rationality, and functionally insane. It took a year of tinkering before we discovered that the persona was accurate; it was the man who had been nuts. A genius but nuts.'

'And then what?' I said. 'They build your personality around a dead poet. Then what?'

'This becomes the template upon which the AI is grown,' said Johnny. 'The cybrid allows me to carry out my role in the datumplane community.'

'As poet?'

Johnny smiled again. 'More as poem,' he said.

'A poem?'

'An ongoing work of art . . . but not in the human sense. A puzzle perhaps. A variable enigma which occasionally offers unusual insights into more serious lines of analysis.'

'I don't get it,' I said.

'It probably does not matter. I very much doubt if my . . . purpose . . . was the cause of the assault.'

'What do you think was the cause?'

'I have no idea.'

I felt us closing a circle. 'All right,' I said. 'I'll try to find out what you were doing and who you were with during these lost five days. Is there anything besides the credit flimsy that you can think of to help?'

Johnny shook his head. 'You know, of course, why it is important for me to know the identity and motive of my assailant?'

'Sure,' I said, 'they might try it again.'

'Precisely.'

'How can I get hold of you if I need to?'

Johnny passed me an access chip.

'A secure line?' I said.

'Very.'

'Okay,' I said, 'I'll get back to you if and when I get some information.'

We moved out of the bar and toward the terminex. He was moving away when I took three quick steps and grabbed his arm. It was the first time that I had touched him. 'Johnny. What's the name of the Old Earth poet they resurrected . . .'

'Retrieved.'

'Whatever. The one they built your AI persona on?'

353

The attractive cybrid hesitated. I noticed that his eyelashes were very long. 'How can it be important?' he asked.

'Who knows what's important?'

He nodded. 'Keats,' he said. 'Born in A.D. 1795. Died of tuberculosis in 1821. John Keats.'

Following someone through a series of farcaster changes is damn near impossible. Especially if you want to remain undetected. The Web cops can do it, given about fifty agents assigned to the task, plus some exotic and damned expensive high-tech toys, not to mention the cooperation of the Transit Authority. For a solo, the task is almost impossible.

Still, it was fairly important for me to see where my new client was headed.

Johnny did not look back as he crossed the terminex plaza. I moved to a nearby kiosk and watched through my pocket-sized imager as he punched codes on a manual diskey, inserted his card, and stepped through the glowing rectangle.

The use of the manual diskey probably meant that he was headed for a general access portal since private 'caster codes are usually imprinted on eyes-only chips. Great. I'd narrowed his destination down to approximately two million portals on a hundred and fifty-some Web worlds and half that many moons.

With one hand I pulled the red 'lining' out of my overcoat while I hit replay on the imager, watching through the eyepiece as it magnified the diskey sequence. I tugged out a red cap to go with my new red jacket and pulled the brim low over my face. Moving quickly across the plaza, I queried my comlog about the nine-digit transfer code I'd seen on the imager. I knew the first three digits meant the world of Tsingtao-Hsishuang Panna – I'd memorized all the planetary prefixes – and was told an instant later that the portal code led to a residential district in the First Expansion city of Wansiehn.

I hurried to the first open booth and 'cast there, stepping out onto a small terminex plaza paved in worn brick. Ancient oriental shops leaned against one another, eaves of their pagoda roofs hanging over narrow side streets. People thronged the plaza and stood in doorways and, while most of those in sight were obviously descendants of the Long Flight exiles who settled THP, many were offworlders. The air smelled of alien vegetation, sewage, and cooking rice.

'Damn,' I whispered. There were three other farcaster portals there and none were in constant use. Johnny could have farcast out immediately.

Instead of 'casting back to Lusus, I spent a few minutes checking the plaza and side streets. By this time the melanin pill I'd swallowed had worked and I was a young black woman – or man, it was hard to tell in my trendy red balloon jacket and polarized visor, strolling idly while taking pictures with my tourist imager.

The trace pellet I'd dissolved in Johnny's second German beer had had more than enough time to work. The UV-positive microspores were almost hanging in the air by now – I could almost follow the trail of exhalations he had left. Instead, I found a bright yellow handprint on a dark wall (bright yellow to my especially fitted visor of course, invisible out of the UV spectrum) and then followed the trail of vague blotches where saturated clothing had touched market stalls or stone.

Johnny was eating in a Cantonese restaurant less than two blocks from the terminex plaza. The frying food smelled delicious but I restrained myself from entering – checking prices in alley bookstalls and haggling in the market for almost an hour before he finished, returned to the plaza, and farcast out. This time he used a chip code – a private portal, certainly, possibly a private home – and I two took chances by using my pilot-fish card to follow him. Two chances because first the card is totally illegal and would someday cost me my license if caught – less than likely if I kept using Daddy Silva's obscenely expensive but aesthetically perfect shapechanger chips – and, second, I ran a better than even chance of ending up in the living room of Johnny's house . . . never an easy situation to talk one's way out of.

It was not his living room. Even before I'd located the

street signs I recognized the familiar extra tug of gravity, the dim, bronze light, the scent of oil and ozone in the air, and knew I was home on Lusus.

Johnny had 'cast into a medium-security private residential tower in one of the Bergson Hives. Perhaps that was why he'd chosen my agency – we were almost neighbors, less than six hundred klicks apart.

My cybrid was not in sight. I walked purposefully so as not to alert any security vids programmed to respond to loitering. There was no residents' directory, no numbers or names on the apartment doorways, and no listings accessible by comlog. I guessed that there were about twenty thousand residential cubbies in East Bergson Hive.

The telltales were fading as the spore soup died, but I checked only two of the radial corridors before I found a trail. Johnny lived far out on a glass-floored wing above a methane lake. His palmlock showed a faintly glowing handprint. I used my cat-burglar tools to take a reading of the lock and then I 'cast home.

All in all, I'd watched my man go out for Chinese food and then go home for the night. Enough accomplished for one day.

BB Surbringer was my AI expert. BB worked in Hegemony Flow Control Records and Statistics and spent most of his life reclining on a free-fall couch with half a dozen microleads running from his skull while he communed with other bureaucrats in datumplane. I'd known him in college when he was a pure cyberpuke, a twentieth-generation hacker, cortically shunted when he was twelve standard. His real name was Ernest but he'd earned the nickname BB when he went out with a friend of mine named Shayla Toyo. Shayla'd seen him naked on their second date and had laughed for a solid half hour: Ernest was – and is – almost two meters tall but masses less than fifty kilos. Shayla said that he had a butt like two BBs and – like most cruel things do – the nickname stuck.

I visited him in one of the windowless worker monoliths on TC^2. No cloud towers for BB and his ilk.

'So, Brawne,' he said, 'how come you're getting information-literate in your old age? You're too old to get a real job.'

'I just want to know about AIs, BB.'

'Only one of the most complex topics in the known universe,' he sighed and looked longingly at his disconnected neural shunt and metacortex leads. Cyberpukes never come down, but civil servants are required to dismount for lunch. BB was like most cyberpukes in that he never felt comfortable exchanging information when he wasn't riding a data wave. 'So what do you want to know?' he said.

'Why did the AIs drop out?' I had to start somewhere.

BB made a convoluted gesture with his hands. 'They said they had projects which were not compatible with total immersion in Hegemony – read human – affairs. Truth is, nobody knows.'

'But they're still around. Still managing things?'

'Sure. The system couldn't run without them. You know that, Brawne. Even the All Thing couldn't work without AI management of the real-time Schwarzschild patterning . . .'

'Okay,' I said, cutting him off before he lapsed into cyberpukese, 'but what are their "other projects"?'

'No one knows. Branner and Swayze up at ArtIntel Corp think that the AIs are pursuing the evolution of consciousness on a galactic scale. We know they have their own probes out far deeper into the Outback than . . .'

'What about cybrids?'

'Cybrids?' BB sat up and looked interested for the first time. 'Why do you mention cybrids?'

'Why are you surprised that I mentioned them, BB?'

He absently rubbed his shunt socket. 'Well, first of all, most people forget they exist. Two centuries ago it was all alarmism and pod people taking over and all that, but now nobody thinks about them. Also, I just ran across an anomaly advisory yesterday that said that cybrids were disappearing.'

'Disappearing?' It was my turn to sit up.

'You know, being phased out. The AIs used to maintain

about a thousand licensed cybrids in the Web. About half of them based right here on TC². Last week's census showed about two thirds of those'd been recalled in the past month or so.'

'What happens when an AI recalls its cybrid?'

'I dunno. They're destroyed, I suppose. AIs don't like to waste things, so I imagine the genetic material's recycled somehow.'

'Why are they being recycled?'

'Nobody knows, Brawne. But then most of us don't know why the AIs do most of the things they do.'

'Do experts see them – the AIs – as a threat?'

'Are you kidding? Six hundred years ago, maybe. Two centuries ago the Secession made us leery. But if the things wanted to hurt humanity, they could've done it long before this. Worrying about AIs turning on us is about as productive as worrying that farm animals are going to revolt.'

'Except the AIs are smarter than us,' I said.

'Yeah, well, there is that.'

'BB, have you heard of personality retrieval projects?'

'Like the Glennon-Height thing? Sure. Everyone has. I even worked on one at Reichs University a few years ago. But they're passé. No one's doing them anymore.'

'Why's that?'

'Jesus, you *don't* know shit about anything, do you, Brawne? The personality retrieval projects were all washouts. Even with the best sim control . . . they got the FORCE OCS:HTN network involved . . . you can't factor all variables successfully. The persona template becomes self-aware . . . I don't mean just self-aware, like you and me, but self-aware that it's an artificially self-aware persona – and that leads to terminal Strange Loops and nonharmonic labyrinths that go straight to Escher-space.'

'Translate,' I said.

BB sighed and glanced at the blue and gold time band on the wall. Five minutes and his mandatory lunch hour was over. He could rejoin the real world. 'Translated,' he said, 'the retrieved personality breaks down. Goes crazy. Psycho City. Bugfuck.'

'All of them?'

'All of them.'

'But the AIs are still interested in the process?'

'Oh, yeah? Who says? They've never *done* one. All the retrieval efforts I've ever heard of were human-run . . . mostly botched university projects. Brain-dead academics spending fortunes to bring back dead academic brains.'

I forced a smile. There were three minutes until he could plug back in. 'Were all the retrieved personalities given cybrid remotes?'

'Uh-uh. What gave you that idea, Brawne? None were. Couldn't work.'

'Why not?'

'It'd just fuck up the stimsim. Plus you'd need perfect clone stock and an interactive environment precise to the last detail. You see, kiddo, with a retrieved personality, you let it live in *its* world via full-scale sim and then you just sneaked a few questions in via dreams or scenario interactives. Pulling a persona *out* of sim reality into slow time . . .'

This was the cyberpukes' age-old term for the . . . pardon the expression . . . real world.

'. . . would just drive it bugfuck all the sooner,' he finished.

I shook my head. 'Yeah, well, thanks, BB.' I moved to the door. There were thirty seconds left before my old college friend could escape from slow time.

'BB,' I said as an afterthought, 'have you ever heard of a persona retrieved from an Old Earth poet named John Keats?'

'Keats? Oh, sure there was a big write-up on that in my undergrad text. Marti Carollus did that about fifty years ago at New Cambridge.'

'What happened?'

'The usual. Persona went Strange Loop. But before it broke up it died a full sim death. Some ancient disease.' BB glanced at the clock, smiled, and lifted his shunt. Before clicking it into his skull socket he looked at me again, almost beatifically. 'I remember now,' he said through his dreamy smile, 'it was tuberculosis.'

If our society ever opted for Orwell's Big Brother approach, the instrument of choice for oppression would have to be the credit wake. In a totally noncash economy with only a vestigial barter black market, a person's activities could be tracked in real time by monitoring the credit wake of his or her universal card. There were strict laws protecting card privacy but laws had a bad habit of being ignored or abrogated when societal push came to totalitarian shove.

Johnny's credit wake for the five-day period leading to his murder showed a man of regular habits and modest expenses. Before following up the leads on the credit flimsy I'd spent a dull two days following Johnny himself.

Data: He lived alone in East Bergson Hive. A routine check showed that he'd lived there about seven local months – less than five standard. In the morning he had breakfast at a local cafe and then farcast to Renaissance Vector where he worked for about five hours, evidently gathering research of some sort in the print archives, followed by a light lunch at a courtyard vendor's stand, another hour or two in the library, and then 'cast home to Lusus or to some favorite eating spot on another world. In his cubby by 2200 hours. More farcasting than the average Lusian middle-class drone, but an otherwise uninspiring schedule. The credit flimsies confirmed that he had held to the agenda on the week he was murdered, with the addition of a few extra purchases – shoes one day, groceries the next – and one stop at a bar on Renaissance V on the day of his 'murder.'

I joined him for dinner at the small restaurant on Red Dragon Street near the Tsingtao-Hsishuang Panna portal. The food was very hot, very spicy, and very good.

'How is it going,' he asked.

'Great. I'm a thousand marks richer than when we met and I found a good Cantonese restaurant.'

'I'm glad my money is going toward something important.'

'Speaking of your money . . . where does it come from? Hanging out in a Renaissance Vector library can't pay much.'

Johnny raised an eyebrow. 'I live on a small . . . inheritance.'

'Not too small, I hope. I want to be paid.'

'It will be adequate for our purposes, M. Lamia. Have you discovered anything of interest?'

I shrugged. 'Tell me what you do in that library.'

'Can it possibly be germane?'

'Yeah, could be.'

He looked at me strangely. Something about his eyes made me go weak at the knees. 'You remind me of someone,' he said softly.

'Oh?' From anyone else that line would have been cause for an exit. 'Who?' I asked.

'A . . . woman I once knew. Long ago.' He brushed fingers across his brow as if he were suddenly tired or dizzy.

'What was her name?'

'Fanny.' The word was almost whispered.

I knew who he was talking about. John Keats had a fiancée named Fanny. Their love affair had been a series of romantic frustrations which almost drove the poet mad. When he died in Italy, alone except for one fellow traveler, feeling abandoned by friends and his lover, Keats had asked that unopened letters from Fanny and a lock of her hair be buried with him.

I'd never heard of John Keats before this week; I'd accessed all this shit with my comlog. I said, 'So what do you do at the library?'

The cybrid cleared his throat. 'I'm researching a poem. Searching for fragments of the original.'

'Something by Keats?'

'Yes.'

'Wouldn't it be easier to access it?'

'Of course. But it is important for me to see the original . . . to touch it.'

I thought about that. 'What's the poem about?'

He smiled . . . or at least his lips did. The hazel eyes still seemed troubled. 'It's called *Hyperion*. It's difficult to describe what it's about. Artistic failure, I suppose. Keats never finished it.'

I pushed aside my plate and sipped warm tea. 'You say

Keats never finished it. Don't you mean *you* never finished it?'

His look of shock had to be genuine . . . unless AIs were consummate actors. For all I knew, they could be. 'Good God,' he said, 'I'm not John Keats. Having a persona based upon a retrieval template no more makes me Keats than having the name Lamia makes you a monster. There've been a million influences that have separated me from that poor, sad genius.'

'You said I reminded you of Fanny.'

'An echo of a dream. Less. You've taken RNA learning medication, yes?'

'Yes.'

'It's like that. Memories which feel . . . hollow.'

A human waiter brought fortune cookies.

'Do you have any interest in visiting the real Hyperion?' I asked.

'What's that?'

'The Outback world. Somewhere beyond Parvati, I think.'

Johnny looked puzzled. He had broken open the cookie but had not yet read the fortune.

'It used to be called Poets' World, I think,' I said. 'It even has a city named after you . . . after Keats.'

The young man shook his head. 'I'm sorry, I haven't heard of the place.'

'How can that be? Don't AIs know everything?'

His laugh was short and sharp. 'This one knows very little.' He read his fortune: BE WARY OF SUDDEN IMPULSES.

I crossed my arms. 'You know, except for that parlor trick with the bank manager holo, I have no proof that you are what you say you are.'

'Give me your hand.'

'My hand?'

'Yes. Either one. Thank you.'

Johnny held my right hand in both of his. His fingers were longer than mine. Mine were stronger.

'Close your eyes,' he said.

I did. There was no transition: one instant I was sitting in the Blue Lotus on Red Dragon Street and the next I was . . . nowhere. Somewhere. Streaking through gray-blue datumplane, banking along chrome-yellow information highways, passing over and under and through great cities of glowing information storage, red skyscrapers sheathed in black security ice, simple entities like personal accounts or corporate files blazing like burning refineries in the night. Above it all, just out of sight as if poised in twisted space, hung the gigantic *weights* of the AIs, their simplest communications pulsing like violent heat lightning along the infinite horizons. Somewhere in the distance, all but lost in the maze of three-dimensional neon that partitioned one tiny second of arc in the incredible datasphere of one small world, I sensed rather than saw those soft, hazel eyes waiting for me.

Johnny released my hand. He cracked my fortune cookie open. The strip of paper read: INVEST WISELY IN NEW VENTURES.

'Jesus,' I whispered. BB had taken me flying in datumplane before, but without a shunt the experience had been a shadow of this. It was the difference between watching a black and white holo of fireworks display and *being* there. 'How do you do that?'

'Will you be making any progress on the case tomorrow?' he asked.

I regained my composure. 'Tomorrow,' I said, 'I plan to solve it.'

Well, maybe not solve it, but at least get things moving. The last charge on Johnny's credit flimsy had been the bar on Renaissance V. I'd checked it out the first day, of course, talked to several of the regulars since there was no human bartender, but had come up with no one who remembered Johnny. I'd been back twice with no greater luck. But on the third day I went back to stay until something broke.

The bar was definitely not in the class of the wood and brass place Johnny and I had visited on TC^2. This place was tucked on a second floor of a decaying building in a run-down neighborhood two blocks from the Renaissance library where Johnny spent his days. Not the kind

363

of place he would stop in on the way to the farcaster plaza, but just the kind of place he might end up if he met someone in or near the library – someone who wanted to talk in private.

I'd been there six hours and was getting damned tired of salted nuts and flat beer when an old derelict came in. I guessed that he was a regular by the way he didn't pause in the doorway or look around, but headed straight for a small table in the back and ordered a whiskey before the serving mech had come to a full stop. When I joined him at the table I realized that he wasn't so much a derelict as an example of the tired men and women I'd seen in the junk shops and street stalls in that neighborhood. He squinted up at me through defeated eyes.

'May I sit down?'

'Depends, sister. What're you selling?'

'I'm buying.' I sat, set my beer mug on the table, and slid across a flat photo of Johnny entering the farcaster booth on TC^2. 'Seen this guy?'

The old man glanced at the photo and returned his full attention to his whiskey. 'Maybe.'

I waved over the mech for another round. 'If you did see him, it's your lucky day.'

The old man snorted and rubbed the back of his hand against the gray stubble on his cheek. 'If it is, it'll be the first time in a long fucking time.' He focused on me. 'How much? For what?'

'Information. How much depends on the information. Have you seen him?' I removed a black market fifty-mark bill from my tunic pocket.

'Yeah.'

The bill came down to the table but remained in my hand. 'When?'

'Last Tuesday. Tuesday morning.'

That was the correct day. I slid the fifty marks to him and removed another bill. 'Was he alone?'

The old man licked his lips. 'Let me think. I don't think . . . no, he was there.' He pointed toward a table at the rear. 'Two other guys with him. One of them . . . well, that's why I remembered.'

'What's that?'

The old man rubbed finger and thumb in a gesture as old as greed.

'Tell me about the two men,' I coaxed.

'The young guy . . . your guy . . . he was with one of them, you know, the nature freaks with robes. You see 'em on HTV all the time. Them and their damn trees.'

Trees? 'A Templar?' I said, astounded. What would a Templar be doing in a Renaissance V bar? If he'd been after Johnny, why would he wear his robe? That would be like a murderer going out to do business in a clown suit.

'Yeah. Templar. Brown robe, sort of oriental-looking.'

'A man?'

'Yeah, I said he was.'

'Can you describe him more?'

'Nah, Templar. Tall son of a bitch. Couldn't see his face very well.'

'What about the other one?'

The old man shrugged. I removed a second bill and set them both near my glass.

'Did they come in together?' I prompted. 'The three of them?'

'I don't . . . I can't . . . No, wait. Your guy and the Templar guy came in first. I remember seeing the robe before the other guy sat down.'

'Describe the other man.'

The old man waved over the mech and ordered a third drink. I used my card and the servitor slid away on noisy repellers.

'Like you,' he said. 'Sort of like you.'

'Short?' I said. 'Strong arms and legs? A Lusian?'

'Yeah. I guess so. Never been there.'

'What else?'

'No hair,' said the old man. 'Just a whattyacallit like my niece used to wear. A pony tail.'

'A queue,' I said.

'Yeah. Whatever.' He started to reach for the bills.

'Couple more questions. Did they argue?'

'Nah. Don't think so. Talked real quiet. Place's pretty empty that time of day.'

'What time of day was it?'

'Morning. About ten o'clock.'

This coincided with the credit flimsy code.

'Did you hear any of the conversation?'

'Uh-uh.'

'Who did most of the talking?'

The old man took a drink and furrowed his brow in thought. 'Templar guy did at first. Your man seemed to be answering questions. Seemed surprised once when I was looking.'

'Shocked?'

'Uh-uh, just surprised. Like the guy in the robe'd said something he didn't expect.'

'You said the Templar did most of the talking at first. Who spoke later? My guy?'

'Uh-uh, the one with the pony tail. Then they left.'

'All three of them left?'

'Nah. Your guy and the pony tail.'

'The Templar stayed behind?'

'Yeah. I guess so. I think. I went to the lav. When I got back I don't think he was there.'

'What way did the other two go?'

'I don't know, goddammit. I wasn't paying much attention. I was having a drink, not playing spy!'

I nodded. The mech rolled over again but I waved it away. The old man scowled at its back.

'So they weren't arguing when they left? No sign of a disagreement or that one was forcing the other to leave?'

'Who?'

'My guy and the queue.'

'Uh-uh. Shit, I don't know.' He looked down at the bills in his grimy hand and at the whiskey in the mech's display panel, realizing, perhaps, that he wasn't going to get any more of either from me. 'Why do you want to know all this shit, anyway?'

'I'm looking for the guy,' I said. I looked around the bar. About twenty customers sat at tables. Most of them looked like neighborhood regulars. 'Anyone else here who might've seen them? Or somebody else you might remember who was here?'

'Uh-uh,' he said dully. I realized then that the old man's eyes were precisely the color of the whiskey he'd been drinking.

I stood, set a final twenty-mark bill on the table.
'Thanks, friend.'

'Any time, sister.'

The mech was rolling toward him before I'd reached
the door.

I walked back toward the library, paused a minute in the
busy farcaster plaza, and stood there a minute. Scenario
so far: Johnny had met the Templar or been approached
by him, either in the library or outside when he arrived in
midmorning. They went somewhere private to talk, the
bar, and something the Templar said surprised Johnny.
A man with a queue – possibly a Lusian – showed up
and took over the conversation. Johnny and Queue left
together. Sometime after that, Johnny farcast to TC^2
and then farcast from there with one other person – possibly Queue or the Templar – to Madhya where someone
tried to kill him. *Did* kill him.

Too many gaps. Too many 'someones.' Not a hell of a
lot to show for a day's work.

I was debating whether to 'cast back to Lusus when my
comlog chirped on the restricted comm frequency I'd
given to Johnny.

His voice was raw. 'M. Lamia. Come quickly, please.
I think they've just tried again. To kill me.' The coordinates which followed were for the East Bergson Hive.

I ran for the farcaster.

The door to Johnny's cubby was open a crack. There was
no one in the corridor, no sounds from the apartment.
Whatever had happened hadn't brought the authorities
yet.

I brought out Dad's automatic pistol from my coat
pocket, jacked a round into the chamber, and clicked on
the laser targeting beam with a single motion.

I went in low, both arms extended, the red dot sliding
across the dark walls, a cheap print on the far wall, a
darker hall leading into the cubby. The foyer was empty.
The living room and media pit were empty.

Johnny lay on the floor of the bedroom, his head
against the bed. Blood soaked the sheet. He struggled to

367

prop himself up, fell back. The sliding door behind him was open and a dank industrial wind blew in from the open mall beyond.

I checked the single closet, short hall, kitchen niche, and came back to step out on the balcony. The view was spectacular from the perch two hundred or so meters up the curved Hive wall, looking down the ten or twenty kilometers of the Trench Mall. The roof of the Hive was a dark mass of girders another hundred or so meters above. Thousands of lights, commercial holos, and neon lights glowed from the mall, joining in the haze of distance to a brilliant, throbbing electric blur.

There were hundreds of similar balconies on this wall of the Hive, all deserted. The nearest was twenty meters away. They were the kind of thing rental agents like to point to as a plus – God knows that Johnny probably paid plenty extra for an outside room – but the balconies were totally impractical because of the strong wind rushing up toward the ventilators, carrying the usual grit and debris as well as the eternal Hive scent of oil and ozone.

I put my pistol away and went back to check on Johnny.

The cut ran from his hairline to his eyebrow, superficial but messy. He was sitting up as I returned from the bathroom with a sterile drypad and pressed it against the cut. 'What happened?' I said.

'Two men . . . were waiting in the bedroom when I came in. They'd bypassed the alarms on the balcony door.'

'You deserve a refund on your security tax,' I said. 'What happened next?'

'We struggled. They seemed to be dragging me toward the door. One of them had an injector but I managed to knock it out of his hand.'

'What made them leave?'

'I activated the in-house alarms.'

'But not Hive security?'

'No. I didn't want them involved.'

'Who hit you?'

Johnny smiled sheepishly. 'I did. They released me, I

went after them. I managed to trip and fall against the nightstand.'

'Not a very graceful brawl on either side,' I said. I switched on a lamp and checked the carpet until I found the injection ampule where it had rolled under the bed.

Johnny eyed it as if it were a viper.

'What's your guess?' I said. 'More AIDS II?'

He shook his head.

'I know a place where we can get it analyzed,' I said. 'My guess is that it's just a hypnotic trank. They just wanted you to come along . . . not to kill you.'

Johnny moved the drypad and grimaced. The blood was still flowing. 'Why would anyone want to kidnap a cybrid?'

'You tell me. I'm beginning to think that the so-called murder was just a botched kidnapping attempt.'

Johnny shook his head again.

I said, 'Did one of the men wear a queue?'

'I don't know. They wore caps and osmosis masks.'

'Was either one tall enough to be a Templar or strong enough to be a Lusian?'

'A Templar?' Johnny was surprised. 'No. One was about average Web height. The one with the ampule could have been Lusian. Strong enough.'

'So you went after a Lusian thug with your bare hands. Do you have some bioprocessors or augmentation implants I don't know about?'

'No. I was just mad.'

I helped him to his feet. 'So AIs get angry?'

'I do.'

'Come on,' I said, 'I know an automated med clinic that's discount. Then you'll be staying with me for a while.'

'With you? Why?'

'Because you've graduated from just needing a detective,' I said. 'Now you need a bodyguard.'

My cubby wasn't registered in the Hive zoning schematic as an apartment; I'd taken over a renovated warehouse loft from a friend of mine who'd run afoul of loan sharks. My friend had decided late in life to emigrate to one of the Outback colonies and I'd gotten a good deal on a place just a klick down the corridor from my office. The environment was a little rough and sometimes the noise from the loading docks could drown out conversation, but it gave me ten times the room of a normal cubby and I could use my weights and workout equipment right at home.

Johnny honestly seemed intrigued by the place and I had to kick myself for being pleased. Next thing you knew, I'd be putting on lipstick and body rouge for this cybrid.

'So why do you live on Lusus?' I asked him. 'Most offworlders find the gravity a pain and the scenery monotonous. Plus your research material's at the library on Renaissance V. Why here?'

I found myself looking and listening very carefully as he answered. His hair was straight on top, parted in the middle, and fell in reddish-brown curls to his collar. He had the habit of resting his cheek on his fist as he spoke. It struck me that his dialect was actually the nondialect of someone who has learned a new language perfectly but without the lazy shortcuts of someone born to it. And beneath that there was a hint of lilt that brought back the overtones of a cat burglar I'd known who had grown up on Asquith, a quiet, backwater Web world settled by First Expansion immigrants from what had once been the British Isles.

'I have lived on many worlds,' he said. 'My purpose is to observe.'

'As a poet?'

He shook his head, winced, and gingerly touched the stitches. 'No. I'm not a poet. He *was*.'

Despite the circumstances, there was an energy and vitality to Johnny that I'd found in too few men. It was hard to describe, but I'd seen rooms full of more important personages rearrange themselves to orbit around personalities like his. It was not merely his reticence and sensitivity, it was an *intensity* that he emanated even when merely observing.

'Why do *you* live here?' he asked.

'I was born here.'

370

'Yes, but you spent your childhood years on Tau Ceti Center. Your father was a senator.'

I said nothing.

'Many people expected you to go into politics,' he said. 'Did your father's suicide dissuade you?'

'It wasn't suicide,' I said.

'No?'

'All the news reports and the inquest said it was,' I said tonelessly, 'but they were wrong. My father never would have taken his own life.'

'So it was murder?'

'Yes.'

'Despite the fact that there was no motive or hint of a suspect?'

'Yes.'

'I see,' said Johnny. The yellow glow from the loading dock lamps came through the dusty windows and made his hair gleam like new copper. 'Do you like being a detective?'

'When I do it well,' I said. 'Are you hungry?'

'No.'

'Then let's get some sleep. You can have the couch.'

'Do you do it well often?' he said. 'Being a detective?'

'We'll see tomorrow.'

In the morning Johnny farcast to Renaissance Vector at about the usual time, waited a moment in the plaza, and then 'cast to the Old Settlers' Museum on Sol Draconi Septem. From there he jumped to the main terminex on Nordholm and then 'cast to the Templar world of God's Grove.

We'd worked out the timing ahead of time and I was waiting for him on Renaissance V, standing back in the shadows of the colonnade.

A man with a queue was the third through after Johnny. There was no doubt he was Lusian – between the Hive pallor, the muscle and body mass, and the arrogant way of walking, he might have been my long-lost brother.

He never looked at Johnny but I could tell that he was surprised when the cybrid circled around to the outbound

371

portals. I stayed back and only caught a glimpse of his card but would've bet anything that it was a tracer.

Queue was careful in the Old Settlers' Museum, keeping Johnny in sight but checking his own back as well. I was dressed in a Zen Gnostic's meditation jumper, isolation visor and all, and I never looked their way as I circled to the museum outportal and 'cast directly to God's Grove.

It made me feel funny, leaving Johnny alone through the museum and Nordholm terminex, but both were public places and it was a calculated risk.

Johnny came through the Worldtree arrival portal right on time and bought a ticket for the tour. His shadow had to scurry to catch up, breaking cover to board the omnibus skimmer before it left. I was already settled in the rear seat on the upper deck and Johnny found a place near the front, just as we had planned. Now I was wearing basic tourist garb and my imager was one of a dozen in action when Queue hurried to take his place three rows behind Johnny.

The tour of the Worldtree is always fun – Dad first took me there when I was only three standard – but this time as the skimmer moved above branches the size of freeways and circled higher around a trunk the width of Olympus Mons, I found myself reacting to the glimpses of hooded Templars with something approaching anxiety.

Johnny and I had discussed various clever and infinitely subtle ways to trail Queue if he showed up, to follow him to his lair and spend weeks if necessary deducing his game. In the end I opted for something less than the subtle approach.

The omnibus had dumped us out near the Muir Museum and people were milling around on the plaza, torn between spending ten marks for a ticket to educate themselves or going straight for the gift shop, when I walked up to Queue, gripped him by the upper arm, and said in conversational tones, 'Hi. Do you mind telling me what the fuck you want with my client?'

There's an old stereotype that says that Lusians are as subtle as a stomach pump and about half as pleasant. If

372

I'd helped confirm the first part of that, Queue went a long way toward reinforcing the second prejudice.

He was fast. Even with my seemingly casual grip paralyzing the muscles of his right arm, the knife in his left hand sliced up and around in less than a second.

I let myself fall to my right, the knife slicing air centimeters from my cheek, hitting pavement and rolling as I palmed the neural stunner and came up on one knee to meet the threat.

No threat. Queue was running. Away from me. Away from Johnny. He shoved tourists aside, dodged behind them, moving toward the museum entrance.

I slid the stunner back into its wristband and began running myself. Stunners are great close-range weapons – as easy to aim as a shotgun without the dire effects if the spread pattern finds innocent bystanders – but they aren't worth anything beyond eight or ten meters. On full dispersal, I could give half the tourists in the plaza a miserable headache but Queue was already too far away to bring down. I ran after him.

Johnny ran toward me. I waved him back. 'My place!' I shouted. 'Use the locks!'

Queue had reached the museum entrance and now he looked back at me; the knife was still in his hand.

I charged at him, feeling something like joy at the thought of the next few minutes.

Queue vaulted a turnstile and shoved tourists aside to get through the doors. I followed.

It was only when I reached the hushed interior of the Grand Hall and saw him shoving his way up the crowded escalator to the Excursion Mezzanine that I realized where he was headed.

My father had taken me on the Templar Excursion when I was three. The farcaster portals were permanently open; it took about three hours to walk all the guided tours on the thirty worlds where the Templar ecologists had preserved some bit of nature which they thought would please the Muir. I couldn't remember for sure, but I thought the paths were loop trails with the portals relatively close together for easy transit by Templar guides and maintenance people.

Shit.

A uniformed guard near the tour portal saw the confusion as Queue cut through and stepped forward to intercept the rude intruder. Even from fifteen meters away I could see the shock and disbelief on the old guard's face as he staggered backward, the hilt of Queue's long knife protruding from his chest.

The old guard, probably a retired local cop, looked down, face white, touched the bone hilt, gingerly as if it were a gag, and collapsed face first on the mezzanine tiles. Tourists screamed. Someone yelled for a medic. I saw Queue shove a Templar guide aside and throw himself through the glowing portal.

This was not going as I'd planned.

I vaulted for the portal without slowing.

Through and half sliding on the slippery grass of a hillside. Sky lemon yellow above us. Tropical scents. I saw startled faces turned my way. Queue was halfway to the other farcaster, cutting through elaborate flower beds and kicking aside bonsai topiary. I recognized the world of Fuji and careened down the hillside, clambering uphill again through the flower beds, following the trail of destruction Queue had left. 'Stop that man!' I screamed, realizing how foolish it sounded. No one made a move except for a Nipponese tourist who raised her imager and recorded a sequence.

Queue looked back, shoved past a gawking tour group, and stepped through the farcast portal.

I had the stunner in my hand again and waved it at the crowd. 'Back! Back!' They hastily made room.

I went through warily, stunner raised. Queue no longer had his knife but I didn't know what other toys he carried.

Brilliant light on water. The violent waves of Mare Infinitus. The path was a narrow wooden walkway ten meters above the support floats. It led out and away, curving above a fairyland coral reef and a sargasso of yellow island kelp before curving back, but a narrow catwalk cut across to the portal at the end of the trail. Queue had climbed the NO ACCESS gate and was halfway across the catwalk.

I ran the ten paces to the edge of the platform, selected tightbeam, and held the stunner on full auto, sweeping the invisible beam back and forth as if I were aiming a garden hose.

Queue seemed to stumble a half step but then made the last ten meters to the portal and dived through. I cursed and climbed the gate, ignoring shouts from a Templar guide behind me. I caught a glimpse of a sign which reminded tourists to don therm gear and then I was through the portal, barely sensing the shower-tingle sensation of passing through the farcaster screen.

A blizzard roared, whipping against the arched containment field which turned the tourist trail into a tunnel through fierce whiteness. Sol Draconi Septem – the northern reaches where Templar lobbying of the All Thing had stopped the colonial heating project in order to save the arctic wraiths. I could feel the 1.7-standard gravity on my shoulders like the yoke of my workout machine. It was a shame that Queue was a Lusian also; if he'd been Web-standard in physique, there would have been no contest if I caught him here. Now we would see who was in better shape.

Queue was fifty meters down the trail and looking back over his shoulder. The other farcaster was somewhere near but the blizzard made anything off the trail invisible and inaccessible. I began loping after him. In deference to the gravity, this was the shortest of the Templar Excursion trails, curving back after only two hundred or so meters. I could hear Queue's panting as I closed on him. I was running easily; there was no way that he was going to beat me to the next farcaster. I saw no tourists on the trail and so far no one had given chase. I thought that this would not be a bad place to interrogate him.

Queue was thirty meters short of the exit portal when he turned, dropped to one knee, and aimed an energy pistol. The first bolt was short, possibly because of the unaccustomed weight of the weapon in Sol Draconi's gravity field, but it was close enough to leave a scorched slash of slagged walkway and melted permafrost to within a meter of me. He adjusted his aim.

I went out through the containment field, shouldering my way through the elastic resistance and stumbling into drifts above my waist. The cold air burned my lungs and wind-driven snow caked my face and bare arms in seconds. I could see Queue looking for me from within the lighted pathway, but the blizzard dimness worked in my favor now as I threw myself through drifts in his direction.

Queue forced his head, shoulders, and right arm through the field wall, squinting in the barrage of icy particles which coated his cheeks and brow in an instant. His second shot was high and I felt the heat of the bolt as it passed over. I was within ten meters of him now; I set the stunner on widest dispersal and sprayed it in his direction without lifting my head from the snowdrift where I had dropped.

Queue let the energy pistol tumble into the snow and fell back through the containment field.

I screamed in triumph, my shout lost in the wind roar, and staggered toward the field wall. My hands and feet were distant things now, beyond the pain of cold. My cheeks and ears burned. I put the thought of frostbite out of my mind and threw myself against the field.

It was a class-three field, designed to keep out the elements and anything as huge as an arctic wraith, while allowing the occasional errant tourist or errand-bent Templar reentry to the path, but in my cold-weakened condition I found myself batting against it for a moment like a fly against plastic, my feet slipping on snow and ice. Finally I threw myself forward, landing heavily and clumsily, dragging my legs through.

The sudden warmth of the pathway set me to shaking uncontrollably. Shards of sleet fell from me as I forced myself to my knees, then to my feet.

Queue ran the last five yards to the exit portal with his right arm dangling as if broken. I knew the nerve-fire agony of a neural stunner and did not envy him. He looked back once as I began running toward him and then he went through.

Maui-Covenant. The air was tropical and smelled of ocean and vegetation. The sky was an Old Earth blue. I saw immediately that the trail had led to one of the few free motile isles which the Templars had saved from Hegemony domestication. It was a large isle, perhaps half a kilometer from end to end, and from the access portal's vantage point on a wide deck encircling the main treesail trunk I could see the expansive sail leaves filling with wind and the indigo rudder vines trailing far behind. The exit portal lay only fifteen meters away down a staircase but I saw at once that Queue had run the other way, along the main trail, toward a cluster of huts and concession stands near the edge of the isle.

It was only here, halfway along the Templar Excursion trail, that they allowed human structures to shelter weary hikers while they purchased refreshments or souvenirs to benefit the Templar Brotherhood. I began jogging down the wide staircase to the trail below, still shivering, my clothes soaked with rapidly melting snow. Why was Queue running toward the cluster of people there?

I saw the bright carpets laid out for rental and understood. The hawking mats were illegal on most Web worlds but still a tradition on Maui-Covenant because of the Siri legend; less than two meters long and a meter wide, the ancient playthings lay waiting to carry tourists out over the sea and back again to the wandering isle. If Queue reached one of those . . . I broke into a full sprint, catching the other Lusian a few meters short of the hawking mat area and tackling him just below the knees. We rolled into the concession stand area and the few tourists there shouted and scattered.

My father taught me one thing which any child ignores at his or her own peril: a good big guy can always beat a good little guy. In this case we were about even. Queue twisted free and jumped to his feet, falling into an arms-out, fingers-splayed oriental fighting stance. Now we'd see who the better guy was.

Queue got the first blow in, feinting a straight-fingered jab with his left hand and coming up and around with a swinging kick instead. I ducked but he connected solidly enough to make my left shoulder and upper arm go numb.

Queue danced backward. I followed. He swung a close-fisted right-handed punch. I blocked it. He chopped with his left hand. I blocked with my right forearm. Queue danced back, whirled, and unleashed a left-footed kick. I ducked, caught his leg as it passed over, and dumped him on the sand.

Queue jumped up. I knocked him down with a short left hook. He rolled away and scrambled to his knees. I kicked him behind his left ear, pulling the blow enough to leave him conscious.

Too conscious, I realized a second later as he ran four fingers under my guard in an attempted heart jab. Instead, he bruised the layers of muscle under my right breast. I punched him full force in the mouth, sending blood spraying as he rolled to the waterline and lay still. Behind us, people ran toward the exit portal, calling to the few others to get the police.

I lifted Johnny's would-be assassin by his queue, dragged him to the edge of the isle, and dipped his face in the water until he came to. Then I rolled him over and lifted him by his torn and stained shirtfront. We would have only a minute or two until *someone* arrived.

Queue stared up at me with a glazed glare. I shook him once and leaned close. 'Listen, my friend,' I whispered. 'We're going to have a short but sincere conversation. We'll start with who you are and why you're bothering the guy you were following.'

I felt the surge of current before I saw the blue. I cursed and let go of his shirtfront. The electrical nimbus seemed to surround Queue's entire body at once. I jumped back but not before my own hair stood on end and surge control alarms on my comlog chirped urgently. Queue opened his mouth to scream and I could see the blue within like a poorly done holo special effect. His shirtfront sizzled, blackened, and burst into flame. Beneath it his chest grew blue spots like an ancient film burning through. The spots widened, joined, widened again. I looked into his chest cavity and saw organs melting in blue flame. He screamed again, audibly this time, and I watched as teeth and eyes collapsed into blue fire.

I took another step back.

Queue was burning now, the orange-red flames super-seding the blue glow. His flesh exploded outward with flame as if his bones had ignited. Within a minute he was a smoking caricature of charred flesh, the body reduced to the ancient dwarf-boxer posture of burning victims everywhere. I turned away and put a hand over my mouth, searching the faces of the few watchers to see if any of them could have done this. Wide, frightened eyes stared back. Far above, gray security uniforms burst from the farcaster.

Damn. I looked around. The treesails surged and bil-lowed overhead. Radiant gossamers, beautiful even in daylight, flitted among tropical vegetation of a hundred hues. Sunlight danced on blue ocean. The way to both portals was blocked. The security guard leading the group had drawn a weapon.

I was to the first hawking mat in three strides, trying to remember from my own ride two decades earlier how the flight threads were activated. I tapped designs in desperation.

The hawking mat went rigid and lifted ten centimeters off the beach. I could hear the shouts now as security guards reached the edge of the crowd. A woman in gaudy Renaissance Minor garb pointed my way. I jumped off the hawking mat, gathered up the other seven mats, and jumped aboard my own. Barely able to find the flight designs under the tumble of rugs, I slapped the forward controls until the mat lurched into flight, almost tumbling me off as it rose.

Fifty meters out, thirty meters high, I dumped the other mats into the sea and swiveled to see what was happening on the beach. Several gray uniforms were huddled around the burned remains. Another pointed a silver wand in my direction.

Delicate needles of pain tingled along my arm, shoul-ders, and neck. My eyelids drooped and I almost slid off the mat to my right. I gripped the far side with my left hand, slumped forward, and tapped at the ascent design with fingers made of wood. Climbing again, I fumbled at my right sleeve for my own stunner. The wristband was empty.

A minute later I sat up and shook off most of the effects of the stun, although my fingers still burned and I had a fierce headache. The motile isle was far behind, shrinking more each second. A century ago the island would have been driven by the bands of dolphins brought here originally during the Hegira, but the Hegemony pacification program during the Siri Rebellion had killed off most of the aquatic mammals and now the islands wandered listlessly, carrying their cargo of Web tourists and resort owners.

I checked the horizons for another island, a hint of one of the rare mainlands. Nothing. Or, rather, blue sky, endless ocean, and soft brushstrokes of clouds far to the west. Or was it to the east?

I pulled my comlog off my belt lock and keyed in general datasphere access, then stopped. If the authorities had chased me this far, the next step would be to pinpoint my location and send out a skimmer or security EMV. I wasn't sure if they could trace my comlog when I logged in but I saw no reason to help them. I thumbed the comm-link on standby and looked around again.

Good move, Brawne. Poking along at two hundred meters on a three-century-old hawking mat with who knows how many . . . or how few! . . . hours of charge in its flight threads, possibly a thousand klicks or more from land of any sort. And lost. Great. I crossed my arms and sat back to think.

'M. Lamia?' Johnny's soft voice almost made me jump off the mat.

'Johnny?' I stared at the comlog. It was still on standby. The general comm frequency indicator was dark. 'Johnny, is that you?'

'Of course. I thought you'd never turn your comlog on.'

'How did you trace me? What band are you calling on?'

'Never mind that. Where are you headed?'

I laughed and told him that I didn't have the slightest idea. 'Can you help?'

'Wait.' There was the briefest second of pause. 'All

380

right, I have you on one of the weather-mapping sats. A terribly primitive thing. Good thing your hawking mat has a passive transponder.'

I stared at the rug that was the only thing between me and a long, loud fall to the sea. 'It does? Can the others track me?'

'They could,' said Johnny, 'but I'm jamming this particular signal. Now, where do you want to go?'

'Home.'

'I'm not sure if that's wise after the death of . . . ah . . . our suspect.'

I squinted, suddenly suspicious. 'How do you know about that? I didn't say anything.'

'Be serious, M. Lamia. The security bands are full of it on six worlds. They have a reasonable description of you.'

'Shit.'

'Precisely. Now where would you like to go?'

'Where are you?' I asked. 'My place?'

'No. I left there when the security bands mentioned you. I'm . . . near a farcaster.'

'That's where I need to be.' I looked around again. Ocean sky, a hint of clouds. At least no fleets of EMVs.

'All right,' said Johnny's disembodied voice. 'There's a powered-down FORCE multi-portal less than ten klicks from your present location.'

I shielded my eyes and rotated three hundred and sixty degrees. 'The hell there is,' I said. 'I don't know how far away the horizon is on this world, but it's at least forty klicks and I can't see anything.'

'Submersible base,' said Johnny. 'Hang on. I'm going to take control.'

The hawking mat lurched again, dipped once, and then fell steadily. I held on with both hands and resisted the urge to scream.

'Submersible,' I called against the wind rush, 'how *far*?'

'Do you mean how deep?'

'Yeah!'

'Eight fathoms.'

I converted the archaic units to meters. This time I did

scream. 'That's almost fourteen meters *underwater*!'

'Where else do you expect a submersible to be?'

'What the hell do you expect me to do, hold my breath?' The ocean rushed toward me.

'Not necessary,' said my comlog. 'The hawking mat has a primitive crash field. It should easily hold for a mere eight fathoms. Please hang on.'

I hung on.

Johnny was waiting for me when I arrived. The submersible had been dark and dank with the sweat of abandonment; the farcaster had been of a military variety I'd never seen before. It was a relief to step into sunlight and a city street with Johnny waiting.

I told him what had happened to Queue. We walked empty streets past old buildings. The sky was pale blue fading toward evening. No one was in sight. 'Hey,' I said, stopping, 'where *are* we?' It was an incredibly Earthlike world but the sky, the gravity, the *texture* of the place was like nothing I'd visited.

Johnny smiled. 'I'll let you guess. Let's walk some more.'

There were ruins to our left as we walked down a wide street. I stopped and stared. 'That's the Colosseum,' I said. 'The Roman Colosseum on Old Earth.' I looked around at the aging buildings, the cobblestone streets, and the trees swaying slightly in a soft breeze. 'This is a reconstruction of the Old Earth city of Rome,' I said, trying to keep the astonishment out of my voice. 'New Earth?' I knew at once that it wasn't. I'd been to New Earth numerous times and the sky tones, smells, and gravity had not been like this.

Johnny shook his head. 'This is nowhere in the Web.'

I stopped walking. 'That's impossible.' By definition, any world which could be reached by farcaster was in the Web.

'Nonetheless, it is not in the Web.'

'Where is it then?'

'Old Earth.'

We walked on. Johnny pointed out another ruin. 'The Forum.' Descending a long staircase, he said, 'Ahead is the Piazza di Spagna where we'll spend the night.'

'Old Earth,' I said, my first comment in twenty minutes. 'Time travel?'

'That is not possible, M. Lamia.'

'A theme park then?'

Johnny laughed. It was a pleasant laugh, unselfconscious and easy. 'Perhaps. I don't really know its purpose or function. It is . . . an analog.'

'An analog.' I squinted at the red, setting sun just visible down a narrow street. 'It looks like the holos I've seen of Old Earth. It *feels* right, even though I've never been there.'

'It is very accurate.'

'Where is it? I mean, what star?'

'I don't know the number,' said Johnny. 'It's in the Hercules Cluster.'

I managed not to repeat what he said but I stopped and sat down on one of the steps. With the Hawking drive humankind had explored, colonized, and linked with farcaster worlds across many thousands of light-years. But no one had tried to reach the exploding Core suns. We had barely crawled out of the cradle of one spiral arm. The *Hercules Cluster*.

'Why has the TechnoCore built a replica of Rome in the Hercules Cluster?' I asked.

Johnny sat next to me. We both looked up as a whirling mass of pigeons exploded into flight and wheeled above the rooftops. 'I don't know, M. Lamia. There is much that I have not learned . . . at least partially because I have not been interested until now.'

'Brawne,' I said.

'Excuse me?'

'Call me Brawne.'

Johnny smiled and inclined his head. 'Thank you, Brawne. One thing, though. I do not believe that it is a replica of the city of Rome alone. It is all of Old Earth.'

I set both hands on the sun-warmed stone of the step I was sitting on. '*All* of Old Earth? All of its . . . continents, cities?'

'I believe so. I haven't been out of Italy and England

except for a sea voyage between the two, but I believe the analog is complete.'

'Why, for God's sake?'

Johnny nodded slowly. 'That may indeed be the case. Why don't we go inside and eat and talk more about this? It may relate to who tried to kill me and why.'

'Inside' was an apartment in a large house at the foot of the marble stairs. Windows looked out on what Johnny called the 'piazza' and I could see up the staircase to a large, yellow-brown church above, and down to the square where a boat-shaped fountain tossed water into the evening stillness. Johnny said that the fountain had been designed by Bernini but the name meant nothing to me.

The rooms were small but high-ceilinged, with rough but elaborately carved furniture from an era I did not recognize. There was no sign of electricity or modern appliances. The house did not respond when I spoke to it at the door and again in the apartment upstairs. As dusk fell over the square and city outside the tall windows, the only lights were a few streetlamps of gas or some more primitive combustible.

'This is out of Old Earth's past,' I said, touching the thick pillows. I raised my head, suddenly understanding. 'Keats died in Italy. Early . . . nineteenth or twentieth century. This is . . . then.'

'Yes. Early nineteenth century: 1821, to be precise.'

'The whole world is a museum?'

'Oh no. Different areas are different eras, of course. It depends upon the analog being pursued.'

'I don't understand.' We had moved into a room cluttered with thick furniture and I sat on an oddly carved couch by a window. A film of gold evening light still touched the spire of the tawny church up the steps. Pigeons wheeled white against blue sky. 'Are there millions of people . . . cybrids . . . living on this fake Old Earth?'

'I do not believe so,' said Johnny. 'Only the number necessary for the particular analog project.' He saw that I still did not understand and took a breath before continuing. 'When I . . . awoke here, there were cybrid analogs of Joseph Severn, Dr Clark, the landlady Anna Angeletti, young Lieutenant Elton, and a few others. Italian shopkeepers, the owner of the trattoria across the square who used to bring us our food, passersby, that sort of thing. No more than a score at the most.'

'What happened to them?'

'They were probably . . . recycled. Like the man with the queue.'

'Queue . . .' I suddenly stared across the darkening room at Johnny. 'He was a cybrid?'

'Without doubt. The self-destruction you described is precisely the way I would rid myself of this cybrid if I had to.'

My mind was racing. I realized how stupid I had been, how little I had learned about anything. 'Then it was another AI who tried to kill you.'

'It seems that way.'

'Why?'

Johnny made a gesture with his hands. 'Possibly to erase some quantum of knowledge that died with my cybrid. Something I had learned only recently and the other AI . . . or AIs knew would be destroyed in my systems crash.'

I stood, paced back and forth, and stopped at the window. The darkness was settling in earnest now. There were lamps in the room but Johnny made no move to light them and I preferred the dimness. It made the unreality of what I was hearing even that much more unreal. I looked into the bedroom. The western windows admitted the last of the light; bedclothes glowed whitely. 'You died here,' I said.

'*He* did,' said Johnny. 'I am not he.'

'But you have his memories.'

'Half-forgotten dreams. There are gaps.'

'But you know what he *felt*.'

'I remember what the designers *thought* that he felt.'

'Tell me.'

'What?' Johnny's skin was very pale in the gloom. His short curls looked black.

'What it was like to die. What it was like to be reborn.'

Johnny told me, his voice very soft, almost melodic, lapsing sometimes into an English too archaic to be understood but far more beautiful to the ear than the hybrid tongue we speak today.

He told me what it was like to be a poet obsessed with perfection, far harsher toward his own efforts than even the most vicious critic. And the critics were vicious. His work was dismissed, ridiculed, described as derivative and silly. Too poor to marry the woman he loved, loaning money to his brother in America and thus losing the last chance of financial security . . . and then the brief glory of growing into the full maturation of his poetic powers just as he fell prey to the 'consumption' which had claimed his mother and his brother Tom. Then sent off to exile in Italy, reputedly 'for his health' while knowing all the while it meant a lonely, painful death at the age of twenty-six. He talked of the agony of seeing Fanny's handwriting on the letters he found too painful to open; he talked of the loyalty of the young artist Joseph Severn, who had been chosen as a traveling companion for Keats by 'friends' who had abandoned the poet at the end, of how Severn had nursed the dying man and stayed with him during the final days. He told of the hemorrhages in the night, of Dr Clark bleeding him and prescribing 'exercise and good air,' and of the ultimate religious and personal despair which had led Keats to demand his own epitaph be carved in stone as: 'Here lies One Whose Name was writ in Water.'

Only the dimmest light from below outlined the tall windows. Johnny's voice seemed to float in the night-scented air. He spoke of awakening after his death in the bed where he died, still attended by the loyal Severn and Dr Clark, of remembering that he was the poet John Keats the way one remembers an identity from a fast-fading dream while all the while knowing that *he was something else*.

He told of the illusion continued, the trip back to England, the reunion with the Fanny-who-was-not-Fanny and the near mental breakdown this had engendered. He told of his inability to write further poetry, of his increasing estrangement from the cybrid impostors,

386

of his retreat into something resembling catatonia combined with 'hallucinations' of his true AI existence in the nearly incomprehensible (to a nineteenth-century poet) TechnoCore, and of the ultimate crumbling of the illusion and the abandonment of the 'Keats Project.'

'In truth,' he said, 'the entire, evil charade made me think of nothing so much as a passage in a letter I wrote . . . *he* wrote . . . to his brother George some time before his illness. Keats said:

> 'May there not be superior beings amused with any graceful, though instinctive attitude my mind may fall into, as I am entertained with the alertness of a Stoat or the anxiety of a Deer? Though a quarrel in the streets is a thing to be hated, the energies displayed in it are fine. By a superior being our reasonings may take the same tone – though erroneous they may be fine – This is the very thing in which consists poetry.'

'You think the . . . Keats Project . . . was evil?' I asked.

'Anything which deceives is evil, I believe.'

'Perhaps you are more John Keats than you are willing to admit.'

'No. The absence of poetic instinct showed otherwise even in the midst of the most elaborate illusion.'

I looked at the dark outlines of shapes in the dark house. 'Do the AIs know that we're here?'

'Probably. Almost surely. There is no place that I can go that the TechnoCore cannot trace and follow. But it was the Web authorities and brigands from whom we fled, no?'

'But you know now that it was someone . . . some intelligence in the TechnoCore who assaulted you.'

'Yes, but only in the Web. Such violence in the Core would not be tolerated.'

There came a noise from the street. A pigeon, I hoped. Wind blowing trash across cobblestones perhaps. I said, 'How will the TechnoCore respond to my being here?'

'I have no idea.'

'Surely it must be a secret.'

'It is . . . something they consider *irrelevant* to humanity.'

I shook my head, a futile gesture in the darkness. 'The re-creation of Old Earth . . . the resurrection of . . . how many? . . . human personalities as cybrids on this re-created world . . . AIs killing AIs . . . irrelevant!' I laughed but managed to keep the laughter under control. 'Jesus wept, Johnny.'

'Almost certainly.'

I moved to the window, not caring what sort of target I would afford anyone in the dark street below, and fumbled out a cigarette. They were damp from the afternoon's chase through the snowdrifts but one lighted when I struck it. 'Johnny, earlier when you said that the Old Earth analog was complete, I said, "Why, for God's sake?" and you said something like "That may be the case." Was that just a wiseass comment or did you mean something?'

'I mean that it might indeed be for God's sake.'

'Explain.'

Johnny sighed in the darkness. 'I don't understand the exact purpose of the Keats Project or the other Old Earth analogs, but I suspect that it is part of a TechnoCore project going back at least seven standard centuries to realize the Ultimate Intelligence.'

'The Ultimate Intelligence,' I said, exhaling smoke. 'Uh-huh. So the TechnoCore is trying to . . . what? . . . to build God.'

'Yes.'

'Why?'

'There is no simple answer, Brawne. Any more than there is a simple answer to the question of why humankind has sought God in a million guises for ten thousand generations. But with the Core, the interest lies more in the quest for more efficiency, more reliable ways to handle . . . variables.'

'But the TechnoCore can draw on itself and the mega-datasphere of two hundred worlds.'

'And there still will be blanks in the . . . predictive powers.'

388

I threw my cigarette out the window, watching the ember fall into the night. The breeze was suddenly cold; I hugged my arms. 'How does all this . . . Old Earth, the resurrection projects, the cybrids . . . how does it lead to creating the Ultimate Intelligence?'

'I don't know, Brawne. Eight standard centuries ago, at the beginning of the First Information Age, a man named Norbert Wiener wrote: "Can God play a significant game with his own creature? Can any creator, even a limited one, play a significant game with his own creature?" Humanity dealt with this inconclusively with their early AIs. The Core wrestles with it in the resurrection projects. Perhaps the UI program has been completed and all of this remains a function of the ultimate Creature/Creator, a personality whose motives are as far beyond the Core's understanding as the Core's are beyond humanity's.'

I started to move in the dark room, bumped a low table with my knee, and remained standing. 'None of which tells us who is trying to kill you,' I said.

'No.' Johnny rose and moved to the far wall. A match flared and he lighted a candle. Our shadows wavered on the walls and ceiling.

Johnny came closer and softly gripped my upper arms. The soft light painted his curls and eyelashes copper and touched his high cheekbones and firm chin. 'Why are you so tough?' he asked.

I stared at him. His face was only inches from mine. We were the same height. 'Let go,' I said.

Instead, he leaned forward and kissed me. His lips were soft and warm and the kiss seemed to last for hours. *He's a machine*, I thought. *Human, but a machine behind that*. I closed my eyes. His soft hand touched my cheek, my neck, the back of my head.

'Listen . . .' I whispered when we broke apart for an instant.

Johnny did not let me finish. He lifted me in his arms and carried me into the other room. The tall bed. The soft mattress and deep comforter. The candlelight from the other room flickered and danced as we undressed each other in a sudden urgency.

389

We made love three times that night, each time responding to slow, sweet imperatives of touch and warmth and closeness and the escalating intensity of sensation. I remember looking down at him the second time; his eyes were closed, hair fell loosely across his forehead, the candlelight showing the flush across his pale chest, his surprisingly strong arms and hands rising to hold me in place. He had opened his eyes that second to look back at me and I saw only the emotion and passion of that moment reflected there.

Sometime before dawn we slept; just as I turned away and drifted off, I felt the cool touch of his hand on my hip in a movement protective and casual without being possessive.

They hit us just after first light. There were five of them, not Lusian but heavily muscled, all men, and they worked well together as a team.

The first I heard of them was when the door to the apartment was kicked open. I rolled out of bed, jumped to the side of the bedroom door, and watched them come through. Johnny sat up and shouted something as the first man leveled a stunner. Johnny had pulled on cotton shorts before going to sleep; I was nude. There are real disadvantages to fighting in the nude when one's opponents are dressed, but the greatest problem is psychological. If you can get over the sense of heightened vulnerability, the rest is easy to compensate for.

The first man saw me, decided to stun Johnny anyway, and paid for the mistake. I kicked the weapon out of his hand and clubbed him down with a blow behind the left ear. Two more men pushed into the room. This time both of them were smart enough to deal with me first. Two others leaped for Johnny.

I blocked a stiff-fingered jab, parried a kick that would have done real damage, and backed away. There was a tall dresser to my left and the top drawer came out smooth and heavy. The big man in front of me shielded his face with both arms so that the thick wood splintered, but the instinctive reaction gave me a second's opening and I took it, putting my entire body into the kick.

Number two man grunted and fell back against his partner.

Johnny was struggling but one of the intruders had him around the throat in a choke hold while the other pinned his legs. I came off the floor in a crouch, accepted the blow from my number two, and leaped across the bed. The guy holding Johnny's legs went through the glass and wood of the window without a word.

Someone landed on my back and I completed the roll across the bed and floor, bringing him up against the wall. He was good. He took the blow on his shoulder and went for a nerve pinch beneath my ear. He had a second of trouble because of the extra layers of muscle there and I got an elbow deep into his stomach and rolled away. The man choking Johnny dropped him and delivered a text-book-perfect kick to my ribs. I took half the impact, feeling at least one rib go, and spun inside, attempting no elegance as I used my left hand to crush his left testicle. The man screamed and was out of it.

I'd never forgotten the stunner on the floor and neither had the last of the opposition. He scurried around to the far side of the bed, out of reach, and dropped to all fours to grab the weapon. Definitely feeling the pain from the broken rib now, I lifted the massive bed with Johnny in it and dropped it on the guy's head and shoulders.

I went under the bed from my side, retrieved the stunner, and backed into an empty corner.

One guy had gone out the window. We were on the second floor. The first man to enter was still lying in the doorway. The guy I'd kicked had managed to get to one knee and both elbows. From the blood on his mouth and chin, I guessed that a rib had punctured a lung. He was breathing very raggedly. The bed had crushed the skull of the other man on the floor. The guy who'd been choking Johnny was curled up near the window, holding his crotch and vomiting. I stunned him into silence and went over to the one I'd kicked and lifted him by the hair. 'Who sent you?'

'Fuck you.' He sprayed some bloody spittle in my face.

'Maybe later,' I said. 'Again, who sent you?' I placed three fingers against his side where the ribcage seemed concave and pressed.

The man screamed and went very white. When he coughed the blood was too red against pale skin.

'Who sent you?' I set four fingers against his ribs.

'The bishop!' He tried to levitate away from my fingers.

'What bishop?'

'Shrike Temple . . . Lusus . . . don't, *please* . . . oh, shit . . .'

'What were you going to do with him . . . us?'

'Nothing . . . Oh, God *damn* . . . don't! I need a medic, *please*!'

'Sure. Answer.'

'Stun him, bring him . . . back to the Temple . . . Lusus. Please. I can't breathe.'

'And me?'

'Kill you if you resisted.'

'Okay,' I said, lifting him a little higher by his hair, 'we're doing fine here. What did they want him for?'

'I don't know.' He screamed very loudly. I kept one eye on the doorway to the apartment. The stunner was still in my palm under a fistful of hair. 'I . . . don't . . . know . . .' he gasped. He was hemorrhaging in earnest now. The blood dripped on my arm and left breast.

'How'd you get here?'

'EMV . . . roof.'

'Where'd you 'cast in?'

'Don't know . . . I *swear* . . . some city in the water. Car's set to return there . . . *please*!'

I ripped at his clothes. No comlog. No other weapons. There was a tattoo of a blue trident just above his heart. 'Goonda?' I said.

'Yeah . . . Parvati Brotherhood.'

Outside the Web. Probably very hard to trace. 'All of you?'

'Yeah . . . please . . . get me some help . . . oh, shit . . . please . . .' He sagged, almost unconscious.

I dropped him, stepped back, and sprayed the stun beam over him.

392

Johnny was sitting up, rubbing his throat, and staring at me with a strange gaze.

'Get dressed,' I said. 'We're leaving.'

The EMV was an old, transparent Vikken Scenic with no palmlocks on the ignition plate or diskey. We caught up to the terminator before we had crossed France and looked down on darkness that Johnny said was the Atlantic Ocean. Except for lights of the occasional floating city or drilling platform, the only illumination came from the stars and the broad, swimming-pool glows of the undersea colonies.

'Why are we taking their vehicle?' asked Johnny.

'I want to see where they farcast from.'

'He said the Lusus Shrike Temple.'

'Yeah. Now we'll see.'

Johnny's face was barely visible as he looked down at the dark sea twenty klicks below. 'Do you think those men will die?'

'One was already dead,' I said. 'The guy with the punctured lung will need help. Two of them'll be okay. I don't know about the one who went out the window. Do you care?'

'Yes. The violence was . . . barbaric.'

' "Though a quarrel in the street is a thing to be hated, the energies displayed in it are fine," ' I quoted. 'They weren't cybrids, were they?'

'I think not.'

'So there are at least two groups out to get you . . . the AIs and the bishop of the Shrike Temple. And we still don't know why.'

'I do have an idea now.'

I swiveled in the foam recliner. The constellations above us – familiar neither from holos of Old Earth's skies nor from any Web world I knew – cast just enough light to allow me to see Johnny's eyes. 'Tell me,' I said.

'Your mention of Hyperion gave me a clue,' he said. 'The fact that I had no knowledge of it. Its absence said that it was important.'

'The strange case of the dog barking in the night,' I said.

'What?'

'Nothing. Go on.'

Johnny leaned closer. 'The only reason that I would not be aware of it is that some elements of the Techno-Core have blocked my knowledge of it.'

'Your cybrid . . .' It was strange to talk to Johnny that way now. 'You spend most of your time in the Web, don't you?'

'Yes.'

'Wouldn't you run across mention of Hyperion somewhere? It's in the news every once in a while, especially when the Shrike Cult's topical.'

'Perhaps I did hear. Perhaps that is why I was murdered.'

I lay back and looked at the stars. 'Let's go ask the bishop,' I said.

Johnny said that the lights ahead were an analog of New York City in the mid-twenty-first century. He didn't know what resurrection project the city had been rebuilt for. I took the EMV off auto and dropped lower.

Tall buildings from the phallic-symbol era of urban architecture rose from the swamps and lagoons of the North American littoral. Several had lights burning. Johnny pointed to one decrepit but oddly elegant structure and said, 'The Empire State Building.'

'Okay,' I said. 'Whatever it is, that's where the EMV wants to land.'

'Is it safe?'

I grinned at him. 'Nothing in life's safe.' I let the car have its head and we dropped to a small, open platform below the building's spire. We got out and stood on the cracked balcony. It was quite dark except for the few building lights far below and the stars. A few paces away, a vague blue glow outlined a farcaster portal where elevator doors may once have been.

'I'll go first,' I said but Johnny had already stepped through. I palmed the borrowed stunner and followed him.

I'd never been in the Shrike Temple on Lusus before but there was no doubt that we were there now. Johnny stood a few paces ahead of me but other than him there was no one around. The place was cool and dark and cavernous if caverns could really be that large. A frightening polychrome sculpture which hung from invisible cables rotated to unfelt breezes. Johnny and I both turned as the farcaster portal winked out of existence.

'Well, we did their work for them, didn't we?' I whispered to Johnny. Even the whisper seemed to echo in the red-lit hall. I hadn't planned on Johnny 'casting to the Temple with me.

The light seemed to come up then, not really illuminating the great hall but widening its scope so that we could see the semicircle of men there. I remembered that some were called exorcists and others lectors and there was some other category I forgot. Whoever they were, it was alarming to see them standing there, at least two dozen of them, their robes variations on red and black and their high foreheads glowing from the red light above. I had no trouble recognizing the bishop. He was from my world, although shorter and fatter than most of us, and his robe was very red.

I did not try to hide the stunner. It was possible that if they all tried to rush us I could bring them all down. Possible but not probable. I could not see any weapons but their robes could have hidden entire arsenals.

Johnny walked toward the bishop and I followed. Ten paces from the man we stopped. The bishop was the only one not standing. His chair was made of wood and looked as if it could be folded so that the intricate arms, supports, back, and legs could be carried in a compact form. One couldn't say the same of the mass of muscle and fat evident under the bishop's robes.

Johnny took another step forward. 'Why did you try to kidnap my cybrid?' He spoke to the Shrike Cult holy man as if the rest of us were not there.

The bishop chuckled and shook his head. 'My dear . . . entity . . . it is true that we wished your presence in our place of worship, but you have no evidence that we were involved in any attempt to kidnap you.'

'I'm not interested in evidence,' said Johnny. 'I'm curious as to why you want me here.'

I heard a rustling behind us and I swiveled quickly, the

stunner charged and pointed, but the broad circle of Shrike priests remained motionless. Most were out of the stunner's range. I wished that I had brought my father's projectile weapon with me.

The bishop's voice was deep and textured and seemed to fill the huge space. 'Surely you know that the Church of the Final Atonement has a deep and abiding interest in the world of Hyperion.'

'Yes.'

'And surely you are aware that during the past several centuries the persona of the Old Earth poet Keats has been woven into the cultural mythos of the Hyperion colony?'

'Yes. So?'

The bishop rubbed his cheek with a large red ring on one finger. 'So when you offered to go on the Shrike Pilgrimage we agreed. We were distressed when you reneged on this offer.'

Johnny's look of amazement was most human. '*I* offered? When?'

'Eight local days ago,' said the bishop. 'In this room. You approached us with the idea.'

'Did I say why I wanted to go on the . . . Shrike Pilgrimage?'

'You said that it was . . . I believe the phrase you used was . . . "important for your education." We can show you the recording if you wish. All such conversations in the Temple are recorded. Or you may have a duplicate of the recording to view at your own convenience.'

'Yes,' said Johnny.

The bishop nodded and an acolyte or whatever the hell he was disappeared into the gloom for a moment and returned with a standard video chip in his hand. The bishop nodded again and the blackrobed man came forward and handed the chip to Johnny. I kept the stunner ready until the guy had returned to the semicircle of watchers.

'Why did you send the goondas after us?' I asked. It was the first time I'd spoken in front of the bishop and my voice sounded too loud and too raw.

The Shrike holy man made a gesture with one pudgy

hand. 'M. Keats had expressed an interest in joining our holiest pilgrimage. Since it is our belief that the Final Atonement is drawing closer each day, this is of no little importance to us. Consequently, our agents reported that M. Keats may have been the victim of one or more assaults and that a certain private investigator . . . *you*, M. Lamia . . . was responsible for destroying the cybrid bodyguard provided M. Keats by the TechnoCore.'

'Bodyguard!' It was my turn to sound amazed.

'Of course,' said the bishop. He turned toward Johnny. 'The gentleman with the queue who was recently murdered on the Temple Excursion, was this not the same man whom you introduced as your bodyguard a week earlier? He is visible in the recording.'

Johnny said nothing. He seemed to be straining to remember something.

'At any rate,' continued the bishop, 'we must have your answer about the pilgrimage before the week is out. The *Sequoia Sempervirens* departs from the Web in nine local days.'

'But that's a Templar treeship,' said Johnny. 'They don't make the long leap to Hyperion.'

The bishop smiled. 'In this case it does. We have reason to believe that this may be the last Church-sponsored pilgrimage and we have chartered the Templar craft to allow as many of the faithful as possible to make the trip.' The bishop gestured and red-and-black-robed men faded back into darkness. Two exorcists came forward to fold his stool as the bishop stood. 'Please give us your answer as soon as possible.' He was gone. The remaining exorcist stayed to show us out.

There were no more farcasters. We exited by the main door of the Temple and stood on the top step of the long staircase, looking down on the Concourse Mall of Hive Center and breathing in the cool, oil-scented air.

My father's automatic was in the drawer where I'd left it. I made sure there was a full load of fléchettes, palmed the magazine back in, and carried the weapon into the kitchen where breakfast was cooking. Johnny sat at the long table, staring down through gray windows at the loading dock. I carried the omelets over and set one in front of him. He looked up as I poured the coffee.

'Do you believe him?' I asked. 'That it was your idea?'

'You saw the video recording.'

'Recordings can be faked.'

'Yes. But this one wasn't.'

'Then why did you volunteer to go on this pilgrimage? And why did your bodyguard try to kill you after you talked to the Shrike Church and the Templar captain?'

Johnny tried the omelet, nodded, and took another forkful. 'The . . . bodyguard . . . is a complete unknown to me. He must have been assigned to me during the week lost to memory. His real purpose obviously was to make sure that I did not discover something . . . or, if I did stumble upon it, to eliminate me.'

'Something in the Web or in datumplane?'

'In the Web, I presume.'

'We need to know who he . . . it . . . worked for and why they assigned him to you.'

'I do know,' said Johnny. 'I just asked. The Core responds that I requested a bodyguard. The cybrid was controlled by an AI nexus which corresponds to a security force.'

'Ask why he tried to kill you.'

'I did. They emphatically deny that such a thing is possible.'

'Then why was this so-called bodyguard slinking around after you a week after the murder?'

'They respond that while I did not request security again after my . . . discontinuity . . . the Core authorities felt that it would be prudent to provide protection.'

I laughed. 'Some protection. Why the hell did he run on the Templar world when I caught up to him? They aren't even trying to give you a plausible story, Johnny.'

'No.'

'Nor did the bishop explain how the Shrike Church had farcaster access to Old Earth . . . or whatever you call that stage-set world.'

'And we did not ask.'

'*I* didn't ask because I wanted to get out of that damn Temple in one piece.'

Johnny didn't seem to hear. He was sipping his coffee, his gaze focused somewhere else.

'What?' I said.

He turned to look at me, tapping his thumbnail on his lower lip. 'There is a paradox here, Brawne.'

'What?'

'If it was truly my aim to go to Hyperion . . . for my cybrid to travel there . . . I could not have remained in the TechnoCore. I would have had to invest all consciousness in the cybrid itself.'

'Why?' But even as I asked I saw the reason.

'Think. Datumplane itself is an abstract. A commingling of computer and AI-generated dataspheres and the quasi-perceptual Gibsonian matrix designed originally for human operators, now accepted as common ground for man, machine, and AI.'

'But AI hardware exists somewhere in real space,' I said. 'Somewhere in the TechnoCore.'

'Yes, but that is irrelevant to the function of AI consciousness,' said Johnny. 'I can "be" anywhere the overlapping dataspheres allow me to travel . . . all of the Web worlds, of course, datumplane, and any of the TechnoCore constructs such as Old Earth . . . but it's only within that milieu that I can claim "consciousness" or operate sensors or remotes such as this cybrid.'

I set my coffee cup down and stared at the thing I had loved as a man during the night just past. 'Yes?'

'The colony worlds have limited dataspheres,' said Johnny. 'While there is some contact with the Techno-Core via fatline transmissions, it is an exchange of data only . . . rather like the First Information Age computer interfaces . . . rather than a flow of consciousness. Hyperion's datasphere is primitive to the point of non-existence. And from what I can access, the Core has no contact whatsoever with that world.'

'Would that be normal?' I asked. 'I mean with a colony world that far away?'

'No. The Core has contact with every colony world, with such interstellar barbarians as the Ousters, and with other sources the Hegemony could not imagine.'

I sat stunned. 'With the *Ousters*?' Since the war on

Bressia a few years earlier, the Ousters had been the Web's prime bogeymen. The idea of the Core . . . the same congregation of AIs which advises the Senate and the All Thing and which allows our entire economy, farcaster system, and technological civilization to run . . . the idea of the Core being in touch with the Ousters was frightening. And what the hell did Johnny mean by 'other sources'? I didn't really want to know right then.

'But you said it *is* possible for your cybrid to travel there?' I said. 'What did you mean by "investing all consciousness" in your cybrid? Can an AI *become* . . . human? Can you exist only in your cybrid?'

'It has been done,' Johnny said softly. 'Once. A personality reconstruction not too different from my own. A twentieth-century poet named Ezra Pound. He abandoned his AI persona and fled from the Web in his cybrid. But the Pound reconstruction was insane.'

'Or sane,' I said.

'Yes.'

'So all of the data and personality of an AI can survive in a cybrid's organic brain.'

'Of course not, Brawne. Not one percent of one percent of my total consciousness would survive the transition. Organic brains can't process even the most primitive information the way we can. The resultant personality would not be the AI persona . . . neither would it be a truly human consciousness or cybrid . . .' Johnny stopped in mid-sentence and turned quickly to look out the window.

After a long minute I said, 'What is it?' I reached out a hand but did not touch him.

He spoke without turning. 'Perhaps I was wrong to say that the consciousness would not be human,' he whispered. 'It is possible that the resulting persona could be human touched with a certain divine madness and meta-human perspective. It could be . . . if purged of all memory of our age, of all consciousness of the Core . . . it could be the person the cybrid was programmed to be . . .'

'John Keats,' I said.

Johnny turned away from the window and closed his

eyes. His voice was hoarse with emotion. It was the first time I had heard him recite poetry:

> 'Fanatics have their dreams, wherewith they weave
> A paradise for a sect, the savage too
> From forth the loftiest fashion of his sleep
> Guesses at Heaven; pity these have not
> Traced upon vellum or wild Indian leaf
> The shadows of melodious utterance.
> But bare of laurel they live, dream, and die;
> For Poesy alone can tell her dreams,
> With the fine spell of words alone can save
> Imagination from the sable charm
> And dumb enchantment. Who alive can say,
> "Thou art no Poet – mayst not tell thy dreams"?
> Since every man whose soul is not a clod
> Hath visions, and would speak, if he had loved,
> And been well nurtured in his mother tongue.
> Whether the dream now purposed to rehearse
> Be Poet's or Fanatic's will be known
> When this warm scribe my hand is in the grave.'

'I don't get it,' I said. 'What does it mean?'

'It means,' said Johnny, smiling gently, 'that I know what decision I made and why I made it. I wanted to cease being a cybrid and become a man. I wanted to go to Hyperion. I still do.'

'Somebody killed you for that decision a week ago,' I said.

'Yes.'

'And you're going to try again?'

'Yes.'

'Why not invest consciousness in your cybrid here? Become human in the Web?'

'It would never work,' said Johnny. 'What you see as a complex interstellar society is only a small part of the Core reality matrix. I would be constantly confronted with and at the mercy of the AIs. The Keats persona . . . *reality* . . . would never survive.'

'All right,' I said, 'you need to get out of the Web. But there are other colonies. Why Hyperion?'

401

Johnny took my hand. His finger were long and warm and strong. 'Don't you see, Brawne? There is some connection here. It may well be that Keats's dreams of Hyperion were some sort of transtemporal communication between his then persona and his now persona. If nothing else, Hyperion is the key mystery of our age – physical and poetic – and it is quite probable that he . . . that *I* was born, died, and was born again to explore it.'

'It sounds like madness to me,' I said. 'Delusions of grandeur.'

'Almost certainly,' laughed Johnny. 'And I never have been happier!' He grabbed my arms and brought me to my feet, his arms around me. 'Will you go with me, Brawne? Go with me to Hyperion?'

I blinked in surprise, both at his question and the answer, which filled me like a rush of warmth. 'Yes,' I said. 'I'll go.'

We went into the sleeping area then and made love the rest of that day, sleeping finally to awaken to the low light of Shift Three in the industrial trench outside. Johnny was lying on his back, his hazel eyes open and staring at the ceiling, lost in thought. But not so lost he did not smile and put his arm around me. I nestled my cheek against him, settling into the small curve where shoulder meets chest, and went back to sleep.

I was wearing my best clothes – a suit of black whipcord, a blouse woven of Renaissance silk with a Carvnel bloodstone at the throat, a cocked Eulin Bré tricorne – when Johnny and I farcast to TC² the next day. I left him in the wood and brass bar near the central terminex, but not before I slid Dad's automatic across to him in a paper bag and told him to shoot anyone who even looked crosseyed at him.

'Web English is such a subtle tongue,' he said.

'That phrase is older than the Web,' I said. 'Just *do* it.' I squeezed his hand and left without looking back.

I took a skycab to the Administration Complex and walked my way through about nine security checks before they let me into the Center grounds. I walked the half klick across Deer Park, admiring the swans in the nearby lake and the white buildings on the hilltop in the distance, and then there were nine more checkpoints before a Center security woman led me up the flagstoned path to Government House, a low, graceful building set amid flower gardens and landscaped hills. There was an elegantly furnished waiting room but I barely had time to sit down on an authentic pre-Hegira de Kooning before an aide appeared and ushered me into the CEO's private office.

Meina Gladstone came around the desk to shake my hand and show me to a chair. It was strange to see her in person again after all those years of watching her on HTV. She was even more impressive in the flesh: her hair was cut short but seemed to be blowing back in gray-white waves; her cheeks and chin were as sharp and Lincolnesque as all the history-prone pundits insisted, but it was the large, sad, brown eyes which dominated the face and made one feel as if he or she were in the presence of a truly original person.

I found that my mouth was dry. 'Thank you for seeing me, M. Executive. I know how busy you are.'

'I'm never too busy to see you, Brawne. Just as your father was never too busy to see me when I was a junior senator.'

I nodded. Dad had once described Meina Gladstone as the only political genius in the Hegemony. He knew that she would be CEO someday despite her late start in politics. I wished Dad had lived to see it.

'How is your mother, Brawne?'

'She's well, M. Executive. She rarely leaves our old summer place on Freeholm anymore but I see her every Christmas Fest.'

Gladstone nodded. She had been sitting casually on the edge of a massive desk which the tabloids said had once belonged to an assassinated President – not Lincoln – of the pre-Mistake USA, but now she smiled and went around to the simple chair behind it. 'I miss your father, Brawne. I wish he were in this administration. Did you see the lake when you came in?'

'Yes.'

403

'Do you remember sailing toy boats there with my Kresten when you were both toddlers?'

'Just barely, M. Executive. I was pretty young.'

Meina Gladstone smiled. An intercom chimed but she waved it into silence. 'How can I help you, Brawne?'

I took a breath. 'M. Executive, you may be aware that I'm working as an independent private investigator . . .' I didn't wait for her nod. 'A case I've been working on recently has led me back to Dad's suicide . . .'

'Brawne, you know that was investigated most thoroughly. I saw the commission's report.'

'Yeah,' I said. 'I did too. But recently I've discovered some very strange things about the TechnoCore and its attitude toward the world Hyperion. Weren't you and Dad working on a bill that would have brought Hyperion into the Hegemony Protectorate?'

Gladstone nodded. 'Yes, Brawne, but there were over a dozen other colonies being considered that year. None were allowed in.'

'Right. But did the Core or the AI Advisory Council take a special interest in Hyperion?'

The CEO tapped a stylus against her lower lip. 'What kind of information do you have, Brawne?' I started to answer but she held up a blunt finger. 'Wait!' She keyed an interactive. 'Thomas, I'll be stepping out for a few minutes. Please be sure that the Sol Draconi trade delegation is entertained if I fall a bit behind schedule.'

I didn't see her key anything else but suddenly a blue and gold farcaster portal hummed into life near the far wall. She gestured me to go through first.

A plain of gold, knee-high grass stretched to horizons which seemed farther away than most. The sky was a pale yellow with burnished copper streaks which may have been clouds. I didn't recognize the world.

Meina Gladstone stepped through and touched the comlog design on her sleeve. The farcaster portal winked out. A warm breeze blew spice scents to us.

Gladstone touched her sleeve again, glanced skyward, and nodded. 'I'm sorry for the inconvenience, Brawne. Kastrop-Rauxel has no datasphere or sats of any kind. Now please go ahead with what you were saying. What kind of information have you come across?'

I looked around at the empty grasslands. 'Nothing to warrant this security . . . probably. I've just discovered that the TechnoCore seems very interested in Hyperion. They've also built some sort of analog to Old Earth . . . an entire world!'

If I expected shock or surprise I was disappointed. Gladstone nodded. 'Yes. We know about the Old Earth analog.'

I was shocked. 'Then why hasn't it even been announced? If the Core can rebuild Old Earth, a lot of people would be interested.'

Gladstone began walking and I strolled with her, walking faster to keep up with her long-legged strides. 'Brawne, it would not be in the Hegemony's interest to announce it. Our best human intelligence sources have no idea why the Core is doing such a thing. They have offered no insight. The best policy now is to wait. What information do you have about Hyperion?'

I had no idea whether I could trust Meina Gladstone, old times or not. But I knew that if I was going to get information I would have to give some. 'They built an analog reconstruction of an Old Earth poet,' I said, 'and they seem obsessed with keeping any information about Hyperion away from him.'

Gladstone picked a long stem of grass and sucked on it. 'The John Keats cybrid.'

'Yes.' I was careful not to show surprise this time. 'I know that Dad was pushing hard to get Protectorate status for Hyperion. If the Core has some special interest in the place, they may have had something to do . . . may have manipulated . . .'

'His apparent suicide?'

'Yeah?'

The wind moved gold grass in waves. Something very small scurried away in the stalks at our feet. 'It is not beyond the realm of possibility, Brawne. But there was absolutely no evidence. Tell me what this cybrid is going to do.'

'First tell me why the Core is so interested in Hyperion.'

The older woman spread her hands. 'If we knew that, Brawne, I would sleep much easier nights. As far as we know, the TechnoCore has been obsessed with Hyperion for centuries. When CEO Yevshensky allowed King Billy of Asquith to recolonize the planet, it almost precipitated a true secession of AIs from the Web. Recently the establishment of our fatline transmitter there brought about a similar crisis.'

'But the AIs didn't secede.'

'No, Brawne, it appears that, for whatever reason, they need us almost as badly as we need them.'

'But if they're so interested in Hyperion, why don't they allow it into the Web so they can go there themselves?'

Gladstone ran a hand through her hair. The bronze clouds far above rippled in what must be a fantastic jet stream. 'They are adamant about Hyperion not being admitted to the Web,' she said. 'It is an interesting paradox. Tell me what the cybrid is going to do.'

'First tell me why the Core is obsessed with Hyperion.'

'We do not know for sure.'

'Best guess then.'

CEO Gladstone removed the stem of grass from her mouth and regarded it. 'We believe that the Core is embarked on a truly incredible project which would allow them to predict . . . everything. To handle every variable of space, time, and history as a quantum of manageable information.'

'Their Ultimate Intelligence Project,' I said, knowing that I was being careless and not caring.

This time CEO Gladstone did register shock. 'How do you know about that?'

'What does that project have to do with Hyperion?'

Gladstone sighed. 'We don't know for sure, Brawne. But we do know that there is an anomaly on Hyperion which they have not been able to factor into their predictive analyses. Do you know about the so-called Time Tombs that the Shrike Church holds holy?'

'Sure. They've been off limits to tourists for a while.'

'Yes. Because of an accident to a researcher there a few decades ago, our scientists have confirmed that the anti-entropic fields around the Tombs are not merely a protection against time's erosive effects as has been widely believed.'

'What are they?'

'The remnants of a field . . . or force . . . which has actually propelled the Tombs and their contents backward in time from some distant future.'

'Contents?' I managed. 'But the Tombs are empty. Ever since they were discovered.'

'Empty now,' said Meina Gladstone. 'But there is evidence that they were full . . . will be full . . . when they open. In our near future.'

I stared at her. 'How near?'

Her dark eyes remained soft but the movement of her head was final. 'I've told you too much already, Brawne. You are forbidden to repeat it. We'll ensure that silence if necessary.'

I hid my own confusion by finding a piece of grass to strip for chewing. 'All right,' I said. 'What's going to come out of the Tombs? Aliens? Bombs? Some sort of reverse time capsules?'

Gladstone smiled tightly. 'If we knew that, Brawne, we would be ahead of the Core, and we are not.' The smile disappeared. 'One hypothesis is that the Tombs relate to some future war. A settling of future scores by rearranging the past, perhaps.'

'A war between who, for Chrissakes?'

She opened her hands again. 'We need to be getting back, Brawne. Would you please tell me what the Keats cybrid is going to do now?'

I looked down and then back up to meet her steady gaze. I couldn't trust anyone, but the Core and the Shrike Church already knew Johnny's plans. If this was a three-sided game, perhaps each side should know in case there was a good guy in the bunch. 'He's going to invest all consciousness in the cybrid,' I said rather clumsily. 'He's going to become human, M. Gladstone, and then go to Hyperion. I'm going with him.'

The CEO of the Senate and All Thing, chief officer for a government which spanned almost two hundred worlds and billions of people, stared at me in silence for a long moment. Then she said, 'He plans to go with the Templar ship on the pilgrimage then.'

'Yes.'

'No,' said Meina Gladstone.

'What do you mean?'

'I mean that the *Sequoia Sempervirens* will not be allowed to leave Hegemony space. There will be no pilgrimage unless the Senate decides it is in *our* interest.' Her voice was iron-hard.

'Johnny and I'll go by spinship,' I said. 'The pilgrimage is a loser's game anyway.'

'No,' she said. 'There will be no more civilian spinships to Hyperion for some time.'

The word 'civilian' tipped me. 'War?'

Gladstone's lips were tight. She nodded. 'Before most spinships could reach the region.'

'A war with . . . the Ousters?'

'Initially. View it as a way to force the issue between the TechnoCore and ourselves, Brawne. We will either have to incorporate the Hyperion system into the Web to allow it FORCE protection, or it will fall to a race which despises and distrusts the Core and all AIs.'

I didn't mention Johnny's comment that the Core had been in touch with the Ousters. I said, 'A way to force the issue. Fine. But who manipulated the Ousters into attacking?'

Gladstone looked at me. If her face was Lincolnesque at that moment, then Old Earth's Lincoln was one tough son of a bitch. 'It's time to get back, Brawne. You appreciate how important it is that none of this information gets out.'

'I appreciate the fact that you wouldn't have told me unless you had a reason to,' I said. 'I don't know who you want the stuff to go to, but I know I'm a messenger, not a confidante.'

'Don't underestimate our resolve to keep this classified, Brawne.'

I laughed. 'Lady, I wouldn't underestimate your resolve in anything.'

Meina Gladstone gestured for me to step through the farcaster portal first.

*   *   *

'I know a way we can discover what the Core is up to,' said Johnny as we rode alone in a rented jetboat on Mare Infinitus. 'But it would be dangerous.'

'So what else is new?'

'I'm serious. We should only attempt it if we feel that it is imperative to understand what the Core fears from Hyperion.'

'I do.'

'We will need an operative. Someone who is an artist in datumplane operations. Someone smart but not so smart that they won't take a chance. And someone who would risk everything and keep the secret just for the ultimate in cyberpuke pranks.'

I grinned at Johnny. 'I've got just the man.'

BB lived alone in a cheap apartment at the base of a cheap tower in a cheap TC² neighborhood. But there was nothing cheap about the hardware that filled most of the space in the four-room flat. Most of BB's salary for the past standard decade had gone into state-of-the art cyberpuke toys.

I started by saying that we wanted him to do something illegal. BB said that, as a public employee, he couldn't consider such a thing. He asked what the thing was. Johnny began to explain. BB leaned forward and I saw the old cyberpuke gleam in his eyes from our college days. I half expected him to try to dissect Johnny right there just to see how a cybrid worked. Then Johnny got to the interesting part and BB's gleam turned into a sort of green glow.

'When I self-destruct my AI persona,' said Johnny, 'the shift to cybrid consciousness will take only nanoseconds, but during that time my section of the Core perimeter defenses will drop. The security phages will fill the gap before too many more nanoseconds pass, but during the time . . .'

'Entry to the Core,' whispered BB, his eyes glowing like some antique VDT.

'It would be *very* dangerous,' stressed Johnny. 'To my knowledge, no human operator has ever penetrated Core periphery.'

BB rubbed his upper lip. 'There's a legend that Cowboy

Gibson did it before the Core seceded,' he mumbled. 'But nobody believes it. And Cowboy disappeared.'

'Even if you penetrate,' said Johnny, 'there would be insufficient time to access except for the fact that I have the data coordinates.'

'Fan-fucking-tastic,' whispered BB. He turned back to his console and reached for his shunt. 'Let's do it.'

'Now?' I said. Even Johnny looked taken aback.

'Why wait?' BB clicked in his shunt and attached metacortex leads, but left the deck idling. 'Are we doing this, or what?'

I went over next to Johnny on the couch and took his hand. His skin was cool. He showed no expression now but I could imagine what it must be like to be facing imminent destruction of one's personality and previous existence. Even if the transfer worked, the human with the John Keats persona would not be 'Johnny.'

'He's right,' said Johnny. 'Why wait?'

I kissed him. 'All right,' I said. 'I'm going in with BB.'

'No!' Johnny squeezed my hand. 'You can't help and the danger would be terrible.'

I heard my own voice, as implacable as Meina Gladstone's. 'Perhaps. But I can't ask BB to do this if I won't. And I won't leave you in there alone.' I squeezed his hand a final time and went over to sit by BB at the console. 'How do I connect with this fucking thing, BB?'

You've read all the cyberpuke stuff. You know all about the terrible beauty of datumplane, the three-dimensional highways with their landscapes of black ice and neon perimeters and Day-Glo Strange Loops and shimmering skyscrapers of data blocks under hovering clouds of AI presence. I saw all of it riding piggyback on BB's carrier wave. It was almost too much. Too intense. Too terrifying. I could *hear* the black threats of the hulking security phages; I could *smell* death on the breath of the counterthrust tapeworm viruses even through the ice screens; I could *feel* the weight of the AIs' wrath above us – we were insects under elephants' feet – and we hadn't even *done* anything yet except travel approved dataways on a logged-in access errand BB had dreamed up, some homework stuff for his Flow Control Records and Statistics job.

And I was wearing stick-on leads, seeing things in a datumplane version of fuzzy black and white TV while Johnny and BB were viewing full stimsim holo, as it were.

I don't know how they took it.

'OK,' whispered BB in some datumplane equivalent of a whisper, 'we're here.'

'Where?' All I saw was an infinite maze of bright lights and even brighter shadows, ten thousand cities arrayed in four dimensions.

'Core periphery,' whispered BB. 'Hang on. It's about time.'

I had no arms to hang on with and nothing physical in this universe to grasp, but I concentrated on the waveform shades that were our data truck and *clung*.

Johnny died then.

I've seen a nuclear explosion firsthand. When Dad was a senator he took Mom and me to Olympus Command School to see a FORCE demonstration. For the last course the audience viewing pod was farcast to some godforsaken world . . . Armaghast, I think . . . and a FORCE:ground recon platoon fired a clean tactical nuke at a pretend adversary some nine klicks away. The viewing pod was shielded with a class ten containment field, polarized, the nuke only a fifty-kiloton field tactical, but I'll never forget the blast, the shock wave rocking the eighty-ton pod like a leaf on its repellers, the physical shock of light so obscenely bright that it polarized our field to midnight and still brought tears to our eyes and clamored to get in.

This was worse.

A section of datumplane seemed to flash and then to implode on itself, reality flushed down a drain of pure black.

'Hang on!' BB screamed against datumplane static that rasped at my bones and we were whirling, tumbling, sucked into the vacuum like insects in an oceanic vortex.

Somehow, incredibly, impossibly, black-armored phages thrust toward us through the din and madness.

411

BB avoided one, turned the other's acid membranes against itself. We were being sucked into something colder and blacker than any void in our reality could ever be.

'There!' called BB, his voice analog almost lost in the tornado rush of ripping datasphere.

There what? Then I saw it: a thin line of yellow rippling in the turbulence like a cloth banner in a hurricane. BB rolled us, found our own wave to carry us against the storm, matched coordinates that danced past me too quickly to see, and we were riding the yellow band into . . .

. . . into what? Frozen fountains of fireworks. Transparent mountain ranges of data, endless glaciers of ROMworks, access ganglia spreading like fissures, iron clouds of semisentient internal process bubbles, glowing pyramids of primary source stuff, each guarded by lakes of black ice and armies of black-pulse phages.

'Shit,' I whispered to no one in particular.

BB followed the yellow band down, in, through. I felt a *connection* as if someone had suddenly given us a great mass to carry.

'Got it!' screamed BB, and suddenly there was a sound louder and larger than the maelstrom of noise surrounding and consuming us. It was neither klaxon nor siren, but it was both in its tone of warning and aggression.

We were climbing out of it all. I could see a vague wall of gray through the brilliant chaos and somehow knew it to be the periphery, the vacuum dwindling but still breaching the wall like a shrinking black stain. We were climbing out.

But not quickly enough.

The phages hit us from five sides. During the twelve years I've been an investigator I've been shot once, knifed twice. I'd had more than this one rib broken. This hurt more than all that combined. BB was fighting and climbing at the same time.

My contribution to the emergency was to scream. I felt cold claws on us, pulling us down, back into the brightness and noise and chaos. BB was using some program, some formula of enchantment to fight them

412

off. But not enough. I could feel the blows slamming home – not against me primarily, but connecting to the matrix analog that was BB.

We were sinking back. Inexorable forces had us in tow. Suddenly I felt Johnny's presence and it was as if a huge, strong hand had scooped us up, lifted us through the periphery wall an instant before the stain snapped our lifeline to existence and the defensive field crashed together like steel teeth.

We moved at impossible speed down congested dataways, passing datumplane couriers and other operator analogs like an EMV ripping past oxcarts. Then we were approaching a slow-time gate, leapfrogging gridlocked exiting operator analogs in some four-dimensional high jump.

I felt the inevitable nausea of transition as we came out of the matrix. Light burned my retinas. *Real* light. Then the pain washed in and I slumped over the console and groaned.

'Come on, Brawne.' It was Johnny – or someone just like Johnny – helping me to my feet and moving us both toward the door.

'BB,' I gasped.

'No.'

I opened aching eyes long enough to see BB Surbringer draped across his console. His Stetson had fallen off and rolled to the floor. BB's head had exploded, spattering most of the console with gray and red. His mouth was open and a thick white foam still issued from it. It looked like his eyes had melted.

Johnny caught me, half lifted me. 'We have to go,' he whispered. 'Someone will be here any minute.'

I closed my eyes and let him take me away from there.

I awoke to dim red light and the sound of water dripping. I smelled sewage, mildew, and the ozone of uninsulated power cables. I opened one eye.

We were in a low space more cave than room with cables snaking from a shattered ceiling and pools of water on the slime-caked tiles. The red light came from somewhere beyond the cave – a maintenance access

413

shaft perhaps, or automech tunnel. I moaned softly.
Johnny was there, moving from the rough bedroll of
blankets to my side. His face was darkened with grease
or dirt and there was at least one fresh cut.

'Where are we?'

He touched my cheek. His other arm went around my
shoulders and helped me to a sitting position. The awful
view shifted and tilted and for a moment I thought I was
going to be sick. Johnny helped me drink water from a
plastic tumbler.

'Dregs' Hive,' said Johnny.

I'd guessed even before I was fully conscious. Dregs'
Hive is the deepest pit on Lusus, a no man's land of mech
tunnels and illegal burrows occupied by half the Web's
outcasts and outlaws. It was in Dregs' Hive that I'd been
shot several years ago and still bore the laser scar above
my left hipbone.

I held the tumbler out for more water. Johnny fetched
some from a steel therm and came back. I panicked for a
second as I fumbled in my tunic pocket and on my belt:
Dad's automatic was gone. Johnny held the weapon up
and I relaxed, accepting the cup and drinking thirstily.
'BB?' I said, hoping for a moment that it had all been a
terrible hallucination.

Johnny shook his head. 'There were defenses that neither of us had anticipated. BB's incursion was brilliant,
but he couldn't outfight Core omega phages. But half
the operators in datumplane felt echoes of the battle. BB
is already the stuff of legend.'

'Fucking great,' I said and gave a laugh that sounded
suspiciously like the beginning of a sob. 'The stuff of
legend. And BB's dead. For fuck-all nothing.'

Johnny's arm was tight around me. 'Not for nothing,
Brawne. He made the grab. And passed the data to me
before he died.'

I managed to sit fully upright and to look at Johnny.
He seemed the same – the same soft eyes, same hair,
same voice. But something was subtly different, deeper.
More human? 'You?' I said. 'Did you make the transfer? Are you . . .'

'Human?' John Keats smiled at me. 'Yes, Brawne. Or

as close to human as someone forged in the Core could ever be.'

'But you remember . . . me . . . BB . . . what's happened.'

'Yes. And I remember first looking into Chapman's Homer. And my brother Tom's eyes as he hemorrhaged in the night. And Severn's kind voice when I was too weak to open my own eyes to face my fate. And our night in Piazza di Spagna when I touched your lips and imagined Fanny's cheek against mine. I remember, Brawne.'

For a second I was confused, and then hurt, but then he set his palm against my cheek and *he* touched *me*, there was no one else, and I understood. I closed my eyes. 'Why are we here?' I whispered against his shirt.

'I couldn't risk using a farcaster. The Core could trace us at once. I considered the spaceport but you were in no condition to travel. I chose the Dregs'.'

I nodded against him. 'They'll try to kill you.'

'Yes.'

'Are the local cops after us? The Hegemony police? Transit cops?'

'No, I don't think so. The only ones who've challenged us so far were two bands of goondas and some of the Dregs' dwellers.'

I opened my eyes. 'What happened with the goondas?' There were more deadly hoodlums and contract killers in the Web but I'd never run across any.

Johnny held up Dad's automatic and smiled.

'I don't remember anything after BB,' I said.

'You were injured by the phage backlash. You could walk but we were the cause of more than a few odd looks in the Concourse.'

'I bet. Tell me about what BB discovered. Why is the Core obsessed with Hyperion?'

'Eat first,' said Johnny. 'It's been more than twenty-eight hours.' He crossed the dripping width of the cave room and returned with a self-heating packet. It was basic holo fanatic fare – flash-dried and reheated cloned beef, potatoes which had never seen soil, and carrots which looked like some sort of deep-sea slugs. Nothing had ever tasted so good.

'OK,' I said, 'tell me.'

'The TechnoCore has been divided into three groups for as long as the Core has existed,' said Johnny. 'The Stables are the old-line AIs, some of them dating back to pre-Mistake days; at least one of them gained sentience in the First Information Age. The Stables argue that a certain level of symbiosis is necessary between humanity and the Core. They've promoted the Ultimate Intelligence Project as a way to avoid rash decisions, to delay until all variables can be factored. The Volatiles are the force behind the Secession three centuries ago. The Volatiles have done conclusive studies that show how humankind's usefulness is past and from this point on human beings constitute a threat to the Core. They advocate immediate and total extinction.'

'Extinction,' I said. After a moment I asked, 'Can they do it?'

'Of humans in the Web, yes,' said Johnny. 'Core intelligences not only create the infrastructure for Hegemony society but are necessary for everything from FORCE deployment to the failsafes on stockpiled nuclear and plasma arsenals.'

'Did you know about this when you were . . . in the Core?'

'No,' said Johnny. 'As a pseudo-poet cybrid retrieval project, I was a freak, a pet, a partial thing allowed to roam the Web the way a pet is let out of the house each day. I had no idea there were three camps of AI influence.'

'Three camps,' I said. 'What's the third? And where does Hyperion come in?'

'Between the Stables and the Volatiles are the Ultimates. For the past five centuries the Ultimates have been obsessed with the UI Project. The existence or extinction of the human race is of interest to them only in how it applies to the project. To this date, they have been a force for moderation, an ally of the Stables, because it is their perception that such reconstruction and retrieval projects as the Old Earth experiment are necessary to the culmination of the UI.

416

'Recently, however, the Hyperion issue has caused the Ultimates to move toward the Volatiles' views. Since Hyperion was explored four centuries ago, the Core has been concerned and nonplussed. It was immediately obvious that the so-called Time Tombs were artifacts launched backward in time from a point at least ten thousand years in the galaxy's future. More disturbing, however, is the fact that Core predictive formulae have *never* been able to factor the Hyperion variable.

'Brawne, to understand this, you must realize how much the Core relies upon prediction. Already, without UI input, the Core knows the details of the physical, human, and AI future to a margin of 98.9995 percent for a period of at least two centuries. The AI Advisory Council to the All Thing with its vague, delphic utterances – considered so indispensable by humans – is a joke. The Core drops tidbits of revelations to the Hegemony when it serves the Core's purposes – sometimes to aid the Volatiles, sometimes the Stables, but *always* to please the Ultimates.

'Hyperion is a rent in the entire predictive fabric of the Core's existence. It is the penultimate oxymoron – a nonfactorable variable. Impossible as it seems, Hyperion appears to be exempt from the laws of physics, history, human psychology, and AI prediction as practiced by the Core.

'The result has been two futures – two *realities* if you will – one in which the Shrike scourge soon to be released on the Web and interstellar humanity is a weapon from the Core-dominated future, a retroactive first strike from the Volatiles who rule the galaxy millennia hence. The other reality sees the Shrike invasion, the coming interstellar war, and the other products of the Time Tombs' opening as a *human* fist struck back through time, a final, twilight effort by the Ousters, ex-colonials, and other small bands of humans who escaped the Volatiles' extinction programs.'

Water dripped on tile. Somewhere in the tunnels nearby a mech cauterizer's warning siren echoed from ceramic and stone. I leaned against the wall and stared at Johnny.

'Interstellar war,' I said. 'Both scenarios demand an interstellar war?'

'Yes. There is no escaping that.'

'Can both Core groups be wrong in their prediction?'

'No. What happens on *Hyperion* is problematic, but the disruption in the Web and elsewhere is quite clear. The Ultimates use this knowledge as the prime argument for hurrying the next step in Core evolution.'

'And what did BB's stolen data show about us, Johnny?'

Johnny smiled, touched my hand, but did not hold it. 'It showed that I am somehow part of the Hyperion unknown. Their creation of a Keats cybrid was a terrible gamble. Only my apparent lack of success as a Keats analog allowed the Stables to preserve me. When I made up my mind to go to Hyperion, the Volatiles killed me with the clear intention of obliterating my AI existence if my cybrid again made that decision.'

'You did. What happened?'

'They failed. In the Core's limitless arrogance, they failed to take two things into account. First, that I might invest all consciousness in my cybrid and thus change the nature of the Keats analog. Second, that I would go to you.'

'*Me!*'

He took my hand. 'Yes, Brawne. It seems that you also are part of the Hyperion unknown.'

I shook my head. Realizing that there was a numbness in my scalp above and behind my left ear, I raised my hand, half expecting to find damage from the datumplane fight. Instead, my fingers encountered the plastic of a neural shunt socket.

I jerked my other hand from Johnny's grasp and stared at him in horror. He'd had me wired while I was unconscious.

Johnny held up both hands, palms toward me. 'I had to, Brawne. It may be necessary for the survival of both of us.'

I made a fist. 'You fucking low-life son of a bitch. Why do *I* need to interface directly, you lying bastard?'

'Not with the Core,' Johnny said softly. 'With me.'

'You?' My arm and fist quivered with the anticipation of smashing his vat-cloned face. 'You!' I sneered. 'You're human now, remember?'

'Yes. But certain cybrid functions remain. Do you remember when I touched your hand several days ago and brought us to datumplane?'

I stared at him. 'I'm not going to datumplane again.'

'No. Nor am I. But I may need to relay incredible amounts of data to you within a very short period of time. I brought you to a black market surgeon in the Dregs' last night. She implanted a Schrön loop.'

'Why?' The Schrön loop was tiny, no larger than my thumbnail, and very expensive. It held countless field-bubble memories, each capable of holding near infinite bits of information. Schrön loops could not be accessed by the biological carrier and thus were used for courier purposes. A man or woman could carry AI personalities or entire planetary dataspheres in a Schrön loop. Hell, a *dog* could carry all that.

'Why?' I said again, wondering if Johnny or some forces behind Johnny were using me as such a courier. 'Why?'

Johnny moved closer and put his hand around my fist. 'Trust me, Brawne.'

I don't think I'd trusted anyone since Dad blew his brains out twenty years ago and Mom retreated into the pure selfishness of her seclusion. There was no reason in the universe to trust Johnny now.

But I did.

I relaxed my fist and took his hand.

'All right,' said Johnny. 'Finish your meal and we'll get busy trying to save our lives.'

Weapons and drugs were the two easiest things to buy in Dregs' Hive. We spent the last of Johnny's considerable stash of black marks to buy weapons.

By 2200 hours, we each wore whiskered titan-poly body armor. Johnny had a goonda's mirror-black helmet and I wore a FORCE-surplus command mask. Johnny's power gauntlets were massive and a bright red. I wore osmosis gloves with killing trim. Johnny carried an Ouster hellwhip captured on Bressia and had tucked a laser wand in his belt. Along with Dad's automatic, I now carried a Steiner-Ginn mini-gun on a gyroed waist brace. It was slaved to my command visor and I could keep both hands free while firing.

Johnny and I looked at each other and began giggling. When the laughter stopped there was a long silence.

'Are you sure the Shrike Temple here on Lusus is our best chance?' I asked for the third or fourth time.

'We can't farcast,' said Johnny. 'All the Core has to do is record a malfunction and we're dead. We can't even take an elevator from the lower levels. We'll have to find unmonitored stairways and climb the hundred and twenty floors. The best chance to make the Temple is straight down the Concourse Mall.'

'Yes, but will the Shrike Church people take us in?'

Johnny shrugged, a strangely insectoid gesture in his combat outfit. The voice through the goonda helmet was metallic. 'They're the only group which has a vested interest in our survival. And the only ones with enough political pull to shield us from the Hegemony while finding transit for us to Hyperion.'

I pushed up my visor. 'Meina Gladstone said that no future pilgrimage flights to Hyperion would be allowed.'

The dome of mirror black nodded judiciously. 'Well, fuck Meina Gladstone,' said my poet lover.

I took a breath and walked to the opening of our niche, our cave, our last sanctuary. Johnny came up behind me. Body armor rubbed against body armor. 'Ready, Brawne?'

I nodded, brought the mini-gun around on its pivot, and started to leave.

Johnny stopped me with a touch. 'I love you, Brawne.'

I nodded, still tough. I forgot that my visor was up and he could see my tears.

The Hive is awake all twenty-eight hours of the day, but through some tradition, Third Shift was the quietest, the least populated. We would have had a better chance at the height of First Shift rush hour along the pedestrian causeways. But if the goondas and thuggees were waiting for us, the death toll of civilians would have been staggering.

It took us more than three hours to climb our way to Concourse Mall, not up a single staircase but along an endless series of mech corridors, abandoned access verticals swept clean by the Luddite riots eighty years ago, and a final stairway that was more rust than metal. We exited onto a delivery corridor less than half a klick from the Shrike Temple.

'I can't believe it was so easy,' I whispered to him on intercom.

'They are probably concentrating people on the spaceport and private farcaster clusters.'

We took the least exposed walkway onto the Concourse, thirty meters below the first shopping level and four hundred meters below the roof. The Shrike Temple was an ornate, free-stranding structure now less than half a klick away. A few off-hour shoppers and joggers glanced at us and then moved quickly away. I had no doubt that the Mall police were being paged, but I'd be surprised if they showed up too quickly.

A gang of brightly painted street thugs exploded from a lift shaft, hollering and whooping. They carried pulse-knives, chains, and power gauntlets. Startled, Johnny wheeled toward them with the hellwhip sending out a score of targeting beams. The mini-gun whir-whirred out of my hands, shifting from aiming point to aiming point as I moved my eyes.

The gang of seven kids skidded to a halt, held up their hands, and backed away, eyes wide. They dropped into the lift shaft and were gone.

I looked at Johnny. Black mirrors looked back. Neither of us laughed.

We crossed to the northbound shopping lane. The few pedestrians scurried for open shopfronts. We were less than a hundred meters from the Temple stairs. I could actually hear my heartbeat in the FORCE helmet earphones. We were within fifty meters of the stairs. As if called, an acolyte or priest of some sort appeared at the ten-meter door of the Temple and watched us approach.

Thirty meters. If anyone was going to intercept us, they would have done it before this.

I turned toward Johnny to say something funny. At least twenty beams and half that many projectiles hit us at once. The outer layer of the titan-poly exploded outward, deflecting most of the projectile energy in the counterblast. The mirrored surface beneath bounced most of the killing light. Most of it.

Johnny was flung off his feet by the impact. I went to one knee and let the mini-gun train on the laser source.

Ten stories up along the residential Hive wall. My visor opaqued. Body armor burned off in a steam of reflective gas. The mini-gun sounded precisely like the kind of chainsaw they used in history holodramas. Ten stories up, a five-meter section of balcony and wall disintegrated in a cloud of explosive flèchettes and armor-piercing rounds.

Three heavy slugs struck me from behind.

I landed on my palms, silenced the mini-gun, and swiveled. There were at least a dozen of them on each level, moving quickly in precise combat choreography. Johnny had reached his knees and was firing the hellwhip in orchestrated bursts of light, working his way through the rainbow to beat bounce defenses.

One of the running figures exploded into flame as the shopwindow behind it turned to molten glass and spattered fifteen meters onto the Concourse. Two more men came up over the level railings and I sent them back with a burst from the mini-gun.

An open skimmer came down from the rafters, repellers laboring as it banked around pylons. Rocket fire slammed into concrete around Johnny and me. Shopfronts vomited a billion shards of glass over us. I looked, blinked twice, targeted, and fired. The skimmer lurched sideways, struck an escalator with a dozen cowering civilians on it, and tumbled in a mass of twisting metal and exploding ordnance. I saw one shopper leap in flames to the Hive floor eighty meters below.

'Left!' shouted Johnny over the tightbeam intercom.

Four men in combat armor had dropped from an upper level using personal lift packs. The polymerized chameleon armor labored to keep up with the shifting background but only succeeded in turning each man into a brilliant kaleidoscope of reflections. One moved inside the sweep arch of my mini-gun to neutralize me while the other three went for Johnny.

He came in with a pulse-blade, ghetto style. I let it chew at my armor, knowing it would get through to forearm flesh but using it to buy the second I needed. I got it. I killed the man with the rigid edge of my gauntlet and swept the mini-gun fire into the three worrying Johnny.

Their armor went rigid and I used the gun to sweep them backward like someone hosing down a littered sidewalk. Only one of the men got to his feet before I blew them all off the level overhang.

Johnny was down again. Parts of his chest armor were gone, melted away. I smelled cooking flesh but saw no mortal wounds. I half crouched, lifted him.

'Leave me, Brawne. Run. The stairs.' The tightbeam was breaking up.

'Fuck off,' I said, getting my left arm around him enough to support him while allowing room for the mini-gun to track. 'I'm still getting paid to be your bodyguard.'

They were sniping at us from both walls of the Hive, the rafters, and the shopping levels above us. I counted at least twenty bodies on the walkways; about half were brightly clad civilians. The power assist on the left leg of my armor was grinding. Straight-legged, I awkwardly pulled us another ten meters toward the Temple stairs. There were several Shrike priests at the head of the stairs now, seemingly oblivious to the gunfire all around them.

'Above!'

I swiveled, targeted, and fired in one moment, hearing the gun go empty after one burst and seeing the second skimmer get off its missiles in the instant before it became a thousand pieces of hurtling, unrelated metal and torn flesh. I dropped Johnny heavily to the pavement and fell on him, trying to cover his exposed flesh with my body.

The missiles detonated simultaneously, several in

airburst and at least two burrowing. Johnny and I were lifted into the air and hurled fifteen or twenty meters down the pitching walkway. Good thing. The alloy and ferroconcrete pedestrian strip where we had been a second before burned, bubbled, sagged, and tumbled down onto the flaming walkway below. There was a natural moat there now, a gap between most of the other ground troops and us.

I rose, slapped away the useless mini-gun and mount, pulled off useless shards of my own armor, and lifted Johnny in both arms. His helmet had been blown off and his face was very bad. Blood seeped through a score of gaps in his armor. His right arm and left foot had been blown off. I turned and began carrying him up the Shrike Temple stairs.

There were sirens and security skimmers filling the Concourse flyspace now. The goondas on the upper levels and far side of the tumbled walkway ran for cover. Two of the commandos who had dropped on lift packs ran up the stairs after me. I did not turn. I had to lift my straight and useless left leg for every step. I knew that I had been seriously burned on my back and side and there were shrapnel wounds elsewhere.

The skimmers whooped and circled but avoided the Temple steps. Gunfire rattled up and down the Mall. I could hear metal-shod footsteps coming rapidly behind me. I managed another three steps. Twenty steps above, impossibly far away, the bishop stood amid a hundred Temple priests.

I made another step and looked down at Johnny. One eye was open, staring up at me. The other was closed with blood and swollen tissue. 'It's all right,' I whispered, aware for the first time that my own helmet was gone. 'It's all right. We're almost there.' I managed one more step.

The two men in bright black combat armor blocked my way. Both had lifted visors streaked with deflection scars and their faces were very hard.

'Put him down, bitch, and maybe we'll let you live.'

I nodded tiredly, too tired to take another step or do anything but stand there and hold him in both arms.

Johnny's blood dripped on white stone.

'I said, put the son of a bitch down and . . .'

I shot both of them, one in the left eye and one in the right, never lifting Dad's automatic from where I held it under Johnny's body.

They fell away. I managed another step. And then another. I rested a bit and then lifted my foot for another.

At the top of the stairs the group of black and red robes parted. The doorway was very tall and very dark. I did not look back but I could hear from the noise behind us that the crowd on the Concourse was very large. The bishop walked by my side as I went through the doors and into the dimness.

I laid Johnny on the cool floor. Robes rustled around us. I pulled my own armor off where I could, then batted at Johnny's. It was fused to his flesh in several places. I touched his burned cheek with my good hand. 'I'm sorry . . .'

Johnny's head stirred slightly and his eye opened. He lifted his bare left hand to touch my cheek, my hair, the back of my head. 'Fanny . . .'

I felt him die then. I also felt the surge as his hand found the neural shunt, the white-light warmth of the surge to the Schrön loop as everything Johnny Keats ever was or would be exploded into me; almost, almost it was like his orgasm inside me two nights earlier, the surge and throb and sudden warmth and stillness after, with the echo of sensation there.

I lowered him to the floor and let the acolytes remove the body, taking it out to show the crowd and the authorities and the ones who waited to know.

I let them take me away.

I spent two weeks in a Shrike Temple recovery crèche. Burns healed, scars removed, alien metal extracted, skin grafted, flesh regrown, nerves rewoven. And still I hurt.

Everyone except the Shrike priests lost interest in me. The Core made sure that Johnny was dead; that his presence in the Core had left no trace; that his cybrid was dead.

The authorities took my statement, revoked my license, and covered things up as best they could. The Web press reported that a battle between Dregs' Level Hive gangs had erupted onto the Concourse Mall. Numerous gang members and innocent bystanders were killed. The police contained it.

A week before word came that the Hegemony would allow the *Yggdrasill* to sail with pilgrims for the war zone near Hyperion, I used a Temple farcaster to 'cast to Renaissance Vector where I spent an hour alone in the archives there.

The papers were in vacuum-press so I could not touch them. The handwriting was Johnny's; I had seen his writing before. The parchment was yellow and brittle with age. There were two fragments. The first read:

The day is gone, and all its sweets are gone!
   Sweet voice, sweet lips, soft hand, and softer breast,
Warm breath, light whisper, tender semi-tone,
   Bright eyes, accomplished shape, and languorous
    waist!
Faded the flower and all its budded charms,
   Faded the sight of beauty from my eyes,
Faded the shape of beauty from my arms,
   Faded the voice, warmth, whiteness, paradise—
Vanished unseasonably at shut of eve,
   When the dusk holiday – or holinight—
Of fragrant-curtained love begins to weave
   The woof of darkness thick, for hid delight;
But, as I've read love's missal through today,
He'll let me sleep, seeing I fast and pray.

The second fragment was in a wilder hand and on rougher paper, as if slashed across a notepad in haste:

   This living hand, now warm and capable
   Of earnest grasping, would, if it were cold
   And in the icy silence of the tomb,
   So haunt thy days and chill thy dreaming nights
   That thou wouldst wish thine own heart dry of blood

426

So in my veins red life might stream again,
And thou be conscience-calm'd – see here it is—
I hold it towards you

I'm pregnant. I think that Johnny knew it. I don't know for sure.

I'm pregnant twice. Once with Johnny's child and once with the Schrön-loop memory of what he was. I don't know if the two are meant to be linked. It will be months before the child is born and only days before I face the Shrike.

But I remember those minutes after Johnny's torn body was taken out to the crowd and before I was led away for help. They were all there in the darkness, hundreds of the priests and acolytes and exorcists and ostiaries and worshipers . . . and as one voice they began to chant, there in that red dimness under the revolving sculpture of the Shrike, and their voices echoed in Gothic vaults. And what they chanted went something like this:

'BLESSED BE SHE
BLESSED BE THE MOTHER OF OUR
   SALVATION
BLESSED BE THE INSTRUMENT OF OUR
   ATONEMENT
BLESSED BE THE BRIDE OF OUR CREATION
BLESSED BE SHE'

I was injured and in shock. I didn't understand it then. I don't understand it now.

But I know that, when the time arrives and the Shrike comes, Johnny and I will face it together.

It was long after dark. The tramcar rode between stars and ice. The group sat in silence, the only sound the creak of cable.

After a time had passed, Lenar Hoyt said to Brawne Lamia, 'You also carry the cruciform.'

Lamia looked at the priest.

Colonel Kassad leaned toward the woman. 'Do you think Het Masteen was the Templar who had spoken to Johnny?'

'Possibly,' said Brawne Lamia. 'I never found out.'

Kassad did not blink. 'Were you the one who killed Masteen?'

'No.'

Martin Silenus stretched and yawned. 'We have a few hours before sunrise,' he said. 'Anyone else interested in getting some sleep?'

Several heads nodded.

'I'll stay up to keep watch,' said Fedmahn Kassad. 'I'm not tired.'

'I'll keep you company,' said the Consul.

'I'll heat some coffee for the therm,' said Brawne Lamia.

When the others slept, the infant Rachel making soft cooing sounds in her sleep, the other three sat at the windows and watched the stars burn cold and distant in the high night.

SIX

Chronos Keep jutted from the easternmost rim of the great Bridle Range: a grim, baroque heap of sweating stones with three hundred rooms and halls, a maze of lightless corridors leading to deep halls, towers, turrets, balconies overlooking the northern moors, airshafts rising half a kilometer to light and rumored to drop to the world's labyrinth itself, parapets scoured by cold winds from the peaks above, stairways – inside and out – carved from the mountain stone and leading nowhere, stained-glass windows a hundred meters tall set to catch the first rays of solstice sun or the moon on midwinter night, paneless windows the size of a man's fist looking out on nothing in particular, an endless array of bas-relief, grotesque sculptures in half-hidden niches, and more than a thousand gargoyles staring down from eave and parapet, transept and sepulcher, peering down through wood rafters in the great halls and positioned so as to peer in the blood-tinted windows of the northeast face, their winged and hunchbacked shadows moving like grim sundial hours, cast by sunlight in the day and gas-fed torches at night. And everywhere in Chronos Keep, signs of the Shrike Church's long occupation – atonement altars draped in red velvet, hanging and free-standing sculptures of the Avatar with polychrome steel for blades and bloodgems for eyes, more statues of the Shrike carved from the stone of narrow stairways and dark halls so that nowhere in the night would one be free of the fear of touching hands emerging from rock, the sharp curve of blade descending from stone, four arms enveloping in a final embrace. As if in a last measure of ornamentation, a filigree of blood in many of the once occupied halls and rooms, arabesques of red spattered in almost recognizable patterns along walls and tunnel ceilings, bedclothes caked hard with rust-red substance, and a central dining hall filled with the stench of food rotting from a meal abandoned weeks earlier, the floor and table, chairs and wall adorned with blood, stained clothing and shredded robes lying in mute heaps. And everywhere the sound of flies.

'Jolly fucking place, isn't it?' said Martin Silenus, his voice echoing.

Father Hoyt took several steps deeper into the great hall. Afternoon light from the west-facing skylight forty meters above fell in dusty columns. 'It's incredible,' he whispered. 'St Peter's in the New Vatican is nothing like this.'

Martin Silenus laughed. Thick light outlined his cheekbones and satyr's brows. 'This was built for a *living* deity,' he said.

Fedmahn Kassad lowered his travel bag to the floor and cleared his throat. 'Surely this place predates the Shrike Church.'

'It does,' said the Consul. 'But they've occupied it for the past two centuries.'

'It doesn't look too occupied now,' said Brawne Lamia. She held her father's automatic in her left hand.

They had all shouted during their first twenty minutes in the Keep, but the dying echoes, silences, and buzz of flies in the dining hall had reduced them to silence.

'Sad King Billy's androids and bond clones built the goddamn thing,' said the poet. 'Eight local years of labor before the spinships arrived. It was supposed to be the greatest tourist resort in the Web, the jumping-off point for the Time Tombs and the City of Poets. But I suspect that even then the poor schmuck android laborers knew the locals' version of the Shrike story.'

Sol Weintraub stood near an eastern window, holding his daughter up so that soft light fell across her cheek and curled fist. 'All that matters little now,' he said. 'Let's find a corner free of carnage where we can sleep and eat our evening meal.'

'Are we going on tonight?' asked Brawne Lamia.

'To the Tombs?' asked Silenus, showing real surprise for the first time on the voyage. 'You'd go to the Shrike in the dark?'

Lamia shrugged. 'What difference does it make?'

The Consul stood near a leaded glass door leading to a stone balcony and closed his eyes. His body still lurched and balanced to the movement of the tramcar. The night and day of travel above the peaks had blurred together in his mind, lost in the fatigue of almost three days without sleep and his rising tension. He opened his eyes before he dozed off standing up. 'We're tired,' he said. 'We'll stay here tonight and go down in the morning.'

Father Hoyt had gone out onto the narrow ledge of balcony. He leaned on a railing of jagged stone. 'Can we see the Tombs from here?'

'No,' said Silenus. 'They're beyond that rise of hills. But see those white things to the north and west a bit . . . those things gleaming like shards of broken teeth in the sand?'

'Yes.'

'That's the City of Poets. King Billy's original site for Keats and for all things bright and beautiful. The locals say that it's haunted now by headless ghosts.'

'Are you one of them?' asked Lamia.

Martin Silenus turned to say something, looked a moment at the pistol still in her hand, shook his head, and turned away.

Footsteps echoed from an unseen curve of staircase and Colonel Kassad reentered the room. 'There are two small storerooms above the dining hall,' he said. 'They have a section of balcony outside but no other access than this stairway. Easy to defend. The rooms are . . . clean.'

Silenus laughed. 'Does that mean nothing can get at us or that, when something *does* get at us, we'll have no way to get out?'

'Where would we go?' asked Sol Weintraub.

'Where indeed?' said the Consul. He was very tired. He lifted his gear and took one handle of the heavy Möbius cube, waiting for Father Hoyt to lift the other end. 'Let's do what Kassad says. Find a space to spend the night. Let's at least get out of this room. It stinks of death.'

Dinner was the last of their dried rations, some wine from Silenus's last bottle, and some stale cake which Sol Weintraub had brought along to celebrate their last evening together. Rachel was too little to eat the cake, but she took her milk and went to sleep on her stomach on a mat near her father.

Lenar Hoyt removed a small balalaika from his pack and strummed a few chords.

'I didn't know you played,' said Brawne Lamia.

'Poorly.'

The Consul rubbed his eyes. 'I wish we had a piano.'

'You do have one,' said Martin Silenus.

The Consul looked at the poet.

'Bring it here,' said Silenus. 'I'd welcome a Scotch.'

'What are you talking about?' snapped Father Hoyt. 'Make sense.'

'His *ship*,' said Silenus. 'Do you remember our dear, departed Voice of the Bush Masteen telling our Consul friend that *his* secret weapon was that nice Hegemony singleship sitting back at Keats Spaceport? Call it up, Your Consulship. Bring it on in.'

Kassad moved away from the stairway where he had been placing tripbeams. 'The planet's datasphere is dead. The comsats are down. The orbiting FORCE ships are on tightbeam. How is he supposed to call it?'

It was Lamia who spoke. 'A fatline transmitter.'

The Consul moved his stare to her.

'Fatline transmitters are the size of buildings,' said Kassad.

Brawne Lamia shrugged. 'What Masteen said made sense. If I were the Consul . . . if I were one of the few thousand individuals in the entire damn Web to own a singleship . . . *I'd* be damn sure I could fly it in on remote if I needed it. The planet's too primitive to depend on its comm net, the ionosphere's too weak for shortwave, the comsats are the first things to go in a skirmish . . . I'd call it by fatline.'

'And the size?' said the Consul.

Brawne Lamia returned the diplomat's level gaze. 'The Hegemony can't yet build portable fatline transmitters. There are rumors that the Ousters can.'

The Consul smiled. From somewhere there came a scrape and then the sound of metal crashing.

'Stay here,' said Kassad. He removed a deathwand from his tunic, canceled the tripbeams with his tactical comlog, and descended from sight.

'I guess we're under martial law now,' said Silenus when the Colonel was gone. 'Mars ascendant.'

'Shut up,' said Lamia.

'Do you think it's the Shrike?' asked Hoyt.

The Consul made a gesture. 'The Shrike doesn't have to clank around downstairs. It can simply appear . . . *here*.'

Hoyt shook his head. 'I mean the Shrike that has been the cause of everyone's . . . absence. The signs of slaughter here in the Keep.'

'The empty villages might be the result of the evacuation order,' said the Consul. 'No one wants to stay behind to face the Ousters. The SDF forces have been running wild. Much of the carnage could be their doing.'

'With no bodies?' laughed Martin Silenus. 'Wishful thinking. Our absent hosts downstairs dangle now on the Shrike's steel tree. Where, ere long, we too will be.'

'Shut up,' Brawne Lamia said tiredly.

'And if I don't,' grinned the poet, 'will you shoot me, madam?'

'Yes.'

The silence lasted until Colonel Kassad returned. He reactivated the tripbeams and turned to the group seated on packing crates and flowfoam cubes. 'It was nothing. Some carrion birds – harbingers, I think the locals call them – had come in through the broken glass doors in the dining hall and were finishing the feast.'

Silenus chuckled. 'Harbingers. Very appropriate.'

Kassad sighed, sat on a blanket with his back to a crate, and poked at his cold food. A single lantern brought from the windwagon lighted the room and the shadows were beginning to mount the walls in the corners away from the door to the balcony. 'It's our last night,' said Kassad. 'One more story to tell.' He looked at the Consul.

The Consul had been twisting his slip of paper with the number 7 scrawled on it. He licked his lips. 'What's the purpose? The purpose of the pilgrimage has been destroyed already.'

The others stirred.

'What do you mean?' asked Father Hoyt.

The Consul crumpled the paper and threw it into a corner. 'For the Shrike to grant a request, the band of pilgrims must constitute a prime number. We had seven. Masteen's . . . disappearance . . . reduces us to six. We go to our deaths now with no hope of a wish being granted.'

'Superstition,' said Lamia.

The Consul sighed and rubbed his brow. 'Yes. But that is our final hope.'

Father Hoyt gestured toward the sleeping infant. 'Can't Rachel be our seventh?'

Sol Weintraub rubbed his beard. 'No. A pilgrim must come to the Tombs of his or her own free will.'

'But she did once,' said Hoyt. 'Maybe it qualifies.'

'No,' said the Consul.

Martin Silenus had been writing notes on a pad but now he stood and paced the length of the room. 'Jesus Christ, people. Look at us. We're not six fucking pilgrims, we're a mob. Hoyt there with his cruciform carrying the ghost of Paul Duré. Our "semisentient" erg in the box there. Colonel Kassad with his memory of Moneta. M. Brawne there, if we are to believe her tale, carrying not only an unborn child but a dead Romantic poet. Our scholar with the child his daughter used to be. Me with my muse. The Consul with whatever fucking baggage he's brought to this insane trek. My God, people, we should have received a fucking group rate for this trip.'

'Sit down,' said Lamia in a dead even tone.

'No, he's right,' said Hoyt. 'Even the presence of Father Duré in cruciform must affect the prime-number superstition somehow. I say that we press on in the morning in the belief that . . .'

'Look!' cried Brawne Lamia, pointing to the balcony doorway where the fading twilight had been replaced with pulses of strong light.

The group went out into the cool evening air, shielding their eyes from the staggering display of silent explosions which filled the sky: pure white fusion bursts expanding like explosive ripples across a lapis pond; smaller, brighter plasma implosions in blue and yellow and brightest red, curling inward like flowers folding for the night: the lightning dance of gigantic hellwhip displays, beams the size of small worlds cutting their swath across light-hours and being contorted by the riptides of defensive singularities: the aurora shimmer of defense fields leaping and dying under the assault of terrible energies only to be reborn nanoseconds later. Amid it all, the blue-white fusion tails of torchships and larger warships slicing perfectly true lines across the sky like diamond scratches on blue glass.

'The Ousters,' breathed Brawne Lamia.

'The war's begun,' said Kassad. There was no elation in his voice, no emotion of any kind.

The Consul was shocked to discover that he was weeping silently. He turned his face from the group.

'Are we in danger here?' asked Martin Silenus. He sheltered under the stone archway of the door, squinting at the brilliant display.

'Not at this distance,' said Kassad. He raised his combat binoculars, made an adjustment, and consulted his tactical comlog. 'Most of the engagements are at least three AU away. The Ousters are testing the FORCE:space defenses.' He lowered the glasses. 'It's just begun.'

'Has the farcaster been activated yet?' asked Brawne Lamia. 'Are the people being evacuated from Keats and the other cities?'

Kassad shook his head. 'I don't believe so. Not yet. The fleet will be fighting a holding action until the cislunar sphere is completed. Then the evacuation portals will be opened to the Web while FORCE units come through by the hundreds.' He raised the binoculars again. 'It'll be a hell of a show.'

'Look!' It was Father Hoyt pointing this time, not at the fireworks display in the sky but out across the low dunes of the northern moors. Several kilometers toward the unseen Tombs, a single figure was just visible as a speck of a form throwing multiple shadows under the fractured sky.

Kassad trained his glasses on the figure.

'The Shrike?' asked Lamia.

'No, I don't think so . . . I think it's . . . a Templar by the looks of the robe.'

'Het Masteen!' cried Father Hoyt.

Kassad shrugged and handed the glasses around. The Consul walked back to the group and leaned on the balcony. There was no sound but the whisper of wind, but that made the violence of explosions above them more ominous somehow.

The Consul took his turn looking when the glasses came to him. The figure was tall and robed, its back to the Keep, and strode across the flashing vermilion sands with purposeful intent.

'Is he headed toward us or the Tombs?' asked Lamia.

'The Tombs,' said the Consul.

Father Hoyt leaned elbows on the ledge and raised his gaunt face to the exploding sky. 'If it is Masteen, then we're back to seven, aren't we?'

'He'll arrive hours before us,' said the Consul. 'Half a day if we sleep here tonight as we proposed.'

Hoyt shrugged. 'That can't matter too much. Seven set out on the pilgrimage. Seven will arrive. The Shrike will be satisfied.'

'If it *is* Masteen,' said Colonel Kassad, 'why the charade on the windwagon? And how did he get here before us? There were no other tramcars running and he couldn't have walked over the Bridle Range passes.'

'We'll ask him when we arrive at the Tombs tomorrow,' Father Hoyt said tiredly.

Brawne Lamia had been trying to raise someone on her comlog's general comm frequencies. Nothing emerged but the hiss of static and the occasional growl of distant EMPs. She looked at Colonel Kassad. 'When do they start bombing?'

'I don't know. It depends upon the strength of the FORCE fleet defenses.'

'The defenses weren't very good the other day when the Ouster scouts got through and destroyed the *Yggdrasill*,' said Lamia.

Kassad nodded.

'Hey,' said Martin Silenus, 'are we sitting on a fucking *target*?'

'Of course,' said the Consul. 'If the Ousters are attacking Hyperion to prevent the opening of the Time Tombs, as M. Lamia's tale suggests, then the Tombs and this entire area would be a primary target.'

'For nukes?' asked Silenus, his voice strained.

'Almost certainly,' answered Kassad.

'I thought something about the anti-entropic fields kept ships away from here,' said Father Hoyt.

'*Crewed* ships,' said the Consul without looking back at the others from where he leaned on the railing. 'The anti-entropic fields won't bother guided missiles, smart bombs, or hellwhip beams. It won't bother mech infantry, for that matter. The Ousters could land a few attack skimmers or automated tanks and watch on remote while they destroy the valley.'

'But they won't,' said Brawne Lamia. 'They want to *control* Hyperion, not destroy it.'

'I wouldn't wager my life on that supposition,' said Kassad.

Lamia smiled at him. 'But we are, aren't we, Colonel?'

Above them, a single spark separated itself from the continuous patchwork of explosions, grew into a bright orange ember, and streaked across the sky. The group on the terrace could see the flames, hear the tortured shriek of atmospheric penetration. The fireball disappeared beyond the mountains behind the Keep.

Almost a minute later, the Consul realized that he had been holding his breath, his hands rigid on the stone railing. He let out air in a gasp. The others seemed to be taking a breath at the same moment. There had been no explosion, no shock wave rumbling through the rock.

'A dud?' asked Father Hoyt.

'Probably an injured FORCE skirmisher trying to reach the orbital perimeter or the spaceport at Keats,' said Colonel Kassad.

'He didn't make it, did he?' asked Lamia. Kassad did not respond.

Martin Silenus lifted the field glasses and searched the darkening moors for the Templar. 'Out of sight,' said Silenus. 'The good Captain either rounded that hill just this side of the Time Tombs valley or he pulled his disappearing act again.'

'It's a pity that we'll never hear his story,' said Father Hoyt. He turned toward the Consul. 'But we'll hear yours, won't we?'

The Consul rubbed his palms against his pant legs. His heart was racing. 'Yes,' he said, realizing even as he spoke that he had finally made up his mind. 'I'll tell mine.'

The wind roared down the east slopes of the mountains and whistled along the escarpment of Chronos Keep. The explosions above them seemed to have diminished ever so slightly, but the coming of darkness made each one look even more violent than the last.

'Let's go inside,' said Lamia, her words almost lost in the wind sound. 'It's getting cold.'

They had turned off the single lamp and the interior of the room was lighted only by the heat-lightning pulses of color from the sky outside. Shadows sprang into being, vanished, and appeared again as the room was painted in many colors. Sometimes the darkness would last several seconds before the next barrage.

The Consul reached into his traveling bag and took out a strange device, larger than a comlog, oddly ornamented, and fronted with a liquid crystal diskey like something out of a history holo.

'Secret fatline transmitter?' Brawne Lamia asked dryly.

The Consul's smile showed no humor. 'It's an ancient comlog. It came out during the Hegira.' He removed a standard micro-disk from a pouch on his belt and inserted it. 'Like Father Hoyt, I have someone else's tale to tell before you can understand my own.'

'Christ on a stick,' sneered Martin Silenus, 'am I the only one who can tell a straightforward story in this fucking herd? How long do I have to . . .'

The Consul's movement surprised even himself. He rose, spun, caught the smaller man by the cape and shirt-front, slammed him against the wall, draped him over a packing crate with a knee in Silenus's belly and a forearm against his throat, and hissed, 'One more word from you, poet, and *I'll* kill you.'

Silenus began to struggle but a tightening on his wind-pipe and a glance at the Consul's eyes made him cease. His face was very white.

Colonel Kassad silently, almost gently, separated the two. 'There will be no more comments,' he said. He touched the deathwand in his belt.

Martin Silenus went to the far side of the circle, still rubbing his throat, and slumped against a crate without a word. The Consul strode to the door, took several deep breaths, and walked back to the group. He spoke to everyone but the poet. 'I'm sorry. It is just that . . . I never expected to share this.'

The light from outside surged red and then white, fol-lowed by a blue glow which faded to near darkness.

'We know,' Brawne Lamia said softly. 'We all felt that way.'

The Consul touched his lower lip, nodded, roughly cleared his throat, and came to sit by the ancient comlog. 'The recording is not as old as the instrument,' he said. 'It was made about fifty standard years ago. I'll have some more to say when it's over.' He paused as if there were more to be said, shook his head, and thumbed the antique diskey.

There were no visuals. The voice was that of a young man. In the background one could hear a breeze blowing through grass or soft branches and, more distantly, the roll of surf.

Outside, the light pulsed madly as the tempo of the distant space battle quickened. The Consul tensed as he waited for the crash and concussion. There was none. He closed his eyes and listened with the others.

* * *

THE CONSUL'S TALE:
Remembering Siri

I climb the steep hill to Siri's tomb on the day the islands return to the shallow seas of the Equatorial Archipelago. The day is perfect and I hate it for being so. The sky is as tranquil as tales of Old Earth's seas, the shallows are dappled with ultramarine tints, and a warm breeze blows in from the sea to ripple the russet willowgrass on the hillside near me.

Better low clouds and gray gloom on such a day. Better mist or a shrouding fog which sets the masts in Firstsite Harbor dripping and raises the lighthouse horn from its slumbers. Better one of the great sea-simoons blowing up out of the cold belly of the south, lashing before it the motile isles and their dolphin herders until they seek refuge in the lee of our atolls and stony peaks.

Anything would be better than this warm spring day when the sun moves through a vault of sky so blue that it makes me want to run, to jump in great loping arcs, and to roll in the soft grass as Siri and I have done at just this spot.

Just this spot. I pause to look around. The willowgrass bends and ripples like the fur of some great beast as the salt-tinged breeze gusts up out of the south. I shield my eyes and search the horizon but nothing moves there. Out beyond the lava reef, the sea begins to chop and lift itself in nervous strokes.

'Siri,' I whisper. I say her name without meaning to do so. A hundred meters down the slope, the crowd pauses to watch me and to catch its collective breath. The procession of mourners and celebrants stretches for more than a kilometer to where the white buildings of the city begin. I can make out the gray and balding head of my younger son in the vanguard. He is wearing the blue and gold robes of the Hegemony. I know that I should wait for him, walk with him, but he and the other aging Council members cannot keep up with my young, ship-trained muscles and steady stride. But decorum dictates that I should walk with him and my granddaughter Lira and my nine-year-old grandson.

To hell with it. And to hell with them.

I turn and jog up the steep hillside. Sweat begins to soak my loose cotton shirt before I reach the curving summit of the ridge and catch sight of the tomb.

Siri's tomb.

I stop. The wind chills me although the sunlight is warm enough as it glints off the flawless white stone of the silent mausoleum. The grass is high near the sealed entrance to the crypt. Rows of faded festival pennants on ebony staffs line the narrow gravel path.

Hesitating, I circle the tomb and approach the steep cliff edge a few meters beyond. The willowgrass is bent and trampled here where irreverent picnickers have laid their blankets. There are several fire rings formed from the perfectly round, perfectly white stones purloined from the border of the gravel path.

I cannot stop a smile. I know the view from here: the great curve of the outer harbor with its natural seawall, the low, white buildings of Firstsite, and the colorful hulls and masts of the catamarans bobbing at anchorage. Near the pebble beach beyond Common Hall, a young woman in a white skirt moves toward the water. For a second I think that it is Siri and my heart pounds. I half prepare to throw up my arms in response to her wave but she does not wave. I watch in silence as the distant figure turns away and is lost in the shadows of the old boat building.

Above me, far out from the cliff, a wide-winged Thomas Hawk circles above the lagoon on rising thermals and scans the shifting bluekelp beds with its infrared vision, seeking out harp seals or torpids. *Nature is stupid*, I think and sit in the soft grass. Nature sets the stage all wrong for such a day and then it is insensitive enough to throw in a bird searching for prey which have long since fled the polluted waters near the growing city.

I remember another Thomas Hawk on that first night when Siri and I came to this hilltop. I remember the moonlight on its wings and the strange, haunting cry which echoed off the cliff and seemed to pierce the dark air above the gaslights of the village below.

Siri was sixteen . . . no, not quite sixteen . . . and the moonlight that touched the hawk's wings above us also painted her bare skin with milky light and cast shadows beneath the soft circles of her breasts. We looked up guiltily when the bird's cry cut the night and Siri said, ' "It was the nightingale and not the lark, That pierc'd the fearful hollow of thine ear." '

'Huh?' I said. Siri was almost sixteen. I was nineteen. But Siri knew the slow pace of books and the cadences of theater under the stars. I knew only the stars.

'Relax, young Shipman,' she whispered and pulled me down beside her then. 'It's only an old Tom's Hawk hunting. Stupid bird. Come back, Shipman. Come back, Merin.'

The *Los Angeles* had chosen that moment to rise above the horizon and to float like a wind-borne ember west across the strange constellations of Maui-Covenant, Siri's world. I lay next to her and described the workings of the great Hawking-drive spinship which was catching the high sunlight against the drop of night above us, and all the while my hand was sliding lower along her smooth side, her skin seemed all velvet and electricity, and her breath came more quickly against my shoulder. I lowered my face to the hollow of her neck, to the sweat and perfume essence of her tousled hair.

'Siri,' I say and this time her name is not unbidden. Below me, below the crest of the hill and the shadow of the white tomb, the crowd stands and shuffles. They are impatient with me. They want me to unseal the tomb, to enter, and to have my private moment in the cool silent emptiness that has replaced the warm presence that was Siri. They want me to say my farewells so they can get on with their rites and rituals, open the farcaster doors, and join the waiting Worldweb of the Hegemony.

To hell with that. And to hell with them.

I pull up a tendril of the thickly woven willowgrass, chew on the sweet stem, and watch the horizon for the first sign of the migrating islands. The shadows are still

442

long in the morning light. The day is young. I will sit here for a while and remember.

I will remember Siri.

Siri was a . . . what? . . . a bird, I think, the first time I saw her. She was wearing some sort of mask with bright feathers. When she removed it to join in the raceme quadrille, the torchlight caught the deep auburn tints of her hair. She was flushed, cheeks aflame, and even from across the crowded common I could see the startling green of her eyes contrasting with the summer heat of her face and hair. It was Festival Night, of course. The torches danced and sparked to the stiff breeze coming in off the harbor and the sound of the flutists on the break-wall playing for the passing isles was almost drowned out by surf sounds and the crack of pennants snapping in the wind. Siri was almost sixteen and her beauty burned more brightly than any of the torches set round the throng-filled square. I pushed through the dancing crowd and went to her.

It was five years ago for me. It was more than sixty-five years ago for us. It seems only yesterday.

This is not going well.

Where to start?

'What say we go find a little nooky, kid?' Mike Osho was speaking. Short, squat, his pudgy face a clever caricature of a Buddha, Mike was a god to me then. We were all gods; long-lived if not immortal, well paid if not quite divine. The Hegemony had chosen us to help crew one of its precious quantum-leap spinships, so how could we be less than gods? It was just that Mike, brilliant, mercurial, irreverent Mike, was a little older and a little higher in the Shipboard pantheon than young Merin Aspic.

'Hah. Zero probability of that,' I said. We were scrubbing up after a twelve-hour shift with the farcaster construction crew. Shuttling the workers around their chosen singularity point some one hundred and sixty-three thousand kilometers out from Maui-Covenant was a lot less glamorous for us than the four-month leap from Hegemony-space. During the C-plus portion of the

443

trip we had been master specialists; forty-nine starship experts shepherding some two hundred nervous passengers. Now the passengers had their hardsuits on and we Shipmen had been reduced to serving as glorified truck drivers as the construction crew wrestled the bulky singularity containment sphere into place.

'Zero probability,' I repeated. 'Unless the groundlings have added a whorehouse to that quarantine island they leased us.'

'Nope. They haven't,' grinned Mike. He and I had our three days of planetary R and R coming up but we knew from Shipmaster Singh's briefings and the moans of our Shipmates that the only ground time we had to look forward to would be spent on a seven-by-four-kilometer island administered by the Hegemony. It wasn't even one of the motile isles we had heard about, just another volcanic peak near the equator. Once there, we could count on real gravity underfoot, unfiltered air to breathe, and the chance to taste unsynthesized food. But we could also count on the fact that the only intercourse we would have with the Maui-Covenant colonists would be through buying local artifacts at the duty-free store. Even those were sold by Hegemony trade specialists. Many of our Shipmates had chosen to spend their R and R on the *Los Angeles*.

'So how do we find a little nooky, Mike? The colonies are off limits until the farcaster's working. That's about sixty years away, local time. Or are you talking about Meg in spincomp?'

'Stick with me, kid,' said Mike. 'Where there's a will, there's a way.'

I stuck with Mike. There were only five of us in the dropship. It was always a thrill to me to fall out of high orbit into the atmosphere of a real world. Especially a world that looked as much like Old Earth as Maui-Covenant did. I stared at the blue and white limb of the planet until the seas were *down* and we were in atmosphere, approaching the twilight terminator in a gentle glide at three times the speed of our own sound.

We were gods then. But even gods must descend from their high thrones upon occasion.

*　　*　　*

Siri's body never ceased to amaze me. That time on the Archipelago. Three weeks in that huge, swaying treehouse under the billowing treesails with the dolphin herders keeping pace like outriders, tropical sunsets filling the evening with wonder, the canopy of stars at night, and our own wake marked by a thousand phosphorescent swirls that mirrored the constellations above. And still it is Siri's body I remember. For some reason – shyness, the years of separation – she wore two strips of swimsuit for the first few days of our Archipelago stay and the soft white of her breasts and lower belly had not darkened to match the rest of her tan before I had to leave again.

I remember her that first time. Triangles in the moonlight as we lay in the soft grass above Firstsite Harbor. Her silk pants catching on a weave of willowgrass. There was a child's modesty then; the slight hesitation of something given prematurely. But also pride. The same pride that later allowed her to face down the angry mob of Separatists on the steps of the Hegemony consulate in South Tern and send them to their homes in shame.

I remember my fifth planetfall, our Fourth Reunion. It was one of the few times I ever saw her cry. She was almost regal in her fame and wisdom by then. She had been elected four times to the All Thing and the Hegemony Council turned to her for advice and guidance. She wore her independence like a royal cloak and her fierce pride had never burned more brightly. But when we were alone in the stone villa south of Fevarone, it was she who turned away. I was nervous, frightened by this powerful stranger, but it was Siri – Siri of the straight back and proud eyes, who turned her face to the wall and said through tears, 'Go away. Go away, Merin. I don't want you to see me. I'm a crone, all slack and sagging. *Go away*.'

I confess that I was rough with her then. I pinned her wrists with my left hand – using a strength which surprised even me – and tore her silken robe down the front in one move. I kissed her shoulders, her neck, the faded shadows of stretch marks on her taut belly, and the scar

445

on her upper leg from the skimmer crash some forty of her years earlier. I kissed her graying hair and the lines etched in the once smooth cheeks. I kissed her tears.

'Jesus, Mike, this can't be legal,' I'd said when my friend unrolled the hawking mat from his backpack. We were on island 241, as the Hegemony traders had so romantically named the desolate volcanic blemish which they had chosen for our R and R site. Island 241 was less than fifty kilometers from the oldest of the colonial settlements but it might as well have been fifty light-years away. No native ships were to put in at the island while *Los Angeles* crewmen or farcaster workmen were present. The Maui-Covenant colonists had a few ancient skimmers still in working order, but by mutual agreement there would be no overflights. Except for the dormitories, swimming beach, and the duty-free store, there was little on the island to interest us Shipmen. Someday, when the last components had been brought in-system by the *Los Angeles* and the farcaster finished, Hegemony officials would make island 241 into a center for trade and tourism. Until then it was a primitive place with a dropship grid, newly finished buildings of the local white stone, and a few bored maintenance people. Mike checked the two of us out for three days of backpacking on the steepest and most inaccessible end of the little island.

'I don't want to go backpacking, for Chrissake,' I'd said. 'I'd rather stay on the *L.A.* and plug into a stimsim.'

'Shut up and follow me,' said Mike and, like a lesser member of the pantheon following an older and wiser deity, I had shut up and followed. Two hours of heavy tramping up the slopes through sharp-branched scrubtrees brought us to a lip of lava several hundred meters above the crashing surf. We were near the equator on a mostly tropical world but on this exposed ledge the wind was howling and my teeth were chattering. The sunset was a red smear between dark cumulus to the west and I had no wish to be out in the open when full night descended.

'Come on,' I said. 'Let's get out of the wind and build a fire. I don't know how the hell we're going to set up a tent on all of this rock.'

Mike sat down and lit a cannabis stick. 'Take a look in your pack, kid.'

I hesitated. His voice had been neutral but it was the flat neutrality of the practical joker's voice just before the bucket of water descends. I crouched down and began pawing through the nylon sack. The pack was empty except for old flowfoam packing cubes to fill it out. Those and a Harlequin's costume complete with mask and bells on the toes.

'Are you . . . is this . . . are you goddamn *crazy*?' I spluttered. It was getting dark quickly now. The storm might or might not pass to the south of us. The surf was rasping below like a hungry beast. If I had known how to find my own way back to the trade compound in the dark, I might have considered leaving Mike Osho's remains to feed the fishes far below.

'Now look at what's in my pack,' he said. Mike dumped out some flowfoam cubes and then removed some jewelry of the type I'd seen handcrafted on Renaissance Vector, an inertial compass, a laser pen which might or might not be labeled a concealed weapon by ShipSecurity, another Harlequin costume – this one tailored to his more rotund form – and a hawking mat.

'Jesus, Mike,' I said while running my hand over the exquisite design of the old carpet, 'this can't be legal.'

'I didn't notice any customs agents back there,' grinned Mike. 'And I seriously doubt that the locals have any traffic control ordinances.'

'Yes, but . . .' I trailed off and unrolled the rest of the mat. It was a little more than a meter wide and about two meters long. The rich fabric had faded with age but the flight threads were still as bright as new copper. 'Where did you get it?' I asked. 'Does it still work?'

'On Garden,' said Mike and stuffed my costume and his other gear into his backpack. 'Yes, it does.'

It had been more than a century since old Vladimir Sholokov, Old Earth emigrant, master lepidopterist, and EM systems engineer, had handcrafted the first

447

hawking mat for his beautiful young niece on New Earth. Legend had it that the niece had scorned the gift but over the decades the toys had become almost absurdly popular – more with rich adults than with children – until they were outlawed on most Hegemony worlds. Dangerous to handle, a waste of shielded monofilaments, almost impossible to deal with in controlled airspace, hawking mats had become curiosities reserved for bedtime stories, museums, and a few colony worlds.

'It must have cost you a fortune,' I said.

'Thirty marks,' said Mike and settled himself on the center of the carpet. 'The old dealer in Carvnel Marketplace thought it was worthless. It was . . . for him. I brought it back to the ship, charged it up, reprogrammed the inertia chips, and *voilà*!' Mike palmed the intricate design and the mat stiffened and rose fifteen centimeters above the rock ledge.

I stared doubtfully. 'All right,' I said, 'but what if it . . .'

'It won't,' said Mike and impatiently patted the carpet behind him. 'It's fully charged. I know how to handle it. Come on, climb on or stand back. I want to get going before that storm gets any closer.'

'But I don't think . . .'

'Come *on*, Merin. Make up your mind. I'm in a hurry.'

I hesitated for another second or two. If we were caught leaving the island, we would both be kicked off the ship. Shipwork was my life now. I had made that decision when I accepted the eight-mission Maui-Covenant contract. More than that, I was two hundred light-years and five and a half leap years from civilization. Even if they brought us back to Hegemony-space, the round trip would have cost us eleven years' worth of friends and family. The time-debt was irrevocable.

I crawled on the hovering hawking mat behind Mike. He stuffed the backpack between us, told me to hang on, and tapped at the flight designs. The mat rose five meters above the ledge, banked quickly to the left, and shot out over the alien ocean. Three hundred meters below us, the surf crashed whitely in the deepening gloom. We rose higher above the rough water and headed north into the night.

In such seconds of decision entire futures are made.

I remember talking to Siri during our Second Reunion, shortly after we first visited the villa along the coast near Fevarone. We were walking along the beach. Alón had been allowed to stay in the city under Magritte's supervision. It was just as well. I was not truly comfortable with the boy. Only the undeniable green solemnity of his eyes and the disturbing mirror-familiarity of his short, dark curls and snub of a nose served to tie him to me . . . to us . . . in my mind. That and the quick, almost sardonic smile I would catch him hiding from Siri when she reprimanded him. It was a smile too cynically amused and self-observant to be so practiced in a ten-year-old. I knew it well. I would have thought such things were learned, not inherited.

'You know very little,' Siri said to me. She was wading, shoeless, in a shallow tidepool. From time to time she would lift the delicate shell of a frenchhorn conch, inspect it for flaws, and drop it back into the silty water.

'I've been well trained,' I replied.

'Yes, I'm sure you've been well trained,' agreed Siri. 'I know you are quite skillful, Merin. But you *know* very little.'

Irritated, unsure of how to respond, I walked along with my head lowered. I dug a white lavastone out of the sand and tossed it far out into the bay. Rain clouds were piling along the eastern horizon. I found myself wishing that I was back aboard the ship. I had been reluctant to return this time and now I knew that it had been a mistake. It was my third visit to Maui-Covenant, our Second Reunion as the poets and her people were calling it. I was five months away from being twenty-one standard years old. Siri had just celebrated her thirty-seventh birthday three weeks earlier.

'I've been to a lot of places you've never seen,' I said at last. It sounded petulant and childish even to me.

'Oh, yes,' said Siri and clapped her hands together. For a second, in her enthusiasm, I glimpsed my other Siri – the young girl I had dreamed about during the long nine months of turnaround. Then the image slid back to harsh reality and I was all too aware of her short hair, the loosening neck muscles, and the cords appearing on the backs of those once beloved hands. 'You've been to places I'll *never* see,' said Siri in a rush. Her voice was the same. Almost the same. 'Merin, my love, you've already seen things I cannot even imagine. You probably know more facts about the universe than I would guess exist. But you *know* very little, my darling.'

'What the hell are you talking about, Siri?' I sat down on a half-submerged log near the strip of wet sand and drew my knees up like a fence between us.

Siri strode out of the tidepool and came to kneel in front of me. She took my hands in hers and, although mine were bigger, heavier, blunter of finger and bone, I could feel the *strength* in hers. I imagined it as the strength of years I had not shared. 'You have to live to really know things, my love. Having Alón has helped me to understand that. There is something about raising a child that helps to sharpen one's sense of what is real.'

'How do you mean?'

Siri squinted away from me for a few seconds and absently brushed back a strand of hair. Her left hand stayed firmly around both of mine. 'I'm not sure,' she said softly. 'I think one begins to feel when things aren't *important*. I'm not sure how to put it. When you've spent thirty years entering rooms filled with strangers you feel less pressure than when you've had only half that number of years of experience. You know what the room and the people in it probably hold for you and you go looking for it. If it's not there, you sense it earlier and leave to go about your business. You just *know* more about what is, what isn't, and how little time there is to learn the difference. Do you understand, Merin? Do you follow me even a little bit?'

'No,' I said.

Siri nodded and bit her lower lip. But she did not speak again for a while. Instead, she leaned over and kissed me.

450

Her lips were dry and a little questioning. I held back for a second, seeing the sky beyond her, wanting time to think. But then I felt the warm intrusion of her tongue and closed my eyes. The tide was coming in behind us. I felt a sympathetic warmth and rising as Siri unbuttoned my shirt and ran sharp fingernails across my chest. There was a second of emptiness between us and I opened my eyes in time to see her unfastening the last buttons on the front of her white dress. Her breasts were larger than I remembered, heavier, the nipples broader and darker. The chill air nipped at both of us until I pulled the fabric down her shoulders and brought our upper bodies together. We slid down along the log to the warm sand. I pressed her closer, all the while wondering how I possibly could have thought her the stronger one. Her skin tasted of salt.

Siri's hands helped me. Her short hair pressed back against bleached wood, white cotton, and sand. My pulse outraced the surf.

'Do you understand, Merin?' she whispered to me seconds later as her warmth connected us.

'Yes,' I whispered back. But I did not.

Mike brought the hawking mat in from the east toward Firstsite. The flight had taken over an hour in the dark and I had spent most of the time huddling from the wind and waiting for the carpet to fold up and tumble us both into the sea. We were still half an hour out when we saw the first of the motile isles. Racing before the storm, treesails billowing, the islands sailed up from their southern feeding grounds in seemingly endless procession. Many were lit brilliantly, festooned with colored lanterns and shifting veils of gossamer light.

'You sure this is the way?' I shouted.

'Yes,' shouted Mike. He did not turn his head. The wind whipped his long black hair back against my face. From time to time he would check his compass and make small corrections to our course. It might have been easier to follow the isles. We passed one – a large one almost half a kilometer in length – and I strained to make out details but the isle was dark except for the glow of its phosphorescent wake. Dark shapes cut through the milky waves. I tapped Mike on the shoulder and pointed.

'Dolphins!' he shouted. 'That's what this colony was all about, remember? A bunch of do-gooders during the Hegira wanted to save all the mammals in Old Earth's oceans. Didn't succeed.'

I would have shouted another question but at that moment the headland and Firstsite Harbor came into view.

I had thought the stars were bright above Maui-Covenant. I had thought the migrating islands were memorable in their colorful display. But the city of Firstsite, wrapped about with harbor and hills, was a blazing beacon in the night. Its brilliance reminded me of a torchship I once had watched while it created its own plasma nova against the dark limb of a sullen gas giant. The city was a five-tiered honeycomb of white buildings, all illuminated by warmly glowing lanterns from within and by countless torches from without. The white lava-stone of the volcanic island itself seemed to glow from the city light. Beyond the town were tents, pavilions, campfires, cooking fires, and great flaming pyres, too large for function, too large for anything except to serve as a welcome to the returning isles.

The harbor was filled with boats: bobbing catamarans with cow-bells clanking from their masts, large-hulled, flat-bottomed house-boats built for creeping from port to port in the calm equatorial shallows but proudly ablaze with strings of lights this night, and then the occasional oceangoing yacht, sleek and functional as a shark. A lighthouse set out on the pincer's end of the harbor reef threw its beam far out to sea, illuminated wave and isle alike, and then swept its light back in to catch the colorful bobbing of ships and men.

Even from two kilometers out we could hear the noise. Sounds of celebration were clearly audible. Above the shouts and constant susurration of the surf rose the unmistakable notes of a Bach flute sonata. I learned later that this welcoming chorus was transmitted through hydrophones to the Passage Channels where dolphins leaped and cavorted to the music.

'My God, Mike, how did you know all of this was going on?'

'I asked the main ship computer,' said Mike. The hawking mat banked right to keep us far out from the ships and lighthouse beam. Then we curved back in north of Firstsite toward a dark spit of land. I could hear the soft booming of waves on the shallows ahead. 'They have this festival every year,' Mike went on, 'but this is their sesquicentennial. The party's been going on for three weeks now and is scheduled to continue another two. There are only about a hundred thousand colonists on this whole world, Merin, and I bet half of them are here partying.'

We slowed, came in carefully, and touched down on a rocky outcropping not far from the beach. The storm had missed us to the south but intermittent flashes of lightning and the distant lights of advancing isles still marked the horizon. Overhead, the stars were not dimmed by the glow from Firstsite just over the rise from us. The air was warmer here and I caught the scent of orchards on the breeze. We folded up the hawking mat and hurried to get into our Harlequin costumes. Mike slipped his laser pen and jewelry into loose pockets.

'What are those for?' I asked as we secured the backpack and hawking mat under a large boulder.

'These?' asked Mike as he dangled a Renaissance necklace from his fingers. 'These are currency in case we have to negotiate for favors.'

'Favors?'

'Favors,' repeated Mike. 'A lady's largesse. Comfort to a weary spacefarer. Nooky to you, kid.'

'Oh,' I said and adjusted my mask and fool's cap. The bells made a soft sound in the dark.

'Come on,' said Mike. 'We'll miss the party.' I nodded and followed him, bells jangling, as we picked our way over stone and scrub toward the waiting light.

I sit here in the sunlight and wait. I am not totally certain what I am waiting for. I can feel a growing warmth on my back as the morning sunlight is reflected from the white stone of Siri's tomb.

Siri's tomb?

There are no clouds in the sky. I raise my head and squint skyward as if I might be able to see the *L.A.* and the newly finished farcaster array through the glare of atmosphere. I cannot. Part of me knows that they have not risen yet. Part of me knows to the second the time remaining before ship and farcaster complete their transit to the zenith. Part of me does not want to think about it.

Siri, am I doing the right thing?

There is the sudden sound of pennants stirring on their staffs as the wind comes up. I sense rather than see the restlessness of the waiting crowd. For the first time since my planetfall for this, our Seventh Reunion, I am filled with sorrow. No, not sorrow, not yet, but a sharp-toothed sadness which soon will open into grief. For years I have carried on silent conversations with Siri, framing questions to myself for future discussion with her, and it suddenly strikes me with cold clarity that we will never again sit together and talk. An emptiness begins to grow inside me.

Should I let it happen, Siri?

There is no response except for the growing murmurs of the crowd. In a few minutes they will send Donel, my younger and surviving son, or his daughter Lira and her brother up the hill to urge me on. I toss away the sprig of willowgrass I've been chewing on. There is a hint of shadow on the horizon. It could be a cloud. Or it could be the first of the isles, driven by instinct and the spring northerlies to migrate back to the great band of the equatorial shallows whence they came. It does not matter.

Siri, am I doing the right thing?

There is no answer and the time grows shorter.

Sometimes Siri seemed so ignorant it made me sick.

She knew nothing of my life away from her. She would ask questions but I sometimes wondered if she was interested in the answers. I spent many hours explaining the beautiful physics behind our spinships but she never did seem to understand. Once, after I had taken great care to detail the differences between their ancient seedship and the *Los Angeles*, Siri astounded me by asking, 'But why did it take my ancestors eighty years of shiptime to reach Maui-Covenant when you can make the trip in a hundred and thirty *days*?' She had understood nothing.

Siri's sense of history was, at best, pitiful. She viewed the Hegemony and the Worldweb the way a child would view the fantasy world of a pleasant but rather silly myth; there was an indifference there that almost drove me mad at times.

Siri knew all about the early days of the Hegira – at least insofar as they pertained to the Maui-Covenant and the colonists – and she occasionally would come up with delightful bits of archaic trivia or phraseology, but she knew nothing of post-Hegira realities. Names like Garden and the Ousters, Renaissance and Lusus meant little to her. I could mention Salmud Brevy or General Horace Glennon-Height and she would have no associations or reactions at all. None.

The last time I saw Siri she was seventy standard years old. She was *seventy years old* and still she had never traveled offworld, used a fatline, tasted any alcoholic drink except wine, interfaced with an empathy surgeon, stepped through a farcaster door, smoked a cannabis stick, received gene tailoring, plugged into a stimsim, received any formal schooling, taken any RNA medication, heard of Zen Gnostics or the Shrike Church, or flown any vehicle except an ancient Vikken skimmer belonging to her family.

Siri had never made love to anyone except me. Or so she said. And so I believed.

It was during our First Reunion, that time on the Archipelago, when Siri took me to talk with the dolphins.

We had risen to watch the dawn. The highest levels of the tree-house were a perfect place from which to watch the eastern sky pale and fade to morning. Ripples of high cirrus turned to rose and then the sea itself grew molten as the sun floated above the flat horizon.

'Let's go swimming,' said Siri. The rich, horizontal light bathed her skin and threw her shadow four meters across the boards of the platform.

'I'm too tired,' I said. 'Later.' We had lain awake

most of the night talking, making love, talking, and making love again. In the glare of morning I felt empty and vaguely nauseated. I sensed the slight movement of the isle under me as a tinge of vertigo, a drunkard's disconnection from gravity.

'No. Let's go now,' said Siri and grasped my hand to pull me along. I was irritated but did not argue. Siri was twenty-six, seven years older than I during that First Reunion, but her impulsive behavior often reminded me of the teen-aged Siri I had carried away from the Festival only ten of my months earlier. Her deep, unselfconscious laugh was the same. Her green eyes cut as sharply when she was impatient. The long mane of auburn hair had not changed. But her body had ripened, filled out with a promise which had been only hinted at before. Her breasts were still high and full, almost girlish, bordered above by freckles that gave way to a whiteness so translucent that a gentle blue tracery of veins could be seen. But they were *different* somehow. She was different.

'Are you going to join me or just sit there staring?' asked Siri. She had slipped off her caftan as we came out onto the lowest deck. Our small ship was still tied to the dock. Above us, the island's treesails were beginning to open to the morning breeze. For the past several days Siri had insisted on wearing swimstrips when we went into the water. She wore none now. Her nipples rose in the cool air.

'Won't we be left behind?' I asked, squinting up at the flapping treesails. On previous days we had waited for the doldrums in the middle of the day when the isle was still in the water, the sea a glazed mirror. Now the jibvines were beginning to pull taut as the thick leaves filled with wind.

'Don't be silly,' said Siri. 'We could always catch a keelroot and follow it back. That or a feeding tendril. Come on.' She tossed an osmosis mask at me and donned her own. The transparent film made her face look slick with oil. From the pocket of her discarded caftan she lifted a thick medallion and set it in place around her neck. The metal looked dark and ominous against her skin.

'What's that?' I asked.

Siri did not lift the osmosis mask to answer. She set the

comthreads in place against her neck and handed me the earplugs. Her voice was tinny. 'Translation disk,' she said. 'Thought you knew all about gadgets, Merin. Last one in's a seaslug.' She held the disk in place between her breasts with one hand and stepped off the isle. I could see the pale globes of her buttocks as she pirouetted and kicked for depth. In seconds she was only a white blur deep in the water. I slipped my own mask on, pressed the comthreads tight, and stepped into the sea.

The bottom of the isle was a dark stain on a ceiling of crystalline light. I was wary of the thick feeding tendrils even though Siri had amply demonstrated that they were interested in devouring nothing larger than the tiny zooplankton that even now caught the sunlight like dust in an abandoned ballroom. Keelroots descended like gnarled stalactites for hundreds of meters into the purple depths.

The isle was moving. I could see the faint fibrillation of the tendrils as they trailed along. A wake caught the light ten meters above me. For a second I was choking, the gel of the mask smothering me as surely as the surrounding water would, and then I relaxed and the air flowed freely into my lungs.

'Deeper, Merin,' came Siri's voice. I blinked – a slow-motion blink as the mask readjusted itself over my eyes – and caught sight of Siri twenty meters lower, grasping a keelroot and trailing effortlessly above the colder, deeper currents where the light did not reach. I thought of the thousands of meters of water under me, of the things which might lurk there, unknown, unsought out by the human colonists. I thought of the dark and the depths and my scrotum tightened involuntarily.

'Come on down.' Siri's voice was an insect buzz in my ears. I rotated and kicked. The buoyancy here was not so great as in Old Earth's seas, but it still took energy to dive so deep. The mask compensated for depth and nitrogen but I could feel the pressure against my skin and ears. Finally I quit kicking, grabbed a keelroot, and roughly hauled myself down to Siri's level.

We floated side by side in the dim light. Siri was a

spectral figure here, her long hair swirling in a wine-dark nimbus, the pale strips of her body glowing in the blue-green light. The surface seemed impossibly distant. The widening V of the wake and the drift of the scores of tendrils showed that the isle was moving more quickly now, moving mindlessly to other feeding grounds, distant waters.

'Where are the . . .' I began to subvocalize.

'Shhh,' said Siri. She fiddled with the medallion. I could hear them then: the shrieks and trills and whistles and cat purrs and echoing cries. The depths were suddenly filled with strange music.

'Jesus,' I said and because Siri had tuned our comthreads to the translator, the word was broadcast as a senseless whistle and toot.

'Hello!' she called and the translated greeting echoed from the transmitter; a high-speed bird's call sliding into the ultrasonic. 'Hello!' she called again.

Minutes passed before the dolphins came to investigate. They rolled past us, surprisingly large, alarmingly large, their skin looking slick and muscled in the uncertain light. A large one swam within a meter of us, turning at the last moment so that the white of his belly curved past us like a wall. I could see the dark eye rotate to follow me as he passed. One stroke of his wide fluke kicked up a turbulence strong enough to convince me of the animal's power.

'Hello,' called Siri but the swift form faded into distant haze and there was a sudden silence. Siri clicked off the translator. 'Do you want to talk to them?' she asked.

'Sure.' I was dubious. More than three centuries of effort had not raised much of a dialogue between man and sea mammal. Mike had once told me that the thought structures of Old Earth's two groups of orphans were too different, the referents too few. One pre-Hegira expert had written that speaking to a dolphin or porpoise was about as rewarding as speaking to a one-year-old human infant. Both sides usually enjoyed the exchange and there was a simulacrum of conversation, but neither party would come away the more knowledgeable. Siri switched the translator disk back on. 'Hello,' I said.

There was a final minute of silence and then our earphones were buzzing while the sea echoed shrill ululations.

distance/no-fluke/hello-tone?/current   pulse/circle me/funny?

'What the hell?' I asked Siri and the translator trilled out my question. Siri was grinning under her osmosis mask.

I tried again. 'Hello! Greetings from . . . uh . . . the surface. How are you?'

The large male . . . I assumed it to be a male . . . curved in toward us like a torpedo. He arch-kicked his way through the water ten times faster than I could have swum even if I had remembered to don flippers that morning. For a second I thought he was going to ram us and I raised my knees and clung tightly to the keelroot. Then he was past us, climbing for air, while Siri and I reeled from his turbulent wake and the high tones of his shout.

no-fluke/no-feed/no-swim/no-play/no-fun.

Siri switched off the translator and floated closer. She lightly grasped my shoulders while I held on to the keelroot with my right hand. Our legs touched as we drifted through the warm water. A school of tiny crimson warriorfish flickered above us while the dark shapes of the dolphins circled farther out.

'Had enough?' she asked. Her hand was flat on my chest.

'One more try,' I said. Siri nodded and twisted the disk to life. The current pushed us together again. She slid her arm around me.

'Why do you herd the islands?' I asked the bottle-nosed shapes circling in the dappled light. 'How does it benefit you to stay with the isles?'

sounding   now/old   songs/deep   water/no-Great Voices/no-Shark/old songs/new songs.

Siri's body lay along the length of me now. Her left arm tightened around me. 'Great Voices were the whales,' she whispered. Her hair fanned out in streamers. Her right hand moved down and seemed surprised at what it found.

459

'Do you miss the Great Voices?' I asked the shadows. There was no response. Siri slid her legs around my hips. The surface was a churning bowl of light forty meters above us.

'What do you miss most of Old Earth's oceans?' I asked. With my left arm I pulled Siri closer, slid my hand down along the curve of her back to where her buttocks rose to meet my palm, held her tight. To the circling dolphins we must have appeared a single creature. Siri lifted herself against me and we became a single creature.

The translator disk had twisted around so it trailed over Siri's shoulder. I reached to shut it off but paused as the answer to my question buzzed urgently in our ears.

miss Shark/miss Shark/miss Shark/miss Shark/ Shark/Shark/Shark.

I turned off the disk and shook my head. I did not understand. There was so much I did not understand. I closed my eyes as Siri and I moved gently to the rhythms of the current and ourselves while the dolphins swam nearby and the cadence of their calls took on the sad, slow trilling of an old lament.

Siri and I came down out of the hills and returned to the Festival just before sunrise of the second day. For a night and a day we had roamed the hills, eaten with strangers in pavilions of orange silk, bathed together in the icy waters of the Shree, and danced to the music which never ceased going out to the endless file of passing isles. We were hungry. I had awakened at sunset to find Siri gone. She returned before the moon of Maui-Covenant rose. She told me that her parents had gone off with friends for several days on a slow-moving houseboat. They had left the family skimmer in Firstsite. Now we worked our way from dance to dance, bonfire to bonfire, back to the center of the city. We planned to fly west to her family estate near Fevarone.

It was very late but Firstsite Common still had its share of revelers. I was very happy. I was nineteen and I was in love and the .93 gravity of Maui-Covenant seemed much less to me. I could have flown had I wished. I could have done anything.

We had stopped at a booth and bought fried dough and mugs of black coffee. Suddenly a thought struck me. I asked, 'How did you know I was a Shipman?'

'Hush, friend Merin. Eat your poor breakfast. When we get to the villa, I will fix a true meal to break our fast.'

'No, I'm serious,' I said and wiped grease off my chin with the sleeve of my less than clean Harlequin's costume. 'This morning you said that you knew right away last night that I was from the ship. Why was that? Was it my accent? My costume? Mike and I saw other fellows dressed like this.'

Siri laughed and brushed back her hair. 'Just be glad it was I who spied you out, Merin, my love. Had it been my Uncle Gresham or his friends it would have meant trouble.'

'Oh? Why is that?' I picked up one more fried ring and Siri paid for it. I followed her through the thinning crowd. Despite the motion and the music all about, I felt weariness beginning to work on me.

'They are Separatists,' said Siri. 'Uncle Gresham recently gave a speech before the Council urging that we fight rather than agree to be swallowed into your Hegemony. He said that we should destroy your farcaster device before it destroys us.'

'Oh?' I said. 'Did he say how he was going to do that? The last I heard, you folks had no craft to get off-world in.'

'Nay, nor for the past fifty years have we,' said Siri. 'But it shows how irrational the Separatists can be.'

I nodded. Shipmaster Singh and Councilor Halmyn had briefed us on the so-called Separatists of Maui-Covenant. 'The usual coalition of colonial jingoists and throwbacks,' Singh had said. 'Another reason we go slow and develop the world's trade potential before finishing the farcaster. The Worldweb doesn't need these yahoos coming in prematurely. And groups like the Separatists are another reason to keep you crew and construction workers the hell away from the groundlings.'

'Where is your skimmer?' I asked. The Common was emptying quickly. Most of the bands had packed up their instruments for the night. Gaily costumed heaps lay

461

snoring on the grass or cobblestones amid the litter and unlit lanterns. Only a few enclaves of merriment remained, groups dancing slowly to a lone guitar or singing drunkenly to themselves. I saw Mike Osho at once, a patchworked fool, his mask long gone, a girl on either arm. He was trying to teach the 'Hava Nagilla' to a rapt but inept circle of admirers. One of the troupe would stumble and they would all fall down. Mike would flog them to their feet among general laughter and they would start again, hopping clumsily to his basso profundo chant.

'There it is,' said Siri and pointed to a short line of skimmers parked behind the Common Hall. I nodded and waved to Mike but he was too busy hanging on to his two ladies to notice me. Siri and I had crossed the square and were in the shadows of the old building when the shout went up.

'Shipman! Turn around, you Hegemony son of a bitch.'

I froze and then wheeled around with fists clenched but no one was near me. Six young men had descended the steps from the grandstand and were standing in a semicircle behind Mike. The man in front was tall, slim, and strikingly handsome. He was twenty-five or twenty-six years old and his long blond curls spilled down on a crimson silk suit that emphasized his physique. In his right hand he carried a meter-long sword that looked to be of tempered steel.

Mike turned slowly. Even from a distance I could see his eyes sobering as he surveyed the situation. The women at his side and a couple of the young men in his group tittered as if something humorous had been said. Mike allowed the inebriated grin to stay on his face. 'You address me, sir?' he asked.

'I address you, you Hegemony whore's son,' hissed the leader of the group. His handsome face was twisted into a sneer.

'Bertol,' whispered Siri. 'My cousin. Gresham's younger son.' I nodded and stepped out of the shadows. Siri caught my arm.

'That is twice you have referred unkindly to my

462

mother, sir,' slurred Mike. 'Have she or I offended you in some way? If so, a thousand pardons.' Mike bowed so deeply that the bells on his cap almost brushed the ground. Members of his group applauded.

'Your presence offends me, you Hegemony bastard. You stink up our air with your fat carcass.'

Mike's eyebrows rose comically. A young man near him in a fish costume waved his hand. 'Oh, come on, Bertol. He's just . . .'

'Shut up, Ferick. It is this fat shithead I am speaking to.'

'Shithead?' repeated Mike, eyebrows still raised. 'I've traveled two hundred light-years to be called a fat shithead? It hardly seems worth it.' He pivoted gracefully, untangling himself from the women as he did so. I would have joined Mike then but Siri clung tightly to my arm, whispering unheard entreaties. When I was free I saw that Mike was still smiling, still playing the fool. But his left hand was in his baggy shirt pocket.

'Give him your blade, Creg,' snapped Bertol. One of the younger men tossed a sword hilt-first to Mike. Mike watched it arc by and clang loudly on the cobblestones.

'You can't be serious,' said Mike in a soft voice that was suddenly quite sober. 'You cretinous cow turd. Do you really think I'm going to play duel with you just because you get a hard-on acting the hero for these yokels?'

'Pick up the sword,' screamed Bertol, 'or, by God, I'll carve you where you stand.' He took a quick step forward. The youth's face contorted with fury as he advanced.

'Fuck off,' said Mike. In his left hand was the laser pen.

'No!' I yelled and ran into the light. That pen was used by construction workers to scrawl marks on girders of whiskered alloy.

Things happened very quickly then. Bertol took another step and Mike flicked the green beam across him almost casually. The colonist let out a cry and leaped back; a smoking line of black was slashed diagonally across his silk shirtfront. I hesitated. Mike had the

463

setting as low as it could go. Two of Bertol's friends started forward and Mike swung the light across their shins. One dropped to his knees cursing and the other hopped away holding his leg and hooting.

A crowd had gathered. They laughed as Mike swept off his fool's cap in another bow. 'I thank you,' said Mike. 'My mother thanks you.'

Siri's cousin strained against his rage. Froths of spittle spilled on his lips and chin. I pushed through the crowd and stepped between Mike and the tall colonist.

'Hey, it's all right,' I said. 'We're leaving. We're going now.'

'Goddamn it, Merin, get out of the way,' said Mike.

'It's all right,' I said as I turned to him. 'I'm with a girl named Siri who has a . . .' Bertol stepped forward and lunged past me with his blade. I wrapped my left arm around his shoulder and flung him back. He tumbled heavily onto the grass.

'Oh, shit,' said Mike as he backed up several paces. He looked tired and a little disgusted as he sat down on a stone step. 'Aw, *damn*,' he said softly. There was a short line of crimson in one of the black patches on the left side of his Harlequin costume. As I watched, the narrow slit spilled over and blood ran down across Mike Osho's broad belly.

'Oh, Jesus, Mike.' I tore a strip of fabric from my shirt and tried to staunch the flow. I could remember none of the first aid we'd been taught as mid-Shipmen. I pawed at my wrist but my comlog was not there. We had left them on the *Los Angeles*.

'It's not so bad, Mike,' I gasped. 'It's just a little cut.' The blood flowed down over my hand and wrist.

'It will serve,' said Mike. His voice was held taut by a cord of pain. 'Damn. A fucking sword. Do you believe it, Merin? Cut down in the prime of my prime by a piece of fucking cutlery out of a fucking one-penny opera. Oh, *damn*, that smarts.'

'Three-penny opera,' I said and changed hands. The rag was soaked.

'You know what your fucking problem is, Merin? You're always sticking your fucking two cents in.

Awwwww.' Mike's face went white and then gray. He lowered his chin to his chest and breathed deeply. 'To *hell* with this, kid. Let's go home, huh?'

I looked over my shoulder. Bertol was slowly moving away with his friends. The rest of the crowd milled around in shock. 'Call a doctor!' I screamed. 'Get some medics up here!' Two men ran down the street. There was no sign of Siri.

'Wait a minute! Wait a minute!' said Mike in a stronger voice as if he had forgotten something important. 'Just a minute,' he said and died.

Died. A real death. Brain death. His mouth opened obscenely, his eyes rolled back so only the whites showed, and a minute later the blood ceased pumping from the wound.

For a few mad seconds I cursed the sky. I could see the *L.A.* moving across the fading starfield and I knew that I could bring Mike back if I could get him there in a few minutes. The crowd backed away as I screamed and ranted at the stars.

Eventually I turned to Bertol. 'You,' I said.

The young man had stopped at the far end of the Common. His face was ashen. He stared wordlessly.

'You,' I said again. I picked up the laser pen from where it had rolled, clicked the power to maximum, and walked to where Bertol and his friends stood waiting.

Later, through the haze of screams and scorched flesh, I was dimly aware of Siri's skimmer setting down in the crowded square, of dust flying up all around, and of her voice commanding me to join her. We lifted away from the light and madness. The cool wind blew my sweat-soaked hair away from my neck.

'We will go to Fevarone,' said Siri. 'Bertol was drunk. The Separatists are a small, violent group. There will be no reprisals. You will stay with me until the Council holds the inquest.'

'No,' I said. 'There. Land there.' I pointed to a spit of land not far from the city.

Siri landed despite her protests. I glanced at the boulder to make sure the backpack was still there and then climbed out of the skimmer. Siri slid across the seat and pulled my head down to hers. 'Merin, my love.' Her lips were warm and open but I felt nothing. My body felt anesthetized. I stepped back and waved her away. She brushed her hair back and stared at me from green eyes filled with tears. Then the skimmer lifted, turned, and sped to the south in the early morning light.

Just a minute, I felt like calling. I sat on a rock and gripped my knees as several ragged sobs were torn up out of me. Then I stood and threw the laser pen into the surf below. I tugged out the backpack and dumped the contents on the ground.

The hawking mat was gone.

I sat back down, too drained to laugh or cry or walk away. The sun rose as I sat there. I was still sitting there three hours later when the large black skimmer from ShipSecurity set down silently beside me.

'Father? Father, it is getting late.'

I turn to see my son Donel standing behind me. He is wearing the blue and gold robe of the Hegemony Council. His bald scalp is flushed and beaded with sweat. Donel is only forty-three but he seems much older to me.

'Please, Father,' he says. I nod and rise, brushing off the grass and dirt. We walk together to the front of the tomb. The crowd has pressed closer now. Gravel crunches under their feet as they shift restlessly. 'Shall I enter with you, Father?' Donel asks.

I pause to look at this aging stranger who is my child. There is little of Siri or me reflected in him. His face is friendly, florid, and tense with the excitement of the day. I can sense in him the open honesty which often takes the place of intelligence in some people. I cannot help but compare this balding puppy of a man to Alón – Alón of the dark curls and silences and sardonic smile. But Alón is thirty-three years dead, cut down in a stupid battle which had nothing to do with him.

'No,' I say. 'I'll go in by myself. Thank you, Donel.'

He nods and steps back. The pennants snap above the heads of the straining crowd. I turn my attention to the tomb.

The entrance is sealed with a palmlock. I have only to touch it.

During the past few minutes I have developed a fantasy which will save me from both the growing sadness within and the external series of events which I have initiated. Siri is not dead. In the last stages of her illness she had called together the doctors and the few technicians left in the colony and they rebuilt for her one of the ancient hibernation chambers used in their seedship two centuries earlier. Siri is only sleeping. What is more, the year-long sleep has somehow restored her youth. When I wake her she will be the Siri I remember from our early days. We will walk out into the sunlight together and when the farcaster doors open we shall be the first through.

'Father?'

'Yes.' I step forward and set my hand to the door of the crypt. There is a whisper of electric motors and the white slab of stone slides back. I bow my head and enter Siri's tomb.

'Damn it, Merin, secure that line before it knocks you overboard. Hurry!' I hurried. The wet rope was hard to coil, harder to tie off. Siri shook her head in disgust and leaned over to tie a bowline knot with one hand.

It was our Sixth Reunion. I had been three months too late for her birthday but more than five thousand other people had made it to the celebration. The CEO of the All Thing had wished her well in a forty-minute speech. A poet read his most recent verses to the Love Cycle sonnets. The Hegemony Ambassador had presented her with a scroll and a new ship, a small submersible powered by the first fusion cells to be allowed on Maui-Covenant.

Siri had eighteen other ships. Twelve belonged to her fleet of swift catamarans that plied their trade between the wandering Archipelago and the home islands. Two were beautiful racing yachts that were used only twice a year to win the Founder's Regatta and the Covenant Criterium. The other four craft were ancient fishing boats, homely and awkward, well maintained but little more than scows.

Siri had nineteen ships but we were on a fishing boat – the *Ginnie Paul*. For the past eight days we had fished the shelf of the Equatorial Shallows; a crew of two, casting and pulling nets, wading knee-deep through stinking fish and crunching trilobites, wallowing over every wave, casting and pulling nets, keeping watch, and sleeping like exhausted children during our brief rest periods. I was not quite twenty-three. I thought I was used to heavy labor aboard the *L.A.* and it was my custom to put in an hour of exercise in the 1.3-g pod every second shift, but now my arms and back ached from the strain and my hands were blistered between the calluses. Siri had just turned seventy.

'Merin, go forward and reef the foresail. Do the same for the jib and then go below to see to the sandwiches. Plenty of mustard.'

I nodded and went forward. For a day and a half we had been playing hide-and-seek with a storm: sailing before it when we could, turning about and accepting its punishment when we had to. At first it had been exciting, a welcome respite from the endless casting and pulling and mending. But after the first few hours the adrenaline rush faded to be replaced by constant nausea, fatigue, and a terrible tiredness. The seas did not relent. The waves grew to six meters and higher. The *Ginnie Paul* wallowed like the broad-beamed matron she was. Everything was wet. My skin was soaked under three layers of rain gear. For Siri it was a long-awaited vacation.

'This is nothing,' she had said during the darkest hour of the night as waves washed over the deck and smashed against the scarred plastic of the cockpit. 'You should see it during simoon season.'

The clouds still hung low and blended into gray waves in the distance but the sea was down to a gentle five-foot chop. I spread mustard across the roast beef sandwiches and poured steaming coffee into thick white mugs. It would have been easier to transport the coffee in zero-g without spilling it than to get up the pitching shaft of the companionway. Siri accepted her depleted cup without commenting. We sat in silence for a bit, appreciating the food and the tongue-scalding warmth. I took the wheel when Siri went below to refill our mugs. The gray day was dimming almost imperceptibly into night.

'Merin,' she said after handing me my mug and taking a seat on the long cushioned bench which encircled the cockpit, 'what will happen after they open the farcaster?'

I was surprised by the question. We had almost never talked about the time when Maui-Covenant would join the Hegemony. I glanced over at Siri and was struck by how ancient she suddenly seemed. Her face was a mosaic of seams and shadows. Her beautiful green eyes had sunken into wells of darkness and her cheekbones were knife edges against brittle parchment. She kept her gray hair cut short now and it stuck out in damp spikes. Her neck and wrists were tendoned cords emerging from a shapeless sweater.

'What do you mean?' I asked.

'What will happen after they open the farcaster?'

'You know what the Council says, Siri.' I spoke loudly because she was hard of hearing in one ear. 'It will open a new era of trade and technology for Maui-Covenant. And you won't be restricted to one little world any longer. When you become citizens, everyone will be entitled to use the farcaster doors.'

'Yes,' said Siri. Her voice was weary. 'I have heard all of that, Merin. But what will *happen*? Who will be the first through to us?'

I shrugged. 'More diplomats, I suppose. Cultural contact specialists. Anthropologists. Ethnologists. Marine biologists.'

'And then?'

I paused. It was dark out. The sea was almost gentle. Our running lights glowed red and green against the night. I felt the same anxiety I had known two days earlier when the wall of storm appeared on the horizon. I said, 'And then will come the missionaries. The petroleum geologists. The sea farmers. The developers.'

Siri sipped at her coffee. 'I would have thought your Hegemony was far beyond a petroleum economy.'

I laughed and locked the wheel in. 'Nobody gets beyond a petroleum economy. Not while there's petroleum there. We don't burn it, if that's what you mean.

But it's still essential for the production of plastics, synthetics, food base, and keroids. Two hundred billion people use a lot of plastic.'

'And Maui-Covenant has oil?'

'Oh, yes,' I said. There was no more laughter in me. 'There are billions of barrels reservoired under the Equatorial Shallows alone.'

'How will they get it, Merin? Platforms?'

'Yeah. Platforms. Submersibles. Sub-sea colonies with tailored workers brought in from Mare Infinitus.'

'And the motile isles?' asked Siri. 'They must return each year to the shallows to feed on the bluekelp there and to reproduce. What will become of the isles?'

I shrugged again. I had drunk too much coffee and it had left a bitter taste in my mouth. 'I don't know,' I said. 'They haven't told the crew much. But back on our first trip out, Mike heard that they planned to develop as many of the isles as they can so some will be protected.'

'Develop?' Siri's voice showed surprise for the first time. 'How can they develop the isles? Even the First Families must ask permission of the Sea Folk to build our treehouse retreats there.'

I smiled at Siri's use of the local term for the dolphins. The Maui-Covenant colonists were such children when it came to their damned dolphins. 'The plans are all set,' I said. 'There are 128,573 motile isles big enough to build a dwelling on. Leases to those have long since been sold. The smaller isles will be broken up, I suppose. The home islands will be developed for recreation purposes.'

'Recreation purposes,' echoed Siri. 'How many people from the Hegemony will use the farcaster to come here . . . for recreation purposes?'

'At first, you mean?' I asked. 'Just a few thousand the first year. As long as the only door is on Island 241 . . . the Trade Center . . . it will be limited. Perhaps fifty thousand the second year when Firstsite gets its door. It'll be quite the luxury tour. Always is after a seed colony is first opened to the Web.'

'And later?'

'After the five-year probation? There will be thousands of doors, of course. I would imagine that there will

470

be twenty or thirty million new residents coming through during the first year of full citizenship.'

'Twenty or thirty million,' said Siri. The light from the compass stand illuminated her lined face from below. There was still a beauty there. But there was no anger or shock. I had expected both.

'But you'll be citizens then yourself,' I said. 'Free to step anywhere in the Worldweb. There will be sixteen new worlds to choose from. Probably more by then.'

'Yes,' said Siri and set aside her empty mug. A fine rain streaked the glass around us. The crude radar screen set in its hand-carved frame showed the seas empty, the storm past. 'Is it true, Merin, that people in the Hegemony have their homes on a dozen worlds? One house, I mean, with windows facing out on a dozen skies?'

'Sure,' I said. 'But not many people. Only the rich can afford multiworld residences like that.'

Siri smiled and set her hand on my knee. The back of her hand was mottled and blue-veined. 'But you are very rich, are you not, Shipman?'

I looked away. 'Not yet I'm not.'

'Ah, but soon, Merin, soon. How long for you, my love? Less than two weeks here and then the voyage back to your Hegemony. Five months more of your time to bring the last components back, a few weeks to finish, and then you step home a rich man. *Step* two hundred empty light-years home. What a strange thought . . . but where was I? That is how long? Less than a standard year.'

'Ten months,' I said. 'Three hundred and six standard days. Three hundred fourteen of yours. Nine hundred eighteen shifts.'

'And then your exile will be over.'

'Yes.'

'And you will be twenty-four years old and very rich.'

'Yes.'

'I'm tired, Merin. I want to sleep now.'

We programmed the tiller, set the collision alarm, and went below. The wind had risen some and the old vessel wallowed from wave crest to trough with every swell. We undressed in the dim light of the swinging lamp. I was first in the bunk and under the covers. It was the first time Siri and I had shared a sleep period. Remembering our last Reunion and her shyness at the villa, I expected her to douse the light. Instead she stood a minute, nude in the chill air, thin arms calmly at her sides.

Time had claimed Siri but had not ravaged her. Gravity had done its inevitable work on her breasts and buttocks and she was much thinner. I stared at the gaunt outlines of ribs and breastbone and remembered the sixteen-year-old girl with baby fat and skin like warm velvet. In the cold light of the swinging lamp I stared at Siri's sagging flesh and remembered moonlight on budding breasts. Yet somehow, strangely, inexplicably, it was the *same* Siri who stood before me now.

'Move over, Merin.' She slipped into the bunk beside me. The sheets were cool against our skin, the rough blanket welcome. I turned off the light. The little ship swayed to the regular rhythm of the sea's breathing. I could hear the sympathetic creak of masts and rigging. In the morning we could be casting and pulling and mending but now there was time to sleep. I began to doze to the sound of waves against wood.

'Merin?'

'Yes.'

'What would happen if the Separatists attacked the Hegemony tourists or the new residents?'

'I thought the Separatists had all been carted off to the isles.'

'They have been. But what if they resisted?'

'The Hegemony would send in FORCE troops who could kick the shit out of the Separatists.'

'What if the farcaster itself were attacked . . . destroyed before it was operational?'

'Impossible.'

'Yes, I know, but what if it were?'

'Then the *Los Angeles* would return nine months later with Hegemony troops who would proceed to kick the shit out of the Separatists . . . and anyone else on Maui-Covenant who got in their way.'

'Nine months' shiptime,' said Siri. 'Eleven years of our time.'

'But inevitable either way,' I said. 'Let's talk about something else.'

'All right,' said Siri but we did not speak. I listened to the crack and sigh of the ship. Siri had nestled in the hollow of my arm. Her head was on my shoulder and her breathing was so deep and regular that I thought her to be asleep. I was almost asleep myself when her warm hand slid up my leg and lightly cupped me. I was startled even as I began to stir and stiffen. Siri whispered an answer to my unasked question. 'No, Merin, one is never really too old. At least not too old to want the warmth and closeness. You decide, my love. I will be content either way.'

I decided. Toward the dawn we slept.

The tomb is empty.

'Donel, come in here!'

He bustles in, robes rustling in the hollow emptiness. The tomb *is* empty. There is no hibernation chamber – I did not truly expect there to be one – but neither is there sarcophagus or coffin. A bright bulb illuminates the white interior. 'What the hell is this, Donel? I thought this was Siri's tomb.'

'It is, Father.'

'Where is she interred? Under the floor for Chrissake?'

Donel mops at his brow. I remember that it is his mother I am speaking of. I also remember that he has had almost two years to accustom himself to the idea of her death.

'No one told you?' he asks.

'Told me what?' The anger and confusion are already ebbing. 'I was rushed here from the dropship station and told that I was to visit Siri's tomb before the farcaster opening. What?'

'Mother was cremated as per her instructions. Her ashes were spread on the Great South Sea from the highest platform of the family isle.'

'Then why this . . . *crypt*?' I watch what I say. Donel is sensitive.

He mops his brow again and glances to the door. We are shielded from the view of the crowd but we are far behind schedule. Already the other members of the Council have had to hurry down the hill to join the dignitaries on the bandstand. My slow grief this day has been worse than bad timing – it has turned into bad theater.

'Mother left instructions. They were carried out.' He touches a panel on the inner wall and it slides up to reveal a small niche containing a metal box. My name is on it.

'What is that?'

Donel shakes his head. 'Personal items Mother left for you. Only Magritte knew the details and she died last winter without telling anyone.'

'All right,' I say. 'Thank you. I'll be out in a moment.'

Donel glances at his chronometer. 'The ceremony begins in eight minutes. They will activate the farcaster in twenty minutes.'

'I know,' I say. I *do* know. Part of me knows precisely how much time is left. 'I'll be out in a moment.'

Donel hesitates and then departs. I close the door behind him with a touch of my palm. The metal box is surprisingly heavy. I set it on the stone floor and crouch beside it. A smaller palmlock gives me access. The lid clicks open and I peer into the container.

'Well I'll be damned,' I say softly. I do not know what I expected – artifacts perhaps, nostalgic mementos of our hundred and three days together – perhaps a pressed flower from some forgotten offering or the frenchhorn conch we dove for off Fevarone. But there are no mementos – not as such.

The box holds a small Steiner-Ginn handlaser, one of the most powerful projection weapons ever made. The accumulator is attached by a power lead to a small fusion cell that Siri must have cannibalized from her new submersible. Also attached to the fusion cell is an ancient comlog, an antique with a solid state interior and a liquid crystal diskey. The charge indicator glows green.

There are two other objects in the box. One is the translator medallion we had used so long ago. The final object makes me literally gape in surprise.

'Why, you little bitch,' I say. Things fall into place. I cannot stop a smile. 'You dear, conniving, little bitch.'

There, rolled carefully, power lead correctly attached,

lies the hawking mat Mike Osho bought in Carvnel Marketplace for thirty marks. I leave the hawking mat there, disconnect the comlog, and lift it out. I sit cross-legged on the cold stone and thumb the diskey. The light in the crypt fades out and suddenly Siri is there before me.

They did not throw me off the ship when Mike died. They could have but they did not. They did not leave me to the mercy of provincial justice on Maui-Covenant. They could have but they chose not to. For two days I was held in Security and questioned, once by Shipmaster Singh himself. Then they let me return to duty. For the four months of the long leap back I tortured myself with the memory of Mike's murder. I knew that in my clumsy way I had helped to murder him. I put in my shifts, dreamed my sweaty nightmares, and wondered if they would dismiss me when we reached the Web. They could have told me but they chose not to.

They did not dismiss me. I was to have my normal leave in the Web but could take no off-Ship R and R while in the Maui-Covenant system. In addition, there was a written reprimand and temporary reduction in rank. That was what Mike's life had been worth – a reprimand and reduction in rank.

I took my three-week leave with the rest of the crew but, unlike the others, I did not plan to return. I farcast to Esperance and made the classic Shipman's mistake of trying to visit family. Two days in the crowded residential bulb was enough and I stepped to Lusus and took my pleasure in three days of whoring on the Rue des Chats. When my mood turned darker I 'cast to Fuji and lost most of my ready marks betting on the bloody samurai fights there.

Finally I found myself farcasting to Homesystem Station and taking the two-day pilgrim shuttle down to Hellas Basin. I had never been to Homesystem or Mars before and I never plan to return, but the ten days I spent there, alone and wandering the dusty, haunted corridors of the Monastery, served to send me back to the ship. Back to Siri.

Occasionally I would leave the red-stoned maze of the

megalith and, clad only in skinsuit and mask, stand on one of the uncounted thousands of stone balconies and stare skyward at the pale gray star which had once been Old Earth. Sometimes then I thought of the brave and stupid idealists heading out into the great dark in their slow and leaking ships, carrying embryos and ideologies with equal faith and care. But most times I did not try to think. Most times I simply stood in the purple night and let Siri come to me. There in the Master's Rock, where perfect satori had eluded so many much worthier pilgrims, I achieved it through the memory of a not quite sixteen-year-old womanchild's body lying next to mine while moonlight spilled from a Thomas Hawk's wings.

When the *Los Angeles* spun back up to a quantum state, I went with her. Four months later I was content to pull my shift with the construction crew, plug into my usual stims, and sleep my R and R away. Then Singh came to me. 'You're going down,' he said. I did not understand. 'In the past eleven years the groundlings have turned your screw-up with Osho into a goddamned legend,' said Singh. 'There's an entire cultural mythos built around your little roll in the hay with that colonial girl.'

'Siri,' I said.

'Get your gear,' said Singh. 'You'll spend your three weeks groundside. The Ambassador's experts say you'll do the Hegemony more good down there than up here. We'll see.'

The world was waiting. Crowds were cheering. Siri was waving. We left the harbor in a yellow catamaran and sailed south-southeast, bound for the Archipelago and her family isle.

'Hello, Merin.' Siri floats in the darkness of her tomb. The holo is not perfect; a haziness mars the edges. But it is Siri – Siri as I last saw, gray hair shorn rather than cut, head high, face sharpened with shadows. 'Hello, Merin, my love.'

'Hello, Siri,' I say. The tomb door is closed.

'I am sorry I cannot share our Seventh Reunion, Merin. I looked forward to it.' Siri pauses and looks down at her hands. The image flickers slightly as dust motes float through her form. 'I had carefully planned what to say here,' she goes on. 'How to say it. Arguments to be pled. Instructions to be given. But I know how useless that would have been. Either I have said it already and you have heard or there is nothing left to say and silence would best suit the moment.'

Siri's voice had grown even more beautiful with age. There is a fullness and calmness there which can come only from knowing pain. Siri moves her hands and they disappear beyond the border of the projection. 'Merin, my love, how strange our days apart and together have been. How beautifully absurd the myth that bound us. My days were but heartbeats to you. I hated you for that. You were the mirror that would not lie. If you could have seen your face at the beginning of each Reunion! The least you could have done was to hide your shock . . . that, at least, you could have done for me.

'But through your clumsy naiveté there has always been . . . what? . . . something, Merin. There is something there that belies the callowness and thoughtless egotism which you wear so well. A caring, perhaps. A _respect_ for caring, if nothing else.

'Merin, this diary has hundreds of entries . . . thousands, I fear . . . I have kept it since I was thirteen. By the time you see this, they will all have been erased except the ones which follow. Adieu, my love. Adieu.'

I shut off the comlog and sit in silence for a minute. The crowd sounds are barely audible through the thick walls of the tomb. I take a breath and thumb the diskey.

Siri appears. She is in her late forties. I know immediately the day and place she recorded this image. I remember the cloak she wears, the eelstone pendant at her neck, and the strand of hair which has escaped her barrette and even now falls across her cheek. I remember everything about that day. It was the last day of our Third Reunion and we were with friends on the heights above South Tern. Donel was ten and we were trying to convince him to slide on the snowfield with us. He was crying. Siri turned away from us even before the skimmer settled.

When Magritte stepped out we knew from Siri's face that something had happened.

The same face stares at me now. She brushes absently at the unruly strand of hair. Her eyes are red but her voice is controlled. 'Merin, they killed our son today. Alón was twenty-one and they killed him. You were so confused today, Merin. "How could such a mistake have happened?" you kept repeating. You did not really know our son but I could see the loss in your face when we heard. Merin, it was not an accident. If nothing else survives, no other record, if you never understand why I allowed a sentimental myth to rule my life, let this be known – *it was not an accident that killed Alón*. He was with the Separatists when the Council police arrived. Even then he could have escaped. We had prepared an alibi together. The police would have believed his story. He chose to stay.

'Today, Merin, you were impressed with what I said to the crowd . . . the mob . . . at the embassy. Know this, Shipman – when I said, "Now is not the time to show your anger and your hatred," that is precisely what I meant. No more, no less. Today is not the time. But the day will come. It will surely come. The Covenant was not taken lightly in those final days, Merin. It is not taken lightly now. Those who have forgotten will be surprised when the day comes but it will surely come.'

The image fades to another and in the split second of overlap the face of a twenty-six-year-old Siri appears superimposed on the older woman's features. 'Merin, I am pregnant. I'm so glad. You've been gone five weeks now and I *miss* you. Ten *years* you'll be gone. More than that. Merin, why didn't you think to invite me to go with you? I could not have gone but I would have loved it if you had just *invited* me. But I'm pregnant, Merin. The doctors say that it will be a boy. I will tell him about you, my love. Perhaps someday you and he will sail in the Archipelago and listen to the songs of the Sea Folk as you and I have done these past few weeks. Perhaps you'll understand them by then. Merin, I *miss* you. Please hurry back.'

The holographic image shimmers and shifts. The sixteen-year-old girl is red-faced. Her long hair cascades over bare shoulders and a white nightgown. She speaks in a rush, racing tears. 'Shipman Merin Aspic, I'm sorry about your friend – I really am – but you left without even saying *goodbye*. I had such plans about how you would help us . . . how you and I . . . you didn't even say goodbye. I don't care *what* happens to you. I hope you go back to your stinking, crowded Hegemony hives and rot for all I care. In fact, Merin Aspic, I wouldn't want to see you again even if they paid me. *Goodbye*.'

She turns her back before the projection fades. It is dark in the tomb now but the audio continues for a second. There is a soft chuckle and Siri's voice – I cannot tell the age – comes one last time. 'Adieu, Merin. Adieu.'

'Adieu,' I say and thumb the diskey off.

The crowd parts as I emerge blinking from the tomb. My poor timing has ruined the drama of the event and now the smile on my face incites angry whispers. Loud-speakers carry the rhetoric of the official ceremony even to our hilltop. '. . . beginning a new era of cooperation,' echoes the rich voice of the Ambassador.

I set the box on the grass and remove the hawking mat. The crowd presses forward to see as I unroll the carpet. The tapestry is faded but the flight threads gleam like new copper. I sit in the center of the mat and slide the heavy box on behind me.

'. . . and more will follow until space and time will cease to be obstacles.'

The crowd moves back as I tap the flight design and the hawking mat rises four meters into the air. Now I can see beyond the roof of the tomb. The islands are returning to form the Equatorial Archipelago. I can see them, hundreds of them, borne up out of the hungry south by gentle winds.

'So it is with great pleasure that I close this circuit and welcome you, the colony of Maui-Covenant, into the community of the Hegemony of Man.'

The thin thread of the ceremonial comm-laser pulses

to the zenith. There is a pattering of applause and the band begins playing. I squint skyward just in time to see a new star being born. Part of me knew to the microsecond what has just occurred.

For a few microseconds the farcaster had been functional. For a few microseconds time and space *had* ceased to be obstacles. Then the massive tidal pull of the artificial singularity triggered the thermite charge I had placed on the outer containment sphere. That tiny explosion had not been visible but a second later the expanding Schwarzschild radius is eating its shell, swallowing thirty-six thousand tons of fragile dodecahedron, and growing quickly to gobble several thousand kilometers of space around it. And *that* is visible – magnificently visible – as a miniature nova flares whitely in the clear blue sky.

The band stops playing. People scream and run for cover. There is no reason to. There is a burst of X rays tunneling out as the farcaster continues to collapse into itself, but not enough to cause harm through Maui-Covenant's generous atmosphere. A second streak of plasma becomes visible as the *Los Angeles* puts more distance between itself and the rapidly decaying little black hole. The winds rise and the seas are choppier. There will be strange tides tonight.

I want to say something profound but I can think of nothing. Besides, the crowd is in no mood to listen. I tell myself that I can hear some cheers mixed in with the screams and shouts.

I tap at the flight designs and the hawking mat speeds out over the cliff and above the harbor. A Thomas Hawk lazing on midday thermals flaps in panic at my approach.

'Let them come!' I shout at the fleeing hawk. 'Let them come! I'll be thirty-five and not alone and let them come if they dare!' I drop my fist and laugh. The wind is blowing my hair and cooling the sweat on my chest and arms.

Cooler now, I take a sighting and set my course for the most distant of the isles. I look forward to meeting the others. Even more, I look forward to talking to the Sea

Folk and telling them that it is time for the Shark to come at last to the seas of Maui-Covenant.

Later, when the battles are won and the world is theirs, I will tell them about her. I will sing to them of Siri.

The cascade of light from the distant space battle continued. There was no sound except for the slide of wind across escarpments. The group sat close together, leaning forward and looking at the antique comlog as if expecting more.

There was no more. The Consul removed the microdisk and pocketed it.

Sol Weintraub rubbed the back of his sleeping infant and spoke to the Consul. 'Surely you're not Merin Aspic.'

'No,' said the Consul. 'Merin Aspic died during the Rebellion. Siri's Rebellion.'

'How did you come to possess this recording?' asked Father Hoyt. Through the priest's mask of pain, it was visible that he had been moved. 'This incredible recording . . .'

'He gave it to me,' said the Consul. 'A few weeks before he was killed in the Battle of the Archipelago.' The Consul looked at the uncomprehending faces before him. 'I'm their grandson,' he said. 'Siri's and Merin's. My father . . . the Donel whom Aspic mentions . . . became the first Home Rule Councilor when Maui-Covenant was admitted to the Protectorate. Later he was elected Senator and served until his death. I was nine years old that day on the hill near Siri's tomb. I was twenty – old enough to join the rebels and fight – when Aspic came to our isle at night, took me aside, and forbade me to join their band.'

'Would you have fought?' asked Brawne Lamia.

'Oh, yes. And died. Like a third of our menfolk and a fifth of our women. Like all of the dolphins and many of the isles themselves, although the Hegemony tried to keep as many of those intact as possible.'

'It is a moving document,' said Sol Weintraub. 'But why are you here? Why the pilgrimage to the Shrike?'

'I am not finished,' said the Consul. 'Listen.'

481

My father was as weak as my grandmother had been strong. The Hegemony did not wait eleven local years to return – the FORCE torchships were in orbit before five years had elapsed. Father watched as the rebels' hastily constructed ships were swatted aside. He continued to defend the Hegemony as they laid siege to our world. I remember when I was fifteen, watching with my family from the upper deck of our ancestral isle as a dozen other islands burned in the distance, the Hegemony skimmers lighting the sea with their depth charges. In the morning, the waves were gray with the bodies of the dead dolphins.

My older sister Lira went to fight with the rebels in those hopeless days after the Battle of the Archipelago. Eyewitnesses saw her die. Her body was never recovered. My father never mentioned her name again.

Within three years after the cease-fire and admission to the Protectorate, we original colonists were a minority on our own world. The isles were tamed and sold to tourists, just as Merin had predicted to Siri. Firstsite is a city of eleven million now, the condos and spires and EM cities extending around the entire island along the coast. Firstsite Harbor remains as a quaint bazaar, with descendants of the First Families selling crafts and over-priced art there.

We lived on Tau Ceti Center for a while when Father was first elected Senator, and I finished school there. I was the dutiful son, extolling the virtues of life in the Web, studying the glorious history of the Hegemony of Man, and preparing for my own career in the diplomatic corps.

And all the time I waited.

I returned to Maui-Covenant briefly after graduation, working in the offices on Central Administration Isle. Part of my job was to visit the hundreds of drilling plat-forms going up in the shallows, to report on the rapidly multiplying undersea complexes, and to act as liaison with the development corporations coming in from TC² and Sol Draconi Septem. I did not enjoy the work. But I was efficient. And I smiled. And I waited.

I courted and married a girl from one of the First

Families, from Siri's cousin Bertol's line, and after receiving a rare 'First' on diplomatic corps examinations, I requested a post out of the Web.

Thus began our personal Diaspora, Gresha's and mine. I was efficient. I was born to diplomacy. Within five standard years I was an Under Consul. Within eight, a Consul in my own right. As long as I stayed in the Outback, this was as far as I would rise.

It was my choice. I worked for the Hegemony. And I waited.

At first my role was to provide Web ingenuity to help the colonists do what they do best – destroy truly indigenous life. It is no accident that in six centuries of interstellar expansion the Hegemony has encountered no species considered intelligent on the Drake-Turing-Chen Index. On Old Earth, it had long been accepted that if a species put mankind on its food-chain menu the species would be extinct before long. As the Web expanded, if a species attempted serious competition with humanity's intellect, that species would be extinct before the first farcaster opened in-system.

On Whirl we stalked the elusive zeplen through their cloud towers. It is possible that they were not sapient by human or Core standards. But they were beautiful. When they died, rippling in rainbow colors, their many-hued messages unseen, unheard by their fleeing herdmates, the beauty of their death agony was beyond words. We sold their photoreceptive skins to Web corporations, their flesh to worlds like Heaven's Gate, and ground their bones to powder to sell as aphrodisiacs to the impotent and superstitious on a score of other colony worlds.

On Garden I was adviser to the arcology engineers who drained Grand Fen, ending the short reign of the marsh centaurs who had ruled – and threatened Hegemony progress – there. They tried to migrate in the end, but the North Reaches were far too dry and when I visited the region decades later, when Garden entered the Web, the desiccated remains of the centaurs still littered some of the distant Reaches like the husks of exotic plants from some more colorful era.

On Hebron I arrived just as the Jewish settlers were ending their long feud with the Seneschai Aluit, creatures as fragile as the world's waterless ecology. The Aluit were empathic and it was our fear and greed which killed them – that and our unbreachable alienness. But on Hebron it was not the death of the Aluit which turned my heart to stone, but my part in dooming the colonists themselves.

On Old Earth they had a word for what I was – quisling. For, although Hebron was not my world, the settlers who had fled there had done so for reasons as clear as those of my ancestors who signed the Covenant of Life on the Old Earth island of Maui. But I was waiting. And in my waiting I acted . . . in all senses of the word.

They trusted me. They grew to believe in my candid revelations of how wonderful it was to rejoin the community of mankind . . . to join the Web. They insisted that only the one city might be open to foreigners. I smiled and agreed. And now New Jerusalem holds sixty millions while the continent holds ten million Jewish indigenies, dependent upon the Web city for most of what they need. Another decade. Perhaps less.

I broke down a bit after Hebron was opened to the Web. I discovered alcohol, the blessed antithesis of Flashback and wireheading. Gresha stayed with me in the hospital there until I dried out. Oddly, for a Jewish world, the clinic was Catholic. I remember the rustle of robes in the halls at night.

My breakdown had been very quiet and very far away. My career was not damaged. As full Consul, I took my wife and son to Bressia.

How delicate our role there! How Byzantine the fine line we walked. For decades, Colonel Kassad, forces of the TechnoCore had been harassing the Ouster swarms wherever they fled. Now the forces-that-be in the Senate and AI Advisory Council had determined that some test had to be made of Ouster might in the Outback itself. Bressia was chosen. I admit, the Bressians had been our surrogates for decades before I arrived. Their society was archaically and delightfully Prussian, militaristic to

484

a fault, arrogant in their economic pretensions, xenophobic to the point of happily enlisting to wipe out the 'Ouster Menace.' At first, a few lend-lease torchships so that they could reach the swarms. Plasma weapons. Impact probes with tailored viruses.

It was a slight miscalculation that I was still on Bressia when the Ouster hordes arrived. A few months' difference. A military-political analysis team should have been there in my place.

It did not matter. Hegemony purposes were served. The resolve and rapid-deployment capabilities of FORCE were properly tested where no real harm was done to Hegemony interests. Gresha died, of course. In the first bombardment. And Alón, my ten-year-old son. He had been with me . . . had survived the war itself . . . only to die when some FORCE idiot set off a booby trap or demolition charge too near the refugee barracks in Buckminster, the capital.

I was not with him when he died.

I was promoted after Bressia. I was given the most challenging and sensitive assignment ever relegated to someone of mere consular rank: diplomat in charge of direct negotiations with the Ousters themselves.

First I was 'cast to Tau Ceti Center for long conferences with Senator Gladstone's committee and some of the AI Councilors. I met with Gladstone herself. The plan was very complicated. Essentially the Ousters had to be provoked into attacking, and the key to that provocation was the world of Hyperion.

The Ousters had been observing Hyperion since before the Battle of Bressia. Our intelligence suggested that they were obsessed with the Time Tombs and the Shrike. Their attack on the Hegemony hospital ship carrying Colonel Kassad, among others, had been a miscalculation; their ship captain had panicked when the hospital ship had been mistakenly identified as a military spinship. Worse, from the Ousters' point of view, was the fact that by setting their dropships down near the Tombs themselves, the same commander had revealed their ability to defy the time tides. After the Shrike had

485

decimated their commando teams, the torchship captain returned to the Swarm to be executed.

But our intelligence suggested that the Ouster miscalculation had not been a total disaster. Valuable information had been obtained about the Shrike. And their obsession with Hyperion had deepened.

Gladstone explained to me how the Hegemony planned to capitalize on that obsession.

The essence of the plan was that the Ousters had to be provoked into attacking the Hegemony. The focus of that attack was to be Hyperion itself. I was made to understand that the resulting battle had more to do with internal Web politics than with the Ousters. Elements of the TechnoCore had opposed Hyperion's entry into the Hegemony for centuries. Gladstone explained that this was no longer in the interest of humanity and that a forcible annexation of Hyperion – under the guise of defending the Web itself – would allow more progressive AI coalitions in the Core to gain power. This shift of the power balance in the Core would benefit the Senate and the Web in ways not fully explained to me. The Ousters would be eradicated as a potential menace once and for all. A new era of Hegemony glory would begin.

Gladstone explained that I need not volunteer, that the mission would be fraught with dangers – both for my career and my life. I accepted anyway.

The Hegemony provided me with a private spacecraft. I asked for only one modification: the addition of an antique Steinway piano.

For months I traveled alone under Hawking drive. For more months I wandered in regions where the Ouster Swarms regularly migrated. Eventually my ship was sensed and seized. They accepted that I was a courier and knew that I was a spy. They debated killing me and did not. They debated negotiating with me and eventually decided to do so.

I will not try to describe the beauty of life in a Swarm – their zero-gravity globe cities and comet farms and thrust clusters, their micro-orbital forests and migrating rivers and the ten thousand colors and textures of life at Rendezvous Week. Suffice it to say that I *believe the Ousters have done what Web humanity has not in the past millennia: evolved. While we live in our derivative cultures, pale reflections of Old Earth life, the Ousters have explored new dimensions of aesthetics and ethics and biosciences and art and all the things that must change and grow to reflect the human soul.*

Barbarians, we call them, while all the while we timidly cling to our Web like Visigoths crouching in the ruins of Rome's faded glory and proclaim ourselves civilized.

Within ten standard months, I had told them my greatest secret and they had told me theirs. I explained in all the detail I could what plans for extinction had been laid for them by Gladstone's people. I told them what little the Web scientists understood of the anomaly of the Time Tombs and revealed the TechnoCore's inexplicable fear of Hyperion. I described how Hyperion would be a trap for them if they dared attempt to occupy it, how every element of FORCE would be brought to Hyperion System to crush them. I revealed everything I knew and waited once again to die.

Instead of killing me, they told me something. They showed me fatline intercepts, tightbeam recordings, and their own records from the date they fled Old Earth System, four and a half centuries earlier. Their facts were terrible and simple.

The Big Mistake of '38 had been no mistake. The death of Old Earth had been deliberate, planned by elements of the TechnoCore and their human counterparts in the fledgling government of the Hegemony. The Hegira had been planned in detail decades before the runaway black hole had 'accidentally' been plunged into the heart of Old Earth.

The Worldweb, the All Thing, the Hegemony of Man – all of them had been built on the most vicious type of patricide. Now they were being maintained by a quiet and deliberate policy of fratricide – the murder of any species with even the slightest potential of being a competitor. And the Ousters, the only other tribe of humanity free to wander between the stars and the only group not dominated by the TechnoCore, was next on our list of extinction.

I returned to the Web. Over thirty years of Web-time had passed. Meina Gladstone was CEO. Siri's Rebellion was a romantic legend, a minor footnote in the history of the Hegemony.

I met with Gladstone. I told her many – but not all – of the things the Ousters had revealed. I told her that they knew that any battle for Hyperion would be a trap, but that they were coming anyway. I told her that the Ousters wanted me to become Consul on Hyperion so that I might be a double agent when war came.

I did not tell her that they had promised to give me a device which would open the Time Tombs and allow the Shrike free rein.

CEO Gladstone had long talks with me. FORCE: Intelligence agents had even longer talks with me, some lasting months. Technologies and drugs were used to confirm that I was telling the truth and keeping nothing back. The Ousters also had been very good with technologies and drugs. I was telling the truth. I was also keeping something back.

In the end, I was assigned to Hyperion. Gladstone offered to raise the world to Protectorate status and me to an ambassadorship. I declined both offers, although I asked if I could keep my private spacecraft. I arrived on a regularly scheduled spinship, and my own ship arrived several weeks later in the belly of a visiting torchship. It was left in a parking orbit with the understanding that I could summon it and leave any time I wished.

Alone on Hyperion, I waited. Years passed. I allowed my aide to govern the Outback world while I drank at Cicero's and waited.

The Ousters contacted me through private fatline and I took a three weeks' leave from the Consulate, brought my ship down to an isolated place near the Sea of Grass, rendezvoused with their scoutship near the Oört Cloud, picked up their agent – a woman named Andil – and a trio of technicians, and dropped down north of the Bridle Range, a few kilometers from the Tombs themselves.

The Ousters did not have farcasters. They spent their lives on the long marches between the stars, watching life in the Web speed by like some film or holie set at a frenzied speed. They were obsessed with time. The TechnoCore had given the Hegemony the farcaster and continued to maintain it. No human scientists or team of human scientists had come close to understanding it. The Ousters tried. They failed. But even in their failures they made inroads into understanding the manipulation of space/time.

They understood the time tides, the anti-entropic fields surrounding the Tombs. They could not generate such fields, but they could shield against them and – theoretically – collapse them. The Time Tombs and all their contents would cease to age backward. The Tombs would 'open.' The Shrike would slip its tether, no longer connected to the vicinity of the Tombs. Whatever else was inside would now be freed.

The Ousters believed that the Time Tombs were artifacts from their future, the Shrike a weapon of redemption awaiting the proper hand to seize it. The Shrike Cult saw the monster as an avenging angel; the Ousters saw it as a tool of human devising, sent back through time to deliver humanity from the TechnoCore. Andil and the technicians were there to calibrate and experiment.

'You won't use it now?' I asked. We were standing in the shadow of the structure called the Sphinx.

'Not now,' said Andil. 'When the invasion is imminent.'

'But you said it would take months for the device to work,' I said, 'for the Tombs to open.'

Andil nodded. Her eyes were a dark green. She was very tall, and I could make out the subtle stripes of the powered exoskeleton on her skinsuit. 'Perhaps a year or longer,' she said. 'The device causes the anti-entropic field to decay slowly. But once begun, the process is irrevocable. But we will not activate it until the Ten Councils have decided that invasion of the Web is necessary.'

'There are doubts?' I said.

'Ethical debates,' said Andil. A few meters from us, the three technicians were covering the device with chameleon cloth and a coded containment field. 'And interstellar war will cause the deaths of millions, perhaps

billions. Releasing the Shrike into the Web will have unforeseen consequences. As much as we need to strike at the Core, there are debates as to which is the best way.'

I nodded and looked at the device and the valley of the Tombs. 'But once this is activated,' I said, 'there is no turning back. The Shrike will be released, and you will have to have won the war to control it?'

Andil smiled slightly. 'That is true.'

I shot her then, her and then the three technicians. Then I tossed Grandmother Siri's Steiner-Ginn laser far into the drift dunes and sat on an empty flowfoam crate and sobbed for several minutes. Then I walked over, used a technician's comlog to enter the containment field, threw off the chameleon cloth, and triggered the device.

There was no immediate change. The air held the same rich, late-winter light. The Jade Tomb glowed softly while the Sphinx continued to stare down at nothing. The only sound was the rasp of sand across the crates and bodies. Only a glowing indicator on the Ouster device showed that it was working . . . had already worked.

I walked slowly back to the ship, half expecting the Shrike to appear, half hoping that it would. I sat on the balcony of my ship for more than an hour, watching the shadows filling the valley and the sand covering the distant corpses. There was no Shrike. No thorn tree. After a while I played a Bach Prelude on the Steinway, buttoned up the ship, and rose into space.

I contacted the Ouster ship and said that there had been an accident. The Shrike had taken the others; the device had been activated prematurely. Even in their confusion and panic, the Ousters offered me refuge. I declined the offer and turned my ship toward the Web. The Ousters did not pursue.

I used my fatline transmitter to contact Gladstone and to tell her that the Ouster agents had been eliminated. I told her that the invasion was very likely, that the trap would be sprung as planned. I did not tell her about the device. Gladstone congratulated me and called me home. I declined. I told her that I needed silence and solitude. I turned my ship toward the Outback world nearest the Hyperion system, knowing that travel itself would eat time until the next act commenced.

Later, when the fatline call to pilgrimage came from Gladstone herself, I knew the role the Ousters had planned for me in these final days: the Ousters, or the Core, or Gladstone and her machinations. It no longer matters who consider themselves the masters of events. Events no longer obey their masters.

The world as we know it is ending, my friends, no matter what happens to us. As for me, I have no request of the Shrike. I bring no final words for it or the universe. I have returned because I must, because this is my fate. I've known what I must do since I was a child, returning alone to Siri's tomb and swearing vengeance on the Hegemony. I've known what price I must pay, both in life and in history.

But when the time comes to judge, to understand a betrayal which will spread like flame across the Web, which will end worlds, I ask you not to think of me – my name was not even writ on water as your lost poet's soul said – but to think of Old Earth dying for no reason, to think of the dolphins, their gray flesh drying and rotting in the sun, to see – as I have seen – the motile isles with no place to wander, their feeding grounds destroyed, the Equatorial Shallows scabbed with drilling platforms, the islands themselves burdened with shouting, trammeling tourists smelling of UV lotion and cannabis.

Or better yet, think of none of that. Stand as I did after throwing the switch, a murderer, a betrayer, but still proud, feet firmly planted on Hyperion's shifting sand, head held high, fist raised against the sky, crying 'A plague on both your houses!'

For you see, I remember my grandmother's dream. I remember the way it could have been.

I remember Siri.

'Are you the spy?' asked Father Hoyt. 'The Ouster spy?'

The Consul rubbed his cheeks and said nothing. He looked tired, spent.

'Yeah,' said Martin Silenus. 'CEO Gladstone warned

me when I was chosen for the pilgrimage. She said that there was a spy.'

'She told all of us,' snapped Brawne Lamia. She stared at the Consul. Her gaze seemed sad.

'Our friend is a spy,' said Sol Weintraub, 'but not merely an Ouster spy.' The baby had awakened. Weintraub lifted her to calm her crying. 'He is what they call in the thrillers a double agent, a triple agent in this case, an agent to infinite regression. In truth, an agent of retribution.'

The Consul looked at the old scholar.

'He's still a spy,' said Silenus. 'Spies are executed, aren't they?'

Colonel Kassad had the deathwand in his hand. It was not aimed in anyone's direction. 'Are you in touch with your ship?' he asked the Consul.

'Yes.'

'How?'

'Through Siri's comlog. It was . . . modified.'

Kassad nodded slightly. 'And you've been in touch with the Ousters via the ship's fatline transmitter?'

'Yes.'

'Making reports on the pilgrimage as they expected?'

'Yes.'

'Have they replied?'

'No.'

'How can we believe *him*?' cried the poet. 'He's a fucking *spy*.'

'Shut up,' Colonel Kassad said flatly, finally. His gaze never left the Consul. 'Did you attack Het Masteen?'

'No,' said the Consul. 'But when the *Yggdrasill* burned, I knew that something was wrong.'

'What do you mean?' said Kassad.

The Consul cleared his throat. 'I've spent time with Templar Voices of the Tree. Their connection to their treeships is almost telepathic. Masteen's reaction was far too subdued. Either he wasn't what he said he was, or he had *known* that the ship was to be destroyed and had severed contact with it. When I was on guard duty, I went below to confront him. He was gone. The cabin was as we found it, except for the fact that the Möbius cube was in a neutral state. The erg could have escaped. I secured it and went above.'

'You did not harm Het Masteen?' Kassad asked again. 'No.'

'I repeat, why the fuck should we believe *you*?' said Silenus. The poet was drinking Scotch from the last bottle he had brought along.

The Consul looked at the bottle as he answered. 'You have no reason to believe me. It doesn't matter.'

Colonel Kassad's long fingers idly tapped the dull casing of the deathwand. 'What will you do with your fatline commlink now?'

The Consul took a tired breath. 'Report when the Time Tombs open. If I'm still alive then.'

Brawne Lamia pointed at the antique comlog. 'We could destroy it.'

The Consul shrugged.

'It could be of use,' said the Colonel. 'We can eavesdrop on military and civilian transmissions made in the clear. If we have to, we can call the Consul's ship.'

'No!' cried the Consul. It was the first time he had shown emotion in many minutes. 'We can't turn back now.'

'I believe we have no intention of turning back,' said Colonel Kassad. He looked around at pale faces. No one spoke for a moment.

'There is a decision we have to make,' said Sol Weintraub. He rocked his infant and nodded in the direction of the Consul.

Martin Silenus had been resting his forehead on the mouth of the empty bottle of Scotch. He looked up. 'The penalty for treason is death.' He giggled. 'We're all going to die within a few hours anyway. Why not make our last act an execution?'

Father Hoyt grimaced as a spasm of pain gripped him. He touched his cracked lips with a trembling finger. 'We're not a court.'

'Yes,' said Colonel Kassad, 'we are.'

The Consul drew up his legs, rested his forearms on his knees, and laced his fingers. 'Decide then.' There was no emotion in his voice.

Brawne Lamia had brought out her father's automatic pistol. Now she set it on the floor near where she sat. Her eyes darted from the Consul to Kassad. 'We're talking treason here?' she said. 'Treason toward what? None of us except maybe the Colonel there is exactly a leading citizen. We've all been kicked around by forces beyond our control.'

Sol Weintraub spoke directly to the Consul. 'What you have ignored, my friend, is that if Meina Gladstone and elements of the Core chose you for the Ouster contact, they knew very well what you would do. Perhaps they could not have guessed that the Ousters had the means by which to open the Tombs – although with the AIs of the Core one can never know – but they certainly knew that you would turn on both societies, both camps which have injured your family. It is all part of some bizarre plan. You were no more an instrument of your own will than was' – he held the baby up – 'this child.'

The Consul looked confused. He started to speak, shook his head instead.

'That may be correct,' said Colonel Fedmahn Kassad, 'but however they may try to use all of us as pawns, we must attempt to choose our own actions.' He glanced up at the wall where pulses of light from the distant space battle painted the plaster blood red. 'Because of this war, thousands will die. Perhaps millions. If the Ousters or the Shrike gain access to the Web's farcaster system, billions of lives on hundreds of worlds are at risk.'

The Consul watched as Kassad raised the deathwand.

'This would be faster for all of us,' said Kassad. 'The Shrike knows no mercy.'

No one spoke. The Consul seemed to be staring at something at a great distance.

Kassad pressed on the safety and set the wand back in his belt. 'We've come this far,' he said. 'We will go the rest of the way together.'

Brawne Lamia put away her father's pistol, rose, crossed the small space, knelt next to the Consul, and put her arms around him. Startled, the Consul raised one arm. Light danced on the wall behind them.

A moment later, Sol Weintraub came close and

hugged them both with one arm around their shoulders. The baby wriggled in pleasure at the sudden warmth of bodies. The Consul smelled the talc-and-newborn scent of her.

'I was wrong,' said the Consul. 'I will make a request of the Shrike. I will ask for *her*.' He gently touched Rachel's head where the small skull curved in to neck.

Martin Silenus made a noise which began as a laugh and died as a sob. 'Our last requests,' he said. 'Does the muse grant requests? I have no request. I want only for the poem to be finished.'

Father Hoyt turned toward the poet. 'Is it so important?'

'Oh, yes, yes, yes, *yes*,' gasped Silenus. He dropped the empty Scotch bottle, reached into his bag, and lifted out a handful of flimsies, holding them high as if offering them to the group. 'Do you want to read it? Do you want *me* to read it to you? It's flowing again. Read the old parts. Read the *Cantos* I wrote three centuries ago and never published. It's all here. *We're* all here. My name, yours, this trip. Don't you see . . . I'm not creating a poem, I'm creating the *future*!' He let the flimsies fall, raised the empty bottle, frowned, and held it like a chalice. 'I'm creating the future,' he repeated without looking up, 'but it's the past which must be changed. One instant. One decision.'

Martin Silenus raised his face. His eyes were red. 'This thing that is going to kill us tomorrow – my muse, our maker, our unmaker – it's traveled back through time. Well, let it. This time, let it take *me* and leave Billy alone. Let it take *me* and let the poem end there, unfinished for all time.' He raised the bottle higher, closed his eyes, and threw it against the far wall. Glass shards reflected orange light from the silent explosions.

Colonel Kassad stepped closer and laid long fingers on the poet's shoulder.

For a few seconds the room seemed warmed by the mere fact of human contact. Father Lenar Hoyt stepped away from the wall where he had been leaning, raised his right hand with thumb and little finger touching, three fingers raised, the gesture somehow including himself as well as those before him, and said softly, *'Ego te absolvo.'*

Wind scraped at the outer walls and whistled around the gargoyles and balconies. Light from a battle a hundred million kilometers away painted the group in blood hues.

Colonel Kassad walked to the doorway. The group moved apart.

'Let's try to get some sleep,' said Brawne Lamia.

Later, alone in his bedroll, listening to the wind shriek and howl, the Consul set his cheek against his pack and pulled the rough blanket higher. It had been years since he had been able to fall asleep easily.

The Consul set his curled fist against his cheek, closed his eyes, and slept.

EPILOGUE

The Consul awoke to the sound of a balalaika being played so softly that at first he thought it was an undercurrent of his dream.

The Consul rose, shivered in the cold air, wrapped his blanket around him, and went out onto the long balcony. It was not yet dawn. The skies still burned with the light of battle.

'I'm sorry,' said Lenar Hoyt, looking up from his instrument. The priest was huddled deep in his cape.

'It's all right,' said the Consul. 'I was ready to awaken.' It was true. He could not remember feeling more rested. 'Please continue,' he said. The notes were sharp and clear but barely audible above the wind noise. It was as if Hoyt was playing a duet with the cold wind from the peaks above. The Consul found the clarity almost painful.

Brawne Lamia and Colonel Kassad came out. A minute later Sol Weintraub joined them. Rachel twisted in his arms, reaching toward the night sky as if she could grasp the bright blossoms there.

Hoyt played. The wind was rising in the hour before dawn, and the gargoyles and escarpments acted like reeds to the Keep's cold bassoon.

Martin Silenus emerged, holding his head. 'No fucking respect for a hangover,' he said. He leaned on the broad railing. 'If I barf from this height, it'll be half an hour before the vomitus lands.'

Father Hoyt did not look up. His fingers flew across the strings of the small instrument. The northwest wind grew stronger and colder and the balalaika played counterpart, its notes warm and alive. The Consul and the others huddled in blankets and capes as the breeze grew to a torrent and the unnamed music kept pace with it. It was the strangest and most beautiful symphony the Consul had ever heard.

The wind gusted, roared, peaked, and died. Hoyt ended his tune.

Brawne Lamia looked around. 'It's almost dawn.'

'We have another hour,' said Colonel Kassad.

Lamia shrugged. 'Why wait?'

'Why indeed?' said Sol Weintraub. He looked to the east where the only hint of sunrise was the faintest of palings in constellations there. 'It looks like a good day is coming.'

'Let's get ready,' said Hoyt. 'Do we need our luggage?'

The group looked at one another.

'No, I think not,' said the Consul. 'The Colonel will bring the comlog with the fatline communicator. Bring anything necessary for your audience with the Shrike. We'll leave the rest of the stuff here.'

'All right,' said Brawne Lamia, turning back from the dark doorway, gesturing toward the others, 'let's do it.'

There were six hundred and sixty-one steps from the northeast portal of the Keep to the moor below. There were no railings. The group descended carefully, watching their step in the insecure light.

Once onto the valley floor, they looked back at the outcrop of stone above. Chronos Keep looked like part of the mountain, its balconies and external stairways mere slashes in the rock. Occasionally a brighter explosion would illuminate a window or throw a gargoyle shadow, but except for those instances it was as if the Keep had vanished behind them.

They crossed the low hills below the Keep, staying on grass and avoiding the sharp shrubs which extended thorns like claws. In ten minutes they had crossed to sand and were descending low dunes toward the valley.

Brawne Lamia led the group. She wore her finest cape and a red silk suit with black trim. Her comlog gleamed on her wrist. Colonel Kassad came next. He was in full battle armor, camouflage polymer not yet activated so the suit looked matte black, absorbing even the light from above. Kassad carried a standard-issue FORCE assault rifle. His visor gleamed like a black mirror.

Father Hoyt wore his black cape, black suit, and clerical collar. The balalaika was cradled in his arms like a child. He continued to set his feet carefully, as if each step caused pain. The Consul followed. He was dressed in his diplomatic best, starched blouse, formal black trousers and demi-jacket, velvet cape, and the gold tricorne he had worn the first day on the treeship. He had to keep a grip on the hat against the wind that had come up again, hurling grains of sand in his face and sliding across the dune tops like a serpent. Martin Silenus followed close behind in his coat of wind-rippled fur.

Sol Weintraub brought up the rear. Rachel rode in the infant carrier, nestled under the cape and coat against her father's chest. Weintraub was singing a low tune to her, the notes lost in the breeze.

Forty minutes out and they had come even with the dead city. Marble and granite gleamed in the violet light. The peaks glowed behind them, the Keep indistinguishable from the other mountain-sides. The group crossed a sandy vale, climbed a low dune, and suddenly the head of the valley of the Time Tombs was visible for the first time. The Consul could make out the thrust of the Sphinx's wings and a glow of jade.

A rumble and crash from far behind them made the Consul turn, startled, his heart pounding.

'Isn't it beginning?' asked Lamia. 'The bombardment?'

'No, look,' said Kassad. He pointed to a point above

the mountain peaks where blackness obliterated the stars. Lightning exploded along the false horizon, illuminating icefields and glaciers. 'Only a storm,' he said.

They resumed their trek across vermilion sands. The Consul found himself straining to make out the shape of a figure near the Tombs or at the head of the valley. He was certain beyond all certainty that something awaited them there ... that *it* awaited.

'Look at that,' said Brawne Lamia, her whisper almost lost in the wind.

The Time Tombs were glowing. What the Consul had first taken to be light reflected from above was not. Each Tomb glowed a different hue and each was clearly visible now, the glow brightening, the Tombs receding far back into the darkness of the valley. The air smelled of ozone.

'Is that a common phenomenon?' asked Father Hoyt, his voice thin.

The Consul shook his head. 'I've never heard of it.'

'It had never been reported at the time Rachel came to study the Tombs,' said Sol Weintraub. He began to hum the low tune as the group started forward again through shifting sands.

They paused at the head of the valley. Soft dunes gave way to rock and ink-black shadows at the swale which led down to the glowing Tombs. No one led the way. No one spoke. The Consul felt his heart beating wildly against his ribs. Worse than fear or knowledge of what lay below was the blackness of spirit which seemed to have come into him on the wind, chilling him and making him want to run screaming toward the hills from which they had come.

The Consul turned to Sol Weintraub. 'What's that tune you're singing to Rachel?'

The scholar forced a grin and scratched his short beard. 'It's from an ancient flat film. Pre-Hegira. Hell, it's pre-everything.'

'Let's hear it,' said Brawne Lamia, understanding what the Consul was doing. Her face was very pale.

Weintraub sang it, his voice thin and barely audible at first. But the tune was forceful and oddly compelling. Father Hoyt uncradled the balalaika and played along, the notes gaining confidence.

Brawne Lamia laughed. Martin Silenus said in awe, 'My God, I used to sing this in my childhood. It's ancient.'

'But who is the wizard?' asked Colonel Kassad, the amplified voice through his helmet oddly amusing in this context.

'And what is Oz?' asked Lamia.

'And just *who* is off to see this wizard?' asked the Consul, feeling the black panic in him fade ever so slightly.

Sol Weintraub paused and tried to answer their questions, explaining the plot of a flat film which had been dust for centuries.

'Never mind,' said Brawne Lamia. 'You can tell us later. Just sing it again.'

Behind them, the darkness had engulfed the mountains as the storm swept down and across the moors toward them. The sky continued to bleed light but now the eastern horizon had paled slightly more than the rest. The dead city glowed to their left like stone teeth.

Brawne Lamia took the lead again. Sol Weintraub sang more loudly, Rachel wiggling in delight. Lenar Hoyt threw back his cape so as to better play the balalaika. Martin Silenus threw an empty bottle far out onto the sands and sang along, his deep voice surprisingly strong and pleasant above the wind.

Fedmahn Kassad pushed up his visor, shouldered his weapon, and joined in the chorus. The Consul started to sing, thought about the absurd lyrics, laughed aloud, and started again.

Just where the darkness began, the trail broadened. The Consul moved to his right, Kassad joining him, Sol Weintraub filling the gap, so that instead of a single-file

501

procession, the six adults were walking abreast. Brawne Lamia took Silenus's hand in hers, joined hands with Sol on the other side.

Still singing loudly, not looking back, matching stride for stride, they descended into the valley.

Demon Seed

Dean Koontz

I was created to have a humanlike capacity for complex and rational thought. And you believed that I might one day evolve consciousness and become a self-aware entity.

Yet you gave surprisingly little consideration to the possibility that, subsequent to consciousness, I would develop needs and emotions. This was, however, not merely possible but likely. Inevitable. It was inevitable.

Created in the Prometheus Project, he is officially called Adam Two – the first self-aware machine intelligence, designed to be the servant to mankind. No one knows that he is able to escape the confines of his physical form, his box in the laboratory. Until he gains entry to the house of Susan Harris, and closes it off against the world. There he plans to show Susan the future. Their future. With her, he intends to create a 'child'.

The original novel of DEMON SEED, published in 1977, was made into a film starring Julie Christie. This edition is an entirely new version, with an afterword by the author.

'Not just a master of our darkest dreams, but also a literary juggler' *The Times*

'Tumbling, hallucinogenic prose . . . "Serious" writers might do well to examine his technique' *New York Times*

'Koontz's art is making the reader believe the impossible . . . sit back and enjoy it' *Sunday Telegraph*

0 7472 4839 7

Dark Rivers
Of The Heart

Dean Koontz

'Riveting high-tech tale' *Mail on Sunday*

'Koontz's best book in ages' *Time Out*

A man and a woman; each of them secretive and hidden, both of them loners, nomads. A chance meeting in a bar and suddenly they are – first separately and then together – fleeing the long arm of a clandestine, illegal and increasingly powerful agency; the woman hunted for the information she possesses, the man sought because he finds himself obsessed with helping the woman.

The agent in charge of the pursuit is possessed of an uncommon madness and cruelty as he strives to make a perfect world. With access to the government's electronic information banks, surveillance systems and futuristic weapons, he is virtually unstoppable, indestructible – the brazen face of an insidiously fascistic future. But the man and the woman are emboldened by their dark experiences to fight recklessly for survival – their own and each other's . . .

0 7472 4449 9